EDGE
OF THE
SAWTOOTH

A Rick Morrand Mystery

Peter J. Ryan

BLACKHAWK
P·R·E·S·S

HUNTINGTON BEACH
CALIFORNIA

EDGE OF THE SAWTOOTH by Peter J. Ryan
Copyright © 2017 by Peter. J. Ryan

This is a work of fiction and a product of the author's imagination. Any similarity to actual persons is purely coincidental. Persons, events, and places mentioned in this novel are used in a fictional manner.

Editor - Susanne Lakin
Cover Design - Tamra Lucia
Interior Layout - Ellie Searl, Publishista®

ISBN-10: 0998887102
ISBN-13: 9780998887104
LCCN: 2017905485

BLACKHAWK
P·R·E·S·S
HUNTINGTON BEACH
CALIFORNIA

To my loving and devoted wife, Derilynn,

and to Bree and Larry, my heroes.

PROLOGUE

THIS TIME, CHLOE MORRAND DID not want to die.

She stood at the edge of the Sawtooth, its angry granite jaw jutting fiercely from a towering cliff deep in Montana's unforgiving wilderness. Densely packed fir and spruce trees swayed below, rising from a forest floor blanketed in darkness, beckoning her with a promise of certain death.

As wind and rain whipped chills across her freezing body, her teeth locked tight as she fought the flood of tears flowing down her face. A sudden gust jolted her toward the edge. She steadied herself against the merciless night air, wincing as razors of shale sliced into her feet.

"You need to jump," a voice said.

She froze. Was it behind her? She clamped her hands onto her shoulders, head hanging forward, arms crossed tightly across her chest.

"I don't want to die," she said, her words trembling. She had wanted to die many times before, but not now.

She heard no answer. Only the howling wind raking drenched hair across her eyes. She didn't dare turn around. What if no one was there?

A freeway of images raced through her head. She slammed the brakes, but no use. Without her meds, her thoughts hauled her wherever they wanted to go. She was along for the wild ride.

Her mind jerked sharply to her daughter. Abby's ninth birthday was only one week away. What would she think if Chloe died? Who would care for her? How could her child endure one final broken promise? Chloe shook her head and sobbed. Her mental illness, its flames fanned by drugs, had snatched Abby's innocence.

There had been a widening window of hope. Chloe had been off drugs and alcohol for two years. Her job as a ranger at Yellowstone National Park was perfect. She was a good single mom. Her bipolar disorder was being held in check by a delicate balance of meds and psychotherapy.

Oh yeah, the meds. She had stopped them. They made her feel bloated, her mind slow and confused. She didn't need them. Manic felt better. More energy. Clear thoughts. Big plans.

For a while, she'd felt *well*.

"You should have done what you were told to do," the voice said.

Chloe winced in remorse. She did what she wanted, never what she was told. If she had done what she was told, listened to her father and others, maybe she wouldn't be here—on this edge, this cliff.

Off her meds, she didn't know what was real. She had these ideas—*theories*—about things that were going on around her. She had told her dad, but she couldn't be sure whether he had listened. How could she blame him? Her thoughts could be undependable—they may or may not be true. Just like the voice she heard behind her.

"You need to jump," the voice said again, this time with impatience.

Chloe looked at the blackness below. She thought of her father. In the absence of a mother stolen by cancer, it was Chloe's father who had always supported her, always believed in her, always been there for her. She had repaid him with unsparing heartbreak and shame.

She couldn't do this to him.

"It'll be worse if you don't jump," the voice said. "A *lot* worse."

Was the voice in her mind? No, that one was different. This voice she had heard before.

She straightened her arms, balling her fists to halt the quivering of her freezing limbs. She summoned anger, knowing it might prove far more useful than fear.

She shook her head. The tears stopped. Her eyes opened wide as she whirled around. "Not happening!" she snarled through clenched teeth.

A stunned silence. Chloe moved forward, away from the edge. She had one more play. Maybe it could work.

She didn't want to die.

CHAPTER 1

Thirty hours earlier

A S HIS DAUGHTER PRATTLED ENDLESSLY about her life going so right, Rick Morrand was certain something must be terribly wrong.

They were seated at The Pines, having their traditional Thursday night supper. Or trying to have it, anyway. The waitress had just come by a third time.

"In a minute," Chloe said in less than a second, forcing the waitress into retreat.

Abby, Rick's granddaughter, had said nothing. How could she? Chloe was talking nonstop, filled with unflinching assuredness. Too much assuredness.

Abby stared blankly at her mother, lips pursed, bored with the episode and wanting to change the channel. Rick tousled her hair, smiling at her innocence.

"I'm *starving*," she said.

Chloe sighed. "You're way too impatient."

"Maybe we should order," Rick suggested.

On the front of its menu, The Pines proclaimed itself "Montana's *Finest* Eatery," the identity of the official pollster not divulged. While the claim of statewide culinary excellence was a stretch, it was generally agreed that the restaurant and saloon offered the best food in the town of Riverton, population 6,742.

"So, I'm thinking I can move into a two-bedroom," Chloe chattered, her eyes opening wide. She was tapping her straw on the bottom of her iced tea, stirring up a seabed formed by six packs of Splenda. "If I have a two-bedroom, then Abby can have her own room, and I can have a place to do my blogging."

They sat at their usual table, the one beneath the mounted head of a bewildered-looking moose, the double victim of a bullet and an unskilled taxidermist. Rick scanned the restaurant. His eyes slithered over his left shoulder, traveling vicariously through an archway that led to a barroom filled with sounds of laughter and a distraught Patsy Cline. It took only a few seconds of gazing at the shrine of liquor behind the bar for him to remember that happy hour had never ended in happiness for him.

"You're still blogging, huh?" he asked, turning back toward Chloe and nodding with narrowed eyes. "You have time?"

"Damn right," Chloe shot back. "Someone has to protect the wildlife around here."

"The wildlife seems fairly protected to me."

"Not the buffalo."

Abby, playing a video game on her mother's iPhone, abruptly stopped and buried her face in her hands. "Buffalo?" Her face popped up, eyebrows cringed. "Again?"

"I was thinking of having a bison burger tonight," Rick teased. "What do you think, Abby?"

"Very funny," Chloe said, scolding her father with her glare. Her eyes darted in search of the waitress. "Rhonda, can we go ahead and order?"

After delivering supper plates to a pair of locals seated at the bar, Rhonda approached the table, notepad in hand.

Rick bit the left side of his lip, studying Chloe as she ordered. Her skin was pale, and her makeup had failed to cover the darkness below her eyes. He was sure she hadn't slept. Still, she had all this energy.

He didn't think it was drugs. *Please, God, not drugs.* A manic episode, maybe?

Chloe flicked glances at him twice, perhaps feeling his stare. His eyes ducked into his menu. "Abby, what would you like?" Rick asked, not looking up.

Maybe he should stop being so damn suspicious, he thought. Chloe had just taken a two-year chip from NA. Her child seemed happy. She said the job at Yellowstone was going well. She really liked her new boss, although perhaps a little more than her father would prefer.

Matt Steelman was the guy's name. He'd only been there a short time, but he'd already hung the moon.

"I'll have my usual, Rhon," Rick said. The waitress nodded, slipped the notepad in her apron, and collected the menus. She leaned closer to Rick, gently squeezing his forearm.

"You need to send me a bill," she whispered. "My final divorce papers came through, and I want to pay you."

Rick shook his head, glancing at Abby as his face flushed. "Not necessary."

"I insist. You're a good lawyer."

"It's really not necessary," he repeated, looking again at Chloe and Abby. "I'm sorry the marriage didn't work out. I . . . was happy to help."

She frowned, placing a hand on her hip. "I mean it," she said, tucking the menus under her arm and walking away.

"Why did Rhonda get divorced?" Abby asked in a loud whisper.

"Abby!" Rick shot back. "You know better than that."

"What's the big deal? Mommy's divorced."

"I'm *not* divorced," Chloe snapped, her tone hard and sharp.

"But you and my dad were together, and now you're not."

"Yes, but I was never married. I *told* you that."

"Enough!" Rick said in a stern whisper, wincing as he raised an open palm. Chloe was right—she and Abby's father, meth addict Chase Rettick, had never married, a fact that brought Rick a fair measure of solace. Still, he loathed the idea of Abby being drawn into adult conversations, and he shuddered to envision what was said to her when he wasn't around. He wanted so badly for Abby to just be a kid.

They sat in silence. Rick looked at his daughter, trying to get a read. Her mood was ricocheting between irritability and bliss. Something wasn't right. Chloe stared back, offering a contrived smile. Her raised eyebrows asked what was on his mind. Rick drew a deep breath, hesitant to broach a subject that was certain to cause a stir.

"You doing okay with your meds?" The words barely left his lips when her face flushed, her eyes raising an angry shield. *Bull's-eye.*

"Why would you ask that?" Her edgy, rising voice caused heads to turn.

"I thought I was *supposed* to ask that."

"You're *supposed* to ask me if I'm taking my meds?"

Rick glanced at Abby, who was staring at her video game and pretending not to listen. His heart ached for her.

"Easy," he said to Chloe. "I thought you wanted me to check on you—hold you accountable." He leaned forward, head tilted, eyes open wide. "Am I right?"

Chloe pressed her lips together, her nostrils drawing short breaths. "You want to check on me . . . or *control* me?" she said too loudly.

Rick gripped his forehead, massaging his temples to summon patience. He knew all too well where Chloe got her temper. "Are we going to go through this again?" he asked wearily.

She prepared to answer but instead narrowed her eyes toward the barroom. "What the hell are you looking at?" she yelled.

Rick looked over his shoulder. Two stools down from the locals was a disheveled man seated alone, a grease-soaked John Deere ball cap resting beside a half-empty glass of beer. He shifted his disturbing glare from Chloe to Rick, his face tightening as his dark eyes deepened with unexplained scorn.

Rick hadn't noticed him earlier, and he wasn't sure he'd seen the man before. He fixed his eyes on him. *What's his deal?* Slowly, Rick turned back toward the table.

"Chloe, take it down a notch—*please*," he said in a loud whisper, a caution carried out many times before. "I didn't mean anything by what I said. You know I just worry about you."

Chloe regained her composure. "You shouldn't worry so much. I'm fine. *Honest.*"

Rick had a sinking feeling, sensing that nothing could be further from the truth.

The arrival of food produced an armistice that lasted until dessert.

"Pa-Pa, can I order some vanilla Wilcoxin's?" Abby asked.

Chloe glared at her daughter. "No desserts during the week," she said abruptly, snatching her iPhone from Abby's small hands. "We've discussed it."

"It's Thursday night, Chloe," Rick offered. "A little ice cream won't—"

"Not during the week," Chloe repeated, hiking her eyebrows. "It was your rule, remember? At least, it was your rule when I was a kid."

Rick glanced away, guilty as charged. "It was a dumb rule," he muttered, shaking his head. He put on a pair of cheaters and began reviewing the dinner tab left by Rhonda. As he reached for his wallet, he noticed the broad torso of a man standing at the edge of the table, hands firmly on hips.

"You don't like fishing anymore?" a booming voice asked.

"Hi, Uncle Jack!" Abby shouted. Jack Kelly winked at her, then turned his buoyant eyes and infectious grin toward Chloe. Unable to resist, she managed to birth a smile, her first of the night. "Hey, Uncle Jack," she echoed softly.

He wasn't their blood uncle—obvious to some, Jack being black—but his warm demeanor and magnetic charm had earned him the term of endearment. His friendship with Rick spanned decades, dating back to their chance meeting as opponents at college football's

East-West Shrine Game, Jack representing Rutgers and Rick playing for San Diego State.

Rick slid from the booth and rose to his feet, vigorously shaking Jack's immense hand as the former tight end swallowed him up in a warm embrace. "Yes, I still do like fishing," Rick said with lament. "I've wanted to get out, but something always seems to come up."

Jack's face brightened. "What are you doing Saturday? I was going to take one last trip out to Shadow Lake. Crack of dawn. Thought maybe I could bring back a few more cutthroats before the lake ices over. You in?"

"Won't work," Rick said, casting a smile toward Abby. "My favorite granddaughter will be with me Friday night."

Abby tilted her head and pursed her lips. "I'm your *only* granddaughter, Pa-Pa," she said. "Why can't I just go with you? I want to fish!"

Chloe frowned. "And what about your school project, young lady? Remember your promise to finish it this weekend?" Abby's lips curled downward as she huffed through her freckled nose.

Rick looked curiously at Jack. "Kind of late in the season to be going to Shadow Lake, isn't it? I heard there might be some weather coming in."

"This is Montana," Jack said with a warm chuckle. "There's *always* weather coming in."

Rick nodded and smiled. "Well, we need to get together—soon. It's been too long." He removed his Stetson from a hook next to the booth and tugged it low over his forehead. "You need a table? We were just leaving."

Jack glanced around the crowded dining room. "Don't mind if I do. Tamara is supposed to meet me for supper. I've been fishing on the Yellowstone all afternoon."

"You're making me jealous."

"Life is short, my friend—don't let it pass you by. You *sure* you don't want to go?"

Rick stood and patted his friend's shoulder as Jack slid his brawny frame into the booth. "I'll take a rain check."

Chloe and Abby each gave Jack a hug, then followed Rick through the bar. The guy who'd been staring at them during supper shook his head in disgust. Rick swallowed hard into a rapid heartbeat, suddenly feeling ill at ease. The guy seemed eerily familiar, but he still couldn't place him.

"Chloe, I'll be right out."

"What are you doing?" She glanced between Rick and the stranger. "What's going on?"

"Outside," he said firmly, gesturing toward the door. Chloe fumbled for Abby's hand, tugging her to her side. She squinted at Rick, looking confused, then shook her head as they walked away.

Rick watched Chloe and Abby leave before fixing a hard stare at the stranger. "Do I know you?"

"You should," the man huffed, his breath filling Rick's nostrils with the stench of alcohol. "My name is Draper Townsend. Ring any bells?"

The last name did, loud and clear. Rick felt heat color his face.

"You and my sister were in an accident," Draper continued. "You recall?"

Dumb question. The accident. Rick couldn't forget it if he wanted to. "That was a long time ago, Mr. Townsend."

Draper took a long draw of beer, wiping his mouth with the back of an unwashed hand. "A long time ago? Not for my family. That accident destroyed my parents . . . They were never the same."

Rick glanced toward the floor, his mind flashing to a rainy Friday night in high school. Bent steel. Shattered glass. Blood . . . *so much blood*. Julianne Townsend died that night. They shouldn't even have been together.

He swallowed again and looked back at Draper. Maybe he'd seen the man's picture in the paper. Julianne had mentioned she had a brother, one with an irrepressible mean streak that had landed him in state prison. Incarceration apparently had done little to burnish Draper's social skills.

"I knew your parents," Rick said. "They offered me their forgiveness—a long time ago."

Draper ignored the remark. He looked toward the front door. "That your daughter and grandkid?" he asked, looking back at Rick. "Must be nice, huh? No telling how many children Julianne might have had."

Rick's eyes sharpened as he moved closer to Draper's face. "You threatening my family?" he asked, the edge in his voice reflecting his rocketing adrenaline.

"Hey, Rick!" a familiar voice said. "This guy bothering you?"

Rick turned his head toward Sleeves. The burly auburn-bearded bartender was leaning forward across the bar, supported by the thick tattoo-covered forearms that inspired his name.

"Dammit, Draper, I warned you," Sleeves scolded. "Do I need to run you out of here? Your P.O. probably wouldn't want you drinkin' anyway."

Draper stared blankly at Sleeves. He turned back toward Rick.

"Look, your sister was a good person," Rick said quietly, his voice heavy with contrition. "I have never forgotten what happened. I am truly sorry."

Draper didn't move, his hateful eyes delivering a chill. Rick stared back at him, his patience quickly drifting away. "Don't *ever* threaten my family," he said through gritted teeth.

He pulled back gradually, putting his hands in the pockets of his canvas vest. With a nod toward Sleeves, Rick burned a final stare into Draper's eyes and headed out the door.

"Daddy, who was that guy?" Chloe asked as she shivered in the crisp evening air outside the restaurant. "He seemed . . . creepy."

Rick didn't answer, his mind still in the bar. Chloe waved her hand impatiently. "Dad! Who *was* he?"

"Just an old friend," Rick muttered, trying not to appear rattled. Chloe frowned. "He didn't look too friendly to me."

Abby tugged on her mother's denim jacket, wanting to say good-bye. Chloe hugged her as she focused her eyes on Rick. "Please *promise* Abby will be in school tomorrow? She can't afford to miss any more days."

Rick shrugged. "You have a problem with my homeschooling?"

"Fly fishing doesn't qualify as homeschooling."

"I'll have her there at 8:20 sharp," Rick said. "Promise."

Chloe turned toward her daughter. "C'mon, princess, give Mommy a hug." She dropped to one knee to allow Abby to put arms around her neck.

Chloe stood and faced her dad. Her hands rested on her hips, which were at least an inch above the beltline of her jeans. Rick could see the St. Christopher medal that she wore around her neck, an indicator that her blouse was open one button too many—just the kind of bait that attracted slugs like Chase Rettick.

"You might want to pull up those pants," Rick said, disregarding the blouse issue.

"Save it, Dad. I'm not twelve."

She avoided eye contact, shifting her weight nervously. Rick's instincts kept screaming that something didn't fit. "You sure you're okay?"

Another brushfire. "What is your *problem*?" Chloe shouted, arms flailing. "Why do you keep asking me that?"

"I only asked you once."

"What makes you think I'm not okay?" she asked. "Am I too freakin' *happy* for you?"

Rick took a step toward her. "Chloe, please."

Chloe threw her arms forward, signaling him to keep his distance. Now she was acting twelve. "Leave me the hell alone!" she said, storming off toward her car.

Rick bit his lip and shook his head. He considered going after her but held back. Not his first rodeo. Nor Abby's either.

Abby shrugged as she looked innocently at her grandfather. Rick knew she'd seen this episode before. Tomorrow would be better. Or not.

Rick put out his hand and Abby clutched it. They headed for his truck. The ranch was twenty-five miles down the valley. It was time to go home.

He forced a smile as he looked into the eyes of his grandchild, who reminded him of the uncomplicated little girl that Chloe had once been.

CHAPTER 2

CHLOE MORRAND WAS RUNNING LATE, but that was the least of her problems.

Despite another night without sleep, she wasn't tired. She'd been awake for nearly an hour before her alarm went off, staring at her window in an anxious plea for daylight as she tried in vain to quiet her mind. When she'd lingered too long in the shower, enjoying the water's warmth, she had fallen behind.

She rubbed the shoulders of her green ranger jacket as her SUV staggered to life, frigid air humming from the vents. She gritted her teeth and winced as she clunked over the curb on her way out of her apartment complex. A column of golden aspens flickered in the gentle morning wind, promising a postcard-worthy late-autumn morning, but Chloe barely noticed. Her eyes focused trancelike as she sped through sleepy Riverton, desperate for a jolt of fresh coffee—the last thing she needed.

Even though he'd only seen her once before—when she was a teenager—Richard Bledsoe was certain that the woman speeding out of the apartment complex had to be Chloe Morrand. Attractive mid- to late-twenties. Different hair color, maybe. But yeah, that was her.

Everything he needed to know was on her Facebook page. She posted all the time about being a ranger at Yellowstone National

Park. Even was dumb enough to take a selfie in front of her apartment complex. Bledsoe shook his head. *Amazing what these stupid kids put on Facebook these days.*

His jaw muscles tightened as he followed her SUV into town. His mind drifted to the time he tailed his son, Christian, when the boy was on his way to make a drug buy. They had quite an argument that night, screamed at each other but good. He recalled the countless shouting matches he'd had with his son, some of them turning physical. He would give anything to argue with Christian now, have him standing there in front of him, the young man's stormy brown eyes framed by his thick black hair. Given that opportunity, Bledsoe would lean forward, hold the boy tightly, never let him go.

Of course, such a thing was no longer possible. Christian was gone. And he could thank Rick Morrand for that.

Bledsoe glanced into his rearview mirror to see lips quivering with heartbreak. He blinked his moist eyes and shook his head, fighting off the rapidly approaching gloom. As he clutched his steering wheel, his mind fueled the igniting flames of his insatiable anger.

Someone would have to pay, that was for sure. Bledsoe could deal with Rick Morrand later, but for now the daughter would do just fine.

He watched Chloe pull off toward a cedar roadside kiosk, its neon sign promising "FRESH BREW" in the dim morning light. Bledsoe hung back, not wanting to draw attention. He would have to be patient, wait for his opportunity. His cold eyes glared at her as she waited in line at the drive-through. Chloe for Christian. *An eye for an eye, a tooth for a tooth.*

A life for a life.

———◆———

"Happy Friday!" the smiling face proclaimed as it poked out the window of the Coffee Cabin. Wanda "Pebbles" Pierce didn't care much for makeup, and her gray roots declared her three weeks tardy for a date with Clairol Nice 'n Easy, but her early morning enthusiasm was nearly as stimulating as her coffee. "I was wondering where you were!"

"Hey, Pebbles," Chloe said, forcing a smile. "Yeah, I guess I'm running a little late."

"Three shots, no cream—right, darlin'?"

Chloe nodded.

They exchanged a few additional niceties, Chloe grateful for the opportunity to communicate with a voice not living rent-free inside her head. As soon as she pulled away from the drive-through, the clamor within her tangled brain resumed, delivering repeated, severe critiques of her behavior from the night before. Yet one more time she had embarrassed herself in front of her father and set a poor example for Abby. They both deserved better.

Her bad. *Again.*

Chloe told herself she needed to make it right—clean off her side of the street, as the saying went. She picked up her cell phone, staring at her thumb on the keypad. She took a deep breath, hesitated, then placed the phone back on the console, just as she had done twice already that morning. She had a fifty-mile drive down the length of the valley to her job at Yellowstone. Plenty of time. Her father probably wasn't awake yet, she lied to herself.

A glance in the mirror. "Nice raccoon eyes," she said aloud. She fumbled for some blush from her purse and liberally swiped away. She couldn't let her boss, Matt Steelman, see her looking like this.

Two long sips from her Americano did little to improve her outlook. It had been easier last night, when she was still pissed and pounded away on the keys of her laptop, focusing on her blog. Now the anger was gone, replaced by a blended cocktail of guilt and remorse.

Her head kept scolding her. As she picked up speed on Highway 89 and descended into the valley, Chloe reached for a CD lying without a jewel case on her passenger seat. Popping the disc into her after-market player, she took a deep breath through her nostrils and welcomed the initial strains of Coldplay's "Yellow." She threw on her twenty-dollar sunglasses, which had been wandering on the dash. Rapping her hand on the steering wheel, she plunged herself into the song's hard, searing guitar riffs, bringing her mind and the world about her to an uneasy yet welcome truce. Much better. Her head nodding with increasing intensity, she focused on the road ahead.

CHAPTER 3

DEPUTY BILLY RENFRO BROKE INTO a broad smile as he emerged from the Wildflour Bakery, his beefy right arm cradling a white paper sack as though it were his firstborn. He settled onto a sidewalk bench—the one propped up by a pair of smiling wood-carved bears—and jammed a prodigious paw into his freshly purchased plunder.

As he buried his dentures into a huckleberry Danish—*extra icing, please*—he closed his eyes, threw back his head, and drew a deep breath through his nostrils, convinced all was well in the world around him.

"So, how's that diet coming?"

Billy shielded his eyes from the late morning sun, confirming the familiar voice of Charlie Duchesne, longtime Dexter County coroner. The deputy repositioned himself on the bench, making room for both Charlie and the treasured pastries. He nodded at the bag. "Dig in."

"None for me—Dora would have a fit," Charlie said as he waved his hand and sat down. Billy flicked crust off the front of his uniform and tugged his jacket closed, hoping to somehow disguise his expansive girth. His beloved Melba, now gone fifteen years, would frown on his diet as well. After a moment, he shrugged and shoved another sizeable bite beneath the bushy gray moustache that canopied his upper lip. "You finish that death report for Harold Mikan?" he mumbled through a mouthful. "The sheriff and I would like to put that one to bed, so to speak."

Charlie seemed to pay him no mind, instead squinting curiously up and down Main Street as though trying to solve a riddle. The coroner's clenched teeth revealed an uneven bite that favored one side of his jaw, a mild stroke having left an oval opening that seemed to anticipate a can of spinach. Charlie released a heavy sigh. "Poor choice of words, my friend."

"Well, that's what happened, isn't it?" Billy pressed, eyebrows raised. "He was in bed with Rae Lynn at the time of his passing, was he not?"

Charlie frowned. "Mr. Mikan perished due to cardiac arrest, which I suppose could be considered natural causes. Of course, I don't suppose it's all that *natural* for an eighty-six-year-old man to be having relations with a forty-one-year-old bride."

"Any foul play?"

Charlie wagged his head, folding his arms across his chest. "Nope. About the only foul play here was Harold marrying four different women several years his junior."

"Was it four? That's a lot of alimony." Billy shook his head in wonder. "And this one will get life insurance—plenty of it." He took a last bite of Danish. "You sure there wasn't foul play?"

"Sorry to disappoint you. Whatever life insurance she's getting, she deserves every penny. Harold was a crusty old coot."

"Another routine investigation."

"Yes—routine," Charlie grumbled, his lips curled downward. "Just like everything else around here."

Billy chuckled. "You telling me you're looking for some kind of excitement?"

"Wouldn't hurt."

"Careful what you wish for."

Billy looked into the white paper bag, reviewing his inventory. "Can I interest you in a blueberry muffin? It's got fruit in it."

"None for me."

Billy pulled out a second Danish, this one apple cinnamon. Before he could sample it, he was interrupted by loud shouting down the sidewalk. He dropped the pastry back in the bag, turning his attention to a pair of women—one of them pregnant—fighting over possession of a bright-red handbag. Using his khaki uniform pants as a napkin, he ambled toward the conflict, Charlie apparently having no interest in accompanying him.

"Let go, bitch!" the pregnant woman shouted.

"Not a chance, you damned thief!"

Melody Hanrahan, proprietor of Melody's Cards and Gifts, had a death grip on the vinyl purse. Billy found Melody attractive, kind of a Dolly Parton look-alike. She normally was pleasant, except when she wasn't. Her crazed, fiery eyes caught sight of Billy as he approached. "She stole a necklace, Deputy!" Melody shouted, gasping for breath. "And it ain't the first time she stole from me!"

Billy closed in, placing both hands on the handbag. "Now, calm down, Melody. Take it easy. Can't you see this woman's with child?"

With child indeed. And not just any child. Tessie Lou Hunter was the fiancée of Sheriff Caleb Tidwell. The pregnancy was unexpected, but nuptials were planned. Caleb had insisted he wanted to do what was right—even if it seemed all wrong.

"I demand you arrest her—I want to press charges!" Melody hissed. Her face bore a hateful sneer, her voice infused with venom. Billy frowned. *Whose idea it was to name her Melody?*

"I said, 'Calm down,'" he repeated, extending an open palm toward the shopkeeper. Melody loosened her grip on the purse, allowing Tessie Lou to snatch it.

"It's in her bag," Melody said, her voice tempered. "There's a turquoise necklace. She was trying it on, and then it was gone. I watch her closely—she's done this before, I swear."

Billy turned toward Tessie Lou, her arms crisscrossed over the purse. "This woman's a liar! I don't have anything of hers!"

Billy drew a deep breath and fixed his eyes on the handbag. "Tessie, would you mind if I—"

Tessie Lou's eyes glazed with rage, her lower lip starting to quiver. "Hell yes, I'd mind! You're not lookin' in my purse, Deputy!"

Billy glanced up and down the sidewalk, wincing as he saw that a small crowd had gathered. Charlie had come over and stood among them, his shrug and raised eyebrows offering empathy but no desire to step inside the henhouse.

"I'm telling you, she stole that necklace!" Melody repeated.

Billy turned toward Tessie Lou, who clutched the purse tighter. "If you want to look in this purse, you'll have to arrest me, Deputy," she snarled through clenched teeth. Her eyes narrowed as she defiantly cocked her head. "Let's just say you're wrong. What would Caleb think about that?"

Billy's head throbbed. He rubbed his temples and looked at Melody. "How much for the necklace?"

"Twenty-five dollars."

Billy reached below his gut into the pocket of his pants, fishing out a pair of crumpled bills. "Here's thirty," he said, handing the money to Melody.

Her eyes burned at Tessie Lou. "You're no longer welcome here, pregnant or not."

Billy fluttered his hands in the direction of the onlookers. "Move along now, folks. Nothing more to see." Glancing once more into Tessie's Lou's smoldering eyes, he began walking beside Charlie back down the sidewalk. "Caleb sure knows how to pick 'em," he muttered. "He's definitely got his hands full with that one."

"He might be a little over-matched."

"Yeah, *over-matched*," Billy huffed. "Wouldn't be the first time, now, would it?"

As they approached the wooden bench, a man in a neatly pressed black suit waited for them. Rev. Richard Williams, popular pastor of the First Christian Church, usually wore a wide toothy grin. His smile was missing, replaced by eyebrows furrowed with contempt.

"You promised to call me, Deputy."

Billy rubbed his sticky fingers together and placed them on his hips. "I apologize for that, Reverend. As I told you over the phone, there's really not much we can do."

Rev. Williams's face appeared joyless and weary, as though hadn't slept in days. He rubbed his close-cropped peppered beard, considering Billy's reply. "You *did* promise to call me," he repeated, as though Billy had committed an unpardonable sin. The pastor held his glare for several awkward seconds before he turned and walked away.

Charlie looked at Billy as they sat on the bench, casting a thumb toward Rev. Williams. "What's with him? You been missing church?"

"I haven't been to church in years—not since Melba passed. I wish it were that simple." Billy swallowed and drew a breath. "Seems the preacher's daughter has voluntarily left home, and he wants us to bring her back. Our hands are tied—she's no longer a minor."

Charlie wrinkled his brow. "Courtney? I thought she had a scholarship."

"Not anymore she doesn't. You might say she's lost her way."

"Do you know where she is?"

"I can't be certain, but I would suspect drugs are involved."

"Methamphetamine?"

"Likely."

Charlie whistled a sigh out of the side of his mouth and stroked his balding pate. "Maybe I will take that muffin." Billy reached in the bag, gave the muffin to Charlie, then rolled the top of the bag shut. He dug into his top pocket for a toothpick, his appetite having abandoned him. Gazing down the sidewalk in the other direction, he spotted Melody standing with hands on hips, staring intently as Tessie Lou crossed the street and got into a pickup.

"You know," Billy said, "sometimes routine ain't such a bad thing."

CHAPTER 4

EVEN THOUGH HE WAS A quarter-mile behind her, Sheriff Caleb Tidwell knew he was trailing Chloe Morrand. Barreling along at eighty-five miles per hour, he could hardly keep pace with the SUV in the distance. He shook his head, a gentle frown giving way to a warm smile.

Once he closed in on the 2001 Dodge Durango, the one with the bent vanity plate that read "BUFFGAL," Caleb glanced at his dash to note that Chloe had slowed down to seventy-seven. As he eased past her, she stared at him with a stunned grimace, forehead furrowed and teeth biting the side of her lip. In addition to her speed, she seemed to further realize that the cell phone she was holding in plain view—though not an illegal activity in Montana—did little to buffer her case.

Caleb simply offered a brief wave to Chloe, pressed his accelerator, and continued down the highway. He shook his head again and chuckled. She likely would assume that he was giving her a pass on a speeding ticket because he had a thing for her, and that was partially true.

He knew Chloe's history better than most. He was well aware she could be dangerous to a man's heart, not to mention his soul. Perhaps that was the odd attraction. The danger.

She had proven an elusive conquest for Caleb, one of the few women in Riverton not swayed by a man in uniform—or, at least, not his uniform. Perhaps it was wishful thinking, but he lately had sensed that the ice had begun to thaw. Under normal circumstances, he definitely would have stopped her and issued a *warning*.

But Caleb had no time for Chloe Morrand. Not right now. He was scheduled to meet two visitors further down the valley, in a place that had been arranged to avoid suspicion.

His heart began pounding. He suddenly felt strangely alone. His mouth tightened into a scowl as he scolded himself for getting involved with outsiders in the first place. He should never have taken their money. Now there was no turning back.

Caleb fixed his eyes intently on the road head. He was running late, and these were the kind of people who didn't like to wait.

"Hello? Hello?"

The voice coming from her cell phone snapped Chloe out of a daze. She hadn't seen Caleb coming up behind her, and she was stunned he didn't pull her over.

"Yeah, hello? Matt?" she said to her boss.

"Chloe? Hi. What's up?"

"I ... uh ... I'm running a few minutes behind," she said. "I apologize. I can make it up at lunch or at the end of my shift." She gave herself a hopeful look in the rearview mirror, awaiting Matt's reply.

"No worries. Everything OK?"

She smiled. His voice was gentle and caring. "Oh yeah, I'm fine."

"Good," Matt said. He paused. "Hey, later today, do you have time to get together?"

Matt's tone sounded serious. At least, her mind said it did. Chloe's heart thumped. Was she in trouble?

"Is everything all right?" she asked.

"Sure. Everything's fine."

"Is it my blog? Did someone complain about my blog?"

Matt laughed. "No, nothing like that. I was just hoping we could go somewhere and, you know, talk."

His tone was soft, disarming her. "Talk, huh?" she said playfully, recalling some of the other times they had *talked.*

Matt laughed again. "Yeah . . . talk."

"See you soon, Boss," Chloe said, ending the call and placing her phone back on the console. She grinned at herself in the rearview, then gunned her Durango to keep pace with Caleb Tidwell. *What could be safer than following the sheriff?*

After a couple of more replays of "Yellow," Chloe felt her morning turning around. Her balky heater, combined with a hint of morning sun, had finally begun to warm up the interior of her SUV, and as she traveled about a quarter-mile behind Caleb, she found him to be a capable escort.

Nodding her head contentedly to Coldplay, Chloe watched a herd of Angus scattered in a lush dew-tipped field along the highway. The distant snow-covered peaks of the Beartooth Mountains were sharp and crisp, a backdrop so perfect it couldn't possibly be real.

As her gaze reached the end of the herd, Chloe stiffened. She took her foot off the gas momentarily, squinting out the window. Separated from the cattle, but within a few feet of a damaged fence line, were two bison. They weren't grazing, but instead appeared to be confused by the newness of their surroundings, uncertain what to do next.

Something wasn't right. If the animals were from the wild Yellowstone herd—and if they were infected—they most certainly would be slaughtered.

Chloe impulsively reached for her cell phone. She wanted to call Matt, tell him what she saw, but she decided it could wait until she arrived at work. She put the phone down and glanced into her rearview, reminding herself she needed lipstick.

She passed another herd on her right, this one mostly red cattle. A few of the animals stopped eating to watch her SUV fly by. She cocked her head, snagged by the sight, as she reached the ranch's fence line, not wanting to believe what she saw.

Two more bison. This time they were standing closer to the cattle.

Chloe needed to call *someone*. Maybe her dad? She had earlier decided she would avoid talking to him until later in the day. That would no longer work. She needed to call him now.

As he got out of the shower, Rick made a mental note that he had about ten minutes before he needed to wake up Abby. They had stayed up late—even had a tablespoon of ice cream, as it turned out—and he wanted her to get as much sleep as possible.

Rick heard the coffeemaker in the kitchen taking final steamy gasps as it finished brewing. His phone rang, causing him to slip out into the kitchen wrapped in a towel. He looked at his Blackberry. *Chloe*. Her photo flashed on the screen, accompanied by the sound of one of those obnoxious songs from Coldplay. Chloe had programmed herself into his contacts—at the time, they'd both thought it was funny.

He didn't touch the phone, instead staring at it as he poured a half cup of coffee. He took a sip, calmly watching the phone run out of rings and vanish into voice mail. *Not now*. He needed a break from all things Chloe.

Sadness flushed over him. He should have answered. He loved his daughter dearly. On most days, especially now that she was *stable*, they truly connected. She was bright and had a great sense of humor. *His* sense of humor.

But, damn, was she ever high maintenance. The events of the previous night still stung.

Rick thought of his late wife, Christine. She would have answered the phone, made things right. She always had. Three years removed from the day of her death, when the vicious breast cancer she'd fought so valiantly had secured its undeserved triumph, Rick's chest still ached with a desolate feeling of loneliness, a desperate void that seemed impossible to fill.

He took another sip of his coffee and set the cup back on the kitchen counter. Abby needed to go to school.

Chloe cringed as she prepared to leave her father a message.

"Dad, it's me," she said between nervous breaths. "Uh . . . sorry about last night. I was kind of tired. I hope . . . Anyway, I just passed the Double-U and Shining Mountain. Both ranches have bison inside the fence with their herds. Makes no sense, does it?"

She paused, her mouth tightening as she clenched her teeth in frustration. She had explained the issue to her father a thousand times, telling him that Yellowstone bison—even when stricken with brucellosis—would not harm local cattle. Plenty of experts agreed with her, and she had the blog to prove it. As the son of a rancher, her dad never took her seriously. She bit the side of her curled bottom lip. Would he even care? Would *anybody* care?

"I . . . uh . . . I'll try to call later," she said, adding a mousy "Love you."

Her mind shifted into overdrive. She needed to *save* these buffalo. *Now.* If she waited until she got to work, it might be too late. The animals would be shot on the spot, with no one bothering to check whether they were infected.

She tried to think, but her brain sparked like a snapped power line. Morning sunlight rushed into the sides of her sunglasses, causing her head to throb. Her heart rate climbed. Anxiety attack?

The meds. I should have taken my meds.

It had been almost six weeks. The meds had made her feel drowsy and bloated. She told her psychiatrist, but he wouldn't listen. Shrinks never listened. He just wrote another scrip and told her to deal with it.

She looked at the road in front of her. Caleb was still up ahead. Maybe he could help.

Caleb wasn't too keen on Chloe's activism, that was for sure. Nobody in town was. Not after every truck at the Fourth of July rodeo had a "Save the Buffalo" flyer placed on its windshield. Ranchers flooded the sheriff's office with complaints. Caleb hadn't been amused.

That was a few months back. Maybe this could work. Caleb had a thing for her, always had. He would definitely help *her*, wouldn't he? She was positive she could trust him.

She pushed her accelerator, the tires of her SUV vibrating as she hit ninety. She closed in on Caleb quickly, mainly because he had turned off of 89 and headed down the gravel road that led into the mountains. The sheriff seemed unaware that she was only a quarter-mile behind him, picking up speed as he eventually disappeared into a canyon.

Chloe gave chase, wagging her head in desperation. She followed a stream of heavy dust for about three miles, slowing only slightly as she wound through hairpins in the national forest. She threw her hands in the air, incredulous. "Where the hell are you *going?*" she shouted to the empty interior of her Durango.

She was familiar with the road that led to the trailhead for Sawtooth Rock and Shadow Lake, a pair of hiking spots her father had taken her as a child. She fumbled for her cell phone, wanting to check the time, but two deep potholes bounced it to the floor. She glanced at the clock on her dash, cursing herself when she remembered it had read 12:37 for the past two years. Time no longer seemed to matter, her desire to catch Caleb having bloomed into a strange obsession.

As she made her way around a corner, Chloe slammed on the brakes and swallowed hard. She spotted Caleb through an opening in a stand of spruce trees, less than one hundred yards ahead. His vehicle sat parked on the side of the road, and he was engaged in an animated conversation with a man and a woman. Chloe turned off her engine, her eyes remaining fixed on the conflict in front of her. She slipped around the front of her Durango, through a narrow roadside ditch and into the trees, hoping to get a closer look.

A Cadillac DTS parked in front of Caleb's SUV said these were out-of-towners, and they were further betrayed by the man's sport coat and open-collared shirt, insufficient attire for the crisp morning air. The woman, dressed in a black leather jacket, was poking her finger menacingly toward Caleb. This was no routine traffic stop.

Caleb nodded nervously, looking more like a misbehaving child than the duly elected Dexter County sheriff.

Chloe eased past the trunk of another spruce, tugging a low-hanging branch out of the way to provide herself a view. She removed her sunglasses and leaned forward, hoping to hear the exchange.

A twig snapped. She froze. Cautiously, she scanned her surroundings. Her eyes widened. Less than fifteen feet away, standing beneath another tree, was a delicate fawn, still in possession of some of its spots, eyes blinking in unblemished innocence.

Chloe raised her index finger to her pursed lips, urging the creature to remain quiet. It worked, but only briefly. The air shattered as a large doe crashed through the brush, startled by unseen danger and eager to protect its young. The mother darted within inches of Chloe and out from the trees, its precious fawn in tow.

Chloe clawed at a tree branch in an effort to maintain her balance, but the limb gave way with a resounding crack. The woman scolding Caleb jerked her head toward the trees, where she immediately spotted Chloe. She didn't look happy.

Chloe shuddered. She backpedaled, tumbling to the ground. She got back on her feet but fell again, her knee cracking against a boulder as she scrambled through the ditch back up to the road. She fumbled in her pocket for her keys, her instincts telling her this was not the time to chat up Caleb about buffalo.

She jumped back into her SUV. Her trembling hand cranked the ignition, but the engine didn't turn over. "Seriously?" she said in a loud, panicked whisper. "Not now!"

On the second attempt, the engine responded. Chloe's SUV lurched across the road as she tried to turn around. Reaching the edge, she hit her brakes and slammed the vehicle into Reverse, her transmission wailing in protest. She punched the gas, sending her rear tires off the edge of the gravel road, but when she shifted forward, her tires only kicked up gravel. Through the trees, she caught sight of Caleb, who was staring directly at her, his mouth tight with displeasure.

Chloe cranked the transmission back into Reverse, this time ramming into a boulder. "Shit!" she whispered loudly, shifting into Drive and trying to rock the vehicle free.

Caleb was now storming toward her, his face reddened and veins bulging from his neck. She put her vehicle in Park and took a deep breath of resignation. When her quivering index finger pressed the button for her power window, she was thankful the glass was only capable of lowering halfway.

"What's up, Chloe?" Caleb said with irritation, placing his hand on the roof above her. She saw her sudden fear in his mirrored sunglasses. His warm exhale delivered the faded odor of eggs and coffee.

Chloe hesitated, turning her eyes first toward his badge, then across his chest to the gold-plated TIDWELL name tag pinned neatly above his pocket. Given her past, she remained uncomfortable dealing with any member of law enforcement, even those she knew. Caleb's anger certainly didn't help.

"I . . . saw you out on 89," she finally stuttered.

"Yeah," he said impatiently, shooting a glance toward the strangers. "What's up?"

She looked through the trees at the pair, then quickly back at Caleb. "I . . . wondered if you saw the buffalo on the—"

"Buffalo?" Caleb snapped. He wiped perspiration off his clean-shaven upper lip and sucked air up his nostrils. "What *buffalo?*"

She panicked. The truth wasn't cutting it. It rarely did, not when she was afraid. Caleb was definitely frightening her. She needed to try something else.

"Actually," she said, "I . . . I saw your car . . . and . . ."

Caleb stared stonily at her. Waiting.

"I . . . I thought maybe we could get together later?"

The young sheriff cocked his head as he pushed back from the SUV. He had made plenty of advances toward Chloe in town, all of which she had rejected. It wasn't that he wasn't attractive—he was. It had more to do with that pregnant fiancée he had at home.

She looked at him hopefully as he considered her proposition.

"Get out of the car, Chloe," Caleb said.

A chill rocketed down the back of her neck. Her forehead tightened. She had heard those words many times before. Never good. *Never good.*

"What?" she asked, her voice shaking. "Why?"

"Get out of the car, Chloe," Caleb repeated. "I need to get you out of this ditch."

Chloe exhaled with temporary relief but remained fearful. She got out of the SUV onto wobbly legs, her search for a deep breath halted halfway by the pounding in her chest. Her eyes wandered toward the strangers near the Cadillac. They glared impatiently, arms folded. She averted her eyes submissively, as though she'd encountered a grizzly.

Caleb stepped past her into the driver's seat. She grimaced as he thrust her delicate transmission between Drive and Reverse, eventually rocking her SUV free and pointing back toward Highway 89.

"Call me later," Caleb ordered as he jumped out of the seat and held the door for Chloe. He waved her into the SUV, appearing irritated, maybe even frightened. Cautiously, she passed him and got in.

"Is . . . is everything OK, Caleb?" she blurted out. "I mean . . . are *you* OK?"

"Call me," Caleb said more forcefully. "Right now, you really need to go."

Chloe was still shaking as she reached Highway 89. A truck's horn blared loudly, letting her know she had pulled onto the roadway without even looking for traffic. She winced at the sound, sliding onto the gravel shoulder before steadying herself and heading south.

She felt bad about leaving Caleb. Something wasn't right. She considered going back. Should she call Billy Renfro, Caleb's deputy? No. Whoever those people were, Caleb didn't want to be disturbed.

Besides, she was late. Really late. Matt wouldn't be happy. She picked up her phone. Should she call work? No. She just needed to get there. As fast as possible.

She began to put her phone down. It rang.

"Dad?"

"No," the voice said with a chuckle. "It's me."

Abby's father. Not now. Definitely not now. She hung up.

The phone rang again. The screen read "Restricted." Her hand reached for it, then pulled back. She shook her head and pushed out a breath. She answered.

"Hello?"

"Hi."

"I thought we agreed there would be no contact," she said, trying not to sound nervous. But she *was* nervous. Her stomach churned. She gasped for air, her anxiety threatening to smother her.

"I need to talk to you," the caller persisted. "In person."

"I . . . I don't think I want to do that," Chloe stammered. She couldn't breathe. She was starting to freak out.

"Please," he said. "It's—"

Silence. Chloe looked at the granite walls that rose up beside Highway 89. She was entering Yankee Jim Canyon. No service. The call was lost.

The canyon was narrow and dark, the highway disappearing beyond the reach of the sun.

Chloe's hand shook as she placed her phone back on the console. She contemplated the haunting voice she had just heard.

In the deep shadows of the canyon, she suddenly felt cold.

CHAPTER 5

CHLOE WAS SURE MATT STEELMAN was *the one*. They had a connection, and it wasn't just physical. He was a good guy, the real deal. She had visions of introducing him to Abby, and Chloe had never introduced any man to Abby. Her daughter would love him, and maybe Chloe and Matt could have kids of their own. They would have Matt's blue eyes, his thick blond hair.

Matt evidently hadn't gotten the memo.

Chloe sensed something was wrong the minute she arrived at work. She was late—*way* late. When she apologized to Matt, he simply shrugged, keeping his eyes fixed on paperwork he was reviewing on his desk. No words. No eye contact. Her stomach churning, she stole a couple of fretful glances as she took her place at the front counter of the Visitor Center.

Things got worse the second time Caleb Tidwell called her. Chloe hadn't provided a cell number—nor contacted Caleb as promised. She hoped he wouldn't notice. No such luck. When she'd batted her eyelashes that morning, she opened a door Caleb was determined to storm his way through.

"Like I told you, Tidwell, she's not allowed to take personal calls," she heard Matt say, plenty of bite in his voice. "You've already said this isn't official business. What do you want with her, anyway?"

Drama! Ooooh, yes! Chloe loved drama. She listened to the testosterone-forged sabers clanking away, the damsel Chloe the ultimate prize. At first, it turned her on, but her brain delivered a stern reminder.

"You can pursue any behavior you would like," her therapist, Annie, once told her, "as long as you are willing to pay the price."

Bledsoe checked into a motel in Gardiner, well south of Riverton and near the entrance of Yellowstone National Park. The last thing he needed was to get too cozy with the residents of the town in which Chloe Morrand lived. He also figured he could track her later in the day, once she got off work at Yellowstone.

His stomach twinged, reminding him that he hadn't eaten in almost twenty-four hours. He splashed water on his face and emerged from his room in search of food. He passed the innkeeper, who was watering a planter filled with sad yellow flowers that were already dead. "Enjoy the afternoon, Mr. Beltran," the man said.

Bledsoe snickered at the greeting. Stephen Beltran. His high school chemistry teacher. The guy at the desk had taken his cash and handed him a key, no questions asked. Maybe it was because they were headed into low season.

People in small towns were way too trusting.

On Caleb's third attempt, Matt let Chloe speak with him. "I want to talk to you about the bison you saw this morning—I think I can provide some information," Caleb said, his cell phone starting to break up. "Can we meet at the Sawtooth trailhead? Say, about six o'clock?"

Chloe grew tense, her defenses rising. The Sawtooth was several miles off Highway 89. "Why the Sawtooth?"

"Because—"

The call dropped. "Damn it!" Chloe looked up from her phone to see Matt glaring at her. She walked briskly outside, punching Caleb's cell number from her call log. *Voice mail.* "It's Chloe. I can meet you at the Sawtooth trailhead at six o'clock. I'll see you then." She stuffed her phone into the pocket of her khakis as she strode back inside, Matt's jealous eyes there to welcome her.

When her shift ended, Matt said he wanted to talk—away from work. She'd welcomed the opportunity to clear the air and ask him about meeting her daughter.

It didn't go well. Matt didn't want to meet Abby, and he no longer wanted Chloe.

Now she found herself alone, parked on side of Highway 89 just north of Gardiner, her lips trembling while waves of emotion gushed forth. As her uneven wailing echoed through the inside of her SUV, she balled her fists and cursed herself for becoming so vulnerable.

As long as you are willing to pay the price . . .

Matt Steelman was her pursuit. This was the price.

Chloe wiped her cheeks with the bottom of her palms and caught her breath. She needed to keep moving. She had to meet Caleb Tidwell—another horrible idea in a day filled with them. She checked her rearview. She was a mess. Mascara streaked below bloodshot eyes. "Nice," she said aloud in a nasal voice, peeking above the tissue squeezing her nose.

She needed to call Caleb and tell him she was running late. She reached for her phone on the console.

It wasn't there.

Bledsoe was sitting calmly in his truck on the northern outskirts of Gardiner, perusing the latest edition of the *Montana Pioneer*, an entertaining local rag he had picked up while having a late-afternoon cup of coffee at the Gateway Cafe. He found himself engrossed in a story that debated whether Canadian wolves were reducing the local elk population. Lucky for him, Chloe Morrand was speeding as she roared out of town, the hole in her muffler making her hard to miss.

Bledsoe tossed the newspaper on his passenger seat. He glanced at his watch: 6:23 p.m. He nodded. Still some daylight left.

His phone rang. He glanced at the screen. It was Susan. Fifth time she had called that day. She probably was worried, and rightly so. They hadn't talked in three days. Before Richard suddenly disappeared, they'd talked every day for thirty years.

Bledsoe couldn't let anyone know where he was, not even his wife. He took a deep, labored breath and closed his eyes. He agonized about not talking to Susan, knowing the pain it would cause her, and Lord knew she had suffered enough. But he'd made a decision. Soon, she would know what happened, how he'd handled things. She would have to understand he was doing this for *them*.

He pulled onto Highway 89 and accelerated. As he stared at the taillights of Chloe's SUV, his head bobbed with the confidence that his opportunity was about to knock.

Draper Townsend was washing down fried chicken with the third beer he'd popped since he started eating.

"How many of those have you had?" Maggie said over her shoulder as she stood at the sink and washed a skillet. She frowned as she stared at the empty bottle of liquid soap in her hand, her eyes squinting as they battled fading sunlight pouring through the kitchen window.

"The chicken?" Draper grunted, his mouth full.

"No, the beer."

"Dunno."

Draper scanned the kitchen, grease stains on the ceiling and lime-green paint peeling from the walls. He didn't care for the place—not that he'd spent much time there. For nearly three decades, he'd been in and out of the state pen, so much so that he was much more comfortable in a prison cell that at home. At least the cinder blocks were painted.

"You shouldn't be drinking at all," Maggie said, continuing to scrub her skillet.

Draper ignored her. Always did. He stared at the apron bow neatly tied above her ample backside, pondering whether every man's wife failed to mind her own business—or just his.

He and Maggie had been together forever, even if they hadn't spent much time under the same roof. She first saw a picture of him in the local paper, when he'd been convicted of armed robbery at age twenty. She began writing letters to him at the prison in Deer Lodge, telling him she was attracted to the childlike innocence in his eyes. Draper had no clue what she was talking about, but the relationship flourished. They married when he received parole, Draper landing a job with a pest control company and the future looking shiny bright.

The honeymoon was brief. Draper went back, this time for attempted murder. Aside from occasional conjugal visits, Draper and Maggie hadn't developed much of a marital bond. They seemed stuck with each other, more than anything else.

"Sleeves called here this morning," Maggie said, casting a glance over her shoulder as she coaxed a noisy, final wheeze of liquid soap into the skillet. "He said you were causing trouble down at The Pines, harassing that Morrand fella."

"Sleeves needs to keep to himself," Draper mumbled in a dark, threatening tone.

Maggie stopped washing and turned toward her husband. She placed a hand on her hip, her wet dishrag dripping onto her dress.

"You're not supposed to drink," she repeated. "You want them to send you back?"

Draper lit a cigarette and took a deep drag, considering the proposition. He and Maggie got along much better when he was behind bars, that was for sure. She had threatened to leave him on occasion, but he knew she'd never follow through. She feared Draper, and she owed him. After all, that attempted murder charge resulted when he confronted her daddy over some things the man had done to Maggie as a child.

Draper was big on settling scores—fellow inmates would attest to that. In his world, no transgression should go unpunished. He felt compelled to level the playing field in a world that treated him unfairly, the cruelest twist being the death of his baby sister, Julianne. Even when his life had drifted into darkness, Julianne had refused to abandon him. She still had talked to him, still seemed to understand him.

Rick Morrand had taken her away and lost nothing. Now it was Morrand's turn to pay.

"Morrand caused the death of my sister," Draper said, flicking an ash among the chicken bones and smear of mashed potatoes on his plate. "He should be held accountable."

Maggie turned back toward the sink, shaking her head.

"You weren't even there," she said. "You were up in Deer Lodge. Maybe if you had been around . . ."

Draper took another drag of his cigarette. His nostrils pulsed as smoke streamed from them. Her words definitely stung. He balled his fist and held it close to his lips, staring intently at her as she finished rinsing the skillet and placed it on the counter. *One good whack and she would be history.*

Maggie turned toward him, her tired expression filled with disappointment. She crossed her arms as she leaned against the counter. She stared coldly at him as he flicked more ash.

"And don't be putting out that cigarette on that plate," she instructed. "That's plastic—it'll leave a mark."

She turned her back on him again, picking up another dish to wash. She should be more respectful toward him, he thought, at least for her own good. He took another gulp of beer and crushed his cigarette into the mashed potatoes. A deep breath seemed to settle him.

Draper was sick and tired of parole. He had some things he needed to handle—scores he needed to settle—that likely would land him in prison for good. He folded his arms across his chest, staring at his wife bent over the sink.

He figured if he was going to be locked away forever—say, on a charge of murder—he sure wasn't going to waste it on Maggie.

Caleb stood outside his SUV at the Shadow Lake trailhead, shivering and stupid. Chloe Morrand had played him on and off since high school, and it looked like she got him again.

He looked toward the sky. Spatters of cool rain tingled his face. His watch told him it was almost seven. She probably wouldn't show. Worse yet, his fiancée would be wondering where he was. He was surprised Tessie Lou hadn't called.

Caleb tugged open the tailgate of his vehicle, staring at a bouquet of flowers. *A real ladies' man.* He'd bought some sandwiches, even a bottle of wine. *Surely Chloe could have one glass of wine . . .*

They had agreed to meet at the trailhead, far out of town. If they had met in public, Tessie would hear about it before he got home. That wouldn't be good. Tessie knew all about Chloe Morrand. She didn't care much for Chloe, nor any other woman who cast eyes toward Caleb. That time he said Chloe's name during sex sure didn't help.

Caleb pushed the tailgate shut, wiping dust on his pants. After checking his watch again, he dropped his head and exhaled, squeezing the bridge of his nose as his irritation with Chloe continued to build. He had a woman at home carrying his child. Yet, here he was once again, resuming his pursuit—his obsession—with Chloe Morrand. He had convinced himself he needed to talk to her about what happened that morning, to find out what she had seen. But he knew it was more than that.

He just had to have Chloe Morrand.

Caleb walked to the front of the parking area, staring down the road that led to the trailhead. Squinting through the canyon's dwindling light, he noticed something he hadn't seen when he had arrived. There was a vehicle, likely a truck, parked in the brush two hundred yards back up the road. He ambled toward it, seeking a better view.

He stopped. He heard the crunch of gravel. Footsteps. Behind him? He turned around.

Too late. Everything went black.

CHAPTER 6

"**D**AMN IT, CHLOE!"

Rick stood in the kitchen of his ranch house, staring at his Blackberry. He had been calling his daughter's cell phone relentlessly, receiving only the same frustrating greeting.

"This is Chloe. You've reached my voice mail. You know what to do!"

What a stupid message. No, he didn't know what to do. And he didn't know what to think.

Was she OK? Was she loaded? Off her meds? With some guy? Drunk? Dead?

Chloe was supposed to have picked Abby up at ten a.m., just like every Saturday. That was the deal. Now, she was more than two hours late. No call. No text. Nothing.

"Damn . . . Dang it, Chloe," he said in a loud whisper. He tried awkwardly to check his language, remembering his granddaughter was in the house.

"You okay, Abby?" Rick called to the bedroom. "Abby?"

"I'm reading my book, Pa-Pa," Abby shouted back. "Is my Mommy coming soon?"

"Sure, baby," Rick said, using the nickname Abby no longer liked. "She'll be here."

But would she?

Chloe's past was her father's prison. Rick had been burned by her behavior so often, he would freefall into despair at the first hint of trouble. Every time Chloe didn't call, every time she didn't pick up her phone, every time she was late, Rick feared the worst.

While Chloe's recent sobriety was ample reason for hope, trust was built with matchsticks. His mind had attended far too many imaginary funerals.

Rick opened the front door and stepped onto the frost-covered porch, rubbing his biceps as he studied the Gallatin Range that bordered the valley to the west. Behind him stood the Beartooth Mountains, guarding the turquoise waters of the Yellowstone River as it made its serpentine journey north from the national park. The autumn sun had been slow to rise over the Beartooths' cathedral peaks, but it was steadily igniting the smooth gilded foothills of the Gallatins.

Clouds waited patiently to the south, revering the cobalt-blue sky that had welcomed the day. For now, all was calm. Storms would come later.

"Can I go see my dad, maybe?" Abby asked, standing in the open front door. She looked at her grandfather with hopeful eyes, her arms crossed tightly as she pressed *Harry Potter* against her pink pajama top. Rick's chest tightened.

Her *dad*. Chase Reddick. No-check Chase. Lowlife sperm donor.

"Baby, we've talked about this—"

"But *why*?"

"Because."

"But he's my dad!" Abby whined. "Why can't I see my dad?"

Why? Well, that was easy, Rick thought. *Your dad is a freakin' drug addict, that's why!* The judge had finally had enough after Chase's last relapse and pulled the plug. Chloe had full custody. But now, of course, Chloe wasn't there.

Rick took a deep, heavy breath. His head pounded. Insanity.

"Baby, why don't you go ahead and get dressed," he said with false calm, his eyes noting her bare feet touching the icy porch. "Maybe you can finish your school project? I'm sure your mom will be here soon."

Abby's lips quivered as she looked at her grandfather. They both had witnessed this episode before. Abby must have been frightened. He definitely was.

He picked up his cell phone as Abby withdrew into the house. Chase Reddick might know *something*. It was worth a try. Rick pounded the keypad.

Four rings. An answer. A delay. Then, a charcoal-scorched voice. "Hullo?"

"Chase, it's Rick Morrand."

"Hey."

Rick bit his curled lip. He hated "Hey." Granted, "Good morning, Mr. Morrand" might be too much to ask. But what was with "Hey"?

"Have you heard from Chloe?" Rick asked. He already regretted this decision.

"Uh, no," Chase said. "Not for about a week. She called, and I forgot . . ."

A sleepy female voice spoke in the background. "Who's that?"

It didn't belong to Chloe. *Thank God.*

"I gotta go," Chase said.

"Chase, if you hear from her, let me know, will you?"

"Sure . . . Yeah."

Rick's nostrils flared. He couldn't help himself. "And, Chase?" he said through gritted teeth, "Don't worry, Abby's fine."

Deadbeat bastard.

Rick dropped his phone into his shirt pocket, shaking his head with disgust. He looked out toward the distant cottonwood trees that ringed the entrance to the ranch. His eyes climbed the road leading from the gate, and he wished Chloe's SUV would miraculously appear. All would be forgiven if she would just get there.

"C'mon, Chloe," he said softly, a plea and a curse.

Rick often wondered whether coming back to Montana had been a mistake. He had left for California when he was eighteen years old—not long after the accident—and vowed never to return. When his father passed away, his mother begged him to come back, but he convinced her to join him on the West Coast instead. She lasted three months, dying of a broken heart, and he was left with the ranch.

By then, Chloe has just attempted suicide for the second time. Rick had finally quit drinking, but there was wreckage to repair. The family was fatigued and sorely in need of a fresh start. He thought the bucolic setting of his childhood might provide them a needed measure of peace.

A decade had passed. Christine fell ill, and she had now been gone three years. Rick was still sober. Chloe was . . .

Rick stared at his phone. He thought about calling the sheriff, but he had been down that road before. On more than one occasion— during Chloe's darker days—Rick had half the valley searching for his daughter, only to have her emerge from some guy's apartment following a night of partying. He cringed at the memory, recalling the disgrace. For now, he would hold off.

"Are you hungry, Abby?" Rick asked as he walked back into the house.

"Mommy promised she would take me for chocolate chip pancakes," Abby said. "Are you sure she's coming soon?"

Rick didn't answer.

His phone rang. The screen read "Private Number." He closed his eyes in despair. His heart raced. "Private Number" usually was a bad sign.

"This is Rick," he said tentatively.

"Rick, how ya doin'?" the deep voice said. "It's Bull Redmond."

Rick exhaled with relief. "Hi, Bull."

Bull sounded impatient. "You still want that chestnut or what?"

Bull had a ten-year-old gelding named Big Sky. The horse had belonged to his son, Ryder, a football star at John Bridger High who went on to study premed on a full ride at the University of Washington. During a visit home the previous Christmas, Ryder rolled his truck as he tried to avoid an elk crossing Highway 89. He was found protruding from his vehicle's shattered windshield, a light dusting of snow gathering on his bloodied young body.

Bull had considered selling Big Sky immediately but kept changing his mind. Rick understood. Seeing Ryder on the gallant horse likely provided a fond memory, and perhaps Bull was reluctant to let that memory drift away.

"I apologize, Bull," Rick said. "I guess we were supposed to get together, weren't we?"

It wasn't the first time Chloe had changed Rick's plans.

"We talked about it," Bull replied softly. "You did say you were interested."

Rick had been interested—real interested—thinking maybe he could buy the horse for Chloe, who wanted to start riding again. It was just fantasy, thinking she would. He always struggled to accept her the way she was.

"I . . . I just can't do it today, Bull," Rick said. "I'm sorry."

"Well, you best call me as soon as possible," Bull said, his tone both friendly and final. "I *do* intend to sell him." He paused a beat. "I gotta go," he added urgently. "I think I just spotted a bison on my property."

The bison comment caused Rick to frown. He shook his head and ended the call, clutching his phone as he went back outside. Far to the north, the wildly random crystal spires of the Crazy Mountains were visible through a narrow canyon. He closely examined the landscape, backtracking toward the entrance of the ranch. A faint trail of dust appeared from just over the hill, indicating the approach of a vehicle from the main road.

A dark-colored SUV! He exhaled with euphoric relief, but it was cruelly short-lived.

The vehicle gradually slowed, turning onto the dirt road leading to the ranch house. As faded foot-high cheat grass disappeared beneath its front license plate, Rick could positively identify the Dodge he had seen so many times before. His neck tensed as he felt blood rushing to his head.

It was definitely an SUV.

The sheriff's SUV.

CHAPTER 7

RICK SWALLOWED HARD AS HE watched Caleb Tidwell step out of his vehicle. He approached the sheriff with trepidation, feeling like a man trudging toward execution.

"Morning, Mr. Morrand," Caleb said in a gravelly voice. He was rubbing the base of his neck as though he'd had a rough night.

"Hello . . . Caleb," Rick replied hesitantly. He braced himself for the news he was convinced Caleb would deliver. Something had happened to Chloe. He could just *feel* it.

"You seen Buddy Rivers around?" Caleb asked, glancing at Rick before quickly turning away.

"Who?"

"Buddy Rivers."

Rick exhaled. The bullet had missed. Still, he was confused. "Buddy Rivers," he repeated pensively.

Caleb cleared his throat. He adjusted his mirrored sunglasses but didn't remove them. "Yes, Buddy Rivers. Your client, Buddy Rivers?"

Buddy Rivers was his "client" all right, but certainly not by choice. Rick had met the eccentric Vietnam veteran in the courtroom of Judge Samuel Wade, where Buddy was facing poaching charges. Buddy had enraged Wade on an earlier occasion when he represented himself on a drunk-driving rap, and the judge demanded Buddy hire a lawyer this time around.

Rick happened to be in the courtroom. Running short on *pro bono* hours, he volunteered his services. Big mistake.

"What did Buddy do?" Rick asked Sheriff Tidwell.

Caleb was leaning against his SUV. He pulled out a pocket knife and began busily burrowing underneath his fingernails. His hands fidgeted, as though he'd overdone the morning coffee.

"Looks like he shot two more buffalo," he said flatly.

"Damn," Rick said, feigning concern. His mind was on Chloe. "Are you kidding me?"

Caleb avoided eye contact, staring intently at the tip of his pocket knife as though he had discovered a valuable piece of dirt.

"I wouldn't joke about something like that, Mr. Morrand. Poaching is a serious offense."

Rick surveyed Caleb, whose mannerisms did little to shield his immaturity. The glasses perched above his sparse moustache covered his bony face in a way that seemed to outsize him, much like the job he had inherited.

His father, J. R. "Big Jim" Tidwell, had been a legend. Though Big Jim's law enforcement methods occasionally seemed unorthodox, his results were beyond question. Over the course of his twenty-three-year watch, not a single local soul had perished during the commission of a crime—at least no soul on the accurate side of the law.

Caleb's ascension to sheriff resulted from an odd twist of fate, Big Jim's oversized heart exploding in mid-cast on the Yellowstone River as he chased his beloved trout. Within days of his father's death, Caleb was elected to replace him. At age twenty-seven, the ink on his criminology diploma barely dry, he won in a landslide. It was as though the valley somehow wanted to keep Big Jim breathing. Thus far, Caleb hadn't fit the bill.

"Buddy Rivers, huh?" Rick said again. "Here I thought you might have some news about my daughter."

"Chloe?" Caleb asked, looking up briefly.

"Only daughter I have."

Rick regretted his remark, but not by much. He had little confidence Caleb could help.

"What's going on with Chloe?" Caleb asked, still fussing with his Montana manicure.

Rick hesitated, wondering how much to disclose. "At this point, I'm not really sure," he finally said. "It seems . . . she's *missing*."

"What makes you think she's missing?"

"She's not here."

Rick drew a rapid breath through his nostrils and tightened his lips. Caleb's first offense was that he was not Big Jim, but it went further than that. The elder Tidwell had possessed a gregarious personality that matched his six-foot-six-inch, 250-pound frame. He would look you in the eye, shake your hand, invite himself warmly into your soul, and provide whatever was needed. Caleb rarely made eye contact, let alone shook anyone's hand. He carried a sense of entitlement and arrogance his father surely would not have sanctioned.

To date, Caleb's grandest accomplishment was possessing clean fingernails.

"We had dinner on Thursday night," Rick said with a long exhale. "She left a voice mail on Friday. She was supposed to be here to pick up Abby this morning, but she hasn't shown up. That's why I said she's missing."

Caleb nodded. If anyone would know the wealth of possibilities that Chloe "missing" entailed, it would be him.

During his senior year, Caleb had worked up the courage to ask her to the prom, and he was stunned when she accepted. He arrived early, pulling up in Big Jim's restored '68 Camaro—the one no one was allowed to drive. A huge bouquet of flowers in hand, he stood proudly on the porch of the Morrand house, his rosy cheeks reeking of English Leather, youthful eyes swimming with anticipation.

Problem was, Chloe wasn't around. She had taken off a few hours earlier, her red velvet prom dress hanging undisturbed in the closet. Two days later, Rick found her strung out on meth at a run-down bungalow in Butte.

Rick would never forget Caleb's dejection that night, his ashen face vanishing into his rented gray tuxedo. Even the carnation pinned to his silk lapel seemed to wilt at the news. Big Jim later insisted that his son had moved on, but Rick wondered if that was true.

"I saw her about a week ago buying groceries at the Town & Country," Caleb said. "Her and Abby. She seemed fine. Real happy."

Rick considered Caleb's words. He never recalled anyone describe his daughter as "real happy," unless you counted her manic episodes.

"Real happy, huh?"

"Real happy," Caleb repeated. After a pause, he added, "Of course, that was a week ago."

Rick knew Chloe's personality changed like mountain weather, and he didn't need Caleb to remind him. His eyes sharpened as veins pulsed in his neck. He allowed the remark to pass.

"What did her message say?" Caleb asked. His jittery fingers fumbled his pocket knife onto the ground, prompting him to put it away.

"Her *what?*" Rick asked in an irritated tone.

"The message. Didn't you say she left a voice mail message?"

Rick had listened to Chloe's voice mail again while watching Caleb's SUV approach the ranch house. The message still hadn't made much sense.

"She said something about passing the Double-U and seeing bison on the property. Same thing at Shining Mountain Ranch. This morning, Bull Redmond said he saw one at his place . . . Why would there be bison that far up the valley?"

Caleb shrugged. He placed his thumbs inside his belt, as if to anchor them. Rick stared at him quizzically, wondering why he was so uneasy.

"I'll check on that with the warden," Caleb offered weakly, looking over his shoulder and once again massaging his neck. He turned his head back toward Rick. "Of course, that doesn't mean people should be shooting 'em."

Rick nodded. "I'll make a point to contact Buddy. Do you want to arrest him, or can I just make sure he shows up in court?"

"Court's fine. The less I deal with him, the better."

The men stood for a moment in silence. Caleb turned to leave, then stopped.

"I guess I could file a report—you know, for Chloe?" he said with little conviction.

Rick considered the offer. Filing a missing person's report might be prudent, but it carried inherent risk. Given Chloe's past, not a lot of time had elapsed.

"Sit tight, Sheriff. I'll make a few more calls."

Caleb nodded but didn't speak. He got into his SUV, waved to no one in particular, and pulled away, gravel grinding under his tires.

Rick heard a tapping on a window behind him. Abby smiled from the other side of the glass. He smiled weakly, then headed for the entrance of the house.

Damn it, Chloe.

CHAPTER 8

BILLY RENFRO AND BULL REDMOND had been close friends for years, so much so that the deputy had served as a pallbearer when Bull's son, Ryder, died in the wreck on Highway 89. If Bull called needing help, Billy didn't ask questions. He just showed up.

When he pulled onto Bull's property, it didn't take him long to see the object of the rancher's concern. Billy fixed his eyes on a large bison pushing hard against a wood-and-wire pen holding three cows. A yellow mutt barked loudly at the buffalo from inside the fence, kicking up dust as it would repeatedly bluff toward the animal and then retreat. The bison ignored the dog, its enormous snout urging the fence to its breaking point. Billy flashed his brights, a technique used by rangers to clear bison off the roads in Yellowstone. The bison didn't stir, intent on reaching the cows.

As Billy slowed to a stop, a deafening shot rang out. He flinched and ducked for cover, peering over his dashboard as Bull Redmond appeared from behind the barn, armed with a shotgun. Bull fired a second shot into the air, then cracked open the weapon to load another pair of shells.

Billy poked his head out. "Damn it, Bull, don't shoot him!"

"I ain't gonna shoot him—at least, not yet," Bull said without looking up. "I just need to keep him away from my cows—not to mention my dog." He snapped the shotgun shut and pumped two more shots skyward, each causing the deputy to recoil. The buffalo took notice, shuffling back a few paces before turning away from the pen, Billy affording him wide berth. As he watched the massive animal slog forward, Billy's eyes drifted into the far distance toward a herd of grazing cattle. The livestock were out of harm's way—for now.

"If he gets close to my herd, I'll need to shoot him," Bull's baritone voice warned as he approached the fence. The rancher presented an imposing figure, towering over Billy with a thick physique that once measured six foot six, his bowed legs now nestling him into a frame of about six four. His jaw was square and firm, coated in a grizzle that looked like heavy-grit sandpaper. He cradled the shotgun loosely across his chest as he folded his massive arms, making him look like a human gun rack. A boxing champion in the military, Bull likely could have set down the weapon and dropped that bison with a solid left hook.

Billy put his hands on his hips and stared at the dirt in front of him. He hesitated, reluctant to deliver the dispiriting news Bull needed to hear. "You realize I'm going to have to call the warden."

Bull's eyes widened. "The warden? Don't you think I could have called the warden?"

Billy shrugged. "The warden will want to test this animal for brucellosis—you know that. And, of course, he'll want to do some testing on your cattle."

Bull shifted the shotgun to his massive right hand and held it pointed toward the ground. He squared his stance, heaved an agitated sigh, and glared at Billy with serious eyes. "You think I don't know that, Billy? Why the hell do you think I called *you*?"

Billy stroked his moustache. He glanced toward the buffalo, charting its sluggish yet steady progress toward the herd. "What do you expect me to do? Put him in my backseat?"

Bull shook his head rapidly. "Not at all. I gave my cowboys the morning off to go to town, but they'll be back this afternoon. I'll have 'em take this buffalo back down to the park."

"Your cowboys will be drunk."

"Maybe a little, but they can help me get him in the trailer. I'll do the rest. I promise I won't kill him."

Billy fumbled in his pocket for a toothpick. He slowly shook his head. "You know we can't do that."

Bull's face grew flush, his jaw muscles tightening. "You don't seem to get it, do you? These cattle are all but sold. The warden comes in here, starts testing, everything stops. If this bison is infected, my cattle will be quarantined." Bull's sad eyes pleaded with Billy. "You can't, you know, look the other way?"

Billy's eyes flared as he took the toothpick from his mouth and flicked it onto the ground. He glared at Bull, friendship only going so far. "No, I *can't* look the other way—that's not the law. I'm set to retire in another year, and I'd just as soon not lose my pension. More important than that, it just ain't the right thing to do."

Billy fished his cell phone out of his jacket and searched for the warden's number. Bull stared at the phone, shook his head, then turned to walk away. "Thanks a lot, Billy," he grumbled. "Glad I called you."

Billy looked out at the buffalo, still making glacier-like headway toward the herd. He'd need to use his SUV to haze it away from the livestock until the warden arrived. As he put the phone to his ear, he watched his crestfallen friend walk toward the ranch house, head bowed and shotgun slung over his shoulder. Given the cards life had dealt him, Bull couldn't be blamed for requesting a new deck.

"Sorry I couldn't help you, Bull," Billy said quietly as he waited for the warden to answer. "I have to do what's right."

CHAPTER 9

B Y MOST ACCOUNTS, THE BEST river to fish in Yellowstone Park during the month of October undoubtedly would be the Madison, where the large browns and rainbows made their way upstream from Hebgen Lake to the Firehole. A second option would perhaps be the Lewis, a densely populated migration thoroughfare between Lewis and Shoshone Lakes.

For Matt Steelman, any river would do. He had been waiting for this Saturday morning for what seemed like forever.

During countless sweltering, dust-choked nights in Baghdad, Matt would allow his mind to float lazily down the fabled Yellowstone streams, dreaming of the brightly colored fish they possessed. He swore to himself that when he got back—*if* he got back—he would return to one of those idyllic waterways to which he had ventured from his childhood home in Salt Lake.

He finally had managed a Saturday off from his job as a supervisor at the Yellowstone Visitor Center. The weather was cooperating magnificently, and his gear was packed. He gleefully welcomed the cool morning air into his nostrils, stopping to admire a pair of antelope grazing near his rented cabin just outside the park. This was the day that he would use to permanently escape the Green Zone.

His phone rang. It was work.

"It's my day off," he said tersely as he climbed into his pickup.

"I'm sorry to bother you, Matt," said Gwen Winther, Saturday manager at the Visitor Center. "Have you heard from Chloe Morrand?"

"She's not working today," Matt said, starting his truck's fussy ignition.

"I realize that," Gwen answered. "Her father called. I guess that Chloe was supposed to come to his house this morning, and she hasn't shown up. He sounded worried."

"She was at work yesterday," Matt offered.

"I know," Gwen said. "I saw her time card, and I told him she worked all day. He wanted your cell number."

Matt turned off the engine. He swallowed hard into a tightened throat.

"My cell number?" he asked, barely squeezing out the words. "Why?"

"I told him you were Chloe's supervisor," Gwen answered routinely. "I said you were probably the last one down here who had seen her."

"W . . . why'd you tell him that?"

"'Cause it's true?"

Matt's mind rewound to Friday afternoon. He and Chloe had left work at the same time, soon after they had finished their shifts. They met a short drive away at the Hellroaring Creek trailhead, their relationship having traveled well beyond the boundaries of the workplace.

Matt sensed Chloe was getting too close, especially when she'd asked him to meet her daughter. He was physically attracted to her—who wasn't?—but she needed far more than he could offer. He had to cut things off.

Of course, his decision to end their affair minutes after they had consummated a sex act didn't sit well with Chloe. His mention of another woman's name complicated matters even further. Chloe had nearly sent the passenger door of Matt's Toyota Tacoma off its hinges when she exited his vehicle. He begged her to calm down and talk, but that was impossible. He recalled her two arms extending into his vehicle, each equipped with a one-finger salute, as though she wanted to double the emphasis of the message she sought to convey. "Fuck off!" she'd screamed.

When Chloe picked up a roadside rock and narrowly missed the rear window of his cab, Matt decided it was time to go. He'd sped off, watching in his rearview mirror as Chloe searched feverishly for another projectile to hurl.

"Do you think she's okay?" Gwen asked. "Her dad seems pretty worried. He said he's been trying her cell phone all morning."

Chloe's *cell phone*. Matt had forgotten all about it. After he had fled Psychoville and left the national park, he'd heard a ring tone. It was the Coldplay song "Yellow."

Chloe had left her phone on the seat. Acting on an angry, ill-conceived impulse, Matt had picked up the phone and tossed it out his passenger window, leaving it bouncing along the shoulder of Highway 89.

"Matt, are you there?" Gwen asked.

He freaked. His breathing picked up. He felt cold but began to sweat. Any concern he had for Chloe was trampled by his mad rush into survival mode. He had *touched* that phone. No one could know they had been together. *No one.*

"You didn't give him my number, did you?" he asked, hoping his trembling voice wasn't betraying him.

"That's against policy," Gwen said, as if Matt cared about policy. "I told him I would contact you if I could."

Images of Chloe flashed through his mind. When he had arrived at Yellowstone a few months earlier, he'd immediately felt a connection to her. A fevered sexual relationship rapidly ensued, but there was more to it than that.

Chloe had seemed to tune in to Matt's PTSD, that unwelcome souvenir from Iraq. She perceived his struggles as though gazing through a spotless window that provided an unobstructed view of the contents of his brain. She had delivered him from peril, speaking openly about her past and her gratitude for her personal redemption. If someone like her could make it safely back from hell, surely he could do the same. Their physical passion seemed to make their physical connection that much more real.

Still, he needed this job. "Did her father leave a number?"

"His cell," Gwen said. "I can text it to you."

"Yeah, do that."

Matt wasn't calling anyone. He tossed his phone onto the passenger seat. It was his day off, the day he had envisioned when he had stood drained of hope on the banks of the murky Tigris River.

Unfortunately, on this day off, he wouldn't be fishing—at least, not for trout. The wheels of his truck kicked up a stream of dust as pulled away from his rental house and sped toward Highway 89.

He needed to find that phone.

Chapter 10

Reiff Metcalf felt so bad, he wanted to die. Sadly, that eventuality would have to wait.

His head pounded mercilessly as he strained to focus on the female bartender about to deliver a Greyhound—Absolut vodka with a splash of grapefruit juice—the devoted concoction that had long served as his salvation and curse. It was approaching high noon in Riverton at a small tavern called The Spur, and Reiff wanted desperately to abate the damage of the previous evening while emboldening himself to endure another day.

"What brings you to Montana?" the bartender asked as she delivered his cocktail. Her smile was forced, but her high tanned cheekbones produced a pleasing allure. At least, Reiff thought so. Squinting through his Maui Jim sunglasses, he nodded at the drink in appreciation, eager to numb his afflicted brain and sooth his troubled soul.

"How do you know I'm visiting?" he groaned, his voice hoarse from shouting the night before. The bartender raised her eyebrows— *Seriously?*—then smirked as she studied his Tommy Bahama print shirt.

"Southern California," he conceded, his hand unsteadily guiding his drink closer to him. "Newport Beach."

She nodded knowingly but seemed less than impressed. "Welcome to the United States."

Reiff offered a tight smile. That was a good one, he thought. He wanted to say something else, but the bartender had already turned away, bending over to wash glasses in a sink filled with murky gray water.

The Spur was narrow and long. A small rectangular front window cast sunlight onto an aging pool table, a lonely cue left abandoned on felt that was faded and worn. The bar counter itself was positioned toward the rear, where daylight surrendered to neon. Dark-brown diagonal slices of barn wood graced the walls, decorated with torn posters of Bud Light girls hawking watered-down beer and Monday Night Football. The almond-colored tin ceiling did little to absorb the bottomless bellows of Johnny Cash, who kept crowing "Folsom Prison Blues" at a volume far louder than Reiff preferred.

He shot quick glances around the bar, wary someone might witness his hand tremble as he took his first sip. He remembered the story of a guy who had the shakes so bad he would strap a belt around his wrist, run it behind his neck, and then tug on it to lever the drink to his lips. Now, *that's* an alcoholic, Reiff reassured himself.

Reiff raised the cocktail to his mouth. He quivered only slightly—the valium and half-pint at the hotel must have helped—and as soon as the burning elixir reached his dry lips, he felt on his way toward emancipation, temporary as it may have been.

A lunch crowd was arriving—assuming that chili dogs and nachos could be considered lunch. The snowy TV in the corner was turned to a hunting channel, the nicer flat screen behind the bar showing a rerun of *Andy Griffith*. Reiff saw no signs of college football, nor any evidence of college degrees.

He took a deep draining sip of his drink, staring at the bartender washing glasses. He briefly wondered how clean his glass was, noticing his cocktail tasted a little soapy, but decided he didn't really care. His eyes focused on the back of her flowered Western skirt, which flowed so flawlessly over her skin that he was convinced her underwear had taken the day off.

She whirled around toward him—perhaps sensing his leer—causing him to quickly avert his eyes. "Can I get you another one of those?" she asked.

"How about a White Russian?" Reiff said, feeling a twinge of discomfort in his stomach. "It's Kahlua—"

"Kahlua, vodka, and cream," she interrupted. "I know how to make a White Russian. I gotta admit, though, we don't see that many of those. Want that in a sipper cup?"

Another good one, he thought. Reiff liked her spunk. She had an edge to her, that was for sure. *A real cowgirl.*

"No, thank you," he said dryly as he watched her fill a shaker with ice. It took her a moment to track down the Kahlua, but soon the drink was in front of him. He took a long sip, dabbing his upper lip with a cocktail napkin.

"I didn't get your name," he said.

The bartender leaned her forearms on the bar in front of her. She smiled, less guarded this time, which Reiff found promising. Her face was smooth, natural, definitely no work done. She had large rich-green eyes that likely had served her well. Her eyes invited him in at first, before wandering to the wedding band on his finger.

"You don't need my name," she said, heading toward customers at the other end of the bar.

Reiff shook his head, accepting another defeat. He removed his sunglasses, massaging his aching temples. He focused on the mirror behind the bar, contemplating the visage of a person he no longer liked. His once-golden hair was now thinning and streaked with gray—Rogaine and Just for Men be damned. His skin was bright red, his eyes a chalky yellow. He covered the face with his glass, draining his cocktail and pushing it forward in a desperate attempt to run further away.

Thirty years earlier, he had enjoyed a meteoric rise as a young trial lawyer, building a teeming practice with help of Rick Morrand, his college roommate at San Diego State. With a dynamic personality to go with his lifeguard looks, Reiff was even tabbed for a future in politics.

He never made it past city council. Alcohol had chipped away at his dreams, eventually destroying his marriage and eroding his reputation. He sent a son and daughter through college and law school, but they rarely returned his calls. They demanded he choose between them and alcohol, not a fair choice at all.

Despite seeking the company of others, he often felt so terribly alone.

The bartender appeared and took Reiff's glass. "Ready?" she asked, her tone much like a nurse delivering a shot of insulin to a diabetic. She had kept the Kahlua nearby, assuming he would need it. She placed the drink in front of him, offering a half-smile tinged with pity.

Reiff thought of Rick Morrand, who used to party right along with him but ended up quitting drinking. During the early evangelical days of his sobriety, Morrand had given Reiff a copy of *The Big Book of Alcoholics Anonymous*. At first, Reiff thought it made a fine coaster, but in darker moments he had picked up the manual and read it.

"More than most people, the alcoholic leads a double life," the Big Book told him. "He is very much the actor. To the outer world he presents his stage character. This is the one he likes his fellows to see. He wants to enjoy a certain reputation, but knows in his heart he doesn't deserve it . . ."

The bartender delivered the drink. Reiff nodded approvingly at her and drank half of it, a shiver chasing down the back of his neck as he returned to the mirror and found the frightened, insecure man who must never be discovered. The 12 Steps seemed to work well enough for Rick Morrand, but they could *never* fly for Reiff Metcalf. That Fourth Step? The one about a "searching and fearless moral inventory"? Uh-uh, no thanks. Reiff had way too much buried wreckage, too many skeletons that must never see the light of day.

He took another long sip from his drink. He barely had a chance to swallow, when pain rocketed through him so sharply that he dropped his glass onto the bar.

Reiff clutched his stomach in agony, snorting air though his nostrils as a thousand needles pierced the interior of his abdomen. Breaking into a sweat, he slid off his barstool and stumbled toward a door marked with a battered metal sign that read "Cowboys." He burst into the bathroom—startling a burly local washing his hands—

and crumpled to his knees as he emptied the liquid contents of his stomach into the nearest toilet.

"You okay there, fella?" the man asked, looking over Reiff's shoulder into a bowl shaded with blood. "You want me to call someone?"

Reiff shook his head and waved his hand weakly. "I'm fine," he grunted, tears of pain falling from the corners of his eyes.

"You don't look fine," the man persisted, wiping his hands with a brown paper towel. "You sure—"

"I'm *fine*," Reiff said, this time with more bite. He spit a mixture of saliva and blood into the toilet, fixing his eyes on a sight that was becoming more frequent. "All I need is a minute, and I'll be fine."

"Suit yourself," the man said, tossing the paper towel into a rusty metal bucket. He yanked open the bathroom door, taking one final glance at Reiff before shaking his head and leaving the bathroom.

"He ain't here."

When the phone rang, Maggie was sitting on the weathered brown sofa, transfixed by a rerun of *Wheel of Fortune*. She was astonished that some rotund blue-hair named Alice needed to buy another vowel when it was plain to see that "TRUST YOUR INSTINCTS" was the answer to the puzzle.

Maggie figured she should have been more polite, considering she was talking to a parole officer, but she didn't really care. She'd about had her fill of Draper Townsend.

"Good morning, Maggie," Brenda Moreland said. "Any idea where Draper might be?"

Maggie paused, using a long drag out of a Marlboro 100 to contemplate the question. She had known Brenda for years and felt no ill will toward her. After all, they had been comrades-in-arms, teaming together in repeated, unsuccessful attempts to keep Draper out of prison.

"No idea, Brenda," Maggie said with disinterest. She adjusted the yellow Slimline phone beneath her chin and sent a billow of smoke skyward.

"I'm hearing he's been drinking," Brenda said.

"No comment."

"He was scheduled for a urine test yesterday but never showed."

"For drugs?"

"Everything," Brenda said, now sounding frustrated. "C'mon, Maggie, you know the drill."

Yeah, Maggie knew the drill all too well. Urine tests didn't mean much to Draper Townsend. Nothing meant much to him—including her. She drew hard on her smoke, pushing a long gray strand of hair off her forehead. She rested her elbow on the corduroy arm of the couch, her cigarette propped in the air. She stared with weary, dull eyes at the heart tattoo on the inside of her wrist, the initials D.T. written in faded script beneath it. Another band of ink surrounded her finger, the closest Draper had ever come to offering her a ring. She felt clouds of gloom swarm over her, realizing that being chained to Draper Townsend had allowed the world to pass her by.

"Maggie, you there?"

"I'm here."

"Is there anything else you can give me that might help?"

"Not if I want to keep this face of mine pretty."

Brenda sighed from the other end of the phone. "I told you to get out of there."

"Yeah, I know."

"Well?"

Maggie drew on her cigarette again, studying the filter before delivering another stream of smoke toward the discolored stucco ceiling. She crushed the butt into a red hard plastic ashtray stolen from a Missoula motel.

"C'mon now, Brenda," she said with an uneasy chuckle. "You and I both know I don't need to go anywhere. Draper Townsend ain't gonna be here long."

Maggie placed the phone back in the cradle. Staring at the TV screen, she rubbed the heart tattoo on her wrist as though she could somehow make it go away. Alice was all atwitter on *Wheel of Fortune*, finally solving the puzzle with an *I* she didn't need.

Trust your instincts. For too many years, Maggie had ignored her instincts—the ones that told her Draper Townsend was an unredeemable cancer of a man who tainted all who came in contact with him. Sure, at one time she'd liked the sweet things he'd say to her, making her feel wanted, but that all ended a long time ago. Draper was gone again—where, she didn't know—and she was alone. Her instincts told her it was time to move on without him.

Draper Townsend needed to go away for good. She was sure of it.

She would do everything in her power to make it happen.

Reiff closed the lid of the toilet and flushed it. Color left his fingertips as he gripped the side of the stall, pulling himself up as though he were dying, which of course he was. He plopped onto the toilet lid, causing it to slide out of place. "Shit!" he muttered. Snaring toilet paper from a bouncing near-empty roll, he dabbed his drenched brow.

He closed his eyes. He breathed. His phone rang.

Reiff fumbled to get his phone out of his pocket, then dropped it on the floor. Another "Shit!" He retrieved the phone and recognized his office number.

"Yeah," he grunted.

"There you are!" his secretary, Jeanine, said. "Hey, you okay?"

"I'm fine." Reiff grunted some more. "What's up?"

"I've been looking all over for you. Are you still in Montana?"

"Yes."

"Do you have your ringer turned on? I've been calling like crazy."

"Yeah . . . I was in the . . . I must not have heard it." *Freakin' Johnny Cash.*

"I thought something might have happened," Jeanine said. "I called Rick, and he said he didn't even know you were coming—"

"You called Rick?" Reiff asked, his eyes opening wide.

"Of course," Jeanine replied. "Doesn't Rick still live in Montana? His cell has a 406 area code, so I—"

"Yeah," Reiff interrupted. "Rick still lives in Montana."

Jeanine had been Reiff's secretary for seventeen years. She was stout and unattractive, which partially explained her lengthy tenure. He tended to ogle the younger, hotter paralegals, and they would soon scatter. Jeanine was all business, punctual and accurate, a true pro. She also was extremely thorough, a trait Reiff judged as being both good and bad.

"Rick doesn't know I'm here yet," he said.

"He doesn't? I thought when you said you were going to Montana—"

"He doesn't know I'm here."

"Oh."

Silence hung in the air. Reiff assumed Jeanine wanted more details, which would not be forthcoming. Only he knew why he was in Montana, and he planned to keep it that way.

Another bar patron entered the bathroom. After briefly looking at Reiff talking in the stall, he proceeded to a urinal.

"It's Saturday," Reiff said to Jeanine, changing the subject.

"I know."

"So, what's up?"

"Well," Jeanine said, "I don't know how to tell you this, but that Bledsoe guy has been calling again. You remember him?"

"I do."

How could he forget? As a personal injury attorney, Reiff didn't see a lot of repeat business. While his advertising implored prospective clients to "Get What You Deserve," they rarely thought they did. A forty-percent cut for the firm did little to change their thinking.

Bledsoe's son, Christian, had been a client of Metcalf & Morrand, back when Rick was still drinking and snorting coke. The Bledsoes claimed that Christian had been molested by a priest, the case representing a rare departure from the firm's customary auto accidents and dog bites. There was a settlement, the priest neither found guilty nor punished, an outcome Richard Bledsoe found unsatisfactory. Bledsoe later discovered that Rick Morrand knew the priest, a clear conflict of interest.

More recently, Christian had died, the victim of an overdose.

"A couple of the girls spotted him in the parking lot, staring at them when they left work," Jeanine said. "I decided to call the police, but he took off before they arrived."

Reiff had never met Bledsoe. About all he knew about the case was that it produced a check. He and Rick each had worked their own stack of files. That one had belonged to Rick, and he never should have taken it. The priest, Father Timothy Doyle, had baptized Chloe Morrand, for Christ's sake. Rick was way out of control in those days. While he hadn't quite reached rock bottom, his shovel wasn't far away.

"Do we still have a restraining order?"

"Yes," Jeanine said. "The police went to his house, but he wasn't there."

"Any idea where he is?"

"His wife told them he left two days ago. Took his hunting gear and left town."

"Hunting gear?" Reiff echoed, feeling the skin on his scalp tighten. "Did she know where he was going?"

"She thought Wyoming, Idaho ... maybe even Montana," Jeanine said. "The guy was pretty creepy. He really seems to hate Rick."

"Did you tell Rick about Bledsoe?"

"No," Jeanine answered. "I didn't talk to him that long. He seemed to be ... preoccupied."

Reiff fell silent. His trip to Montana was getting complicated.

"I did tell Rick I would ask you to call him when I found you," Jeanine said. She paused. "You know, you probably shouldn't be traveling—"

"I'll call him," Reiff answered, ending the call and placing his phone is his pocket. He drew a deep breath through his nostrils, then pushed himself to his feet. He staggered to the sink and turned on the faucet, staring at the water running though his cupped trembling hands. He splashed water on his face.

He wished Jeanine hadn't contacted Rick Morrand. He hadn't traveled to Montana to see his ex-partner.

He needed to see someone else.

CHAPTER 11

ABBY WAS STARING OUT THE passenger window of Rick's truck, her forefinger tapping the glass to count cows dotting the landscape as they sped north on Highway 89. Rick had instructed her to bring *Harry Potter* along, but she wasn't reading.

"Where are we going?" she asked, sounding both bored and impatient. She began fumbling with the power window, lowering it halfway in an apparent search for fresh air, instead filling the cab with an unpleasant bouquet courtesy of the cattle.

"Please don't do that," Rick said flatly as he raised the window.

"Where are we *going*?"

"I want to stop by the apartment."

"*Our* apartment? Why?"

Rick didn't immediately answer her, his mind drifting to his former law partner, Reiff Metcalf. He hadn't talked to Reiff for months, nor seen him in years. Still, Rick had received a curious phone call from Jeanine Marconi, their former secretary at Metcalf & Morrand, saying she was trying to locate Reiff in Montana, a place he had never been. Why didn't Reiff tell him he was coming? If he was here, why hadn't he called?

"Pa-Pa!" Abby repeated, increasing her volume. "Why are we going to the apartment?"

"You don't have to shout," Rick said, his eyes fixed on the road.

"You're not even listening to me!"

Abby's mood had been sour since breakfast. Considering that her mother had promised chocolate chip pancakes, Rick couldn't expect her to be tickled by Lucky Charms. But this wasn't about cereal. It was about Chloe.

"Why do I have to go?" Abby protested.

"Because you are eight years old, and I can't leave you alone at the ranch."

"I'm almost nine," she said somberly.

Rick's stomach dropped. He remembered Abby's birthday, only one week away. Her mother had planned a big party, even sent invitations to Abby's classmates. Chloe was excited about it, convinced she would be making amends for lost time.

"Was Sheriff Tidwell talking to you about Mommy?" she asked.

"No."

"What did he want?"

Rick studied her, rubbing the stubble on his unshaven chin. "You sure are a curious one, aren't you?"

Abby shrugged, her raised eyebrows saying, *I am almost nine, you know!* She pushed her brown silky hair behind her ears, just like her mother would do. Her open mouth displayed an array of confused teeth that would someday make peace and evolve into an attractive smile. Her cheekbones tightened as she squinted at him, blue eyes fighting the afternoon sun.

"He wanted to talk to me about Buddy Rivers," Rick finally said.

Abby considered the name. "Isn't he the guy who's always getting in trouble?"

Rick chuckled uneasily. "I suppose you could say that."

"What did he do now?"

"Well," Rick said slowly, "the sheriff says he killed a couple of buffalo."

"Is that bad?" Abby asked. "You eat buffalo burgers on Thursday nights. *Somebody* has to kill them."

"The buffalo from Thursday night were raised on a ranch," Rick said. "Buddy is killing—or, at least, he is accused of killing—buffalo that wandered up from Yellowstone. Those buffalo are protected."

"Protected?"

"The government says you're not supposed to kill them."

Abby appeared confused. Maybe a little bored.

"Is Mr. Rivers crazy?" she asked curiously.

"What makes you say he's crazy?" Rick asked, adding dismissively, "He just has some issues."

"What kind of issues?"

"He's just a little . . . Maybe we should talk about something else?"

Abby rolled her eyes. Rick knew she didn't like it when she asked a question and an adult changed the subject. She wanted to learn something, and he wasn't taking the time to explain.

"All I wanted to know was what the issues are," she said, drawing a perturbed breath. "Guess I'll just have to Google it."

Abby opened the book on her lap and started reading. A paragraph later, she snapped it shut.

"Is *Mommy* crazy?"

Rick shot her an icy look. He glanced in his rearview mirror, then pulled onto the shoulder of the road, the truck skidding to a stop on the gravel.

"What makes you say that?"

His tone was deathly stern, which made Abby ease toward the passenger door, fright in her eyes. She hesitated to speak but finally found secure words.

"I heard Mrs. Denton say that Mommy was crazy."

Rick rolled his eyes and sighed. He had turned toward Abby, his left wrist slung over the top of the steering wheel.

"When did she say that?" he asked more gently.

"We were at the Town & Country. Mommy forgot bread and went back to get it. Mrs. Denton told the next person in line to be patient, that Mommy was crazy. She was making a circle with her finger around her ear."

Rick stared at the roof of his pickup. Barbara Denton was a part-time cashier at Town & Country, but she had a full-time job as town gossip.

"Your mommy's not crazy, Abby. She's had some troubles in the past. You already know that. But she's doing better now."

At least, he hoped. As he and his granddaughter sat in silence, Rick retraced the path of the previous evening, regretting that it had ended badly. He should have never asked Chloe about the meds, but he just couldn't help himself. Now she was gone.

Her disappearances were challenging, to say the least. She could be anywhere. She might be safe, or not. It wasn't so much a matter of tracking her down as waiting for her to surface.

Abby bowed her head, staring ruefully at her lap.

"Pa-Pa?" she asked, tears forming in her eyes. "Where *is* she?"

Rick's chest ached, his mind dueling between sadness and anger. He had convinced himself that Chloe could cause no more pain.

He waved his hand toward Abby, urging her closer so he could put his arm around her slender shoulders. She hesitated, then gradually edged over, burying her face in her small, trembling hands. He felt her body shudder as she started to cry.

"Seven Up is fine," Reiff told the bartender as he climbed back onto his barstool. She nodded quizzically, as though she expected an explanation for his behavior, but Reiff was in no mood to elucidate.

The attacks—acute pancreatitis—had been going on for about a year. Some were worse than others. On three occasions, he'd landed in the hospital. His doctor told him that if he didn't quit drinking, he would die. What the doctor didn't realize was that, without alcohol, Reiff didn't know how to live.

The doctor's admonitions were now moot, of course. Reiff had developed full-blown pancreatic cancer. The alcohol consumption that began in his youth and imprisoned him for decades had finally landed him on death row.

"Can I get you anything else?" the bartender asked as she placed the 7 Up in front of him. Reiff shook his head with resignation, his eyes fixed on his glass.

He took a pair of Vicodin tablets out of his pants pocket and tossed them into his mouth. He washed them down with the soda, then wiped his hand on his sleeve. He had a growing tolerance for the medication, but it seemed to work when he took enough of it.

He stared into the mirror behind the bar, his thoughts turning to Chloe Morrand. He hadn't seen her in person in nearly a decade. He wondered what she was like, how much she had changed. He looked her up on Facebook once but saw only one picture. Nothing about her daughter. Rick Morrand had said once that the girl's name was Abby.

Reiff drained his 7 Up and placed it in front of him, staring at the glass, unimpressed. He considered adding Seagrams but figured he'd better not chance it so soon after an attack. He'd have to ride the Vicodin for now.

The anonymous bartender pressed the soda gun to refill his glass, using her other hand to grab a remote and turn up the volume on the TV behind the bar. Reiff recognized it as a plasma, a lofty accessory for an establishment like The Spur. A faded Moose Drool sticker had been placed in the center of the metal frame below the screen, probably to disguise the fact that it was a Samsung or Mitsubishi.

A female newscaster was reporting from Gardiner, with the historic Roosevelt Arch visible in the background. The story attracted the attention of the patrons seated at the bar, who interrupted their conversations and fixed their eyes on the screen.

"Montana authorities are examining the remains of a bison from Yellowstone National Park found dead under suspicious circumstances on Wednesday," the reporter began. "The bison death comes one day after at least two other buffalo were illegally killed ten miles north of the park.

"The killings occurred less than a week after the state and federal agencies that oversee the nation's last purebred herd of wild buffalo struck a deal to allow the animals to roam into some parts of Montana without facing capture or slaughter."

A cowboy seated next to Reiff—a guy everyone was calling Levi—took a sip of his beer. "We didn't agree to no deal," he grunted toward the screen as though the reporter might hear him.

Reiff's instincts sharpened. He sensed controversy. Where there was controversy, there were adversaries, and adversaries needed lawyers.

"What's this about?" Reiff asked, nodding toward the TV as he leaned closer to Levi's ear.

"What this is about," Levi said, "is that there are too many bison in the damn park. They're all over the place. They need to have a hunt and thin 'em out." He shook his head in disgust, his tone flooding with derision. "Of course, that'll never happen. Environmental types wanna to protect their innocent little buffalo."

Reiff needed more information. "So, what's the big deal letting buffalo roam into Montana?"

Levi appeared astonished. He removed his hat and scratched his head as though Reiff's inquiry had activated a bad case of psoriasis.

"The big deal is that the bison carry brucellosis," he said. "Ever hear of it?"

Reiff shook his head.

"It causes pregnant cows to abort. If your cows can't have calves—"

"You have no cattle to raise, and the cows lose their value," Reiff said, finishing the sentence.

Levi formed his left hand into a pistol and fired it at Reiff. "There you go," he said. "Considering I work on a ranch, that ain't all that good for my livelihood."

"Shh," the bartender said, nodding back toward the TV.

"Wildlife activists are outraged by the killings," the reporter continued, "and they have vowed to stage protests in Gardiner and Riverton until they receive assurances the bison are protected."

Levi buried his face in his hands. "You gotta be kiddin' me."

Reiff smiled, taking a sip of his 7 Up. His pain was gone. The Vicodin was working.

"Looks like you guys are headed for 'Occupy Montana,'" he said with a slight chuckle.

No one seemed amused. Reading the facial expressions around him, Reiff figured it was time to go. He placed a twenty on the bar and adjusted his Maui Jims.

Thanks to Jeanine, he had to call Rick Morrand.

CHAPTER 12

CHLOE RARELY INVITED HER FATHER to her apartment, claiming she needed to clean it first. She had given him a key—possibly worried she might lock herself out—but he'd never used it. Today would be different.

Rick tapped on the door but heard no sound. He tried again, this time louder.

He drew a deep breath. He glanced back at the truck, where Abby sneered at him from the front seat. She wanted to go inside, but he had ordered her to stay back, unsure what he might find. He wasn't sure exactly what he was afraid of, only that he was.

He turned the key, his heart pounding as he heard the thud of the deadbolt. "Chloe?" he said, pushing the door open a sliver. "Chloe? It's Dad."

No response. *Not good.*

Rick swallowed, his throat suddenly dry, his mind overrun by a flash flood of worst-case scenarios. "Chloe? You in here?" The door creaked as he pushed it forward into darkness, the curtains drawn shut. He fumbled for the light.

The place was spotless—and deathly quiet.

He eased into the living room of the one-bedroom apartment. No signs of distress or turmoil. Instead, he saw peace and happiness.

A watercolor of a chestnut horse was neatly trimmed and stuck to the refrigerator, Chloe proudly showcasing one of her daughter's latest works of art. Next to it, a recent math test boasted a circled red *A* across the top.

A photo on the wall recalled the day Chloe received her National Park Service uniform. She had been so ecstatic she couldn't make it home without first stopping by to show the uniform to Rick, who insisted she try it on. They had marked the occasion with a selfie.

Abby's face was everywhere. One picture among the tidy crescent of wooden frames on the coffee table showed mother and child at the Fourth of July parade, their cheeks pressed tightly together as if they were trying to make their smiles as large as possible and still jam them into a five-by-seven. Rick picked up the photo, pushed forth a burdened chuckle, then gently put it back down.

The apartment also claimed hope. On a desk in the living room, taped neatly to the base of her lamp, Chloe proudly displayed a bright-blue medallion she received to commemorate two years of sobriety. Next to her laptop, arranged in a tidy stack, were printouts detailing the requirements needed to become a licensed paramedic.

Rick felt a temporary burst of pride, but it quickly gave way to gloom. He still didn't know where his daughter was.

He proceeded to her bedroom. Chloe's bed had been made with precision. Her therapist, Annie, had instructed her to *never* leave her apartment without making her bed. If she made her bed before she left, a symbol of discipline and organization, Chloe's thought process throughout the day seemed to be more consistent and fluid. What began as a habit became an obsession.

Rick drew air into his nostrils, trying to relieve the mournful ache in his chest. It agonized him to think about how his daughter had to live her life. Though buoyed by a delicate balance of medication, counseling, and stringent rituals, Chloe still had to summon unflagging perseverance to chart her way through days that others navigated with ease. It seemed she was never quite sure what she would encounter—or how her brain might behave—once she stepped outside her door.

"I would rather have anything—*anything*—besides this," she once said of her mental illness. "Why does it have to be my *brain*?"

Rick had thought many times about what she said. She'd rather be deaf? Blind? Paraplegic? Surely, she didn't mean it. Perhaps she did.

Rick circled the bed, moving toward a wooden dresser covered by a spotless lace doily. A small heart-shaped frame contained yet another photo of Abby, when she was about three. Next to the picture was a black book with gold letters, titled *Twenty-Four Hours a Day.*

He stared at the top drawer, recalling Chloe's adolescence, when Christine would check her dresser and backpack for drugs. That was *then*, he assured himself, and this is *now*. Things are different, aren't they?

Rick cast a glance over his shoulder, convinced someone might be watching him inside the empty, soundless apartment. Placing his hands on the drawer handles, he hesitated briefly, ashamed that he did not trust his daughter. He slid the drawer open.

To the left was a neat pile of three CDs, each with the same typewritten label: "Chloe's Coldplay Mix." Next to the CDs was a checkbook from Wells Fargo. Rick had recommended that Chloe open an account there, mainly because he visited the local branch once a week and he could deposit gas money for her. She had resisted his generosity at first, but he insisted, telling her how proud he was that she had landed her job at Yellowstone.

When Rick picked up the checkbook, a deposit slip fell out. He checked the date. Chloe had been to the bank on Thursday. His forehead tightened into a confused frown. Chloe had put fifteen hundred dollars in the bank—a chunk of change for someone who was accepting Daddy's gas money. He folded the receipt and stuffed it in his shirt pocket.

As he replaced the checkbook, his eyes were lured to a pair of orange plastic bottles lying in the drawer. He felt a haunting chill, as though his arteries had filled with ice water. Prescription drugs. Were they her meds—or something else?

He picked up one of the bottles and read the prescription. *Seroquel.* Following several years of medication roulette, Chloe had landed on a sometimes controversial antipsychotic prescribed for the treatment of both schizophrenia and bipolar disorder. Despite initial weight gain and leg tremors, she had adjusted to *Seroquel*, and it was working for her. Rick stared at the bottle and exhaled.

His reprieve was short-lived. He squinted at the label. The prescription had been processed two weeks earlier, and the pills hadn't been touched. He snatched the other bottle from the dresser and checked the prescription date. Filled at the start of the previous month, it was more than half full.

Chloe stopped taking her meds.

With a prescription bottle clutched in each hand, he slammed his fists on the top of the dresser. His eyes clamped shut, his mind filled with anguish that was quickly shoved aside by fear.

He no longer was alone in the room.

The sound of breathing made him stiffen, afraid to move. He heard a menacing growl coming from only a few feet behind him and growing more intense by the second. Chest pounding, he slowly turned around.

A Rottweiler was glaring at him, baring its teeth. As Rick prepared to speak, the dog moved closer, its thick muscles revealing an angry tremor.

"Eaaasy," he whispered quietly.

The animal responded with a pair of thick harsh barks, saliva foaming on each side of its mouth. Rick pushed himself against the dresser, causing it to tilt backward and hit the wall.

"There you are!"

Rick caught his breath. Chloe's landlady, Minnie, was entering the room.

"Dammit, Saddam, where's your manners?" Minnie said.

Rick had heard of Saddam but never seen him. Chloe had mentioned the dog once, Rick wondering why anyone would christen a man's best friend with the name of the deceased Iraqi dictator. Chloe explained Minnie had inherited the dog from a cousin, and the landlady likely had no idea who the real Saddam was.

"You caught me off guard," Rick said, sliding the twin prescription bottles into his coat pockets.

Chloe gleefully claimed that Minnie had a thing for Rick. On more than one occasion, the landlady had intimated to Chloe that she "wanted to get with her daddy," a comment Rick found almost as inappropriate as his daughter found it amusing.

Minnie weighed well north of two hundred pounds. She possessed hard, leathery skin and was plagued by a plethora of dental deficiencies. Her large stomach plunged over her torn, faded jeans, which featured a worn circle on the right back pocket where she housed her Copenhagen.

"Your daughter out of town?"

"No ... at least, not that I know of," Rick answered. "I just haven't seen her."

They stood for a moment in silence, the empty air becoming awkward. The only thing worse than being alone with Minnie was being joined by Saddam. The dog continued to stare menacingly at Rick, mouth dripping with drool. Finally, Rick cast a thumb over his shoulder toward the dresser.

"I was looking for the extra key to our guest cabin, and I thought Chloe might have one," he said. He paused for a moment, then looked pleadingly at the landlady. "When was the last time you saw her, Minnie?"

Minnie pulled out her Copenhagen and stared at it, contemplating a snuff. Rick prayed she'd postpone. No luck.

"Late Thursday evening," she said, taking a dip and jamming it somewhere between her fleshy cheek and random rust-colored teeth. "I had to come over here to put an end to a ruckus."

"What kind of ruckus?"

"The baby's daddy was over here," Minnie explained. "He came by once when she wasn't here, and then again when she got home. He was definitely on *something*. He kept shouting about having a right to see Abby."

Rick's eyes narrowed as he folded his arms tightly across his chest. He replayed his conversation with Chase Rettick—the one in which Chase claimed he hadn't seen Chloe in more than a week.

"Did they argue?"

"Oh, they did more than argue," Minnie answered. "It was physical."

"*Physical,*" Rick echoed, practically spitting out the word.

"There was some shovin' goin' on. I even had a mind to call the sheriff."

Rick's glanced away briefly, then turned back toward Minnie, nostrils flared.

"He was *pushing* her?"

"To be honest, it was tough to tell who was shovin' who."

"What happened next?"

"He came out the door with his shirt torn. I told him to get off the property. Saddam was with me, and of course I had my .22. To his credit, he took my advice."

CHAPTER 13

JACK KELLY WAS NERVOUS, AND he had good reason to be. He was walking down a trail in the Beartooth Wilderness, holding a stringer of trout ranging in size from eighteen to twenty-two inches. A blustery Friday night rainstorm had given way to a morning filled with bright sunshine, providing an ideal interlude for Jack to coax a half-dozen fish to the Shadow Lake shore. The speckled cutthroats were shiny and plump, destined to make a fine supper for anyone equipped with butter, lemon juice, and wild onions.

As dark clouds rolled over the high peaks, shrouding the afternoon sun and auguring an unwelcome storm, Jack's immediate concern was whether his fish would make it to the frying pan. Aside from volatile weather, the trail to Shadow Lake was notorious for bear activity, especially in autumn, when grizzlies were aggressively fattening up in anticipation of winter hibernation. A former detective who'd served thirty years on the force in Newark, New Jersey, Jack had pretty much seen it all, and there was little left to faze him—except, perhaps, grizzly bears.

When he had left home at daybreak, he was carrying his shotgun, an appeasement to his wife, Tamara, who didn't like him hiking solo—especially with a heart condition. The shotgun remained in the car, of course, Jack figuring his lower back would be challenged enough on his eight-mile trek without hauling any additional cargo. He hit the trail armed with his .357 and accompanied by his dog Cedar, a Lab mix he had rescued from a cold, dark Newark tenement reeking of vomit and littered with crackheads.

"Solo my ass," he had told his dog.

Now, he was much less brazen. He was walking bear bait, the scent of his fish detectable for miles. He thumbed along his belt until he felt the leather case holding his revolver, a ritual he had been repeating about every ten minutes since he left the lake. He was convinced that emptying six chambers into a six-hundred-pound bear would be enough to stop it, but he wasn't eager to test the theory.

Jack had been introduced to Shadow Lake by Rick Morrand, the same man who'd exposed him to Montana. After meeting as college football players at the East-West Shrine game, their friendship grew over the years, and Jack began visiting Montana as his law enforcement career wound down. Despite Tamara's initial reservations about how their interracial marriage might fly in a rural area, they eventually agreed to retire there.

As he walked down the trail, Jack found himself stopping often, convinced he heard sounds behind him. On each occasion, he turned to discover harmless wind murmuring through giant spruce trees, or perhaps tired, moaning creaks emanating from standing deadwood.

After crossing an exposed ridge, Jack descended back into the forest, making a mental note that he was just over a mile from the trailhead. Shifting the weighty stringer from one hand to the other, he eagerly hastened his pace with assurance. He envisioned a triumphant return home, where he would build a warm fire, change clothes, and put his fish on the grill, his wife watching him with pride as she sipped her Sauvignon Blanc.

Suddenly, he froze. He searched the ground around him and scanned the trees, his stomach starting to churn.

"Cedar," he said in a loud whisper, panic filtering into his voice. "Cedar?"

The dog had been splashing through creeks and running into the brush with limitless energy, reappearing each time with his tongue gleefully dangling from the side of his mouth. Jack realized he hadn't seen him in nearly twenty minutes.

"Cedar!" he shouted, his heartbeat accelerating. "Cedar! Here, boy!"

Jack looked back down the trail. Convinced the dog was ahead of him, he pounded forward. "Cedar!" he yelled again.

After a hundred yards, he thought he heard something. He stopped. He listened.

"A bark," Jack said to no one. "I think I heard him bark. Cedar!"

Jack picked up his pace and continued to listen. More barks. His panic receded. He breathed. "Cedar," he told himself. Then louder, "Cedar!"

Why isn't he coming back?

Jack stormed ahead, listening intently as he walked. He was getting closer. The dog could be heard on one side of the trail. There was a small footpath that led from the main route up toward Sawtooth Rock. Jack broke into a jog, his back causing him to grimace.

Sawtooth Rock—or the Sawtooth, as it was called—jutted from the trees an easy mile from the trailhead, its imposing sheer wall rising straight up from the forest depths. The hike to the top was a challenge, but was well worth it, affording a view of the valley that was hard to equal.

As Jack approached, Cedar stood in some underbrush. His bark had descended into a pained howl, as though he felt pity for the object that had drawn his interest. Jack's forehead tightened. Cedar *never* howled. The stringer of cutthroats dropped from his hand. Jack instinctively drew his pistol and inched forward.

Lying among the scrub, partially covered by a few scattered wet leaves, was the body of a woman. She was on her back, her khaki shirt torn and her limbs flung wildly askew like a discarded marionette. Her eyes were open but lifeless, her skin milky white. There was no need to check her pulse.

"Oh, God, no," he said aloud, his voice choking with emotion as he buried his square jaw into the fur on Cedar's head.

Jack's chest tightened. He felt nauseated, but not because he had never seen a dead body before—Newark had shown him plenty of those. This appeared to be a woman he knew, even though he wasn't ready to admit it.

Cedar continued his plaintive wail. Jack holstered his gun, dropped to his knees, and wrapped his arm tightly around his dog, attempting to quiet him. He followed the rock wall up beyond the tip of the Sawtooth, where the approaching storm clouds had now produced a yellow-gray sky. He coaxed his eyes back down to the body. It appeared she hadn't been gone long, easily less than twenty-four hours, but he couldn't be certain. Bloody scratches stemmed from each of her eyes, as well as what appeared to be talon marks below her neck, indicating that one or more birds may have landed on the body before Cedar's barks had frightened them away.

Jack shivered, the late-afternoon wind suddenly chilling his sweat-soaked skin. Air abandoned his lungs, his eyes filling with tears as he was suddenly found himself reliving the cruel, unremitting torture that accompanies the loss of a child.

Cedar offered a soft whimper and leaned toward the body, seemingly recognizing the victim himself. "No!" Jack said, pulling him away. "Back!" The dog retreated a few paces, circling twice and then shifting side to side as he restlessly watched his master.

Jack's eyes once again chased up the moss-covered stone leading to the top of the Sawtooth. A pair of ravens hovered above the cliff, maintaining a haunting vigil. As he squinted through freezing rain that had begun to fall, he resisted listening to the voice telling him with assurance what had happened.

He looked again at the young woman, searching for signs of bruises or fractures. Her head rested on a rock lying in the grass. He leaned forward, noticing her hair was soaked in the reddish brown color of dried blood. He closed his eyes tightly, pinching the bridge of his nose. Perhaps she had *fallen*, he persuaded himself.

Jack scanned the ground, searching for evidence of foul play. The scene would need to be secured so an investigation could take place. He had to somehow alert local law enforcement.

His fatherly instincts made him rifle through his backpack for a plastic rain poncho he had never used. He unfurled it and laid it neatly across her. A gust of wind slipped underneath the poncho, sliding it off the woman. Jack lunged forward, snared the plastic, and put it back in place, securing it with whatever small rocks were within reach. As much as he hated to disrupt his surroundings, he wanted to ensure that wildlife would leave the body undisturbed. He examined each rock as he placed it on the poncho, glancing at the top of the cliff as he wondered whether they had broken loose from above.

Waging war with his emotions, Jack pulled out his cell phone, clinging to the hope he might find a signal. His heart sank as he read the words "No Service" across the top of the screen. He knelt for several moments in the dreary gray silence, the only sound coming from the steady patter of freezing rain hitting the poncho.

Cedar started a slow growl, hearing something Jack could not. "What is it, boy?" he said anxiously.

The dog disappeared down the footpath toward the main trail. Glancing at the body, Jack stood and followed Cedar. Another hiker? A deer? A grizzly?

Jack recalled seeing a lone overnight camper on the other side of Shadow Lake. He had waved at the man but received no response. The temperature was now plummeting, and thick, ominous clouds rushed in. Perhaps the man had decided to pack up and call it a weekend.

"Cedar!" Jack yelled, drawing his .357 and peering down the footpath. He picked up his pace, swatting branches out of his way as he hurried toward the main trail.

Cedar was barking now, looking down the trail in the direction of the lake. There was a lone backpacker, a gray cotton hood over his head shielding his face. He held a silver chain of about four or five plump cutthroats, the lake apparently as kind to him as it had been to Jack. His pace slowed as he approached the dog, whose barks had returned to a soft, rumbling growl.

"How ya doing?" Jack said, eager to get initial formalities out of the way.

The man didn't answer. He delivered a chilling stare, his gray lifeless eyes drifting to the .357 Jack was holding at his side.

"I need your help," Jack said, placing his gun in its holster. "I need someone to contact the sheriff. There's a . . . *situation* . . . out here that needs attention."

More silence. The man stared at him, as if sizing him up. A former tight end in college, Jack stood six foot four and still carried 250 pounds. His cavernous, urban voice was more intimidating than welcoming. He wondered whether the man was considering his physical stature, or perhaps his skin color.

"What kind of situation?" the man finally mumbled from a mouth of scattered teeth.

Jack hesitated, swallowing hard. *This dude is creepy.* He found himself resting his palm on the butt of his gun.

"I'm an ex-cop," Jack said. "Someone is . . . severely hurt. I need to get the sheriff out here right away. And an ambulance."

The word *cop* seemed to catch the man's attention, perhaps made him uneasy. He shifted his pack and began walking. He brushed past Jack, his eyes fixed on the ground. "I prefer to try to keep to myself."

Jack's eyes widened as he shook his head. He opened his palms, his arms outstretched. He'd never met an asshole in the backcountry, but there was a first time for everything.

"Are you *serious*?" he shouted, blood rushing to his forehead. "C'mon, man! I need your help!"

"We'll see," the man said over his shoulder, continuing down the trail.

Jack stared in disbelief, Cedar pressing up against his thigh. Something wasn't right with this guy—perhaps he knew more than he was letting on. Jack started to follow the man, intent on demanding his name. After a few steps, he resisted. *I'm not a cop anymore.* He rested his hand back on his gun, one of the few times it had ever been useless.

Wagging his head in disgust, he retreated on the footpath, taking a mental inventory of the contents of his backpack. He always brought enough food and gear to last him through a night, in case there was an emergency. There had never been one. Until now.

The sky had turned a carbon color, the freezing rain wandering its way into wet snow. As he returned to the body, he reached into his backpack for another layer. He didn't know how long he would have to stay, but he knew for sure he wasn't going to leave.

Jack tugged the poncho off the woman's face, stopping at the top of her chest. He shook his head as he looked through watery eyes at the St. Christopher medal resting below her neck.

He covered her again, his heart aching for his good friend Rick Morrand.

CHAPTER 14

SAGE FONTENOT WAS STANDING OUTSIDE as Rick and Abby pulled into her driveway. Rick caught her vigorously rubbing her two front teeth, probably checking to make sure there wasn't any lipstick on them. She didn't wear lipstick often, so Rick noticed when she did.

Rick had barely spoken to Abby during the ride over from Chloe's apartment, probably because his jaw was clenched shut, teeth grinding, his eyes searing the road as his mind focused on Chase Rettick.

He should have known better. Given Chase's track record, it was no surprise that he'd lied about the last time he'd seen Chloe. Rick's first inclination was to go directly to the meth-head's house and get in his face. But he realized a confrontation likely would ensue—at least, he *hoped* it would—and that couldn't happen in front of Abby.

"You'll have fun with Auntie Sage," Rick mumbled as he prepared to lower his window. "I won't be gone too long."

Abby didn't answer, which made sense. He wasn't exactly good company.

"Hey, you two," Sage said as the truck rolled to a stop. She had fluffed her thick hair nicely, even though it was a little wet. Rick must have called when she was getting out of the shower. "I hope this little girl's hungry. I'm going to make chicken tacos."

Rick offered a half-smile, all three of them knowing that chicken tacos represented the full range of Sage's culinary skills. "That's sounds pretty good, doesn't it, Abby?" he said with limited enthusiasm.

Auntie Sage wasn't actually family, but she was close enough, having known Rick forever. Commencing when she was five, Sage told anyone who would listen that she was going to someday marry her brave and gallant hero, eight-year-old Rick Morrand. The way she still looked at him, he knew her feelings hadn't changed.

Sage's family had roots in Louisiana, her grandfather an unskilled New Orleans gambler who'd moved to Montana to escape his debts and the hazards that came with them. Her daddy was part Cajun, her mother part Crow, and together those parts produced some fairly exotic features as Sage blossomed into womanhood.

Abby jumped out of the passenger seat and ran around the truck. She threw her arms around Sage's waist. "Auntie Sage, do you have Wilcoxin's?"

"I have your favorite—Moose Tracks. But the tacos are going to come first."

Abby smiled for the first time all day, tightening her grip on Sage.

"Why don't you go on inside?" Sage said. "The TV's on. I'll be along in a minute."

Abby nodded and scurried toward the house. She suddenly stopped, turned back toward the truck to offer a brief wave to her grandfather, then resumed running. Rick raised an open palm, his weak smile doing little to mask the torment he felt inside.

"I really appreciate you doing this," he said to Sage with a labored sigh, his fist wrapping tightly over the top of his steering wheel. "Sure you don't mind?"

Sage shook her head. She leaned toward the truck window and lowered her voice.

"You okay? You look a little . . . tense."

Tense? He was ready to blast out of his skin. He doubted he would find Chloe at Chase Rettick's—especially after the altercation Minnie had described—but he definitely planned to get some answers.

"I'm fine," he said unconvincingly.

"How long has she been gone?" Sage asked. She knew Chloe's patterns as well as anyone.

Rick stared out his windshield, a sick feeling invading his stomach. *Gone.* He couldn't believe it. Nor accept it.

"Since this morning. She just didn't show up."

Sage rubbed Rick's forearm gently as he stared sadly into her deep, desirable eyes. He had always found her attractive, but their relationship had never progressed beyond friendship. She had been supportive following the accident, when everyone in the valley had turned their back on him, but he left her behind when he moved to California.

By age twenty-three, she had been divorced twice and had sworn off marriage. Female problems prevented her from having children. A talented guitar player, she threw herself into her music and became an icon of local honky-tonks. She wrote and sang of cowgirls, Indians, and anyone else who'd been screwed. Her four-person band was appropriately named "Broken Dreams."

When Rick returned to the valley, his wife, Christine, warmed to Sage immediately. The women became close friends, and when Christine finally succumbed to cancer, she demanded that Sage be at her bedside.

Unfortunately for Sage, she could not replace Christine. No one could. Especially at times like these, when Rick was adrift in a turbulent sea of anger, doubt, and worry. He longed for Christine to steady him, but she was no longer there.

"Did Chloe call . . . text—*anything*?" Sage asked.

Rick hesitated, her voice taking a moment to filter into his thoughts. "She left a voice mail early Friday morning," he said. "Something about a couple of bison inside the fence at the Double-U."

"Those the ones that were shot?"

"No, that happened closer to the park, near Tom Miner Basin. I guess there's buffalo showing up all over."

"Did Buddy shoot the ones down near Tom Miner?"

"Who else?"

Rick's eyes lingered on Sage's gentle smile. She had always been there. Now, in many ways, she was all he had. "Thanks for doing this," he repeated. "I'll be back as soon as I can."

Sage tapped his forearm. "Abby will be fine here with me," she said. "Do what you need to do."

He forced a smile he didn't feel. *Do what you need to do?* Oh, he planned on it.

Having borrowed a few of Draper's longnecks out of the fridge, Maggie felt emboldened when her husband returned home and the subject turned to his most recent whereabouts.

"Where the hell you been?" she snarled, her tone far from delicate.

Draper didn't answer. He dumped a backpack next to the door and made a beeline to the fridge, no doubt anxious to grab a beer. When he tugged the door open, his expression quickly soured, signaling his displeasure with the current inventory.

"Where's all my beer?" he sneered, his angry, unshaven face smoldering in the light from the Frigidaire.

"I left you one," Maggie replied without concern. "Besides, you shouldn't be drinking anyway. Remember?"

Draper grabbed the lone remaining Bud. He slammed the refrigerator door shut, twisted the bottle cap, and twirled it toward the garbage, not even close. His face reddened as he pointed threateningly at Maggie.

"You're gonna go get me some more beer."

"Hell I am."

"What'd you say?"

Maggie lit a cigarette and took a long drag.

"Brenda called. Said you missed your piss test."

"Fuck Brenda."

"You'd like that, wouldn't you?"

Draper didn't bite. He placed a hand on his hip and took a long draw from his longneck, his narrow, scornful eyes focused on Maggie.

"How'd she sound?" he asked curiously, wiping his foamy mouth with the back of his soil-smeared fist.

"She said you'd better get in there on Monday." Nodding at the bottle he was holding, she added, "Your prospects ain't lookin' too good."

Draper took another drink of his beer. "I go back up to Deer Lodge, it makes Brenda look bad," he said confidently, discharging a lengthy belch for punctuation. "It means she's doing a poor job rehabilitating me."

Maggie sucked on her cigarette, cocking her head to one side as she exhaled. "You never said where you've been the last twenty-four hours."

Draper ignored her, just like before. He finished his beer and slammed the bottle on the table. He walked to the kitchen counter, snaring Maggie's purse.

"I gotta go get some more beer," he said. "Monday's still a long way off."

Maggie jumped from her chair and clamped down on his hand, which was holding a twenty-dollar bill. "Gimme that!" she said. "I work hard for my money."

Draper's lips tightened as his dark eyes delivered a grim, menacing stare. Maggie received the message, slowly releasing his hand and returning meekly to her chair.

She took a drag of her cigarette as Draper stuffed the bill in his pocket and headed out the back door. A moment later, he returned, as though he had forgotten something. She felt her heart start to race. She gripped the metal edge of the kitchen table, averting her eyes and cowering as he walked back into the kitchen. She heard a clinking noise that sounded like a chain.

He walked past her to the sink, where he dropped a metal stringer of fish under the faucet and turned on the water. She exhaled.

"You're gonna need to clean those," he said as he left.

CHAPTER 15

JACK VIGOROUSLY RUBBED HIS BICEPS, warding off a deepening chill as the wet snow maintained its persistence. Kneeling beside Chloe's covered body, holding Cedar tightly in an effort to steal some warmth, he calculated how long it would take the strange camper to hike to the trailhead, locate a cell phone signal, and call the police. That assumed, of course, the man owned a cell phone and was inclined to use it, neither of which was certain.

He scanned the dreary, ashen sky above him. It would be dark soon, maybe an hour. He was never late coming out of the wilderness, so Tamara would be worried. That could tip in his favor. Perhaps she might call someone.

Jack pushed paralyzed fingers into his pants pockets, searching for a Bic lighter he always carried on hikes. It was wet and produced a weak spark, but it could work. He rose to his feet, football knees cracking in revolt. His eyes searched his surroundings. He needed a fire, but it had to be a fair distance from Chloe's body.

He moved beneath the cover of the forest, finding a spot below the lower branches of a giant spruce. He stopped, convinced he'd heard something but dismissed it. He assembled some small twigs on top of a piece of cardboard that had come with his poncho. After several attempts, and a liberal abundance of curse words, he was able to coax a flame from his lighter, and his fire crackled to life. He foraged the area for dry deadwood, stacking it nearby.

Jack leaned against the tree and slid down its bark onto the freezing ground. He took a long sip from a water bottle, praying hydration might generate warmth. He fished in his backpack, producing a pair of thin fleece gloves, scolding himself as he recalled the warmer pair he had rejected and left on the kitchen table. The only remaining item was a Mylar blanket, still in its plastic package. He considered it briefly before tossing it back into the pack. He could have used another layer or two of clothing, but when he'd set out that morning, he had no intentions of spending the night.

His shoulders slumped as he warmed his hands over the fire and stared at the rain poncho shielding his friend's daughter. His chest ached dully, thick with grief. His vigil had assured that no other creatures would tamper with her body, and regardless of what might happen with the weather, he was determined not to leave.

Jack was well aware of the difficulties Rick had experienced with Chloe, having had a troubled daughter himself. He also knew Chloe had a well-worn reputation in the valley, and there would be instant assumptions about her manner of death. By all appearances, she had fallen from the cliff. Whether or not she had done so willingly was the burning question.

He refused to make assumptions. In his mind, this was a crime scene, and it would remain so until proven otherwise.

He found his eyes continuing to scan the stern face of the Sawtooth, squinting into the snow that landed methodically onto his face. If he could hike up top, take a look around, perhaps he could gather more information. He would look for tracks, clothing, signs of a struggle. There was no telling how long it would be before help arrived. The more the weather worsened, the greater chance any evidence would be compromised.

He placed larger pieces of wood on the fire, watching anxiously as they puffed billows of dense smoke before giving birth to fresh flames. Bitter cold was no friend, not with a heart condition. He would need this fire to stay alive.

"C'mon, boy," Jack said, extending his hands one last time over the fire. "Let's go see what's up top."

He walked stiffly as he approached Chloe's body, realizing the fire had done little to warm his frozen toes. After checking the rocks that secured the edges of the poncho, he scanned the area and listened, convincing himself no animals were nearby. Futilely massaging the sleeves of his thin jacket to ward off the chill, tilting his face downward to shield it from the biting wind, he trudged forward on a muddy path flecked with snow.

Rick nearly ran over a dog—or a coyote, maybe—as he splashed into the muddy pothole-specked driveway leading to Chase's double-wide. He could hear music pulsing from the trailer—that hip-hop crap he hated so much—and the din only worsened as he drew closer.

He had tried to calm himself on the way over, even taking a crack at reciting the Serenity Prayer, an old trick from AA. He couldn't make it past the first line before his head ignited, fanning a fresh wildfire of rage. *God, grant me the serenity to accept the things I cannot change?* Oh, no, there was plenty he planned to change.

Rick's truck had barely rolled to a stop before he jumped out, fists balled tightly and jaw muscles corded like steel cable. He stormed toward the trailer, rapping on the flimsy door twice before checking the handle to see if it was locked.

It wasn't.

He stepped inside, his senses overwhelmed by a smell similar to burning plastic. His eyes stung as he raced through the kitchen area, where he spotted a methamphetamine pipe on the counter. He shook his head with anger and disgust.

Rick looked down the hallway. Chase was standing with his back to him while picking at his face in a bathroom mirror. He didn't have time to react before Rick turned him around, gripped his throat tightly beneath his jaw, and slammed him hard against the mirror, causing it to break into a roadmap of cracks.

"I understand you like to push women around," Rick said. "Care to tell me about it?" He caught a glimpse of his own rage in the fractured mirror, his face turning a deep crimson and blood vessels throbbing in his neck.

Chase was loaded, seemingly too stunned to process what was happening. Rick glared into the addict's dilated pupils, gloomy black pits descending into nothingness.

"I . . . I didn't do nothin'!" Chase said weakly. "She attacked *me!*"

Chloe did have a short fuse. It was hereditary.

"You lied to me!" Rick yelled, tightening his grip. "You said you hadn't seen Chloe for a week."

Rick didn't wait for an answer. He moved closer, stopping two inches away from Chase's twitching nose and flickering eyes. He reached into the sink and picked up a shard that had fallen from the mirror.

"I want to know everywhere you've been since Thursday night," he shouted, holding up the jagged piece of glass. "You lie to me, and I'll slit your throat!"

Chase's eyes filled with terror. He wriggled his neck, attempting vainly to escape the death grip, but Rick crashed Chase's head into the medicine cabinet, smashing glass shelves. The loud music blared, adding to the confusion.

The music stopped.

"He's been with me!" a female voice yelled from behind him. "Get off him! Leave him alone!"

As Rick continued to clutch Chase's neck, he rotated his head to identify the voice. It was high-pitched, as though it belonged to a child. He turned to discover a gaunt teenage girl glaring at him, her right arm extended and a butcher knife in her hand.

"Courtney, what are you doing here?" he asked, eyes wide with disbelief.

Courtney was the daughter of Rev. Richard Williams, the popular local pastor who occasionally tagged along with Rick and his friend Jack Kelly when they fished the Yellowstone. Rick had seen Courtney at various occasions, and he knew she played piano at the church. Her father had always beamed when he spoke of her, saying he wanted her to attend music school back east.

Rick tried to speak, but he struggled to find words. He stared blankly, his stomach tightening as he futilely attempted to process how Courtney Williams had ended up with Chase Rettick in a double-wide reeking with the chemical odor of crank.

He released Chase's throat, dropped the slice of mirror glass into the sink, and gently eased toward Courtney. Her once-immaculate skin was flecked with tiny sores, and dark circles draped below her weary cinnamon-colored eyes. It appeared as if she hadn't slept for a week.

"Courtney, you need to come with me," he pleaded. "Your dad—"

"No!" she screamed, her pupils flaring as she jabbed the knife in Rick's direction. "I'm not going anywhere with you! I'm eighteen! I can go where I want!"

Rick stared at Courtney as though she were possessed. "You're going to stay here?" he asked incredulously. "With *him*?"

Rick looked at Chase, who hadn't moved and seemed to have no plans to do so.

"She told you the truth," Chase finally muttered in a cautious, desperate whisper. "She's been here with me since Thursday night."

Rick cocked his head. "Did you tell her you went to Chloe's apartment?"

Courtney's eyes widened. "You went to her *apartment*?"

"I was trying to see my daughter."

Rick shoved Chase in the chest, sending him banging once more into the medicine chest. Chase's muscles tensed as if to retaliate, but apparently he thought better of it.

"You are not *allowed* to see Abby," Rick said sternly. "Court order. Remember?"

"She's my daughter!"

"Well, you're no father!"

Rick's eyes burned with hatred for Chase. He wondered at times why he so despised this troubled young man bedeviled by drug abuse. Perhaps part of his anger was directed at himself, since he remained remorseful for the years his drinking and cocaine use had prevented him from being a better role model for Chloe.

Courtney was still glaring at Chase. "You went to her apartment?" she repeated. The knife had dropped to her side, giving Rick an opportunity to grab it. Holding her wrist, he stared at her bony forearm, which had abrasions from where she had picked her skin. She pulled away.

When Rick took one final look into the eyes of the two young addicts, he saw dark and barren hopelessness—nothing more. He walked down the hallway, sending the knife clattering across the kitchen table as he headed for the door.

As he jumped into his truck and threw it into Reverse, he nearly hit a car parked next to the double-wide. It was a lime-green Toyota Corolla, given to Courtney by her father for her sixteenth birthday. Rick had been there when he gave it to her, the clergyman bursting with pride. To see his daughter now would shatter the man's heart.

Rick pursed his lips and shook his head mournfully. He wondered whether Richard Williams would see his daughter again. If he did, he might not know who she was.

Jack's pounding heart echoed within his rib cage as he labored for oxygen. Reaching the top of the Sawtooth, his head swam with dizziness, causing him to buckle at the waist, hands clasped above his knees. He remained that way for a full minute, using the respite to closely observe the crushed gravel surrounding him.

Despite the strenuous hike to the top, the Sawtooth received a fair amount of traffic. Footprints were everywhere. Jack would focus his efforts toward the front of the cliff, considering ways that Chloe might have fallen.

After ordering Cedar to sit, Jack squinted toward the gun-metal sky, following the falling snowflakes as they floated to the ground. The snow had yet to accumulate, but Jack knew that would soon change as the temperature continued to plummet. He wondered how long the storm would last and how it might affect potential evidence.

He inched forward, scanning his surroundings for any possible signs of struggle. His eyes first spotted a pair of hiking boots, scattered about a foot apart approximately fifteen feet from the edge of the cliff. One of the boots lay on its side, and only one sock was visible, indicating the boots had been removed with haste. Jack fished his cell phone out of his pocket, opened the camera app, and snapped several shots.

He moved a few steps back, looking at the ground as he took a wide, circular route a safe distance from the edge of the cliff. He suddenly froze, his eyes fixed on a flat stone just in front of his feet. A drop of blood, about the size of a half-dollar, stained the rock. A second drop, this one smaller, had splattered on a rock nearby. He took a couple of photos, reminding himself that the blood could belong to anyone, human or beast.

Drawing a deep breath, Jack traced a visual path from the edge of the cliff back to the place where he stood. His eyes captured a shiny object glinting in the day's fading light. He moved closer, forearms resting on the front of his thighs.

Lying in the gravel was a gold-colored anklet. Its surface had tarnished, but it still had a glimmer that indicated it hadn't spent much time in the elements. Attached to a flimsy chain, the jewelry piece consisted of a name written in formal script: *Desiree.*

Jack remembered a girl named Desiree, an informant back in Jersey. She described herself as a professional dancer, and she would wear a similar anklet during her *performances.* Jack never got to know her very well, but he doubted Desiree was her real name.

During his time in Montana, Jack had never met anyone named Desiree.

As he clicked a few shots of the anklet, he wondered how local enforcement might view his efforts. He knew a couple of deputies in town, and they weren't exactly warm and fuzzy. Perhaps they wouldn't appreciate a retired black guy from Jersey sticking his nose into local business. They might make a few calls, ask for a peek inside his personnel jacket, and come away less than enamored with what they found. Sure, Jack had used plenty of force during his career, but only when needed. He retired as a good cop. He decided he didn't care what the local deputies thought.

Instead, he trusted his experience and instincts, remaining concerned that severe weather could impair any serious investigation. He wanted to make sure they got it right. After all, this was the daughter of Rick Morrand.

Glancing at Cedar, who was sitting obediently at the top of the trail, Jack continued to circle. He was cautious to avoid the tip of the cliff and the saber-shaped slice of granite that gave the place its name. But he wanted to see whether the smaller rocks on the edge had been disturbed, indicating that Chloe may have somehow skidded to her death, as opposed to making the tormenting and tenebrous decision to jump.

What was she doing there, in bare feet and clad only in the uniform of the National Park Service? Had she been up there alone?

Leaning over the towering cliff, he was distracted by a noise below him—a deep, groaning bellow. He squinted through the rising smoke produced by his fire, shaking his head in disbelief.

"Shit!" Jack yelled, his pulse quickening as he stuffed his phone in his pocket and drew his firearm. "No! Get the hell out of there!"

An adolescent grizzly was a few feet from Chloe's body, munching on the cutthroats that Jack had set aside in the tall grass. Jack had completely forgotten about the fish, but the bear was appreciative. Depending how hungry he was, he could finish the fish and move on to something else.

Cedar had instinctively rushed to Jack's side, yelping at the bear while dancing perilously close to the edge of the cliff. "Back, Cedar!" Jack shouted, waving at him. "Get back!"

Cedar turned and made a beeline for the footpath, deciding he would engage the bear face-to-face. *Damn it, Cedar!* Knowing the dog would be sorely overmatched, Jack called after him, but his efforts were useless. Flooding with adrenaline, he dropped to one knee. He focused on the bear, which had glanced briefly at the top of the cliff before resuming his meal.

Jack needed to act. Cedar would be down in less than a minute. He found a target—the base of a fir just behind the bear—and aimed his .357. A thundering shot shattered the silence of the wilderness, wood splintering from the tree that stood only a few feet from the bear. The grizzly flinched momentarily but continued to eat. Jack shook his head in disbelief. *Stupid-ass bear!*

Jack's chest grew tight, his head swimming with fear. He could hear Cedar barking as the dog made his way down the trail. Jack aimed again, this time a little closer. Another ear-splitting crack rang out.

Too close. The bear let out a short, sharp wail. Jack must have grazed him. Either way, it worked. The animal took a few steps backward, spun around, and disappeared into the brush. Jack bent forward, hands on knees, exhaling with relief.

Cedar appeared fifteen seconds later, looking skyward toward his master as he stood sentry over Chloe's body. "Stay!" Jack yelled, holding out a flat hand. "Sit . . . and stay!" Cedar complied instantly, thumping his tail twice to punctuate his obedience.

Jack rose to his feet, his lower back screaming for Advil. He attempted to steady his breathing, the cold mountain air stinging his nostrils. He reviewed the area around him, noticing that the hard-driving snow was blanketing the ground on top of the Sawtooth.

He started back down, walking gingerly on the steep path made treacherous by the wet snow. As darkness drifted in, he briefly considered the stranger he'd encountered, his spirits plummeting as he accepted that the man had been of no use. He would need to rely on Tamara—his dear, sweet Tamara. Loneliness cascaded over him as he yearned for his wife.

The smoke he had seen told Jack that the grizzly had lumbered through his fire, and it would need to be rebuilt. The bear had gone for now, but it could always return. The temperature seemed to be dropping by the second.

It was going to be a long night.

CHAPTER 16

A S HE PERUSED THE MENU at the Gateway Café, debating the merits of chicken fried steak versus baby back ribs, Richard Bledsoe wondered whether his luck had begun to turn.

"Would you care for another Heineken?" asked a cheery-faced woman in her early forties, her smile so wide that it exposed the silver fillings in her back teeth. She wore a red apron over her tidy blue jeans, and her pleated white blouse bore an acrylic name tag that read "FAWN," a peculiar appellation for someone living and working in the heart of grizzly country.

"Another Heineken would be just fine."

Bledsoe had left California in a dark and dour temperament, intent on exacting justice for the death of his only son, Christian. The boy, who would have been twenty-seven, had died of a drug overdose, ruled intentional, although Richard Bledsoe knew better. By his verdict, blame belonged squarely on the shoulders of a Catholic priest, Father Timothy Doyle, and the law firm that had defended him.

"Have you decided, or do you need more time?" Fawn asked as she tilted a Heineken into a fresh frosted glass.

"Chicken fried steak," Bledsoe replied, "with the mashed potatoes."

"It comes with a salad."

"Thousand Island."

"I'll get you some bread," Fawn said, flashing another buoyant smile as she took his menu.

The Gateway Café, a stone's throw from the entrance of Yellowstone Park, seemed to be catching its breath after a turbulent six-month crush of nonstop tourism. Aside from the lighthearted laughter of a young couple two tables away, the restaurant was empty and quiet.

Bledsoe studied the shiny pine-covered walls, which reflected light off their countless coats of varnish. Assorted posters cluttered the restaurant, advertising events that had long since passed. A weathered sign near the cash register told patrons that credit cards required a purchase of ten dollars or more.

"Here you go," Fawn said as she appeared with a red plastic basket filled with dinner rolls. "Your salad will be up in a minute."

Bledsoe nodded and took a sip of his beer. The place reminded him of Vermont, where he spent memory-filled summers as a kid growing up outside Boston. He had tried to replicate the experience with Christian, traveling to cabins in California's Eastern Sierras, but it never seemed to work out. A once-cheerful toddler, the boy suddenly became taciturn in adolescence, deathly afraid of strangers and seemingly adrift in a perpetual state of melancholy. It wasn't until Christian was sixteen that Richard discovered the reason—or, at least, he believed he did.

His chest grew tight as he turned his thoughts to his son, drawing fresh blood from a festering wound that itched often and seemed impossible not to scratch. His grief seeped down deep into his stomach, creating that nauseating feeling that comes to those who discover they had unexpectedly lost all of their riches, which indeed Bledsoe felt he had.

He forcefully punctured a stale dinner roll with his thumb, cracking it open and stuffing half in his mouth. He washed it down with another long sip of beer.

"Here we are!" Fawn said, approaching the table with a dinner salad and small dish of Thousand Island. "Let me know if that's enough dressing—"

"This is fine," he replied sharply. He was quickly growing tired of Fawn and her gleeful disposition, reasoning that he was answering way too many questions for someone who just wanted to eat. He drew a deep breath, calmed himself, offering the waitress a taut, polite smile and remembering she was *innocent*. Like a fawn. Like Christian.

Bledsoe had never settled up with Father Tim, who steadfastly proclaimed himself sinless as he was spirited away by the church and forever hidden in one of those faraway places where he could do no further harm. Bledsoe's focus had turned to The Law Offices of Metcalf & Morrand, and specifically Rick Morrand, whose previous association with the priest should have precluded the firm from accepting Christian's case.

Bledsoe had heard that Morrand had a daughter, but he hadn't given her much thought until recently, when he determined he could best repay the lawyer by forcing him to endure the agony a parent experiences when he outlives his child. The thought had come to him as a glowing epiphany, an apparition that promised perfect justice, a denouement he felt obligated to embrace.

"Now, careful, this is hot," Fawn said cautiously as she reappeared carrying a large oval plate with stream rising from it. Bledsoe shoved his salad aside, making room for a chicken-fried steak bathed in oily gravy. His cardiologist would hardly condone such a meal, but Bledsoe was no longer overly concerned about his health—or anything else.

In so many ways, he had nothing left to lose, Christian's death having sapped all purpose for existence. He found himself fluctuating violently between depression and anger, which cost him friendships and left his marriage in cinders. He determined that he badly needed to balance the slate with Rick Morrand.

An engineer by trade, he had devised the flawless plan, one built with precision and immune to failure. Much to his dismay, the first phase of its execution was not what he had envisioned—not even close. But he had achieved his desired result nonetheless.

He took a long celebratory drink from his Heineken. He never anticipated Chloe Morrand's death would require so little effort.

If Rick knew anything about Reiff Metcalf, it was that he always needed a drink. He had received no indication that anything had changed.

Rick had barely pulled away from Chase Rettick's double-wide when he received a phone call. Reiff was in town, urgently needing to meet with his ex-partner regarding a matter that somehow couldn't be handled over the phone. Rick suggested The Pines, which had food that Rick enjoyed, as well as the familiar altar of inebriants that Reiff would so urgently crave.

Rick's truck crept along Main Street, slowed by snarling traffic more suited for the Fourth of July weekend than a Saturday night in October. Pedestrians were everywhere, walking briskly about as cold rain fell. As he sat waiting for the second of Riverton's three traffic lights to turn green, he noticed a series of plain white vans parked along the side of the street. A stream of men and women, some of them holding handmade signs, were piling into the vehicles.

Rick glanced at his watch as he pulled into the bank parking lot across from The Pines. He was running late, but he figured Reiff probably wouldn't notice. Wind-driven raindrops stung his face as he exited his truck. He hunched his shoulders, pushed his Stetson tightly onto his head, and crossed Main Street toward the neon sign lighting the entrance to the restaurant.

Before going in, he stopped on the sidewalk and scanned the dark, stormy skies, his chest heavy as he fixed his mind on Chloe. He was no closer to finding her than he had been that morning. He remembered that her temper had flared on Thursday night, but the incident had seemed benign. That, of course, was before he had found she was off her meds.

He yanked open the restaurant's wooden door and was immediately greeted by the Saturday night conviviality of a saloon. He brushed the rain off his hat and nodded at Sleeves behind the bar. His thoughts trailed to Draper Townsend, the man who confronted him on Thursday. Draper had already been locked up when the tragic accident involving his sister, Julianne, had occurred. In fact, Draper and Rick had never even met. Julianne had warned Rick that her brother could be mean-spirited and disagreeable, and her assessment proved accurate.

Chloe, Draper, Julianne, the accident. Unpleasant, sorrowful images paraded nonstop through Rick's mind, undying film clips that hauntingly refused to remain on the cutting room floor. His stomach wrung with uneasiness, his soul filling with dread.

Rick glanced around the saloon and saw no sign of Draper, fortunate for all parties concerned. He did, however, hear the booming voice of Reiff Metcalf.

"Partner!" Reiff shouted, spotting Rick at the entrance. "There you are!"

Reiff ambled toward him, wrapping Rick in a bear hug. Rick patted his ex-partner gently on the back and forced a smile. Vociferous greeting aside, Reiff was a weathered barn. His eyes were swollen and yellow, his nose a deep crimson, his face as rutted as a backcountry fire road. While he was loud and slightly intoxicated, at least Reiff wasn't falling-down drunk. Rick was relieved.

"Why don't you grab your drink," he said, nodding at Reiff's station at the bar. "We'll get a table."

As he stared into the mirror, Matt Steelman's face reflected a pitched battle between anger and fear. Twisting sideways, he winced as he slowly raised his T-shirt—the washed-out gray one with the cracked "ARMY" across the front—and braced for what he was about to discover.

His suspicions were valid. The discomfort he had tried to ignore all day was rooted in two long, deep scratches that extended from the back of his boxers around the side of his sinew-strapped rib cage. His brow furrowed as he examined the streaks, which resembled a pair of contrails from one of the countless F-16 fighter jets that had scoured the skies of Iraq. He turned his body to examine his other side. Two more scrapes, not quite as deep.

His efforts to find Chloe Morrand's cell phone had been futile, but the scratches he'd uncovered could prove far more troublesome. He was convinced that the skin cells violently peeled from his bruised torso—along with his DNA—now resided beneath Chloe's fingernails. As much as he could claim that the abrasions were the result of passionate lovemaking—a burdensome admission in itself—it was unlikely law enforcement would ever buy his account of Friday's altercation, if they were to visit.

He opened the medicine cabinet, searching for an ointment to salve his wounds. The shelves were bare, the cabin sorely lacking a woman's touch. Shaking his head as he twisted one of the ceramic faucet handles, he splashed icy water on his fevered face, desperately trying to steady his churning mind. He stared once again into the mirror, his nostrils swelling his chest with oxygen as he dabbed his chin with a towel.

He stopped. His eyes narrowed as he turned his head toward the bathroom door. Senses heightened, he turned off the water and listened. The front door had opened. Floorboards creaked in the living room as an intruder entered the cabin. His heartbeat quickened as he glanced around the bathroom, caught in his boxers with no weapon in sight.

He pulled down his shirt. Slowly, quietly, he opened the door to the bathroom. He squinted in disbelief before he released a labored sigh.

"Sur-prise!"

"Amie," he muttered.

She glanced briefly at the infant she carried in her arms. Her large blue eyes glistened as she brushed rich-golden hair off of her shoulder. "Are you happy to see us?"

Matt stood frozen for several seconds before lurching nervously forward, bypassing Amie's full lips as he kissed her on the cheek. The joy on her face melted away, Matt having pierced her fragile veneer. Her eyes flooded with sadness and hurt. He meekly raised his hand to stroke the silky blond hair of the infant but abruptly pulled back, as though the child was somehow stricken. Looking at Amie again, Matt forced an artificial smile, hardly pleased.

"I thought you were coming up in a couple of weeks. That's what we agreed," he said.

"I know," Amie murmured. "It's just that I . . . *we* . . . missed you."

Matt glanced at the baby, wondering how an infant could possibly *miss* anyone. "I wish you would have called—let me know you were coming. This . . . isn't a good time."

Matt felt queasy, his throat barren and dry. She stared at him with suspicion. "What's wrong?" she asked, gently placing the back of her milky hand on his cheekbone. "Are you sick?"

He jerked his face away and took a step back. "I'm *fine*," he said, his tone sharp. "I just wish you would have called."

His muscles growing tense, Matt pursed his lips as he tried to reel in his smoldering temper. He needed to maintain control, especially in the presence of the baby. He stared at Amie with disdain. *Why does she always make me feel this way?*

He walked to the refrigerator, reached inside, and twisted the cap off of a longneck. He took a long draw, which seemed to steady him.

Amie surveyed the room, cautiously taking a couple of steps forward. "So, this is where you've been living?"

"Yes."

"It was hard to find."

"I like it that way."

"Do you have TV?"

"Nope."

"Internet?"

"None."

"How are people able to ... you know ... *reach* you?"

Matt shrugged. "I have cell service, but it's sketchy."

More awkward silence. Matt took another long swig of beer. Amie adjusted the child in her arms, her confused face unable to choose wrath or sorrow. "Maybe we should leave."

Matt took a final sip from the bottle and placed it on the counter. He shook his head in surrender as he released a lengthy exhale. "No,

it's late. You need to stay." He motioned to a faded green felt couch
in the living room. "Please . . . sit down."

He couldn't let them leave. Not his wife and son.

The voice on the telephone line was quivering with worry, enough so
that Deputy Billy Renfro saw fit to remove his boots from his desktop
and pull his chair forward.

"I'm calling about my husband," the woman said.

Billy considered her words and required more information.
During the course of his forty years as a law enforcement officer, he
had heard women calling about their husbands for all manner of
reasons—a few jealous wives even reporting their husbands had been
freshly shot dead.

"How can I be of help, ma'am?"

"This is Tamara Kelly. My husband, Jack, went fishing this
morning up at Shadow Lake. He should have been home hours ago."

"Jack Kelly?" Billy asked. "Isn't he the bl—"

Billy tried to catch himself. Too late.

"Yeah, the *black* ex-cop," Tamara said, her voice thick with
exasperation.

"I didn't mean anything by it," Billy said, and indeed he hadn't.
At sixty-six years old and well past the sunset of his career, he was
still having trouble wrapping his arms around this relatively new
concept called "political correctness." He looked at his watch,
wondering what detour the regular dispatcher, Helen Prichard, may
have taken when she stepped out to fetch them some dinner a half
hour earlier.

"I've met your husband—a detective, wasn't he?" Billy said,
trying to rally. "Where did you say he was?"

"Shadow Lake. He left early this morning."

Billy leaned forward, bending over his ample girth to place his
elbows on the desk. He wore a thick handlebar moustache, which had
turned gray decades before. It was fairly well-manicured, at least by
Montana standards, and a point of pride. He sometimes claimed the

moustache made him a killer with the ladies, even though he hadn't enjoyed the company of a woman in all the years since losing Melba. He framed himself as the Montana version of a Renaissance man, eschewing George Strait for Vivaldi and spending his free hours exploring the literary classics. He had sent Helen for meatloaf and mashed potatoes from Roxanne's, and it was his full intention to spend the evening hours completing Joyce's *Ulysses*—never mind the tome's overwhelming tediousness.

Billy looked toward his office window, freezing rain pelting the panes of glass. Twirling the edge of his moustache, a cherished habit, he glanced toward the front door of the station, searching for Helen.

"It looks pretty nasty out there," Billy said into the phone as he stared out the window. "I would imagine it's snowing pretty good up near the trailhead."

His words did little to calm Tamara. "That's why I'm calling!" she said, tremors of emotion flooding into her voice. "Can't you call Search and Rescue?"

"Search and Rescue?" Billy asked with an uneasy chuckle. "Now, let's not get ahead of ourselves. After all, you said he's only a couple of hours late. Could he have gone somewhere else? You know, maybe a bar or—"

"He doesn't drink. Or, at least, he barely drinks. And no, he doesn't have a mistress. Are you going to help or what?"

Sheriff Tidwell had summoned another deputy to head out to Highway 89, where a gathering of protesters were said to be blocking the road. The sheriff hadn't provided a lot of details, but, judging by the weather, it sure didn't seem to be a good night for protesting. Billy placed the phone beneath his fleshy, grizzled neck and leaned back in his squeaky metal chair. He interlocked his fingers across his stomach, which lately had been challenging the buttons on his uniform shirt. If someone was going to help Tamara Kelly, it would have to be him.

He picked a pack of Chesterfields off the top of his desk and stared at them, convincing himself he'd only smoked two all day when he damn well knew he'd already passed his limit of three.

"He's never late . . . and he's a heart patient," Tamara implored him. "He drives a green Ford F150. Can you help me . . . *please*?"

Billy pulled out a cigarette, waved it underneath his nostrils, then returned it harmlessly to the pack. Placing the Chesterfields on the desk, he took another look at the disagreeable weather outside. His eyes roamed from the window to a wooden coat rack, where he had hung his heavy green jacket and hat. His badge, first pinned on his chest by Big Jim Tidwell, was in plain view, urging him to act.

"I'm going to go out there and take a look, Mrs. Kelly," he said. "You just sit tight until you hear from me."

CHAPTER 17

REIFF METCALF HAD BEEN A stud quarterback at San Diego State, leading the Aztecs to the 1982 Western Athletic Conference Championship. But as Rick studied his old dormitory roommate across the table at The Pines, it was clear Reiff's once-radiant star was now in full descent.

The spirited blue eyes of his youth, which had beckoned many a chaste coed, were replaced with lifeless, sallow orbs tempered with a defeated sadness. His six-foot-one-inch frame, at one time a sculpture of sinewy muscle, was supplanted by sagging, rounded shoulders and a noticeable paunch, the latter likely made worse by a distended liver.

Rick placed his cell phone on the table. If he didn't hear it in the din of The Pines, he figured he could at least see it ring. He fidgeted in his chair, unable to get comfortable with the memory of his daughter sitting right in front of him only forty-eight hours earlier. He bit the side of his lip as his eyes darted around the restaurant, wishing Chloe would miraculously walk through the front door, or perhaps suddenly stroll unharmed out of the ladies' room.

He turned his attention back toward Reiff, who was drinking a milky beige-colored concoction that Rick didn't immediately recognize—until Reiff ordered another. "White Russian, please," he said, offering a procedural smile to Rhonda, the same waitress from Thursday night.

"Iced tea, right, Mr. Morrand?" Rhonda asked, and Rick nodded with a tight smile.

Reiff's eyes followed Rhonda as she walked away from the table. He appeared ready to make a comment but was deterred by the humorless expression on Rick's face. He winced as he finished the drink he had transported from the bar, gently placing his hand on his stomach.

"You alright?" Rick asked without emotion, tilting his head and looking at Reiff's midsection.

"Fine," Reiff said, raising his right hand to take an oath. "I must have eaten something earlier that didn't agree with me. I'm okay now." Rick nodded in agreement, even though he assumed Reiff had been on a liquid diet all day.

Rhonda appeared with the new cocktail, which Reiff stirred nervously. Rick stared at the glass, a fitting symbol of the barrier that stood between two men who once were hugely successful business partners and inseparable best friends. Reiff was a lead character in a script Rick no longer followed. Just being around his ex-partner made him squirrelly. Chloe's disappearance made things that much worse.

"So, when did you get in?" Rick asked.

"Just got here."

"You said there was something you needed to talk to me about?"

Reiff stopped stirring and took a quick sip. "C'mon, Partner, we just sat down," he said in a gentle tone, the one that could charm sparrows from the trees. "We haven't seen each other in years. Why don't we order, maybe catch up a bit?"

Rick lifted his chin, eyes fixed on his ex-partner. He recalled Reiff using that same delicate timbre when he would inform a client—say, a guy who had lost a limb—that he wouldn't quite be receiving the monetary settlement the firm had forecast. Following a few initial protests, the client eventually would accept his check and leave the office as though he had won the lottery.

"You probably could have just called," Rick said, irritation creeping into his voice. With Chloe missing, he was in no mood for casual dining.

"How has your daughter been?" Reiff asked. "She and the baby still living up here?"

"That 'baby' is eight years old—almost nine," Rick said. "And yeah, Chloe is still here. I haven't heard from her in a day or so though."

"Is that unusual?"

"For her it is. We usually talk once a day."

Reiff jabbed a swizzle stick back into his drink, his hand showing a slight tremor, his face signaling sudden distraction. Rick glanced at his Blackberry. No calls, no texts. He looked squarely at Reiff.

"What brings you to Montana?" he persisted.

Reiff took a long sip from his White Russian, draining half the glass. It seemed to provide a degree of fortitude. "Remember that thing with the priest? The guy who was accused of abuse?"

"Sure. Father Tim," Rick said with a shrug. "He was cleared of the accusations, and our client still received a settlement. Half-mil, wasn't it?" Rick surprised himself with "half-mil." He hadn't spoken like that in a while.

"That's correct. Four hundred fifty thousand dollars, to be exact. Out of which we received about forty percent."

"I remember," Rick nodded. "And the client got two hundred seventy thousand even though he lost, right?"

Rhonda reappeared at the table, notepad in hand. Rick started to open the menu, then handed it to her instead. "Pork chop, medium well, baked potato," he said. "Blue cheese on the salad."

She looked toward Reiff, who appeared to have forgotten about food. He scanned the menu briefly. "I'll have the same thing as him."

"Another drink?" Rhonda asked.

Reiff shook his head. "Not right now."

The waitress walked away, but this time Reiff didn't watch her. He turned his eyes toward Rick. Alcohol seemed to have ushered in a measure of calm, at least for the moment.

"There was a problem with that case."

"What kind of problem?"

"Well, I'm not sure you would recall," Reiff said slowly, searching for the right words. "Those were the days you were in . . . you know . . . the Fog."

The Fog. That was Reiff's charming way of saying his ex-partner was so whacked out on booze and blow that he had no clue what was going on around him. Rick figured the Fog would roll into the conversation at some point.

Details were sketchy, but Rick did remember what happened. Reiff had interviewed a potential client for a sexual abuse case against Father Tim and hadn't discussed it with Rick. In those days, Reiff wasn't asking his partner much of anything, focusing instead on carrying the firm.

Problem was, Father Tim had baptized Chloe. It was Christine's idea, and Rick went along with it, even though he was hardly a practicing Catholic at the time. Perhaps his cocaine-induced psychosis had convinced him that his infant was going to die any second and needed to be shielded from eternal damnation. Reiff was out of town during the ceremony and was unaware of the connection. He signed up the case and worked the file.

Father Tim swore he was innocent. However, as the matter approached trial, an agreement was reached that limited both sides' risks. If a jury found the accusations to be true, the church would pay a settlement no higher than $1.45 million. If the jury found all accusations to be false, the plaintiffs still would receive $450,000.

The jury ended up exonerating Father Tim. But thanks to the deal Reiff negotiated with the church's lawyers, he still secured his client a decent consolation prize.

"Apparently, the family found out that you knew the priest," Reiff continued. "They did have a point—about it being a conflict of interest and all—but we did get them a nice check. They should have been *grateful*."

Rick suddenly felt clammy, like he needed a shower. This was the sleazy existence he had left behind in California, where passing the state bar had given him nothing more than a license to steal, and alcohol, drugs, and frivolous lawsuits were all part of the same package. He had sought a simple existence in Montana, drawing up land contracts and trust agreements, or perhaps navigating an occasional free divorce for a waitress like Rhonda.

"How did they find out?" Rick asked.

"Doesn't matter," Reiff replied. "The bar was all over my ass, but I handled them. That's not what I'm worried about."

"What *are* you worried about?"

"Well, it gets worse."

"How?"

Reiff leaned forward, placing his elbows on the table. He glanced around the restaurant. "The kid, our client, is dead—overdose," he said in a somber, hushed tone. "The father blames us. He says we threw the case."

"*Threw* the case?" Rick said, his eyes opening wide in disbelief. "Father Tim was found innocent, and he probably was innocent. Contrary to popular belief, not all Catholic priests are pedophiles."

"Easy," Reiff said, holding up an open hand. "Don't shoot the messenger." His eyes perused the room, likely in search of Rhonda. Rick guessed Reiff had reassessed his earlier refusal of a drink.

"Wasn't that kid an addict?" Rick asked in an intense, loud whisper.

"Sure was. He was on drugs from the get-go, and he apparently never stopped. His problems have nothing to do with us." Reiff paused to take a sip of ice water, his hand showing a mild quiver. He quickly put the glass down. "Of course, the old man doesn't see it that way. He's made some threats."

A chill raced up Rick's spine. He had a dull, sickening pain in his chest, as if Reiff had slammed his sternum with an iron mallet.

"What *kind* of threats?"

"He's been calling the office for a while. At first, it was the usual stuff we always get from pissed-off clients. But then he started following some of the office girls in his car."

"Did you call the cops?"

"Of course. Restraining order, the whole bit. Still, he wouldn't quit."

"Where is he now?" Rick asked, cocking his head as he leaned forward.

Reiff scanned the restaurant again, his search for Rhonda seemingly growing desperate. She was nowhere to be found. He tried to pick up his glass of water, the shaking of his fingers now worse. He returned the glass to the table, his hand resembling a wobbly plane aborting takeoff.

"That's why I'm here," he said. "When I called the cops, they said they haven't been able to locate him. He left town."

"Where did he go?"

"Not sure," Reiff shook his head. "Cops talked to the guy's wife, but she wouldn't give 'em much." He paused, casting his eyes downward to the hardwood table. "All she said was that he was headed for Montana."

Rick tried to swallow, but his throat felt blocked, as though someone had placed a vise grip on his windpipe. A shadowy dread drifted over him as he thought of his missing daughter. He heard desperation in his voice as he struggled to speak. "Montana?" he muttered. "What . . . the hell . . . for?"

Rhonda suddenly appeared and placed a White Russian in front of Reiff. He smiled warmly. She winked and walked away. He took a long sip of the cocktail, staring at it in apparent worship.

"Why Montana?" Rick persisted, still laboring to get his words out. "Did his wife say *why* he was coming here?"

Reiff took another swallow, using his napkin to dab his upper lip. He seemed calmer now, almost oblivious to Rick's concern. He turned his empty eyes directly toward his ex-partner.

"Why Montana?" Reiff shrugged. "According to her . . . he was going huntin'."

CHAPTER 18

FOLLOWING ANOTHER SOUNDLESS SUPPER, CALEB Tidwell rose from the kitchen table, leaving most of his meal untouched.

"I need to go back out," he informed Tessie Lou as he fastened his gun belt and grabbed his hat.

Tessie raised her fork slightly, then released it into a free fall, the utensil clanging onto her ceramic plate. It was a miracle she didn't scratch her fine tableware, proudly acquired with bonus stamps at Town & Country.

"You're not serious," she said, folding her arms across the top of her pregnant belly. "Why?"

"I'm meeting Clint Roswell out on Highway 89," Caleb answered, avoiding eye contact. "Those buffalo protesters are everywhere. I'm told they're blocking the road."

Tessie tilted her head and raised her eyebrows. "Protesters? On a night like this? You ain't going to see no protesters."

"Where do you *think* I'm going?" Caleb asked, still not looking at her. Pulling his jacket off a wooden hook on the wall, he shook his head and let out a deep sigh.

Tessie rose from her chair and began loudly removing dishes from the table. "Why don't you tell *me*? Who are you *really* going to see?"

Caleb felt blood rushing to his forehead. He had tried to be patient, hoping to slip out the door without conflict. Tessie was spoiling for a fight, unwilling to allow him to go peacefully into the night, obsessed with extracting her pound of flesh.

It had been this way ever since she became pregnant. They had been dating less than two months when Tessie broke the news. The gossips in town insisted he'd been set up, but Caleb sought to do the honorable thing. He moved out of his apartment, rented a small house in the valley, and even pledged marriage.

That's when they got to know each other. They'd been miserable ever since.

"I'm leaving," Caleb said as he slipped on his jacket. He glanced at Tessie only briefly and walked out the door. As he approached his SUV, he patted his pockets and realized he forgot his cell phone. Only a half-minute had elapsed before he got back into the house, but it was too long. When he came through the door, Tessie was staring intently at the display screen of his Samsung.

"Who the hell is this?" she shouted, pointing at the phone. "Huh? Huh?"

"Who the hell is who?" Caleb asked, moving toward her.

"This!" Tessie screamed, her finger stabbing the screen. "Who does this number belong to? I seen it before. Area code 212!"

"What about area code 212?" he asked, struggling to take his phone from her.

"It's New York!"

"How do you know it's New York?"

"My uncle lives in New York."

Caleb rolled his eyes. "Then maybe it's your uncle. Gimme my phone!"

"Screw you," Tessie said, keeping the phone away from him. "I called that number before. I heard a voice mail for a cell phone—a *woman's* cell phone. You have something going on with one of those tourist bitches from New York?"

"What? Are you crazy?"

Tessie was a looker for sure, but the wiring was flawed. When it came to women, Caleb seemed to attract that combination. She'd been the jealous type before the pregnancy, but now she was out of control.

Caleb grinded his teeth, his lips pursed tight, head filling with fury.

"Give. Me. The. Phone!" he shouted. He raised his hand, which quickly closed into a fist. Tessie winced reflexively, like an abused stray.

She dropped the phone on the floor. Caleb stood, breathless, trying to straighten his jacket and uniform shirt.

"You gonna hit me?" Tessie taunted him. "Go ahead, *Sheriff*! I swear—I'm going to make your life miserable!"

"You need help," Caleb said in a trembling voice, pointing his shaking finger at her as he clutched the phone. "You are crazy."

Heaving deep breaths, his glare trailed down toward Tessie's protruding abdomen. He shook his head helplessly, then returned to her wrathful face, his eyes squinting with scorn.

"Haven't you done enough?" he shouted. "I mean, haven't you done *enough*?"

"I hate you!" Tessie yelled. "I hate you!"

Caleb stormed out, jumped into his vehicle, and slammed the door as quickly as he could, desperate to drown out the sounds and thoughts of his sorrowful home.

CHAPTER 19

THE LOBBY OF THE RIVERTON Grand Hotel was traditionally serene, the elegant room nurtured by soft melodies rising warmly from an antique player piano located beside the large parlor stove. It presented an ideal spot for guests to curl up on one of the worn yet lavish velvet chairs and read a timeless volume plucked off the expansive walnut bookshelf nearby.

As Saturday evening approached, Amanda Westin Cobb decided to change all that.

"I thought I made it clear that I wanted a suite!" Amanda shouted as she stabbed her finger against the glass countertop of the front desk. "Did you hear me? A suite! Or, should I say, whatever this place *considers* a suite!"

Amanda wore tight pricey jeans, high heels, and far too much makeup, at least by local measures. The top of her blouse was unbuttoned far enough to expose cleavage that trailed to slightly mismatched aftermarket breasts, ones for which she once had demanded a refund.

She was glaring at Phyllis Danielson, a seemingly docile five-foot-tall woman whose refreshed, confident face appeared comfortable surrounded by a head of thick gray hair.

"There's really no need to shout," Phyllis whispered as she peered curiously out of her round silver-rimmed glasses. "I am confident something can be worked out. We just happen to be a little bit crowded is all."

Amanda rolled her eyes and released an exasperated sigh as she scanned the lobby of the hotel. The Grande was not quite as majestic as she recalled as a child growing up in Riverton, but it was the only hotel she found anywhere close to suitable.

"The fact that you are crowded has absolutely nothing to do with me!" Amanda scolded. "My office called ahead and reserved a room for my cameraman, plus a suite for *me!*"

She threw a quick glance at her cameraman, Thomas Eckert, who was standing a few feet away, equipment in hand. When Amanda had first raised her voice, he had turned his eyes toward the front door, as if he wanted to be someplace else.

"Amanda, why don't you take the room, and I'll sleep in the van?" he muttered meekly. He cast a nod out the wood-framed lobby window toward a white vehicle with a satellite dish on top and the words "Eyewitness News Denver" painted in blue on the side. "I really don't mind."

Amanda's eyes widened as she stared at Thomas in disbelief. She looked out the window, where windblown freezing rain was pelting their news van. Thomas was capable at his craft, but his ass-kissing was tiresome.

"Thomas, I'm not going to try to shoot a segment with a frozen cameraman," Amanda snapped. "You are staying in a hotel room, and I am staying in a suite! Period."

When the network executives asked their Denver affiliate to send a crew to cover a brewing animal rights controversy in Montana, Amanda's roots made her the natural choice. At first she'd resisted the assignment, reluctant to return to a tiny town that held a tainted past better left forgotten. Then came some breaking developments, fueling her sudden desire to see her one-time flame, Rick Morrand. In her mind, she had to go back to Riverton. It was time.

"I am sorry," Phyllis said. "We've had all kinds of media come to town to cover these protests about the buffalo. It appears that the suite you reserved was given to someone else."

"That's not *my* problem," Amanda said sternly through clenched white veneers.

"Actually, it is."

"This is unacceptable!"

"Well, I'm guessing you'll have to learn to accept it."

Amanda slammed an open palm on the counter. Her temples throbbed. She felt the thick, unstoppable drumbeat of an advancing migraine.

"Why should I be surprised?" she exclaimed, lifting her hands in the air. "Who could possibly expect anything else from this hick town!"

Her eyes bore down on Phyllis. "Do you have any idea who I am?"

Phyllis removed her glasses and pushed back her hair. "You're damn right I know who you are," she said, an edge creeping into her voice as she walked around the counter. "You're Mandy Westerfield, and just like me, you went to John Bridger High. You're the hot-shit cheerleader who used to pick on my little sister Annie, so much so that one day I had to put you on the ground. You happen to recall?"

Amanda took a deep breath. "My name is Amanda Westin Cobb," she said definitively. "I am a highly respected *journalist*."

Phyllis huffed. "You're still just Mandy to me."

Amanda paused for a moment, then squinted at her adversary's face. "Phyllis! Phyllis Danielson!" she said. "You pulled my hair!"

"Pulled your hair and bitch-slapped you silly," Phyllis corrected. She stepped closer. "Now, I've had a busy day. How about you and your cameraman take these two nice rooms I was kind enough to offer you?"

Amanda dropped her chin and swallowed. She looked at the guests in the lobby, who pretended to return to their reading. Thomas fidgeted nervously as he looked again toward the front door, perhaps calculating an escape route.

Amanda shook her head as she fumbled in her purse, watching warily as Phyllis put her glasses back on and returned to her station behind the desk. "Is American Express okay?" she asked with a deep sigh.

"Visa or MasterCard."

Amanda dug deeper into the purse, tossing a Visa on the counter. Phyllis cast a cautionary glare over the top of her glasses, then picked up the plastic.

Amanda wished she had never come back. Three decades away from Riverton had not been enough. But fate had intervened.

She was a journalist all right. A professional, genuine newswoman.

And she definitely had news for Rick Morrand.

CHAPTER 20

A WHITE VAN WITH A broken taillight stopped suddenly, causing Billy Renfro to swerve off Highway 89 and go bounding down the side of a muddy incline. Eyes wide and bloodless knuckles gripping the wheel, he prepared for the barrel roll his SUV was certain to take.

By some miracle, the vehicle remained upright, Billy exhaling as two wheels that had been airborne returned harmlessly to the ground. "God damn it!" Billy said, following that with, "Sorry, Melba," an apology to his deceased wife for forgetting his religion.

His aging heart still pounding, Billy turned on his squad lights and began to negotiate his way back onto the highway—no easy task, even with four-wheel drive. As he crested onto the road surface, Billy discovered that the white van he had avoided was one of several vehicles stopped on the road, which was also cluttered with pedestrians.

"What the f—?" Billy said aloud. "Sorry, Melba."

When he cautiously inched forward and spotted another Sheriff's Department vehicle, he fully expected to find Caleb Tidwell working to restore order. Instead, the only officer on hand was Clint Roswell, a high-strung rookie who appeared woefully out of his depth.

Freezing rain blasted into Billy's face as he pulled over to Clint and lowered his window. Through the din, he was able to make out an unremitting chant.

"Stop the flood of bison blood! Save the buff-a-lo! Stop the flood of bison blood! Save the buff-a-lo!"

Billy averted his eyes when the rookie's flashlight temporarily blinded him, raising his hand to deflect the glare. Clint was six feet tall, but weighed 145 pounds dripping wet. He tended to wear his uniform trousers high on his wispy frame, the shafts of his boots exposed. The sparse moustache above his upper lip said he was more suited for teaching Freshman Algebra than handling crowd control.

"I was hoping you were Sheriff Tidwell," Clint said, panic embedded in his shivering voice. He hiked up his pants, likely pressuring his privates. Fright glazed his eyes as he warily watched the protesters. "None of these people will listen to me."

Billy largely ignored Clint, choosing instead to consider the scene. He could definitely confirm that there was a demonstration going on, judging by repeated chants and the placards being carried by the people blocking the highway. From what he'd understood, they'd started with a small group in the afternoon, their legions growing steadily in spite of the worsening weather.

Two protesters, a man and a woman, moved closer to Billy's SUV, brazenly staring into his headlights. The woman held a sign that read "End the Slaughter!" Billy noticed another piece of cardboard nearby that read "The Bison and Sitting Bull Were Here First!"

"Stop the flood of bison blood! Save the buff-a-lo!"

"Jesus Christ," Billy said, his voice blending wonder and disgust. *Sorry, Melba.*

He glanced at Clint, trying to determine whether it was the cold air or nerves that kept the green deputy shifting from side to side. He concluded it was both. Billy reached into his top pocket, locating a toothpick left over from lunch. He placed it in his mouth, twirling it beneath his considerable moustache.

"Any idea where they're from?" he asked calmly.

"Not from here—I can tell you that," Clint said. "I guess they started out down south this morning, and now they're headed toward town. They've walked the length of the valley, like they're on some kind of . . . pilgrimage."

Clint rubbed his scrawny biceps, continuing to shuffle as he nervously watched the crowd. "Do you think you can help me with this?"

Billy looked at Clint, wondering what Big Jim Tidwell would think of such a deputy. Big Jim never would have hired him, gently but firmly encouraging the young man to pursue another vocation.

"No can do," Billy said, removing the toothpick from his mouth. "I need to head up toward the Sawtooth, check on a hiker who's missing. I tried Caleb a few minutes ago, but I got voice mail. He'll be here soon. Be sure to tell him where I am."

Clint's jaw dropped, his eyes filling with dread. He muttered something, but Billy paid him no mind. He raised his power window, bringing silence and warmth to the interior of the SUV. He sounded his siren in short bursts, clearing a path in front of him. Looking in his rearview mirror, he felt a pang of sympathy for Clint, who was largely ignored by the protesters returning to the middle of the highway. He convinced himself Caleb would arrive soon.

Billy's SUV picked up speed, passing a trail of northbound cars on his left before disappearing into the face of the worsening storm.

Jack Kelly stared in despair at his flickering fire, which was gasping desperately for life as it fought the cruel Montana winds. He knew that the flames were the precious key to his survival, but he struggled to muster the energy to gather more fuel.

Cedar pushed close against his ribs, offering warmth to Jack's tremoring body. The canine even had gathered a few twigs for the fire, imitating the earlier movements of his master, but Jack scolded him when he presented wood covered with wet snow. Feeling remorse, Jack had tugged the animal underneath his bicep.

The thick storm was beginning to cover Chloe's tranquil corpse, leaving only patches of the yellow poncho still visible. Jack wondered whether the blowing drifts would eventually provide him with a similar tomb. The decision to remain with Chloe's body had been simple and steadfast, predicated on his loyalty to Rick Morrand and his confidence that Tamara—or perhaps that peculiar stranger he had encountered—would notify authorities. But Jack had failed to bargain on the pace of the storm. While he was well acquainted with Montana's fickle weather, especially in the backcountry, he had been caught off guard by the haste and ferocity of the current front.

As his shivering increased, his breathing grew slow and tedious. His chest throbbed with a heavy ache, the arteries of his rewired heart laboring against the freezing temperatures. He was most concerned about his sudden fatigue and his growing apathy toward movement, which were certain signs that hypothermia was creeping in. Fighting his growing feelings of despair, his scrambled brain clung to visions of seeing his wife again, urging him to find out what happened to Chloe Morrand rather than share her ultimate fate.

Billy made good time when he first turned off the highway, his tires holding onto gravel as he headed toward the trailhead. When he gained altitude, he was forced to slow considerably, his SUV slamming into foot-deep snowdrifts like a fishing boat meeting heavy swells.

He used the trees flanking the road to negotiate his path, his failing eyes barely unable to distinguish the ground surface from the relentless white wall of falling snow. He was forced to swerve suddenly as a mule deer ran past his driver's side door and across his high beams, his measured speed allowing the animal to somehow race unharmed into the darkness. Billy considered a cuss word but declined, figuring he had apologized to Melba enough for one evening. Instead, he inhaled deeply through his nostrils and clutched his steering wheel, his mind lying to him that he wasn't afraid.

If in fact Tamara Kelly was right, that her husband had been trapped somewhere in the backcountry, the man's chances of survival appeared increasingly grave. Billy glanced at his passenger seat, where he had tossed his handheld radio when he left the sheriff's office. He picked up the device and inspected it, wondering whether it would be of any use.

Billy was distracted by a pinging sound coming from the dash. He glanced down to see an indicator light tell him he was low on gas. He slammed an open palm on the top of the steering wheel—and managed to bite his tongue—ruing his decision not to stop for fuel late that morning, when the autumn sun had been pleasant and warm.

His SUV crept forward, now less than a quarter-mile from the trailhead. Strong gusts of menacing wind whirled snow in front of his headlights, the storm showing no signs of remorse or retreat. As he finally drew close to the parking lot, Billy spotted a dark-green Ford truck.

He grabbed his gloves and flashlight off the console and zipped his jacket, keeping his high beams trained on the vehicle. When he pushed his door open, it immediately slammed shut, hammered by a gust of frigid wind. He shoved the door open again, this time kicking it with his feet to allow room to exit his vehicle.

Billy felt his ankles sink into six inches of snow. As he squinted into the driving storm, his mind roamed to thoughts of Tamara Kelly, her haunting, panicked voice echoing in his mind with a mix of desperation and gloom. He lunged forward, gripping the side rail of the truck and aiming his flashlight at the back of the cab. He saw nothing, the window glazed over with ice.

His heart sank as he weighed the considerable odds against Jack Kelly still being alive. If the storm continued to rage, Billy wondered whether his own life would be in the balance as well.

Cedar suddenly backed away from Jack, the dog pacing back and forth in front of the fire as though performing an odd ritual. He startled Jack with a series of loud barks, trying to pump life into his faltering master. Head tilted, Cedar's hazel eyes studied Jack's face curiously before the animal raised his snout and unleashed a piercing howl. A series of plaintive whimpers followed.

"What is it, boy?" Jack asked in a voice sluggish and slurred. Cedar shuffled from side to side once again. The dog looked toward the wavering fire.

Then, suddenly, he was gone, disappearing through swirling snow and into the darkness.

"Cedar!" Jack said weakly. "Cedar . . . No. Come back. Please, come back. Cedar . . ."

Jack clumsily felt for his gun, then scanned the area around him. He considered the grizzly, wondering whether it had left the area. He thought of wolves, considered they may have somehow been attracted by Cedar's sudden howl. As the plastic of the poncho whistled loudly in the wind nearby, he thought of his friend, Rick, and Chloe's young child, Abby. He thought of Tamara—his precious Tamara. Finally, he thought of his faith, and a relationship with God that had lain fallow since Jack's early days on the force.

He felt the brief warmth of his tears as they crept onto his cheekbones. He bowed his head, his chin landing in defeat on his upper chest.

Then he closed his eyes.

Clint was relieved to see Caleb, figuring the sheriff could help restore some measure of order to stormy Highway 89. Along with a handheld radio, Caleb was carrying a prickly mood.

"Where the hell is Billy?" he shouted. "I called back to the office, and Helen said he was gone. He's not answering his cell, his radio—"

"He just came by here," Clint answered nervously. "He said he was going to the Sawtooth."

Caleb's eyes widened momentarily before he looked away. He began rubbing the back of his neck and scanning the freezing asphalt of Highway 89. He shook his head as he turned back toward Clint. "The Sawtooth? Why?"

The deputy shrugged. "He said there was a missing hiker."

"A hiker? Who?"

"Dunno."

Caleb turned to look at the protesters cluttering the highway but appeared unconcerned. His mind seemed elsewhere.

"I gotta go."

Clint blinked rapidly, his head quaking in disbelief. "Go where?"

"The Sawtooth."

"But . . . what about these people?"

Caleb was walking toward his SUV, but he whirled toward Clint, glaring with contempt.

"Grow some balls!" Caleb shouted through gritted teeth. "They need to allow traffic through. Just treat 'em like freakin' buffalo, goddammit!"

Clint stood in stunned silence as Caleb walked away, his mouth opened wide and the weather dripping from his chin. In the brief time he had worked for the department, he had never heard the sheriff speak that way.

Caleb's tires produced an irritated whir on the glassy road before gripping and lurching his SUV into motion. Strobes flashing and siren blaring, the sheriff vanished as quickly as he had arrived.

Clint felt his knees quiver as he turned toward the unruly crowd. The mob appeared to have no intention of dispersing. Instead, they seemed to be drawing closer to him.

"Stop the flood of bison blood! Save the buff-a-lo!"

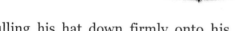

Pulling his hat down firmly onto his head, Billy inched his way toward the cab of the green truck. Tamara Kelly had mentioned that her husband was a heart patient, and Billy half-expected to see a corpse sitting comfortably behind the wheel. His flashlight rattled on the passenger window glass as he examined the bench seat. He exhaled. The cab was empty.

As Billy turned away from the window, his body stiffened at the sound of a deep, murmuring growl. He remained motionless for several seconds, staring into blackness as the flashlight pointed downward at the snow. His heart pounding beneath his jacket, he worked up the courage to turn the beam toward the source of the ominous bellow.

Staring at him in the light, shifting from side to side, was a chocolate Labrador retriever, his mouth agape with eagerness, his eyes glistening with hope.

CHAPTER 21

RICK STARED AT HIS BLACKBERRY, clinging to the fading prospect of positive news about his daughter. He felt his neck and shoulder muscles stiffen with deep anger, which he labored to replace with feelings of fatherly concern. As much as he wished otherwise, it appeared Chloe had done it again, hurtling his brain into a familiar clumsy dance between fear for her well-being and the potential anguish of another false alarm.

He shot a glance at Reiff as his ex-partner suddenly released a loud, chilling moan. Abruptly concluding an extended dissertation on the detriments of tort reform, Reiff was grabbing his side as though someone had stabbed him with a bayonet and twisted it through his organs. His forehead beaded with sweat, his frightful eyes reaching out helplessly to Rick, somewhat like a drowning man pitifully wishing for oxygen as he recedes into the ocean's depths.

"Reiff!" Rick watched his ex-partner crumple on the other side of the booth. "What's—Are you okay?"

Reiff tried to raise his hand with an apparent signal of reassurance, but he quickly snared his soiled napkin from the table and put it to his mouth. He unleashed a sickening death rattle, his deep cough dense with fluid. As he removed his hand from his lips, Rick could see that the napkin was stained with blood. Rhonda, the waitress, had returned to check on their table, and her eyes quickly filled with terror.

"Should I call a doctor?" she asked, looking at Rick as she placed her hands over her mouth. Rick had begun to slide out of his side of the booth. Onlookers glared at their table, The Pines now filled to capacity with the Saturday night supper crowd.

"No doctors!" Reiff shouted, causing nearby heads to turn. "I've had enough of damn doctors." He gripped the side of the table and gradually tugged himself upright. "Just gimme a minute and I'll be fine."

Rhonda disappeared briefly, returning with a pitcher of ice water and fresh napkins. Reiff grabbed a handful of them, nodded in appreciation, and covered his mouth as he unleashed another sickening hack. He winced in agony and lowered the napkins, revealing more blood. Straightening himself in his seat, he seemed to calm himself with deep breaths through his nostrils. "All I need is a minute," he repeated, stabbing at this mouth to wipe away reddish spittle.

Rick dropped to one knee and sidled up to his one-time closest friend, his earlier impatience replaced by compassion. He squinted curiously into Reiff's watery yellow eyes.

"Reiff," he said softly, inches from the tormented man's face. "What the hell is going on?"

CHAPTER 22

CALEB'S FISTS WRUNG THE TOP of his steering wheel, his eyes wide with wrath as he sped through the canyon toward the Sawtooth. He was trying to follow Billy's tire tracks, which were quickly disappearing as they filled with snow in the punishing storm.

He had tried Billy twice more on the radio, receiving no response. Either Billy's radio wasn't on or a repeater tower had been knocked out by the storm. Caleb reached into his pocket to retrieve his cell phone, which told him something he already knew: no signal.

He curled his bottom lip and bit down on it, cursing himself for not asking Clint more about this phantom "missing hiker" Billy had gone to find. It was strict policy that no officer should ever leave headquarters without telling the dispatcher where he was headed. If anyone should know that, it was Billy.

Caleb stomped on the accelerator, causing his SUV to fishtail as he rounded a curve and clipped the heavy branches of a dense roadside spruce. After he managed to straighten his vehicle, he hunched forward, desperately peering out of an icy windshield.

"Bad move, Billy," he muttered under his breath. "You should have stayed in town."

The Labrador raced up the trail, then stopped and circled, barking loudly as he urged Billy forward through the snow.

"Easy, dog, I'm coming," Billy gasped, his lungs stinging as he drew short breaths of the thin, icy air. He stopped to retrieve his breath, but that only prompted the animal to bark even louder.

Billy didn't recognize the dog, but he assumed the animal belonged to Jack Kelly. The Lab was clearly excited, a little agitated perhaps, as he shifted and danced up the trail, its eyes glinting in the glow of Billy's flashlight. When they had started out from the trailhead, the dog had barely given him a chance to grab his radio—useless as it was in the storm—as well as an emergency rucksack he kept in his SUV.

Billy figured he had covered just less than a mile on the flat trail, leaving him about two hundred yards shy of the turnoff to the Sawtooth. He used to take the route to Shadow Lake as a younger man, even spent the night a few times, in the days when he still had his original knees and his gut wasn't overtaxing his lower spine. Even his beloved Chesterfields hadn't seemed to affect him as much back then.

As Billy attempted to quicken his pace, the toe of his boot struck a tree root buried beneath the snow. He stumbled forward, his flashlight soaring into the air like a drum major's baton. His knee slammed into a sharp rock on the trail, producing an unnatural thud of synthetics hitting stone.

"Ahhh!" he shouted, a paralyzing shudder of pain shooting through his bones. He collapsed to the ground and rolled onto his back, his rucksack propping him up like an upended tortoise.

"God!" he yelled, his teary eyes blinking in agony. "Shit! Damn! Piss! Oh, sweet Jesus . . ."

The Lab stopped barking, apparently waiting for Billy to consummate his cussing and issue subsequent apologies to Melba. He lay motionless, staring at the blinding snow falling from the night sky. The dog offered a muted, sympathetic yowl as Billy's pain gradually tempered.

"Heeeeeey!"

Billy thought he heard something. He winced as he rolled onto his belly, looking up the trail. The dog was bouncing again, excited by the sound.

"Cee-der," a strained, doleful human voice cried out. "Cee-der?"

The dog barked sharply in the direction of the noise, dashing into the darkness. Billy struggled to his feet, dusting the snow off his jacket. He spotted a faint glimmer beneath the snow beside the trail, and he grunted and groped until his hand gripped his flashlight. His eyes tightened in agony as he began limping forward.

"I'm coming!" Billy said, adrenaline suppressing his pain. "I got you! Almost there!"

As he bounded across the trailhead parking lot, Caleb spotted Billy's SUV parked awkwardly next to a snow-covered F150. His tires made a spongy, Styrofoam sound as he rolled to a stop in the fresh snow. He reached for his flashlight and shoved open the door to his SUV, a punishing gust of wind sending a stinging burst of icy crystals into the vehicle. After shutting off the engine, he paused for several seconds, reluctant to bid farewell to the vehicle's warmth.

He squeezed out of the SUV into the frigid night, the wind crashing the door hard off his shoulder before it slammed shut. Pointing his flashlight into the whirling squall in front of him, Caleb spotted tracks leading away from Billy's SUV. Two sets, one made by boots, another made by an animal. As his gloved hand rubbed his throbbing shoulder, he shook his head in disgust. He reluctantly began trudging up the trail, the path that lay before him growing rapidly deep.

CHAPTER 23

BILLY FOUND JACK KELLY PROPPED against a tree, staring helplessly at what looked to be the faded remnant of a fire. Jack showed no movement as his dog poked a wet nose against his frozen cheek.

Billy's face tightened in pain, his artificial knee throbbing as he crouched to take a closer look. The man's breathing was slow and labored, and he struggled to push sound from his lips. He was still shivering, a good sign—it meant that his body was still fighting for warmth.

"Cee-dar," the man finally said.

Billy hunched closer, using a gloved hand to shield his face from the biting, swirling wind.

"Jack Kelly, I presume?"

Jack's head jerked, his eyes blinking as though he was startled by Billy's presence. He looked at the badge on Billy's chest and nodded slowly.

"Tamara . . . ?" Jack breathed out a shaky breath, barely audible among the angry gusts.

"Tamara?" Billy repeated quizzically. He hesitated. "Yes, yes! Your wife. Yes, Tamara called us."

Jack managed a contented smile as Cedar's snout continued to poke against his face. The ex-detective clumsily lifted his arm to caress the dog, but his hand dropped weakly to the ground. Billy pointed his flashlight toward Jack's vacant eyes. Hypothermia was beginning to take hold.

Jack's windbreaker felt stiff, as if it had been wet and turned to ice. Despite some initial protests, Billy got Jack to remove it. Billy tugged a wool blanket from his rucksack and tucked it around Jack, urging him to keep his arms close to his body. Billy wondered whether it would be enough.

The deputy felt his own fingers growing numb, his watery eyes blinking as the merciless storm refused to relent. With his knee screaming in pain, Billy wondered how he could ever get Jack out alive. How would *either* of them get out alive?

He turned at the smoldering fire and fumbled for his lighter, wondering whether he could somehow resurrect the dormant coals. Gripping his wounded limb, Billy inched toward a pair of large, thick spruce trees, beneath which there was less snow cover. He grunted through gritted teeth as he lowered himself onto his remaining good knee. Brushing snow aside, he desperately searched for pine needles, dry grass, and twigs, anything that might be dry enough to burn.

Gingerly placing tinder on the fire, he blew gently on the coals, allowing himself a cautious smile as he managed to coax a small flame. The fire gradually came to life as he fed it fuel. Billy scanned his surroundings, searching feverishly for more timber. As he brought an armful of fallen branches toward the fire, he suddenly stopped, the wood falling at his feet. Only steps away, he spotted a snow-covered yellow poncho flapping in the wind. It appeared to be wrapped around something . . . or someone.

As he raised his flashlight, Billy's hand trembled, a combination of cold and nerves. The beam of light revealed a human forearm protruding from the poncho, as well as the sole of a bare foot. Both limbs were an unmistakable lifeless purple.

Billy shot a glare toward Jack Kelly, the man still appearing delirious as he slumped against the tree. *Had there been a struggle? An accident?* According to Tamara Kelly, Jack was hiking alone. Billy guessed that the one-time detective was keeping vigil over the body—a friend to the deceased, as opposed to a foe.

His knee still throbbing, Billy edged toward the corpse. He reached for the top edge of the windblown plastic, delicately pulling it back. A thick ache rumbled across his chest. He was certain he recognized the woman's face. *Everyone* knew her face. Billy covered her and stepped toward Jack.

"Chloe Morrand?" he shouted, his voice fighting the wind.

Jack nodded.

Billy swallowed, his shoulders slumping as the hand holding his flashlight went limp. He looked skyward into the dark, turbulent night, his eyes climbing the snow-spattered face of the Sawtooth. He drew a deep breath through his nose, shaking his head as he let out a sigh. He edged closer to Jack, who was staring at Chloe's body.

"Did she jump?"

Jack jerked his head toward Billy, his eyes widening as though the question had lifted him from his lethargy. "I don't know," Jack said sharply. "At this point, *no one* knows."

Billy raised a defensive palm, nodding his head. "I realize that." He reached for some wood and placed it on the fire. "It's just that, you know, she had a past."

Jack huffed weakly, edging forward toward the crackling timber. As he turned his head back toward Billy, flames flickered in his dark eyes. "Don't we *all* have a past?"

Billy considered Jack's words, wondering whether the ex-cop was a mind reader. He recalled his high school reunion in Billings, the one he attended when Melba was ill. Billy had gone alone and ran into Sara Rawlings. After a few cocktails, Billy convinced himself he was lonely. One thing led to another. Melba never knew. "I suppose we all do," Billy mumbled with remorse, ushering the unpleasant memory back into the recesses of his subconscious.

Billy tossed his rucksack in front of the fire and sat on a piece of fallen deadwood, flexing his sore knee so it wouldn't stiffen. The men watched the flames in silence, enjoying a temporary reprieve from the storm. Cedar edged closer, chin resting on his paws, studying the men quizzically as though awaiting their next move.

"Do you have a radio?" Jack asked. Billy nodded as he pulled the handheld from his back pocket and turned it on. "We can try it," he said with little confidence, staring at the unit as it came to life.

"Seven-four-zero—two," Billy said loudly, calling out the last three numbers of the station identifier, following by his badge number. "Deputy Billy Renfro. Seven-four-zero—two."

A pause. Nothing.

"Seven-four-zero—two. Helen, you there?"

Still nothing.

The wind whistled. Billy tried to ignore the chill that shot up his spine, his jacket and uniform shirt woefully insufficient. He guessed the temperature was in the teens. He didn't believe in wind chill. It was cold, he reasoned, but he'd seen worse.

He reached into his rucksack and produced a bottle of water. He twisted off the cap and pushed it toward Jack. The ex-detective wagged his head in refusal, but Billy didn't budge. "You're dehydrated," Billy said. "You've got to drink. It'll warm you up." Jack nodded, pushing a shaky hand from beneath the blanket and clutching the bottle. He took a sip, but gagged as he seemed to choke on it.

"Easy—nice and slow." Billy took the bottle and placed it to Jack's lips. "How long you figure you've been here?"

Jack swallowed, wiping his mouth with the back of his hand. "Late afternoon," he muttered. "I was on my way back from Shadow Lake. I had to stay with her . . . Couldn't leave her like this."

"I assume you know Rick Morrand?"

Jack swallowed more water and nodded. "Good friend of mine—real good friend." He cast his mournful eyes toward Chloe's body. "I had to stay."

Billy drew a deep breath. He surveyed Jack, who likely required medical attention. The area around Chloe's body needed to be secured so a coroner's investigation could take place. Jack Kelly was right—no one should draw conclusions.

Billy's eyes climbed the rock wall once more. He remembered a warm, pleasant day in mid-August, when he took his granddaughter to the top of the Sawtooth. As they were enjoying the view, Billy's phone suddenly rang—somehow, he had connected to a cell tower.

It was worth a try.

He disappeared briefly into the forest, returning with more spruce branches. He placed them on the fire, the flames fighting the howling wind, which now seemed as fierce as ever.

"I'll be back."

Jack looked at Billy with dazed, confused eyes. Cedar barked, tilting his head to the side.

Billy looked toward the footpath, as if sizing it up. His eyes trailed to his injured leg, as rigid and unpliable as a lodgepole. Casting a final glance at the warm fire, he brazenly hobbled off into the darkness.

Caleb's face was covered with sweat. He stopped on the trail, his pulsing nostrils pushing clouds of vapor into the mountain air. His eyes, watery from the cold, darted about fretfully as his mind searched for answers he so urgently needed.

The tracks he had been following were erratic, covered in spots by blowing snow. Gusts of wind blurred his vision, causing him at times to lose the trail. His cowboy boots were ill suited for such a trek, forcing him to constantly lose his footing. He shook his head with rancor, knowing he would have prepared better had Tessie's fury not forced such a rapid departure from his home.

Caleb's jaw tightened as he thought of Billy Renfro, the relic left over from his father's regime. When Big Jim passed, Billy was considered a prudent choice as successor, but the aging deputy declined to run for office. Rather than consider him a worthy mentor, Caleb viewed Big Jim's best friend more as an affliction—a living, breathing reminder of the size twelve boots Caleb would never quite fill.

Still breathing heavily, Caleb reached into his holster and pulled out his gun, a long-barreled Smith and Wesson .44 inherited from his father. The gun measured nearly fourteen inches in length and was awkward to carry and even more uncomfortable to shoot. Caleb carried it nonetheless, lest anyone discover he was pretending to be someone he clearly was not.

He flipped open the cylinder, checking to make sure all chambers were full. He put the gun back in his holster and aimed his flashlight toward the trail. The Sawtooth wasn't far away. He heard a noise and listened. Buried beneath the vicious wind was an animal's howl, perhaps a wolf or maybe just a dog.

Caleb wished Billy had talked to him first. The deputy would have been ordered to stand down, stay back in Riverton. Billy had a knack for blazing his own trail, and he may have stuck his ripened nose where it didn't quite belong.

Caleb blew out a breath as he continued his trek, hand resting on the handle of his gun, thumb nervously tapping the hammer. His jaw muscles tensed as he shook his head, his wary mind wondering just exactly what Deputy Billy Renfro had found.

Billy Renfro's arms flailed as he wheezed and waddled his way up toward the Sawtooth, tightly clutching his cell phone in his gloved hand. He repeatedly stopped to check the device, releasing a discouraged snort each time he read the words "No signal," and then continued digging his way up the trail.

He arrived at the top to find the ground mostly barren, relentless wind gusts whipping snow across the shale-covered surface. Unlike that pleasant day in August, the place now had a lonely, ominous feeling about it, somewhat like the dark side of the moon.

Billy used his flashlight to scan his surroundings, trying to recall where he'd been standing when he received the summer phone call. It was a longshot getting connected now, especially given the weather, but it might work. As he trudged forward, he spotted a pair of hiking boots, lying askew. Assuming they belonged to Chloe, he snapped a photo and moved on.

Occasionally glancing up to check his footing, Billy moved around the top of the Sawtooth, begging his phone to give him a bar.

His balky, frozen fingers keyed the number of the sheriff's office. He stared intently at the screen, the surrounding blizzard sending a swarm of snowflakes onto its surface. Words appeared.

"Dialing . . . Dialing . . . Dialing . . . Connected."

Three rings later, Helen answered.

CHAPTER 24

WHENEVER HE HEARD THE PHONE ring, Charlie Duchesne always assumed it was Dora. Even though two decades separated the Dexter County coroner from his last gambling wager, his wife still remained anxious during the advent of football season, when Charlie used to communicate far more intimately with his bookie than he did with her.

Charlie had just taken a final look at the death report for Harold Mikan, the eighty-six-year-old rancher who'd expired while having relations with his fourth spouse, Rae Lynn. Heart attack was the final determination. Charlie shrugged and shook his head, offering himself a light chuckle as he dropped the file into his ancient gunmetal file cabinet. Pushing the drawer closed, he turned and picked up the phone on his desk.

"I'm just leaving."

"Charlie, it's Helen from the sheriff's office," the voice on the line said. Charlie's head dipped as he eased around the side of the desk and slid into his chair, realizing he might not be going home anytime soon. He brushed a knuckle across his furrowed brow. As he clenched his teeth, a heavy sigh hissed from the opening in his mouth left by his stroke.

"Yes, Helen?"

"I just got a call from Billy up at the Sawtooth. You're needed up there."

Charlie once had been a well-respected physician with a teeming medical practice outside Rochester, New York. That is, before the Buffalo Bills and Black Jack tore everything to shreds. He now sat in a cramped linoleum-floored office in the basement of Riverton Memorial Hospital, surrounded by walls constructed of cold yellow-painted bricks, his lone view the steel table in the morgue, the only time anybody needing him was when someone was dead.

"Male or female?"

"Female."

"Do you know who it is?"

"Billy said . . . he *thinks* . . . it might be Chloe Morrand."

The skin on Charlie's forehead tightened, his eyelids slamming tightly shut as he began rhythmically wagging his head. He'd met Rick Morrand years earlier at a local AA meeting, sticking his hand out when the native son returned to the valley equipped with a dual addiction to alcohol and cocaine.

Charlie had never been much of a drinker, but with no Gamblers Anonymous meetings available in tiny Riverton, Dora had insisted that he go to AA. As long as the Duchesnes were living in the shadow of Indian casinos, Dora figured any 12-Step program would do.

Charlie quickly became a loyal friend and selfless mentor, always available at a moment's notice. He had been indispensable when Rick endured Chloe's methamphetamine problems, as well as the difficult death of Christine.

"Does . . . Rick know yet?"

"No. There hasn't been a positive ID."

Charlie huffed. "Billy's known Chloe for years," he said impatiently. "Is it her or not?"

Helen hesitated. "It's her."

Charlie's chin fell onto his chest. Rick's attendance at meetings had become sporadic, their conversation sparse. Last Charlie had heard, Chloe was doing well.

"I've already requested two ambulances to head up there," Helen said. "They're bringing a couple of Stokes baskets."

"Two ambulances?"

"Billy has a hiker up there as well. That's who found the body."

"Who's the hiker?'

"A guy named Jack Kelly. Black guy. Ex-cop? You know him?"

"Yeah, I know Jack," Charlie said. "He's a buddy of Rick's."

Charlie's mind flashed to the countless cups of coffee he'd had with Rick over the years, Chloe the most frequent topic on the table. Charlie's head slumped in sadness as he recalled the dread that seemed to reside in Rick's eyes, a father heartsick with worry as he witnessed his daughter's erratic behavior one day at a time—sometimes one minute at a time—Chloe capable of ushering in the thrill of victory and agony of defeat all in the same afternoon.

Charlie reached to the side of the desk and began sifting through the contents of a weary rust-colored duffel bag. "I'm on my way."

Helen paused a moment. "I know Billy asked for you, but the weather's bad up that way," she cautioned. "I mean, it's *really* bad. You sure maybe it wouldn't be better to—"

"I'm on my way," Charlie repeated, and hung up the phone.

CHAPTER 25

WHILE SHE WOULD HAVE FAVORED a stiff drink in the wake of her close encounter with high school classmate Phyllis Danielson, Amanda Westin Cobb joined her cameraman, Thomas, on a ride out to the valley, their stated mission to gather filler footage for their investigative report on the buffalo controversy. Hardly her chosen activity for a stormy Saturday night.

Although protesters were clogging the road when they first arrived, the crowd quickly made room for Amanda's van and those of two other news crews, fervently welcoming coverage of their cause. "Just like Jesus coming into Nazareth," Amanda proclaimed as she watched the sea of people part in front of them. Protesters danced signs in front of her window, accompanied by the muffled sound of their rhythmic chants.

"Stop the flood of bison blood! Save the buffalo!"

"Clever," Amanda deadpanned, nodding her head in mock approval. "Very clever."

The van came to a stop in front of a harried young deputy, his doe eyes squinting into the headlamps of the van. All three vehicles emptied, crews converging on the overwhelmed officer as blinding LEDs illuminated the swirling snow that continued to pummel the road.

A young female reporter in knee-high leather boots, her microphone held in front of her like a sacred crosier, scurried across the slippery pavement, determined to reach the deputy first. Amanda shrugged as she calmly closed the passenger door and flipped up her coat collar, girding herself against the unrelenting wind. She shook her head as she recalled herself as a naïve, uninitiated journalist, aggressively chasing delusional visions of superstardom.

Now in her early fifties, she considered herself a seasoned, trusted newswoman, even if her dreams of the bright lights had been reduced to a flicker. She would execute her assignment with the highest proficiency and integrity. She sneered at the young reporter—only a young girl, really. Amanda wasn't interested in some young deputy or a banal local traffic report.

She was there to deliver something that would get noticed in New York.

Sage was standing in front of an open freezer door, reaching for a carton of Moose Tracks ice cream, when Abby asked a question that stopped her cold.

"Why do so many people hate Mommy?"

They had been watching a movie on the Lifetime channel, one in which a man traveled back and forth to visit two wives who lived in different cities. Sage had it taped on her DVR, and Abby had insisted they watch it. Sage assumed Chloe and Rick likely wouldn't approve of the content, but she reasoned that it was never too early to tutor a young lady on the nuances of handling two-timing men.

"What do you mean? Why are you saying that?"

"It's just, people always seem to be mad at her," Abby said.

Sage put the ice cream on the kitchen counter next to a pair of yellow ceramic bowls. She sat down beside Abby, putting her arm around the child and pulling her close. "People aren't mad at her, baby. They just don't quite understand her."

Abby buried her head against Sage's ribs. "Why not?"

Sage released a long sigh. She stared at the two plates lying on the coffee table. Abby had eaten only half of a chicken taco.

"When people don't understand something, they tend to be afraid of it," Sage said. "A lot of people just don't know what your mom has been through, or they haven't taken the time to get to really know her."

Abby raised her head, furrowing her brow as she resolutely stared into Sage's eyes. "Well, I know my mommy, and I really love her."

"I know, baby. I love her too."

Sage could never have children, a hysterectomy at age twenty-three delivering a dolorous punctuation mark on that possibility. Many of her relationships over the years had never lasted long enough to discuss adoption, or they quickly dissipated when the subject was broached. Chloe—who acted more like a younger sister to the zestful Sage—and later, Abby, were the closest Sage had come to having children. She had fallen in love with both of them, and they only intensified her concealed, carnal attraction to Rick Morrand.

Sage tapped Abby on the hip. "Ready for some Moose Tracks?"

"Can I scoop it?" Abby asked, jumping off the couch.

"Only if you remember to include a pool of chocolate syrup!" Sage said cheerfully as she handed Abby the dinner plates off the table. "There's Hershey's in the fridge."

Abby carefully balanced the dishes and went into the kitchen. Sage smiled when she heard them clatter into the sink, right on schedule, followed by a "Sorry!" from Abby. She picked up the remote off the coffee table and began flipping through the channels.

She leaned forward on the couch, turning up the sound as she spotted a report on the local news. Clint Roswell, the rosy-cheeked rookie deputy, was standing in front of TV cameras, being interviewed by a shouting young female reporter trying to be heard over clamor caused by the combination of a noisy crowd and inclement weather.

"Deputy, you say that you've been out here for hours," the reporter said. "Is it fair to say that the protests have been peaceful?"

Clint squinted vacantly into the bright camera lights, his mouth open but producing no sound. He turned to the young newswoman, whose large seductive eyes proved equally intimidating.

"Pardon me, ma'am?" he finally stuttered.

"The protesters," the reporter said. "Have they been peaceful?"

Clint wagged his head, peeking at the camera before addressing the young woman. "No ma'am. I wouldn't say they've been peaceful at all. They're blocking traffic!"

The reporter hesitated, seemingly unsure where to go next. An ambulance siren squawked loudly in the background, causing Clint to hop backward like a scared rabbit. The reporter tugged him aside as the vehicles eased past them. Clint glanced at her arm beneath his and smiled at her.

"This crowd does appear enthusiastic, and you look like you're out here all alone. Is there additional law enforcement on the way?"

"I'm pretty much it," Clint said. "The dispatcher told me I might get some help from Gardiner, but the sheriff and our other deputy are up at the Sawtooth."

The reporter tugged back long strands of hair blowing across her face, as if to ensure Clint had a clear view of her features. "The Sawtooth? What's happening up there?"

"Missing hiker," Clint responded, suddenly appearing more comfortable. "Dispatcher just told me they might even have a 10-54."

"A 10-54?"

Sage shuddered as chills raced through her body. Among her suitors over the years had been an overly conversant Bozeman cop, convinced that his path to winning her affections was to flaunt his knowledge of law enforcement codes.

Ten-fifty-four was code for a possible dead body.

She put her fingers to her open lips, fear pouring into unblinking her eyes as she stared at the TV. Clint had stopped talking, apparently realizing that his impromptu press conference had gone too far.

"Auntie Sage, do you have any sprinkles?" Abby asked from the kitchen.

Sage breathlessly fumbled for the remote, turning off the TV. She picked up her cell phone and headed for the back door of the house. Abby stood beneath the arch leading into the kitchen, a confused frown on her face.

"Auntie Sage, where are you going?"

"Just a moment, baby—I'll be right there," she said. "I ... I'm going to have a cigarette."

"But I thought you quit."

Sage didn't answer. She stepped out the back door, careful to hide the tears flowing from her eyes. She walked to the end of a stack of wood, where she and Chloe would stash cigarettes—often to Rick's chagrin. She shook the pack vigorously, a half-dozen cigarettes falling to the ground. She picked one up and put it in her mouth, then jammed a couple of fingers beneath the cellophane on the pack, retrieving a weathered pack of matches.

Her panicked mind flooded with an untamed river of disturbing images. She envisioned Chloe lying wide-eyed and motionless somewhere in the frigid backcountry, her face ashen and lips a ghoulish purple-blue. "No, no, no, no!" Sage said aloud, her voice quaking as her face tightened in anguish.

Her hands trembled violently as she tried to light her cigarette. She stabbed at the matchbook. One match, then two, then three. Each match head crumbled as soon as it struck the flint, leaving a faint smell of sulfur in its wake. She threw the cigarette and matches on the ground, covering her face as her head jerked into deep sobs.

She stopped. She breathed. Glancing through a sliver in the curtains leading into the house, she could see Abby looking through cabinets in the kitchen. Sage brushed the wetness from her cheeks, wiping smeared eyeliner and makeup on the back of her jeans. She drew another deep breath.

She needed to take care of Abby. And she needed to call Rick Morrand.

Against Reiff's ardent protests, he was taken to Memorial Hospital, located only two blocks from The Pines. Even while an IV was being inserted into a vein on his left hand, Reiff argued that a Vicodin and a 7 Up was all he needed to placate his ailing abdomen.

"Doctors!" he exclaimed. "I told you—I'm sick of damn doctors!"

The ER doctor who appeared at his bedside appeared unfazed by Reiff's remonstrations, preferring to allow an intravenous sedative to take hold.

"How long have you been sick?"

"I was diagnosed six months ago," Reiff said, his dispirited voice barely above a whisper. "I started having anxiety attacks, then pancreatitis, and finally the doc dropped the 'C' word on me."

Reiff turned toward Rick, who was standing a few feet from the bed. "Partner, you ever have an anxiety attack?"

"Not since I quit drinkin'."

"I know I should quit drinking."

"Couldn't hurt," the doctor piped in.

"It's not easy."

"No, it ain't," Rick agreed. He stared at his friend, arms folded tightly across his chest. Reiff's arrival had been more than a nuisance, what with Chloe gone missing. But now Rick felt a rush of sympathy, his one-time partner having lingered too long at the well of liquor and drugs.

"Reiff, why didn't you tell me what was going on?"

He received no answer. The doctor was dabbing his stethoscope in various locations on Reiff's shoulder blades, asking him to breathe deeply, a request Reiff seemed to find difficult to heed.

"I'm going to keep you overnight, Mr. Metcalf. I'll check on you in the morning, and we can take it from there." He placed the stethoscope in his pocket and looked at a clipboard he had placed on the bed. "I see you're from California," he said. "What brings you up here? You really shouldn't be traveling—and you certainly shouldn't be drinking."

"Look, Doc, you don't understand. I need—"

"You need to listen to the doc," Rick interjected. "One night ain't gonna kill ya."

As Reiff started to protest, Rick's phone shook to life. He quickly fished it out of his shirt pocket, taking a brief look at the screen.

"Sage," he said, putting the phone to his ear. He tightened his brow. Sage sounded like she was about to cry. Not good. Sage *didn't* cry, at least as far as he knew. "What's wrong?"

"They . . . the sheriff . . . they might have found someone," she muttered, her voice shaking.

He listened intently, eyes squinting in confusion. "Found who? Where?"

"The Sawtooth. They said there was a missing hiker . . . Maybe a body."

Rick's breaths became shorter, adrenaline gushing into his veins. "Wait . . . slow down. Where did you hear this?"

"The news!" Sage said, breaking into sobs. "A deputy said it on the news!"

"I'm leaving now," Rick said, his broken voice quaking. "Keep Abby away from the TV—and off that damned Internet!"

Rick felt like someone had just pulled a plastic bag over his head. His mind flashed to Chloe as a young child, when he took her to the Sawtooth during a visit home. She loved it there.

The yellow block walls of the ER seemed to spin. He stood stunned, like a dazed boxer out on his feet. Reiff's face appeared in his field of vision. "What's wrong? You look like you've seen a ghost."

"I gotta go," Rick muttered.

Reiff raised his eyebrows. "Go? Go where? What's going on?"

"Something's . . . wrong. I think something might have happened with my daughter."

Reiff swallowed. His yellow eyes blinked as his face grew flush. "What do you mean?"

"My daughter. I think something's happened to Chloe."

Reiff shook his head. "How . . . How do you know?"

"I gotta go."

The sedative in the IV had produced a slight slur in Reiff's voice. "I'm going with you!" he proclaimed. He started pawing at his IV, preparing to yank it free. The doctor pounced on his hand. "Mr. Metcalf, please!"

Rick glanced at the doctor, then back at Reiff. "You're not going anywhere."

He darted from the ER, searching for the rear exit, somehow completely lost in the hospital where Abby was born and Christine had spent her final days. He ran down the hallway and burst through an emergency exit, leaving a clanging alarm in his wake as he stumbled into the biting wind and wet, cold air. He jumped into his truck, started it, and hit the gas, his tires kicking up loose gravel as he swerved violently to avoid an SUV backing out of a nearby parking space. His mind raced as he brushed the back of his wrist across his eyes, tears causing his vision to blur.

Damn it, Chloe!

CHAPTER 26

MAGGIE STARED IN THE BATHROOM mirror, pressing a blood-soaked washcloth against her swollen lip as she tried to mitigate the damage caused by Draper Townsend's handiwork. She had a corresponding welt below her left eye, which caused her to squint as she surveyed her wounded visage. As usual, she blamed herself.

Draper had gone out for more beer, as well as his dreaded whiskey, and he'd obviously sampled the goods on the drive back home. He had burst through the door of the house in a surly, cruel mood, demanding to know why supper was late.

Maggie's egregious error had been to question the source of the fish he had brought home earlier that day. Standing in front of a skillet at the stove, she had commented that they reminded her of the ones he would bring home from Shadow Lake, trying to calm her husband with the illusion of happier times. Draper insisted the fish were caught in the Yellowstone River.

When Maggie asked whether it was legal to remove native cutthroat from the Yellowstone, Draper's rage rained down on her, and she wound up at her current station in front of the bathroom mirror.

"This damned fish is burnt!" came an ornery bellow from the other room, which made Maggie ponder how exactly Draper expected her to cook when she was getting the living shit kicked out of her. She wisely declined to address his complaint.

Maggie gingerly brushed her fingertips across her cheekbone, knowing she would need to wear her oversized sunglasses for two weeks or more as she waited for an ugly plum-colored bruise to subside to the point that it could be disguised by heavy makeup. Her eyes moistened, but she was determined to fight back those familiar tears of despair that had fallen so many times before.

Instead, she walked calmly into the bedroom. She reached beneath the mattress on her side of the bed, where she stored the Colt Cobra .38 Special she had spirited away from a gun safe belonging to her brother Sean. She glanced over her shoulder in the direction of the kitchen, listening for the clinking sound of Draper's fork as he stabbed at his food.

Maggie opened the cylinder of the revolver, spinning it a few times playfully. Six bullets—more than enough. She clicked the cylinder shut.

The pain in her face subsided as her lips eased into a smile.

Bledsoe lingered at the diner in Gardiner, the three Heinekens in his belly telling him there was no particular rush to return to his stark, empty motel room. He even treated himself to a generous slice of huckleberry pie, which he quickly devoured down to the crust.

He surveyed the restaurant with righteous contentment, knowing that Rick Morrand would now share the pain—*his* pain—of losing an only child. Bledsoe was aware there still was work to be done—he still had unfinished business with Morrand himself—but that could wait a day or so.

"One more Heineken?" Fawn asked as she approached his table. Bledsoe nodded eagerly, his smile cheerful. Bledsoe ogled Fawn as she walked away, taking a final swig from his green bottle of beer.

His mood suddenly darkened when bells on the front door of the restaurant jingled to herald the arrival of a Hispanic man in his early forties. As the visitor unbuttoned his long coat, Bledsoe spotted a large cross on his chest of his open-collared clerical shirt.

"Hi, Father Ernie," Fawn said enthusiastically as the priest sat down at the counter. "Would you like your usual?"

Bledsoe was unable to hear details of their conversation, but he gathered the priest was having dinner following Saturday evening Mass. He stared at the man with cold rage, teeth tightly clenched. Bledsoe thought he had left all thoughts of clergymen—not to mention Hispanics—back in California, but perhaps he was wrong.

"Aquí está su café, Padre," Fawn said in an upbeat voice as she placed a cup of coffee in front of him.

"Gracias," the priest answered. "Muy bien."

"Tu cena estará lista . . ." Fawn said.

"Pronto?"

"Pronto!" Fawn said, snapping her fingers in mock disappointment. "I always forget *pronto*. Yes. Your dinner will be ready *soon*."

"Mui bien," the priest repeated, and they both burst into delightful laughter.

Bledsoe fumed. He shifted in his seat, every muscle tightening as he glared at the priest. He recalled the occasions his young family had gone to church on Saturday night—provided Father Tim was saying Mass—and then enjoyed a carefree evening together at a local Italian restaurant. After they put Christian to bed, he and Susan would stay up late, perhaps even make love, feeling spiritually sound and almost giddy with the knowledge they would sleep in on Sunday morning. Bledsoe wondered whether the priest in the diner was a Jesuit or Dominican or perhaps even a Franciscan, like Father Tim.

Lord, make me an instrument of thy peace. Where there is hatred, let me sow love. Where there is injury, pardon . . .

Bledsoe was in no mood for pardon. His steel eyes remained fixed on Father Ernie, so intently that he didn't notice when Fawn placed a fresh Heineken in front of him. The priest, still relishing his exchange with the waitress, smiled broadly as his deep-brown eyes scanned the restaurant. He offered a friendly nod toward Bledsoe, but his smile faded into a cautious stare.

Bledsoe took a long draw from his Heineken, holding his glare until the priest turned away. Licking beer from his lips, he stared at the thick raven hair trailing down the back of Father Ernie's head. There would be more work to do in Montana than he originally thought.

CHAPTER 27

A S HE HOBBLED OFF THE trail at the Sawtooth, Billy stopped in his tracks. He spotted Caleb down on one knee, pointing a flashlight at Chloe's corpse, his gloved hand replacing the flapping plastic poncho over her face.

Caleb slowly rose from his crouch. With his hand resting on his sidearm and a menacing expression on his face, he glared at Jack Kelly. The ex-detective still seemed out of it, his head wobbly as he squinted up at Caleb. Cedar bared his teeth and growled, as though prepared to protect his master.

When he caught sight of Billy, Caleb jerked his hand from his gun. He rocked from one leg to another, eyes darting in scattered directions. He seemed rattled. Everyone knew that Caleb once had a thing for Chloe Morrand. Maybe that was it.

"What we got here, Billy?" Caleb shouted, his voice dueling the wind. He edged toward his deputy, sneaking a glance at Chloe's body before sweeping a suspicious scowl over Jack.

"Not sure, Sheriff," Billy panted, his hike up the Sawtooth still taxing his lungs. "Mr. Kelly here found—"

"Found?" Caleb asked, now inches from Billy's face. "What makes you so sure he just *found* her?"

Billy jerked his head back, frowning in confusion. "Sheriff, this guy's a good friend of Rick Morrand's. He's an ex-cop. I would assume—"

"I'm not assuming anything, Billy, and neither should you," he snapped. "How about telling me what you *know*?"

Billy drew a deep breath and anchored his fists on his hips. "This guy was out of water and he's got a bad ticker," he said, nodding toward Jack. "If he harmed her, I highly doubt he'd hang out in this storm just so everyone could find the body."

Dumb shit. Sorry, Melba.

The deputy's insubordination seemed to rattle Caleb. "Okay, so he *found* her," the sheriff said. "What else?"

Billy narrowed his eyes. Caleb could get like this, talking down to others at a crime scene. The deputy half-expected him to reach into his pocket and whip out a copy of his criminology degree. Billy exhaled steamy air beneath his thick, frozen mustache. He had been second in command to Big Jim for well over a decade before Caleb could even wipe his own snot. He resented the lack of respect, even if Caleb technically outranked him.

"I managed to reach Helen," Billy eventually said in a calm voice. "She was going to send a couple of ambulances and call the coroner, so we can conduct a full investigation."

Caleb tilted his head and huffed a derisive laugh. "Charlie? You expect *Charlie* to come up here and get something done, in this weather? This storm is getting worse. No one else is coming up here tonight."

"But Sheriff, if I might suggest—"

"There's nothin' to suggest, *Deputy*," Caleb said, reminding Billy of hierarchy. "You take Mr. Kelly down to the trailhead—he looks like he could use medical attention. Hopefully, the ambulance techs will have the good sense to bring along a basket. We'll need to move this body out of here."

Billy's eyes opened wide. Charlie Duchesne was pretty territorial about his crime scenes, especially since his crime scenes were so rare. *The body is mine*, he would say. "Charlie won't want you moving the body before he's had a look," Billy cautioned.

"I don't care what Charlie wants—I'm the sheriff! No one else is coming up here tonight—it's not safe. And we sure as hell can't just leave her up here." Caleb put his hands on his hips, studying Billy's scowl. "Is there something you'd like to say, Billy?"

The deputy moved in tight, his narrowed eyes speaking volumes. Caleb swallowed, trying to hold his ground. "It's my responsibility to make sure no one else gets hurt," he said with an unsteady voice. He looked up at the rock wall of the Sawtooth. "I'm going to stay up here and look around. I'll go up top, gather what I can."

They stared at each other for several seconds before Caleb released a deep sigh. "Billy, this *is* Chloe Morrand." He cast a nod toward the body. "Look where she is and the way she is lying there. We pretty much know what happened, don't we?" He paused, tilting his head forward and raising his eyebrows. "I mean . . . *Don't we?*"

Billy studied the callow sheriff in front of him. Big Jim Tidwell would have never handled things this way, casting assumptions before an investigation had even taken place. Every victim deserved their due—even victims like Chloe Morrand. It didn't what matter the circumstances were or how long it took.

Billy trudged forward, brushing past Caleb to help Jack Kelly to his feet, hoisting the burly detective's muscular arm around his shoulder. He took one long last look at Chloe's body, then turned toward Caleb.

"If that's what you *assume* happened, Sheriff," he said. "As for me, I don't *know.*"

The interior of Rick's truck felt lonely and barren as he accelerated out of town, the only sound coming from the rhythmic slap of overworn wipers slurring an icy film across his windshield. His gloveless white knuckles squeezed the steering wheel as his brain swirled with a surreal series of events that had been rehearsed way too many times in his randomly agonized mind.

Three deer scampered away into the shadows on the side of the road, Rick barely noticing them. A glance at his dashboard told him he was passing eighty-five miles per hour, but his only response was to focus his unblinking vision on Highway 89, somehow fighting back a flood of tears eagerly wishing to cascade into his eyes. He kept reminding himself that he needed to breathe—*breathe!*—his vacant chest aching as though he had absorbed an unobstructed blow from a spirited sledgehammer.

Up ahead, perhaps a half-mile away, he could see flashing lights from a sheriff's department SUV. Something was blocking the road.

"What the hell is this?" Rick told the empty vehicle. "Jeez-zus Christ!"

As he drew nearer, he saw a crowd of people, some holding signs. Others were sitting on the icy pavement in the middle of the highway, apparently with no plans to move. Rick recognized young Clint Roswell, the deputy Sage had spotted on TV. He was being interviewed by a young female reporter. Clint ignored the crowd around him, no doubt awash in the penultimate moments of his fifteen minutes of fame.

Several protesters moved in front of Rick's truck, their lips pantomiming slogans he couldn't make out from inside his cab. He honked his horn, stunning the protesters momentarily, but they refused to move. One of them used both hands to pound the hood of Rick's truck, a flagrantly unacceptable gesture even on a good day.

This was not a good day.

"Have it your way," Rick muttered through clamped teeth. He threw the vehicle into Park and reached into the back of the cab to grab a Winchester 100 from the gun rack. The rifle had belonged to his father, and Rick always appreciated the way it would pierce the air with a thundering echo it when it discharged.

It would do just fine.

He knocked a protester to the pavement as he threw open the door of the truck, then fired two shots into the moonless sky. A couple of women let out screams, and demonstrators raced from the road. "What are you—freakin' crazy?" a man shouted as he dove into a darkened ditch.

Rick picked up his pace. Two more shots quickly rang out from the lever-action repeater. The shots drew notice from Clint, who fell into a crouch, his craven eyes begging for a place to take cover, the safety of the female reporter seeming of little concern.

Rick stormed toward Clint, unleashing a couple of more shots into the air for good measure.

"Mr. M-M-Morrand," Clint said. A pause, then, "Mr. Morrand!"

The reporter stared at Rick, mouth open wide but suddenly speechless. Her cameraman boldly moved forward, focusing his lens on Rick's face as he approached the deputy. Rick turned toward the cameraman, using the barrel of his rifle to lower the camera toward the ground.

"Don't even think about it," he seethed through clamped teeth. He turned his eyes back toward Clint. "I need to know what's going on up at the Sawtooth."

Clint stepped back, nearly losing his footing on the slick pavement. "I . . . I really don't know, Mr. Morrand."

Rick lunged forward, snatching Clint's collar. "Sage Fontenot tells me you're quite the television celebrity. Now, I'll ask you again: What is going on at the Sawtooth?"

Clint's cherubic face was agape with fright. He searched for breath as Rick tightened his grip.

"Tell me, damn it!" Rick shouted. "Is it my daughter? Is it Chloe?"

Blood vessels bulged on Clint's trembling forehead, and his hat toppled onto the pavement as his scrawny legs flailed as limply as a rag doll's. "I swear, I don't know, Mr. Morrand," he sputtered, saliva dripping from the edges of his mouth. "Dispatch just told me there was a body—that's it!"

"Stop it!" the female reporter shouted. "You're hurting him!" Her words seemed to jar Rick from his trance. He loosened the grasp on Clint's neck, allowing the deputy to achieve more favorable footing. Rick nodded briefly as he brushed snow off the deputy's lapels.

"Looks like you need to learn a thing or two about crowd control, Clint. Somebody's liable to get killed out here."

Rick fired a final shot into the air. The road was clear.

Clint shook his head. "This ain't the way to handle it, Mr. Morrand."

Rick had already slung the barrel of his Winchester over his shoulder and was walking toward his truck. "Go home, son. It's past your bedtime."

He tossed his rifle in the cab, jumped behind the wheel, and slammed the door. He yanked the transmission into gear and took off down Highway 89.

His truck sped into the night, darkness swallowing him.

Having dismissed Billy, Caleb climbed eagerly up the Sawtooth. The storm was worsening, snow continuing to pound the forest as the temperature plummeted toward zero.

Emerging from the shelter of the trees as he reached the top of the trail, Caleb was rocked by a gust that nearly threw him off his feet. With one hand clutching his hat, he used his flashlight to pan his surroundings. The snow had begun to drift, with much of the gravel surface lying beneath a thin white cover. He noticed faint footprints being dusted away by the severe wind, and judging by their size, he assumed they belonged to Billy. The thought of the aging deputy caused Caleb to shake his head. *Old bastard needs to retire.*

As he moved to his right, Caleb spotted a pair of hiking boots, a closer examination revealing they belonged to a woman. A sock was protruding from the top of one of the boots, frozen in place. Using his gloved hands, Caleb clumsily placed the boots together and picked them up, careful not to disturb the untied laces. He figured he would face enough of Charlie Duchesne's wrath for moving Chloe's body, and he didn't want to be accused of mishandling evidence.

Pulling his hat down tight around his head, Caleb edged closer to the edge of the Sawtooth, steadying himself as the swirling wind continued to shove him in scattered directions. His arms went slack, and he stared into black nothingness, a chill racing up his spine as he felt the stark emptiness of his solitude. His chest grew thick as his thoughts drifted to Chloe—not the Chloe he knew but rather the one he had always imagined. She was forever gone, leaving her life and young child behind. His body felt paralyzed, weighted by sadness and gloom. He shook his head rapidly, trying to chase Chloe away.

His slowly lifted his right wrist, allowing his flashlight to roam the edge of the cliff, the jagged rock leading to an ominous drop into darkness and doom. He studied the labyrinth of footprints surrounding him, assuming most of those that remained would belong to him or Billy Renfro. The storm likely would cover any reliable evidence, perhaps erase it completely.

As Caleb turned to head back toward the trail, he stopped. His flashlight's beam caught on a glint of metal sparkling on the gravel. He dropped into a crouch and studied a piece of gold-plated jewelry. It was an ankle bracelet with a nameplate that spelled out "Desiree."

Caleb's blinking eyes darted around the top of the Sawtooth, as though someone might be watching him. He tried to clutch the anklet with his glove but failed twice. Removing a glove, he picked up the piece of jewelry and stuffed it deep into his pocket. He released a heavy sigh.

After scanning his desolate surroundings one last time, he started back down the trail.

Maggie waited in the bedroom, biding her time as she listened to Draper throw his plate into the sink in disgust. The refrigerator door opened, followed by the hiss of the metal cap coming off a bottle of beer.

As she peeked out from behind the bedroom door, she saw Draper plop onto the couch and turn up the volume on the TV. Montana State was playing somewhere in California. Draper was always crowing about the Bobcats—*his* team—as if the school had awarded him an honorary degree. The only affiliation Draper Townsend had to anything called Montana State was the Deer Lodge pen.

With Draper focused on the TV screen, Maggie slipped out of the bedroom and began inching her way down the hall. Her heart pounded as she tried to steady the gun with both hands. Her eyes blinked rapidly, attempting to focus on her target. Her nostrils widened, her face reddening as she remembered that she had been waiting for this moment for a long time.

She gently pulled the trigger. An ear-splitting shot rang out.

As Billy Renfro and Jack Kelly stumbled toward the trailhead, they were met by two paramedics from Search and Rescue. The men were struggling through the snow with a Stokes basket, the storm giving no quarter.

"Is this the man who went missing?" asked Ronnie Cates, one of the paramedics.

"Jack Kelly," Billy shouted through the wind. "His name's Jack Kelly."

The paramedics moved toward Jack, but he waved them off. "I'm fine," he mumbled, even though he didn't look it. "I'm a little dehydrated, that's all."

Ronnie flicked a nod toward the ambulances, then turned toward Billy. "We best get him into one of those units, Deputy. We can give him an IV, get him some fluids."

"I'm *fine*!" Jack's thick voice bellowed, his narrowed eyes saying he meant it.

Ronnie looked at Billy. "We're told there's a 10-54?"

Billy released a sad sigh and nodded. "Affirmative."

"Charlie Duchesne is on his way. Should we hold off until he gets here?"

Billy wagged his head. "Sheriff Tidwell is up there waiting for you, at the base of the Sawtooth. He wants you to bring her down now."

Ronnie frowned. "Charlie contacted our dispatch and told them not to move the body. He was pretty insistent."

"I agree with him," Billy said. He squinted into the piercing sheets of snow pelting his face, raising his thick forearm to shield his frozen eyebrows. "Caleb insisted he wants the body moved out. He says the storm is too bad."

Ronnie glanced around. "Late October in Montana," he said with a shrug. "I've seen worse."

Billy lowered his forearm, nodding in agreement. "Not the way I would do it—for that matter, not the way Big Jim would have, either." He glanced over his shoulder up the trail. "But right now, Caleb is the sheriff, and those are his orders."

"We'll head up now," Ronnie said. "In the meantime, you two should help yourselves to the back of one of those ambulances. Get yourselves warm."

"We will." He patted Jack on the shoulder and started to walk away before Ronnie stopped him.

"Hey, Deputy?" he asked, tilting his head. "Is it true? You know, is it Chloe?"

Billy paused. His eyes blinked, beating back sadness. A dense heaviness descended upon his chest. He nodded.

"It's Chloe. It's definitely Chloe."

After Thomas damn near got her killed, Amanda was craving a cocktail more than ever. But as she stared at the flashing lights of the ambulances parked at the Sawtooth trailhead, she found herself a long way from the comfort of her hotel room, let alone a suite.

They'd barely missed a local news van that had lost control and bounded down off the side of the road two miles back. Amanda wanted to abort the mission right then and there, but Thomas forged ahead, insisting they'd have an *exclusive*, even if Amanda had no idea what that exclusive might be. Another tired tale of human misery, more than likely. She was reasonably certain the *exclusive* would have nothing to do with buffalo, which was the reason they were sent to Montana in the first place.

"We're lucky we're not the ones in that ditch," Amanda seethed as they rolled to a stop.

She leaned forward, peering through the ice-covered windshield at the blinding storm. Gusts of wind whistled past the van, snow raking its metal sides like blasting sand. She remembered the Sawtooth from her high school days, when it was a popular gathering spot for young locals who ranged from lovers to losers. She had a surplus of memories about the place, few of them pleasant. "I'm not so sure this was a good idea."

Thomas looked at her and shrugged. "You heard that rookie cop back on Highway 89. There's a missing hiker, and maybe even a 10-54. Good stuff."

"Good stuff?"

"You know what I mean."

Amanda drew a deep breath and stared out the window. "It's got Emmy written all over it," she mumbled.

She turned toward Thomas, who was eagerly tapping the top of the steering wheel, the lights of the ambulances flashing across his unshaven face. She'd met him when he was just an intern, a bright kid out of Columbia. He'd worked in New York for a while but eventually ended up in Denver following a rough breakup with his boyfriend. She recalled how quickly his innocence and youthful ideals had abandoned him, the economic necessities of the rapidly decaying news industry leaving him weary, dishonest, and jaded—just like the rest of them.

Amanda shifted in her seat, vigorously rubbing the arms of her coat as she shivered. The storm frightened her. She never should have come to the trailhead. As she prepared to once again demand that they leave, she spotted two men staggering through the wind to step inside one of the ambulances.

"Go," she said, pointing at them. "One of those guys looks like he's in uniform. See what you can find out."

Thomas's eyes opened wide. "You want *me* to go?" he asked. "I'm a cameraman."

"No, you're a *journalist*," Amanda said, snickering at the thought. "Go see what's going on."

"But—"

"Look," Amanda snapped, accessing her best bitchiness. "You dragged my ass up here against my better judgement. I'm not going out in this storm unless there's a good reason to. Now go!"

"But I don't have any gloves."

"I said go, Geraldo!" she shouted, flicking her hand at him. "Now!"

Charlie Duchesne moved quickly down Highway 89, the protesters having decided it was time to disperse. It wasn't long before he had turned onto the road leading to the trailhead, and he caught up to the taillights of a Dodge truck spitting snow and gravel. Looking at the license plate, Charlie quickly realized that he was following Rick Morrand.

"What's he doing here?" Charlie said aloud. His heart sank. Based on the information from Helen, he was convinced he was going to retrieve the body of Chloe Morrand. He knew he would eventually have been assigned the grim task of informing his close friend of his daughter's death, but he had managed to somehow set that aside, like stuffing an overdue bill into a desk and pretending it might go away.

"What is it now—Facebook?" Charlie muttered to himself, still wondering how Rick might have learned about the 10-54. "Or, I'll bet it was that freakin' Twitter," he added, even though he wasn't quite certain what Twitter was.

As they moved further into the canyon, the snow on the road quickly grew deeper. Charlie watched Rick slam on his brakes, nearly skidding into a ditch. Charlie instantly followed suit, fishtailing as he struggled to regain control. Just as he was about to crash into Rick's tailgate, his friend kept moving, maneuvering past an SUV parked haphazardly on the side of the road. Further up ahead, down an embankment, a news van lay on its side, its satellite dish having snapped off its roof.

"Damn media," Charlie spit out. "Shouldn't be back here anyway."

He spotted a few people milling about the crash site, but he forged ahead. Rick had no plans to stop, and neither did he.

Billy found a stack of blankets in the corner of the ambulance, unfurled one of them, and handed it to Jack Kelly. The ex-detective's eyes drooped with exhaustion, his head bowed and forearms propped on his thighs as he sat on a gurney.

"Believe it or not, they don't keep a ton of drinking water in these things, in case a patient needs surgery," Billy said as he fished through shelves of equipment and supplies. He spotted a chemical icepack, perfect for his knee, and tossed it on the padded bench across from Jack. Releasing a lengthy groan, courtesy of his wounded limb, Billy crouched down toward the lower shelves. "Here we go," he said as he emerged with two bottles of Montana Treasure.

"I really appreciate your efforts," Jack said as he took a drink of water. "If you hadn't shown up when you did, there's no telling what might have happened."

Billy shook his ice pack, then pressed it with his thumbs to loosen its contents. "Something tells me you're the kind of guy who would have done the same." He shook the compress again and placed it on his knee. After removing his wet uniform jacket, Billy draped a wool blanket over his shoulders and looked at Jack. "If you're up for it, I'd like to ask you a few questions about what you found, given you were the first person at the scene."

Jack nodded. "Fire away."

"When you discovered Chloe's body, did you happen to notice any tracks?"

Jack paused in thought. "It was off the trail. She was lying among some vegetation—huckleberry bushes, I guess they were. There was some freezing rain falling, so there really weren't any tracks. Maybe some trampled grass, but that's about it."

Billy nodded. "I assume you didn't touch the body?"

Jack shook his head. "I've processed hundreds of scenes during my career, Deputy," he said. "All I did was place a plastic poncho over her. As you may or may not know, Rick Morrand is a good friend of mine."

Billy nodded with vigor, indicating he meant no offense. "Did you see anyone in the area anyone who might have seemed unusual?"

Jack rubbed his stubbled chin. "There was that guy," he said, eyebrows tightened.

"What guy?"

"Real creepy-looking dude. I heard someone coming, so I ran out to the main trail looking for help. This guy comes along and barely talks to me. I asked him to go call someone, but he blows me off. I'm thinking he's either a white supremacist or maybe just psycho. He was carrying a stringer of fish, so it's possible he was coming from the lake."

Billy impatiently tapped his compress, wondering why it wasn't cold. "Would you be able to identify this guy if you saw him?"

"He kind of hid his face, but it's possible," Jack said with a rapid nod.

Billy closed his eyelids and bared his teeth as he tried to flex his knee. He shook the compress again. "Thanks for your help. Maybe we can talk again in the next day or so, when we've both had some rest."

Jack tilted his bottle toward Billy. "Affirmative." He took a long drink of water, wiping his lips with the back of his hand. "This unit has a radio, doesn't it?"

Billy gazed toward the cab. "I'm sure it does—so does my SUV. The tough part is finding a tower to get a signal through."

Jack tightened his lips, shaking his head as he stared at the ambulance floor. "I'd sure like to contact my wife. She's gotta be a nervous wreck."

Maggie's intention was to put a bullet into Draper's Townsend's head, but she only succeeded in murdering his TV and wounding his remote.

Just as she was about to open fire, the game had gone to commercial. Draper had lifted the remote to change the channel, and the errant bullet caught him square between his index and middle fingers, causing him to release a spine-crawling wail that Maggie would likely cherish in future years—provided she lived to see future years.

After the bullet struck Draper's hand, it continued its journey across the top of the remote and into the TV set, pretty much deeming the Montana State game over. As Draper writhed in pain on the floor, squealing like a castrated swine, Maggie knew she should finish the job while his position was compromised.

Instead, she froze.

"Damn, baby," Draper whimpered, using that tone that always had drawn sympathy from her lonesome, unwanted heart. "Now, why would you go and do a thing like that?"

Maggie shook her head, suddenly forgetting all the countless reasons this rabid dog in front of her needed to be put down. She placed the .38 on the coffee table, rushed to Draper's side, and wrapped his bleeding hand in her cotton dress.

"I'm so sorry, baby," she said, tears gushing forth. "I didn't mean it, I swear. I love you, Draper—you know that."

Draper exhaled several deep breaths, squeezing the wound on his hand. As his initial shock ebbed, he realized she had only grazed him.

"Go on ahead and get me a towel. And, while you're at it, bring me that bottle of whiskey."

Maggie rose slowly, Draper staring at his hand as he unwrapped it from her dress. He watched her closely as she walked to the kitchen. "Damn!" she heard him say as she left him in the living room.

Maggie let the water run in the sink, waiting for it to become ice cold. She removed a glass from the cupboard and filled it with three fingers of whiskey. As she ran a towel under the water in the sink, she heard a distinct click.

She turned to find Draper standing in the kitchen doorway, gripping her .38 in his bloody hand.

CHAPTER 28

THE SEDATIVE ADMINISTERED TO REIFF at the ER was so profoundly effective that he determined the hospital's services were no longer required. He removed the pulse oximeter from his fingertip and inched toward the edge of his bed, only to be startled moments later when the machine measuring his vitals emitted a shrill beeping noise. He quickly placed the sensor back on his finger, took a deep breath through his nostrils, and pensively examined his surroundings, reevaluating his exit strategy.

No more doctors. No more hospitals.

Reiff cautiously slid off the bed and peeked through a drawn curtain. Convinced no one had heard the alarm, he began peeling the tape that connected an IV to his left hand. Eyes slammed shut, he yanked the needle from his vein. The various cancer medications he'd been taking made him somewhat of a bleeder. He snatched a Kleenex from a box near his bedside, using it to plug the wound. He reused the IV tape to hold the tissue in place.

He tore off his hospital gown before he realized he couldn't find his clothes. Buck-naked except for his gray hospital socks, he searched frantically until he found a plastic container inside a cabinet next to the bed. He dressed rapidly, awkwardly misaligning the wood buttons of his flowered Tommy Bahama. He threw on his leather jacket and slipped into his loafers.

"Mr. Metcalf, what are you doing?" a stern voice said behind him.

Reiff froze momentarily, then turned to find a buxom Native American nurse staring at him, her fist balled on her ample hip. He squinted at her name tag, which was covered with a piece of white tape that read "Crystal."

"Hello . . . Crystal. Actually, I . . . I was just leaving."

Crystal cocked her head backward in disbelief. "Leaving?" she huffed. "And just where exactly do you think you are going? You're in no condition to go anywhere."

Reiff zipped up his jacket and proffered a smile. "I'll be fine."

Crystal turned toward the opening in the curtain. "You won't be fine. I'm going to get the doctor."

Reiff shook his head. No more doctors. No more hospitals.

He pulled back the curtain and spotted a door marked "EXIT" no more than twenty feet away. He walked down a hallway, exchanging nods with a maintenance worker mopping the floor. Moments later, he burst out of a door into the desolate parking lot. He heaved a deep breath of icy air, welcoming the waves of sleet whipping into his eyes. *Free at last.*

He needed to get to his hotel. More specifically, he needed to get to the hotel bar. A stiff drink—maybe a few—might slow the freight train of thoughts thundering through his mind.

No matter how hard he tried, he just couldn't stop thinking about Chloe Morrand.

Rick figured he was within a mile of the trailhead, so he hit the gas. Bad decision.

As he entered a tight curve, he raced past a yellow warning sign that suggested twenty miles per hour on a bright sunny day. In the midst of the storm, Rick was doing no less than forty. His tires pawed helplessly at the road, unable to grip the slick surface. His truck began sliding sideways down a steep pitch, seemingly destined to crash into a deep, icy creek before a sturdy spruce intervened. The side of the vehicle slammed hard into the tree, deploying a passenger side airbag Rick didn't know he had. The impact jolted him from the driver's seat but left him unharmed, at least as far as he could tell. He shook his head rapidly as he stared at his cracked windshield, gathering his wits and remembering his mission.

A loud rapping sound came from the driver's side window. Someone was tugging on the door, which appeared to be stuck—likely frozen. Squinting at the frosted window, Rick twisted his legs around and gave the door a meaningful kick, enabling the good Samaritan to open it.

"Rick, are you okay?" Charlie Duchesne asked.

Rick cocked his head, confused. "Charlie? What are you doing out here?"

Charlie hesitated. His poker face was lacking, one of the many failings of his gambling career. "I . . . I was just . . ."

Rick grabbed the steering wheel, frantically pulling himself across the bench seat. He moved within an inch of Charlie's troubled face. "Charlie, *what* are you doing here?" he said more forcefully.

"I . . . I got a call," Charlie stammered. "That's it. I got a call."

"A call about what?" Rick shouted, his fists wrapping around the top of Charlie's coat. "You're the damn coroner, for Chrissakes! Is it true? Did they find a body? Is it Chloe?"

Charlie gripped Rick's wrists, his dispirited eyes pleading with his friend. "I don't know anything, not for sure—not until I get there," he whispered. "Rick . . . *please.*"

Rick slowly released his grip on Charlie's coat and lowered his eyes. Charlie could be telling the truth, but Rick doubted it. He felt his entire body begin to tremor. "Please, God, no," he begged through clenched teeth, as though he was calling in one final favor. His eyes blinked back emotion. "Please, God, no."

After several seconds, he whipped his eyes past Charlie up the embankment, spotting the headlights of the coroner's SUV, its engine running. Shoving his friend out of the way, he scrambled onto the road, fixing his eyes on the vehicle in a hypnotic glare. "Rick, wait!" Charlie shouted, clawing his way through the snow behind him. "Don't do this! Please!"

Rick jumped into the driver's seat and threw the SUV into gear. He slammed his foot on the gas pedal, all four wheels whirring loudly as the vehicle edged sideways in search of traction. Had Charlie not snatched the door handle on the passenger side, he would have been left behind. Rick slammed his palms violently against the top of the steering wheel, urging the SUV forward.

"Please God, no!"

Amanda had her hands cupped over one of the van's heating vents when Thomas returned. He was shivering noticeably, his Eyewitness News windbreaker far insufficient for conditions.

"Close the door!" Amanda shouted as a gust of wind and snow filled the van. She rolled her eyes, watching impatiently as Thomas blew warm breath onto his fingers. "So? What did you find out?"

"Not much," Thomas answered haltingly, his teeth chattering.

"Not much?" Amanda asked, turning toward him. "Who was the guy with the cop?"

"The *cop*, as you call him, is a sheriff's deputy. The guy with him was the hiker."

Amanda glanced toward the ambulance, barely visible through the driving snow. "So the hiker is going to live. Anything else?"

Thomas rubbed his hands together. "There definitely is a 10-54."

"Yeah?" Amanda said without emotion. "Who is it?"

Thomas shook his head. "They wouldn't tell me. They said they haven't notified next of kin. The deputy wasn't very friendly."

"He wasn't *friendly*? A cop? Welcome to my world." Amanda leaned toward the front windshield, using her coat sleeve to wipe off some of the frost. The storm was merciless. "We should go—there's no good reason to even be here." She shook her head with disgust. "Does this thing even have four-wheel drive?"

"No."

"It doesn't?"

"No, it doesn't have four-wheel drive. And no, we're not leaving."

Amanda squinted as him. "Excuse me?

"They'll be down soon, and I want to get footage," Thomas said. "If we don't use it, maybe I can sell it to a local station."

"Management doesn't like that kind of thing."

"Management hasn't seen my bills."

Amanda released a long sigh. Her decision to return to Montana had been ill conceived, a compulsive and tragic error in judgment. Here she was, wandering aimlessly once more in the wilderness, a fitting metaphor for her entire life. She stared at the window where her warm breath had steamed the glass. Her mind drifted to her childhood, to those cold Montana winter mornings when she would draw on the window of her mother's car on the way to school. Her small finger would trace the shape of a heart, maybe add an arrow with feathers, and she would dream about a cute boy in school who might fill the empty space. There was no one filling her heart now— hadn't been for some time.

"Wait—I think that's them," Thomas said, peering out the driver's side window. "I think I see their flashlights."

Amanda leaned toward him for a better look. It appeared he was right. She could see lights flickering above the trailhead, as though a group was making its way down.

Thomas reached behind her seat for his camera. "You coming?"

Amanda blew out an exasperated breath, then buttoned the top of her coat. As she turned to open her door, she shielded her eyes from the bright headlights of a vehicle bounding into the trailhead parking lot. An SUV was swerving uncontrollably in the snow, traveling way too fast for conditions.

The vehicle somehow skidded to a stop. A man jumped out of the driver's side and began running toward the trail. A second man emerged from the passenger side, stumbling behind him in pursuit.

As he raced through the snow-covered parking lot at full speed, his heart pounding in his chest and lungs begging for oxygen, Rick felt like he was traveling in slow motion. He focused his blurry vision on two paramedics carrying a metal basket that contained a body—a body he was certain would be his daughter, Chloe Morrand.

He wanted to pray it wasn't Chloe, but he was done praying, certain that he'd been forsaken by a God who had carried him though so many trials only to abandon him. He found himself painfully alone, isolated in his emptiness, left in a private, excruciating agony about to be born and destined to last a lifetime. His aching chest and heavy legs pleaded with him not to continue, to resist this sentence no father should ever have to accept, but he stumbled forward, his arms flailing wildly as he slammed his eyes closed in anguish.

Releasing a thick, rueful groan through his tightened jaw, Rick stormed past Caleb Tidwell, the young sheriff's arms outstretched as loud, garbled words tumbled from his mouth. The paramedics stared at Rick in shock for several seconds before lowering the basket to the ground, against their better judgment and Caleb's fervent wishes.

Rick dropped to his knees, slumping over the body covered in a gray wool blanket flecked with ice and snow. His hands moved gingerly along the inside edge of the basket, reluctant at first to touch and feel the reality that lay before him. He finally began to feather his trembling fingers over the blanket, stroking it as though he might somehow compel the motionless body back to life.

He pulled back the covering to reveal Chloe's gray, frozen face. As air left his chest, he was overcome with an odd feeling that he had been in this place before, as though his constant fears about his daughter's well-being had foreshadowed this very moment. In a strange way, perhaps in the interest of self-preservation, he thought he had prepared himself, but no quantity of prescient dress rehearsals could have possibly equipped him for this.

A hand touched Rick's shoulder. He forcefully pushed it away. His eyes darted about, catching glimpses of the faceless observers standing around him. He knew what they were thinking—each and every one of them.

As he felt his face twist into a snarl, he leaned closer to Chloe's body, shielding it from these circling demons. Nobody could touch her, he thought. He mustn't let them touch her. Drawing a short breath, he pushed a labored huff of steam from his mouth, his body suddenly fatigued, emotions on empty. He felt the wind, he smelled the storm, but he could hear no sound beyond a dull ringing in his ears. He could see no one except Chloe.

His body remained paralyzed, his lungs spent, seemingly unable—or unwilling—to draw even a solitary breath. *Why should I breathe? For what purpose?*

Rick's lips quivered as he watched his tears fall onto his child's ashen cheeks. He collapsed on her, pressing his forehead against hers as his shoulders jerked in uncontrollable grief. His vision blurred, he lifted his head ever so slightly to study her features, the long, thick hair she had received from Christine, the nose and lips she had passed on to Abby.

His stomach roiled as his thoughts turned to Abby, his sweet granddaughter, days away from her ninth birthday and suddenly without a mother. A child so full of love, and so deserving of love, thrust into a pitiful circumstance outside her power of choice and far beyond her power to control. *Now, just what kind of God would allow this?*

Rick snapped from his daze upon hearing loud shouting behind him. He recognized the voice of Charlie Duchesne.

"What the hell is the matter with you?" Charlie shouted, his voice trembling. "Who said you could move that body?"

Rick looked over his shoulder to see Charlie straddling the upper torso of Caleb Tidwell, hands maintaining an iron grip on the sheriff's uniform jacket.

Caleb clutched Charlie's wrists, trying to unfasten them from his clothing. "Dammit, Charlie," he shouted. "Look at the weather! It's unsafe to go up there. I *had* to move the body."

"That's not your decision!" Charlie shouted, flicking a nod toward Rick. "Now look what you've done." Charlie released Caleb's jacket and struggled to his feet. The sheriff glared at him as he rose and dusted snow off his pant legs.

Rick returned his eyes to his daughter. He began to place the blanket back over her, then stopped. He stared at her longer, unable to let her go.

A blinding beam of light came across Chloe's face, making her seem almost ghoulish, whereas moments before she had appeared serene. Rick whipped his head toward the light, squinting into its intrusive glare. A man was standing only a few feet away, holding a television camera on his shoulder.

"Turn off that goddamned light—now!" he shouted. "What the hell is the matter with you?"

Thomas had moved quickly from the van, not bothering to wait for Amanda. The tall heels of her leather boots weren't much help as she tried to catch him.

She watched in stunned silence when she saw a man kneeling in the snow, grieving over a female body in a Stokes basket. He seemed desperately alone as he shouted at Thomas, the camera's shocking glare having shattered a sacred moment of life-altering anguish. Her heart ached as she studied him, his contorted features betraying a face that was oddly familiar.

"Turn off the camera!" she shouted at Thomas.

He ignored her, continuing to roll.

Amanda hurled a gloved fist at the side of the camera, dislodging its light and smashing the viewfinder into Thomas's face. He stared at her in shock, clutching his nose briefly before looking at his hand, as though checking for blood.

"What is *wrong* with you?"

"Go wait in the van," Amanda snapped.

"But—"

"Go!"

Thomas shook his head and sulked away. Amanda turned back toward the heartbroken man, who now had a young uniformed officer and an older man standing behind him. "C'mon, Rick," the older man said. "Let's let these boys do their job."

Rick?

Rick slowly placed a wool blanket over the woman, staring at her for several seconds before brushing the back of his hand over his eyes. A gust of wind lashed snow across Amanda's face, her entire body suddenly overpowered by a penetrating chill.

She walked away, unable to take her eyes off Rick Morrand.

CHAPTER 29

RICK CLUTCHED THE SIDE OF the metal basket as the paramedics carried Chloe across the parking lot to the rear door of an ambulance. He stood in stunned silence for several seconds before a hand gently touched his wrist, urging him to let go. Rick's chest muscles wrenched as he released the cold steel.

A familiar voice called his name. His eyes lifted to see Jack Kelly cloaked in a red wool blanket as he emerged from a second ambulance. Deputy Billy Renfro followed closely behind.

"I'm sorry, Rick," Jack said as he wrapped his longtime friend in an embrace. Rick nodded, senses dull and body limp, lifeless arms dangling at his side. Jack's tone was soft and compassionate, his eyes warm and gentle. Still, Jack and the world around him seemed a million miles away.

Rick studied his good friend. "Why . . . What are you doing here?"

Billy stepped forward, placing a hand on Rick's shoulder. "Mr. Kelly was fishing out at Shadow Lake," he said in a soothing voice. "He's the one who found Chloe and stayed with her."

Rick nodded. His mind flashed to Thursday, Jack inviting him to Shadow Lake when they saw each other at the Pines. That was the night Rick ran into Draper Townsend, the felon's eyes following Chloe and Abby as they walked out the front door.

Rick took short breaths, his heart pulsing as a haunting chill chased up the back of his neck. How about that ex-client, Richard Bledsoe, the guy Reiff Metcalf had warned him about? He shook his head in disbelief as he blinked into the driving snow, his stomach sickened by the possibility of having somehow induced his daughter's doom.

He looked up at Billy and Jack, both men studying him quizzically, as though he'd just touched down from a distant galaxy. "Wh . . . Where was she, Jack?" Rick asked, his lips quivering. "Where did you find her?"

"Below the Sawtooth."

Rick's eyebrows pinched as he considered Jack's answer. *Below the Sawtooth?* His chest pounded. What was she doing there? Did she jump? There was no way she would jump. She'd been happy—he was sure of it. He felt color leave his face. *But she wasn't taking her meds . . .*

A short-circuit of thoughts sparked inside his brain. If Chloe didn't take her own life, then what did happen? Was it an accident? Did she lose her footing and fall? Why was she at the Sawtooth? Was she there to meet someone? Were drugs involved? Someone may have harmed her, but who? Chase Rettick? Did she push him too far? Chase had lied about the last time he saw Chloe, but Courtney Williams gave him an alibi. *Maybe.*

Billy's voice jolted him. "Me and Charlie will conduct a proper investigation," the deputy said loudly, bracing himself against a gust of wind. "We'll get to the bottom of it."

"Get to the bottom of it? When?"

Billy glanced upward, acknowledging the storm. "As soon as possible."

Rick's eyes hardened. "You need to get on this now!" he barked. "We need to find out who did this!"

"Did what?"

Rick stared at the two men, both of them silent, their eyes seeming to conceal some kind of forbidden secret. He cocked his head. "What do you *think* happened?"

Billy sighed, as if buying time. He nodded toward Sheriff Caleb Tidwell, who was talking to a reporter across the trailhead parking lot. "Well, Caleb figures—"

Jack grabbed Billy's arm and cast a sharp glare at him, head wagging rapidly. "Like Billy said, Rick, they'll do an *investigation.*"

Rick looked at Billy, eyes direct. "What does Caleb *figure*, Deputy?"

Billy hesitated. "Well, given Chloe's history—"

Rick edged closer, inches from Billy's face. "What history is that?"

Billy winced as though he'd stepped on a rusty nail. "Don't shoot the messenger, Rick," he said, holding his ground. "You asked me a question, and I answered it."

Rick shook his head and turned away in disgust, drawing a deep breath as he peered through the driving snow toward the Shadow Lake trailhead. He and Chloe had hiked the trail on plenty of occasions, even a few times with Abby, picking huckleberries along the way on warm and tranquil summer days. Chloe loved the lake, and she loved the Sawtooth, although she was reluctant to get too close to the edge.

He closed his eyes tightly as he fought back emotion, his jumbled mind clawing for reasons she might have traveled up that trail one final time.

The wind suddenly ebbed, the snow easing into a serene gentleness, as if the mountain gods had proffered a temporary reprieve. Rick could hear Billy talking behind him, his voice directed toward Jack in a loud whisper. "How the hell do I know what happened?" Rick heard the deputy say. "You know this as well as anyone. I mean, we just found her. All I mentioned to him was that she had a history. I mean, I don't see—"

Billy stopped talking abruptly as Rick turned around, the deputy averting his eyes in guilt. Rick ignored him, gazing beyond the two men toward the towering spruce and fir trees bordering the parking area, their swaying branches aglow in the twirling ambulance lights. His eyes slowly trailed down toward the ground, where he spotted Charlie Duchesne trudging through a foot of snow, cradling a roll of yellow crime scene tape, five feet of it dancing behind him like the tail of a kite. The coroner was bound for a full-sized SUV parked at the edge of the forest, half of the vehicle shielded from view.

It looked like Chloe's SUV.

"Is that her car?" Rick asked, cocking his head. "That's her car!"

He purposefully strode toward the car before being intercepted by Billy. The deputy turned toward the trees, pitching his head forward and squinting at the vehicle as though seeing it for the first time. "Can't let you go over there, Rick," he said. "If that's Chloe's vehicle, it's evidence. I'm sure you know that."

Rick stopped, staring at the Dodge Durango in the distance. It was a beater, all right—the right front fender loose, a dent creasing the passenger door. He had offered to help Chloe get a newer model, something that wasn't such a gas hog, but she had refused. The Dodge had been purchased with her own money, and she told Rick she was proud of that fact. He was proud, too, that a young mother had bought a car while living from paycheck to paycheck. At least, he'd *thought* she was living paycheck to paycheck. The deposit slip he had found at her apartment made him wonder. Between that discovery and her untouched meds, he wondered about a lot of things.

He felt a hand on his shoulder. "What do you say I drive you home, Rick?" Billy said quietly. "We'll get someone out here in the morning to round up your truck."

"Sage's house," Rick mumbled, turning his eyes toward the rear lights of the ambulance holding his daughter, the vehicle slowly pulling away. "I left Abby with Sage."

Abby! Rick's head swam with dizziness, the frigid reality hitting him that his granddaughter no longer had a mother. A young child with limitless potential had just been issued a life that would never be the same. *None* of their lives would ever be the same.

"I need to go to Sage's," he whispered again, his words drenched with defeat.

The clock on Billy's dashboard crossed midnight by the time he and Rick turned onto the gravel road leading to Sage's house. The fiercest portion of the storm had passed, leaving only a lazy snowfall prancing across the headlights of the SUV.

The men had barely spoken on the ride from the Sawtooth, Billy granting Rick the dubious courtesy of sifting alone through a mental landslide of torment and anguish. As the vehicle rolled to a stop, Rick unglued his eyes from the front windshield and turned toward the deputy.

"Billy, there are some things you need to know."

Billy used his thumb and forefinger to stroke his bushy moustache, perhaps even disguise a yawn. "Such as?"

"I had run-in with Draper Townsend down at The Pines on Thursday night."

Billy huffed a breath. "You and everyone else."

"He'd been drinkin', and we got into it about the accident . . . you know, the thing with Julianne? He made some threats."

"What kind of threats?"

Rick sighed. "Okay, so maybe not threats. He made mention of my family."

Billy nodded patiently. "I see."

"There's also this guy from California."

Billy turned toward Rick, eyes squinting and head cocked. "A guy from California? Who?"

"My former law partner came to town and told me an ex-client had been harassing the legal clerks at the office. Apparently, the guy didn't like the way we handled his case."

"And?"

"There's a chance the guy might have come to Montana."

Billy drew a deep sigh. "So you think—"

"One of these guys might be involved in what happened to Chloe," Rick said, his voice growing urgent. "You need to take a look at both of them."

Billy's gloved hands massaged the top of his steering wheel, his weary eyes saying he would much rather be home in bed. "So you're assuming someone harmed your daughter . . . that she was murdered?"

Rick felt warmth flood into his face, his forehead tighten. "Of course that's what I think," he scowled. "How do you see it?"

Billy paused, shaking his head slowly. "We've already been through this, Rick," he mumbled with fatigue. "Like I told you, we're going to conduct an investigation."

"Yeah, but what do you think happened?" Rick pressed. "You already told me what Caleb said, and I could give a damn about that. We've known each other a long time, Billy. I want to know what *you* think. You have to be thinking *something*."

"Okay, so maybe I do," Billy said, his tone betraying agitation, the day having run far too deep for a man his age. "You weren't up there at the Sawtooth, Rick. *I was.* I saw the body. We both know that Chloe . . . I mean, the way she was positioned—"

"Stop right there, Billy," Rick said, his voice rising. "I'm telling you that Chloe was happy. She was clean. She didn't do this to herself!" His chin fell onto his chest as he tried to swallow into his locked throat. He struggled to breathe, suddenly feeling as though air was being twisted out of his lungs. Closing his eyes, he tried to summon patience. Maybe Billy was right. Maybe Rick was in—what did they call it?—denial? That was it. *Denial.* After all, there was that bottle of meds . . . and that bank deposit. Maybe—

"You okay, Rick?" Billy asked. Rick looked up, but didn't answer. The deputy squared his shoulders toward him, eyes direct and sincere. "Look . . . It's been a long night for all of us. Is there anything else you need to tell me right now?"

Rick wagged his head. He pawed for the door handle and shoved it open, a burst of cold night air snapping him alert like a whiff of smelling salts. Gripping the roof of the SUV, he bent down and peered inside.

"I'm telling you, Billy, Chloe didn't harm herself," he said, his words as firm as oak. "I'm sure of it."

The deputy didn't reply.

Rick didn't know how long Sage had been standing on the porch.

She had her arms folded, her face a tangle of sorrow and dread as she shivered beneath the dull yellow glimmer of a lonely porch light. Rick wasn't sure exactly what she knew, but it looked like she knew enough.

Her eyes welled with tears as he approached her. They embraced in silence, Sage's breasts pressing tightly against his chest. She buried her face at the base of his neck, her warm tears flowing onto his skin. They held each other tighter and longer than ever before. He didn't want to let her go.

"Abby's sleeping," Sage finally said. "I kept her away from the TV and computer. She doesn't know."

Another numbing blow hit Rick as he once again thought of his granddaughter. He felt himself swirling in a dreadful timeless void, staring into a future where happiness could never possibly exist.

They walked inside, then sat on the couch and stared at the fire, paralyzed in silence. The only sound was an occasional crack from burning wood chasing embers up the flue. "It just doesn't make sense," Rick said, slightly above a whisper. "She was doing well. She was happy."

Sage touched Rick's hand, her skin silky and warm. "What do they say happened?"

"She was at the bottom of the Sawtooth," Rick said, taking a labored breath. "Jack Kelly found her. He didn't say what he thought happened, but based on where she was—"

"You don't think she . . ." Sage started to say. "I'm sorry. I—"

"Never," Rick said. "She would never do that to Abby. *Never.*"

His eyes remained fixed on the fire before the sound of a bedroom door snapped him from his trance. "Hi, Pa-Pa," Abby said, squinting as she walked into the living room. "Where's Mommy?"

Rick didn't answer. He sat motionless, his throat tight and dry. He glanced in desperation toward Sage, then looked back at Abby. "Come here, baby," he said, opening his arms.

Abby froze. She remained where she stood, her fearful eyes staring at her grandfather as though he were a horrifying alien intent on doing her harm.

"What's wrong? Is it Mommy? Is something wrong with Mommy?"

Rick extended his arms toward her. "Come here, baby."

"It's Mommy, isn't it?" she shouted, tears beginning to flood down her cheeks. "I *knew* she would do this to me. I *knew* she would leave again!"

Abby turned and fled back into the darkness of the bedroom, Rick and Sage chasing her. Rick sat on the bed and pulled Abby against his chest. She resisted him at first, finally surrendering into his arms, her tiny shoulders jerking violently as she wailed against his shattered heart.

Sage sat on Abby's other side, placing one hand on Rick's lower back and using the other to stroke Abby's hair. Rick held his granddaughter tightly, rocking in an attempt to control her heaving sobs.

She would cry forever.

The loneliness of her hotel room chased Amanda down to the hotel lounge, where alcohol could provide the proper panacea for all she had witnessed at the Sawtooth. She settled into a tall padded leather stool, noticing the tiredness in her face as she studied her reflection in the mirror behind the bar.

The bartender smiled, placed a cocktail napkin in front of her, and introduced himself as Rowdy. She offered a taut, meaningless smile and ordered a Cadillac Margarita, which she briefly sipped before asking him to add a second shot of Grand Marnier.

Rowdy was twenty-something, tall, with a fairly decent build. Amanda watched him closely as he walked away from her, studying his upper thighs. Her mind began to wander, and even wonder, until a second glance at her weary reflection reminded her that she hardly qualified as a cougar.

"Long day?" she heard a voice say. She looked to her right to see a ruddy-faced man whose marginal dye-job put him somewhere beyond fifty. His forearms rested on the leather padding that lined the front of the bar, his hand clutching a colorless drink accented with a wedge of lime.

"Long enough," Amanda said dismissively, turning her attention back to the unfriendly mirror.

"My name is Reiff. Reiff Metcalf."

Amanda hesitated briefly before delivering an irritated glance. "Nice to meet you," she said, declining to offer her name. Her empty hotel room was looking better all the time.

Rowdy reappeared. "How is that Grand Marnier helping out? Is that drink tasting a little better?"

She looked down at her glass, which she was rotating ever so slowly in a clockwise direction. "The drink's fine. Thank you."

Amanda couldn't stop thinking about the grieving man at the trailhead, the man they called Rick. She was positive it was Rick Morrand. She replayed the vision of him wailing over the young woman's corpse. *His daughter, maybe?*

Before her arrival in Riverton, she had been apprehensive about seeing him, wondering whether she was doing the right thing. But as time went on, she had almost become eager, even fantasizing that their encounter would go well. Whatever happened at the Sawtooth—and whoever that woman was—had changed things.

"Do you need anything else?" Rowdy asked.

His voice startled her. She shook her head as her eyes roamed behind him toward a colorful oil painting of a buffalo standing alone in tall rust-colored grass. The painting reminded her of the reason her employer had sent her to Montana.

"Wait! Yes, I do," Amanda said, taking a sip of her cocktail. "What can you tell me about a guy named Buddy Rivers? Ever heard of him?"

Rowdy pitched his head back for a moment. He shrugged as he began wiping the bar. "Buddy? Everyone's heard of Buddy. What do you want to know?"

Amanda stirred her drink. "I guess he's fond of murdering buffalo?"

"*Murdering* buffalo?" Rowdy asked with a frown. "Buddy Rivers isn't the only one who's ever killed a buffalo. He just gets a lot of attention since he's kind of a loose cannon."

"Loose cannon?"

"Okay." Rowdy chuckled. "So maybe he's kind of a nut."

Rowdy poured a shot of Grand Marnier and placed it next to Amanda's glass. "Why are you interested in the buffalo? You don't look like one of those protesters."

Amanda splashed the Grand Marnier into her glass. "I'm a newswoman from the ABC affiliate in Denver. I'm covering the buffalo controversy for our network."

"You're a reporter?" Reiff Metcalf interjected, his voice slightly slurred.

Amanda ignored him. She leaned toward Rowdy. "You want to be interviewed?"

"Sure," Rowdy answered enthusiastically. "When?"

"Tomorrow, perhaps," Amanda answered. She reached in her purse and handed him her card.

Rowdy stared at the card. He began to speak, but Reiff interrupted him.

"Hey, can you turn that up?" Reiff asked, pointing toward a TV in the corner of the bar. Rowdy nodded and grabbed the remote. Amanda stared at the screen as Rowdy increased the volume.

A red banner across the bottom of the news report read "BULLETIN." A trailer beneath it read "Woman's body found in Beartooth Wilderness." On the screen was a mug shot of Chloe Morrand.

Amanda looked toward Reiff, who was staring at the TV in stunned silence. His eyes opened wide, and his lower lip trembled. "She's . . . dead?" he finally said to no one.

"You know this girl?" Amanda asked. Reiff offered a slow, somber nod.

"We all know her," Rowdy said, flicking a glance toward Amanda. "Everybody knows Chloe Morrand."

CHAPTER 30

MATT AROSE EARLY ON SUNDAY morning, eager for daylight that seemed reluctant to come. His night of sleep had been woefully fitful, caused by a combination of lying next to a woman he no longer loved and enduring the wounds administered by a lover he could no longer have.

He hovered above the portable bassinet that held his son, Aaron. The child had slept like a baby, so quiet and peaceful that Matt feared at times he was no longer breathing. Aaron had awakened only once, offering a soft, gurgling murmur to alert his mother he was hungry.

"Don't you want to hold him?"

Matt jerked sharply toward the bed, Amie's voice startling him. She shifted her body into a sitting position, tugging covers toward her neck to ward off the morning's chill. "You *should* hold him. After all, Matthew, he is your son."

Matthew. Matt hated when she called him that. Only his mother had ever called him Matthew—as a child, when he was being scolded. He drew a deep sigh and turned toward the baby. Amie had wanted to call the boy Matthew as well, but Matt had resisted. "Baby Matthew" would be something he just couldn't endure. He had persuaded her to choose a good Mormon name—a salute to their Salt Lake heritage, he claimed—and she picked the first one on the list.

He had once loved Amie, or perhaps lusted for her, back when they were in high school. She was bright and beautiful, a flawlessly sculpted goddess, her azure eyes brimming with temptation, her thick blond hair cascading like a wild waterfall across her shoulders. He would stare across the classroom, studying her features, convinced he must have her.

They married after graduation, both going on to attend Brigham Young. Her first pregnancy, a miscarriage, did its share of damage. They drifted apart. She was a good, faithful Mormon. He was not. Matt badly wanted a break—*needed* a break—and 9-11 offered one. He enlisted in the Army, his focus on Special Forces.

When he got back, things were worse. Much worse. They slept in separate rooms, a necessity after Amie awoke one night to find Matt's powerful hands wrapped around her neck, his thumb pressed firmly against her windpipe. His nightmares were frequent. She urged him to talk about them. He couldn't—not with her.

He strayed from the marriage, but Amie pretended not to know. Divorce was not an option. After all, their union had been sealed for eternity in a Mormon temple. The job at Yellowstone came up, and Matt promised it would offer them a fresh start. He would get established, then send for her. They made love the night before he left, Amie hoping the bountiful pleasures of her flesh might somehow keep her husband captive. In an entire year, Matt had returned to Salt Lake a total of three times—twice for brief visits and once when Aaron was born.

He stared at his son in the bassinet, the infant tranquil and innocent. "He's still sleeping," Matt whispered. "I don't want to wake him."

In truth, Matt didn't want to touch the child at all. In his tainted mind, he had no right. His thoughts flashed to a sweltering morning in Fallujah, when he served as a spotter for an overly ambitious sniper called Omaha. A woman shuffled down the street below them, concealing something beneath her garments. Matt begged Omaha to hold his fire until they could identify what she was carrying. When she drew near a group of soldiers, the sniper dropped her with a single shot to the chest. She was carrying an infant.

The ear-splitting blast from Omaha's .50-caliber rifle had replayed in Matt's mind thousands of times. Wherever he was—in his truck, at his desk, on an isolated trail in Yellowstone—the sound would haunt him. Chloe Morrand knew all of this—the flashbacks, the panic attacks, the unremitting fear. Amie knew nothing.

Matt swallowed hard as he heard the shot echo in his head yet again, blinking back sorrow as he stood in front of Aaron on a Sunday morning in the peaceful cabin.

"He needs to wake up anyway," Amie persisted, her voice now whiny and shrill. "He *needs* you to hold him."

"Not now!" Matt snapped. The baby's eyes opened, his face crinkling as he began to cry. Amie huffed an exasperated sigh as she rose from the bed and picked up Aaron. "Now look what you've done!" The infant's cry turned into a loud wail. Amie's forehead tightened with scorn. "This cabin is cold! Don't you have any heat?"

Matt began to sweat, the bedroom seeming to shrink around him. His heart pounded as he struggled to breathe. He stumbled toward the door, his head wavering as though he were clawing his way through smoke. "I'll get wood," he muttered. "I'll start the stove."

Amy said nothing, and Matt wouldn't have heard her anyway. His vision blurred as he staggered across the living room toward the front door. He lunged for the doorknob and burst onto the front porch, doubling over and dropping to one knee. Thrusting an arm forward, he clutched a railing of aging, splintered wood.

Finally, mercifully, he managed to fill his lungs with the clean, crisp October air.

Maggie's head was throbbing, her burning, wounded skull feeling as though it was about to detonate. Even though she had fully expected Draper to put a bullet into her, finally excusing her from her life of endless misery, he instead had chosen to strike her with the butt of her pistol, perhaps deciding that he wasn't quite ready to return to prison.

Draper wanted more beer, and the only place open on a Sunday morning was The General Store in Cottonwood, a small hamlet located halfway down the valley. As the bald tires of her '95 Ford

Taurus rolled to a stop, Maggie exhaled and rested her forehead on the steering wheel, tears welling in her eyes as she considered her latest descent into her forever deepening cellar of despair. She would have preferred to go somewhere else besides The General Store, knowing that her cousin, Clarissa, likely would be standing behind the front counter, prepared to pass judgment when Maggie showed up bearing evidence of yet another regrettable—and unreported—domestic disturbance.

"Hey," Maggie said as she walked through the front entrance.

Clarissa was standing in front of the cash register, counting one-dollar bills. "Hey," she replied, recognizing Maggie's voice but keeping her eyes fixed on the bills.

When she glanced at Maggie, Clarissa stopped counting, her mouth open wide. Maggie was wearing her oversized sunglasses—standard equipment after a run-in with Draper—but she had added a hooded Montana State sweatshirt, the hood designed to cover the large knot her husband had raised on the top of her head.

"That bastard did it again, didn't he?"

"Did what?"

"Are you *serious*?" Clarissa asked, placing the bills back in the till and slamming it shut. "You come in here dressed like the Unabomber, and you expect me not to notice? Tell you what—why don't you take off those sunglasses and let's have a look?"

"No," Maggie said, starting to walk toward the beer cooler. "I'm fine."

When she returned a few minutes later, placing a twelve-pack and a bottle of generic aspirin on the counter, Maggie tugged at the sleeves of her sweatshirt, trying to cover bruises on her wrists. Her mouth felt as dry as a desert wash, and the pounding in her head was growing worse by the second. She wanted to buy the beer and leave the store as soon as possible, but her cousin wouldn't cooperate.

Clarissa stared at her, arms folded across her chest. "You want to end up like Chloe Morrand?"

"What happened to Chloe Morrand?" Maggie mumbled with disinterest as she pulled a crumpled twenty-dollar bill out of the front pocket of her jeans.

"You haven't heard? They found her last night—at the bottom of the Sawtooth. That's what happens when you run with the wrong crowd."

Maggie stopped smoothing out the bill. "The Sawtooth? Isn't that on the way to Shadow Lake?"

"The same. No one is sure what happened. Suicide, I would guess."

Clarissa picked up the bill on the counter. "That girl always seemed to run with the wrong crowd," she repeated, shaking her head.

Maggie had stopped listening to Clarissa, her brain swimming with thoughts of the previous afternoon, when Draper had brought home the fish from Shadow Lake—and how piqued he became when she questioned their origin. "How long was she dead?"

Clarissa had opened the till to get Maggie some change, but she suddenly stopped, her face tightening into a frown. "How the hell do I know how long she was dead? I ain't Columbo. All I know is she's dead."

She proceeded to count out Maggie's change. "You know, domestic violence is a crime, Maggie, whether you think so or not. It ain't necessarily *your* decision whether or not to prosecute."

Maggie tilted her head with curiosity, wondering what her cousin had in mind. She trusted Clarissa and knew she usually meant well. In high school, they had been inseparable, two winsome girls with grand designs on the future. Clarissa never fulfilled her dream of going to college, but she did eventually meet a nice guy—a fireman—and they had two beautiful children. Maggie wound up becoming Draper Townsend's bride, sentencing herself to life without parole.

"You call the sheriff and you'll only make my life worse," Maggie said, barely above a whisper.

"Worse than what?" Clarissa asked, gesturing toward Maggie with a jut of her fleshy chin. "Worse than this?"

Maggie took a cigarette out of her sweatshirt pocket and stuck it in her mouth. She pulled out a pink Bic lighter, which offered only a few feeble sparks.

"No smokin' in here," Clarissa said.

Maggie dropped her hand from her mouth, leaving the unlit cigarette dangling from her lips. She heaved an exasperated sigh as she stuffed the lighter in her pocket.

"So, say I call the cops," Maggie said. "The prison's overcrowded. Draper violates parole, and he might go back for, what, a couple months? Then what?"

Maggie's voice trembled as she spoke, tears beginning to trickle down her face. She wiped her eyes beneath the sunglasses, wincing in pain as her fingers brushed across her aching, bruised cheekbones.

Clarissa's lips thinned as she tilted her head. "I'm just worried about you, that's all."

"Well, don't," Maggie said, picking up the beer and aspirin. "This is my problem. I'll handle it."

"You need to get away from Draper Townsend," Clarissa warned, "or you need to get him away from you."

Maggie acted like she wasn't listening. She dug her hand into a jar of Bic lighters next to the register, then pulled out a yellow one. "How much I owe you?"

Clarissa blew out a breath as she slammed shut the drawer of the till. "On the house."

Maggie walked outside and lit her cigarette. The blinding sunshine crept beneath her sunglasses, still causing her head to throb, though not a bad as before. She got in her car, threw back a few of the generic aspirin, and washed them down with one of Draper's beers. She couldn't get her mind off of Chloe Morrand being found at the bottom of the Sawtooth.

Draper was as mean as a snake, no doubt about it, but Maggie never figured him for a killer. When he got slapped with that attempted murder charge after firing a shot toward her daddy, Maggie was sure Draper had missed on purpose. He was a coward, more than anything else, the way he was fond of battering women. Maggie had taken her lumps, but she'd never feared Draper was going to kill her, lest he'd no longer have an insect from which he could pull wings.

She didn't see him as a rapist either, if that was what happened to Chloe Morrand. Of course, it was always possible, rape being another form of assault. While Draper had never forced himself on Maggie, even when he was fresh out of prison, the sex was nothing to write home about. No foreplay or romance, just a quick poke before casting her aside, as though he was changing the oil on a high-mileage vehicle. A newer model like Chloe Morrand may well have attracted his eye.

But a murderer? Uh-uh. Maggie just couldn't see it.

She lifted the sunglasses and examined the swollen maroon-and-yellow bruises on her face, her right cheekbone looking like a rotten Georgia peach. She should have seen that one coming, knowing full well Draper was a lefty. Her eyes moistened as she shook her head in shame, disgusted that she would blame herself for the way Draper Townsend threw a punch.

The words Clarissa had told her continued to play in her head. *"You need to get him away from you."* Staring in the mirror, Maggie watched her dry, cracked lips flatten, her eyes turning into a determined glare. It really didn't matter whether she thought Draper was a murderer. If law enforcement happened to see him as a murderer, he would go away for good.

At long last, justice would be served.

When Amanda opened her eyes, she found herself in a bed she didn't recognize. The sound of a flushing toilet in the bathroom only heightened the mystery. She froze momentarily, refusing to move until she had a more thorough grasp on her circumstances.

The bathroom door opened. She heard a male voice. "Good morning."

Her brain still adrift in tequila, Amanda groped for details from the night before. There was the bartender. She'd liked the bartender. He was too young. There were margaritas. Lots of margaritas. Also, lots of shots. Now she was lying in a strange bed, clad only in her bra and panties.

Did she have sex? She certainly didn't *feel* like she had sex. That was strange. She usually had sex. For her, that was a problem, one she had discussed with her therapist ad infinitum. After two years of weekly sessions at $150 a pop, the best the woman could come up with was that Amanda should attend Sexaholics Anonymous. She'd gone to one meeting, but all it did was make her horny.

"Did you sleep okay?"

No! The guy sitting at the bar? *Seriously?*

Slowly, cautiously, Amanda looked over her shoulder. Through a bloodshot, glaucomatous left eye, she confirmed her deepest fears. There he stood, sipping coffee and appearing perfectly relaxed in neatly pressed navy slacks and a crisp blue-striped shirt. Amanda whipped her head back into the makeup-stained pillow, her mind searching for an expedient way to die.

"Relax," Reiff Metcalf said. "Nothing happened. I slept on the couch."

Amanda wasn't buying it—at least not yet. "How did I get here?"

Reiff took a sip of coffee. "You showed up at my door and said you had lost your key," he said with a slight chuckle. "I suggested you go to the front desk, but you mumbled something about someone named Phyllis and barged right in."

Amanda carefully maneuvered her way onto her back, pulling the bedsheet tightly beneath her chin. "Where are my clothes?"

"Right there on the floor, where you left them."

"*Nothing* happened?"

"Nothing happened."

Amanda managed a half-swallow, but her throat felt desperately dry. His systematic reply made her feel old and undesirable. She watched as Reiff walked toward a coffeepot resting on top of a small refrigerator, his manner suggesting he was bored with the discussion.

"Care for some coffee?" he asked.

"Yes, please."

Reiff picked up a cup, peered inside it, then began filling it with coffee. "I was wondering what you could tell me about Chloe

Morrand," he said in a grave tone. "You said last night that you were at the place where she was found."

More details from the previous night trickled into her head. Reiff had been hitting on her—at least she *thought* he'd been hitting on her. There was the newscast. His mood had suddenly changed. He sat at the bar quietly, staring at his drink. The bartender began feeding her shots.

"The Sawtooth," Amanda said.

"The what?"

"The Sawtooth. She—Chloe—was found at the bottom of the Sawtooth."

Reiff handed Amanda her coffee. She wanted cream, but he didn't offer and she didn't ask. As she wrapped her fingers around the cup, she noticed she had broken a nail.

"Do you know what happened?" Reiff asked as he sat down on the upholstered cream-colored couch where he claimed he had slept. He seemed rested and alert. Business casual suited him better than Hawaiian chic.

Amanda shook her head. "I just saw the EMTs bringing her down. She was covered with a blanket. Some guy got into it with the sheriff—pretty much attacked him. Then, I saw Rick, her dad—

"You know Rick Morrand?"

Amanda nodded. "We dated in high school."

Reiff cocked his head to the side. "Funny, he never mentioned you. It's Amanda, right?'

Another nod, this one hesitant. She felt nauseated.

"Nope," Reiff said. "Never mentioned you."

Amanda stared at her black coffee, contemplating her insignificance. She watched as Reiff put his cup on a table, stood, and put on a sport coat. "Take your time," he said as he walked toward the door. "You can stay as long as you like."

"How do you know Rick?" she asked.

Reiff stopped, holding the brass knob of the half-open door. He forced a smile, his eyes appearing to mask an underlying sadness. He hesitated, choking back emotion.

"Rick Morrand," he finally said, "is the best friend I ever had."

Rick stood on Sage's back porch, staring at the Yellowstone as it eased past snow-covered banks. The temperature was just below freezing at best, and the bright morning sun provided little warmth. Despite wearing only a T-shirt, he ignored the chill as he took a long drag of a cigarette. He wasn't cold, but he was numb.

"You don't smoke," a voice behind him said. It was Sage.

"I know," he replied, taking another drag.

Rick had slept only a few hours, after they had finally coaxed Abby to sleep. He awoke sitting on the couch, his arm around Sage and his face buried in her soft almond hair. They had been sitting and staring at the fire, his grief finally giving way to exhaustion and eventual sleep.

Rick awakened to the kind scent of Sage's perfume, surprised to be sitting so close to her. He experienced only a few brief seconds of peacefulness before he was slapped coldly with the harsh knowledge of what was real.

Chloe is dead.

She isn't coming back.

He had gone outside and found a half-pack of cigarettes stashed beneath a piece of firewood. Either Sage or Chloe put them there.

"Guess you found our smokes," Sage said.

"Third log from the left, same as always."

"You used to hate it when we smoked. I'm surprised you didn't throw them out."

"I couldn't," Rick said. "Watching the two of you giggle when you snuck a cigarette . . . it always made me happy." He shrugged. "I didn't want her to smoke, but I was grateful she was clean."

They stood in silence, staring at the river.

She isn't coming back.

"You hungry?" Sage asked, squinting at him in the sunlight. "You must be."

Rick had plenty of thoughts, none of them about food.

"You know, next Saturday is Abby's birthday," he said, studying what was left of his cigarette. "Chloe and I planned a party for her, out at my house. It was all Chloe would talk about. Do you really think Chloe would do this to her?"

"Do what to her?"

"You know . . . Leave her behind like this."

Sage turned toward him, shielding her eyes from the rising sun. "What do you mean?" What are you saying?"

Rick took a final drag. "Caleb is trying to say she took her own life."

Sage tightened her eyebrows. "What?"

He flicked his cigarette onto the gravel in front of the porch. "That's what I mean. It makes no sense. She was happy. And there's no way she would do that to Abby."

"She loved that child," Sage whispered.

Rick drew a deep breath. "I just don't get it. Why was she up there on a Friday night? Was she alone?" He shook his head as he stared at the river, as though the slow-moving current might divine an answer.

Sage gently rubbed his bicep and pushed closer to him. "I'm here for you—you know that, don't you? Whatever you need, I'm here for you."

Rick noticed her touch, but he didn't respond, not as much as he wanted to. Her eyes told him to hold her, maybe never let her go, but he resisted. His phone rang, and he tugged it out of the front pocket of his jeans.

"Morrand."

"Rick, it's Charlie. I'm sorry to call so early—"

"It's okay, Charlie. What's up?"

"I was wondering whether you can meet me out at Chloe's apartment this afternoon. Maybe answer a few questions."

Rick chest went numb, his head feeling dizzy. *Chloe's apartment.* He had been there the previous afternoon, when he was sure his daughter was alive. Charlie's words stung him with a finality that was way too raw.

"I can meet you, Charlie," he said, his voice unsteady. "Who's handling the investigation for the sheriff's office?"

"Billy Renfro—at least, for now. I guess Caleb's wrapped up with everything else going on in town. Suits me just fine. Billy and I work well together."

Rick nodded. Billy was fair-minded. "Where's Billy now?"

"I'm on my way to meet with him at the Sawtooth."

"I'll meet you there."

"Bad idea, Rick. You need to let us handle this. I'll try to keep you in the loop."

Rick drew a deep breath of frustration. "What do *you* think happened, Charlie?"

"No comment."

"That's not an answer."

Charlie sighed. "It's the only one I can give right now. Can we meet at the apartment around one?"

"I'll be there."

Rick stuffed his phone into his jeans. He prepared to speak but was interrupted by a wail from inside the house. It was Abby. Sage disappeared through the doorway.

A chill trickled down Rick's neck, dread pouring over him as he considered his motherless granddaughter. He recalled when Chloe became pregnant. She was hopelessly enslaved by addiction and mental illness, and Rick wondered how she could possibly care for a child. It was Abby—beautiful, innocent Abby—who pushed Chloe to eventually get clean. It was as though the child had given Chloe reason to live.

Would Chloe have wanted this?

He needed answers. He owed it to Chloe.

She isn't coming back.

Sunday morning Mass in Gardiner was scheduled for ten fifteen, but as the clock inched toward ten thirty, no ceremony had begun. Father Ernesto Herrera appeared to be in no hurry, casually welcoming members of his modest congregation, many of whom he knew by name and greeted with a warm embrace.

Bledsoe sat stone-faced in the back row of the church, offering a dispassionate nod to any of the locals who approached him. He declined to acknowledge Father Herrera, instead focusing his eyes on the altar, where a large crucifix was flanked by elongated stained-glass windows. The church was lit by dim lamps contained in blue-and-red glass cylinders hanging from chains that dropped from the high wood-planked ceiling. In many ways, the structure resembled the ornate New England churches of his youth, save for the liberal use of timber as opposed to stone. A part of him longed for the warmth and safety of those cathedrals—and the unshakable faith they had offered him—but they now felt irretrievably distant.

Bledsoe continued to stare straight ahead, his lament turning to a seething bitterness. He was startled by a hand that touched his shoulder.

"My name is Father Ernesto Herrera—most people call me Father Ernie," the priest said to him, extending his hand. "You look familiar. Have we met before?"

Bledsoe hesitated, offering his hand but no name. "No, we haven't met. Hello, Father."

"Ooh, your hand feels cold—so very cold," Father Herrera said, causing a few nearby parishioners to turn their heads. As he continued to grasp Bledsoe's hand, the priest stared intently into his eyes, as though scanning the contents of Bledsoe's soul.

"It's cold outside this morning," Bledsoe said, reclaiming his hand and offering a weak smile. Father Herrera turned to walk away, but Bledsoe stopped him.

"Father, do you offer confession?"

"Of course," the priest answered, nodding toward two ornately carved confessionals clinging to the left side of the church. "We have regular confession Saturday at five p.m., but I'm usually here almost every afternoon. You are welcome anytime."

Bledsoe nodded. "Thank you, Father."

———◆———

Amanda had only been back in her room a few seconds when she heard a knock on the door. It was Thomas, who immediately tried to hand her his cell phone.

"It's Harvey," he said, jabbing the phone toward her. Harvey Eggleston was her station manager in Denver.

Amanda waved her hands frantically while repeatedly mouthing, "No!"

Thomas continued to jab.

"He's been calling all morning," he said in a loud, frantic whisper. "He told me to track you down."

Amanda stared at Thomas, shaking her head. She reluctantly accepted the phone and covered the mouthpiece.

"Pussy!" she said to him, and let the door close in his face.

"Harvey!" Amanda said, feigning enthusiasm. "How are you?"

Harvey wasn't happy. "Where the hell have you been?" he shouted. "Why haven't you filed anything?"

Amanda rolled her eyes. "Harvey, I just got here. I'm working on it."

"I'll bet you're *working on it*. Why haven't I been able to reach you?"

Amanda hated herself. *Rule No. 1: Never screw your boss.* "I haven't been able to set up any interviews yet."

"You haven't met the buffalo killer yet?" Harvey asked. "Have you talked to his lawyer?"

"Actually, I know the lawyer."

"Oh, yeah? How?"

"He's my former boyfriend," Amanda told him, immediately wishing she hadn't.

"Former boyfriend? Guess that doesn't make *him* all that unique."

Amanda released an exasperated sigh. "Something happened to his lawyer's daughter. They found her dead. It might be a suicide."

"Suicide?" Harvey repeated, his voice devoid of sympathy. He quickly moved on. "What's going on with the protests? The network is really interested in this story. It's . . . *unique.*"

Amanda remained silent, her mind fixed on the fate of Chloe Morrand.

"Are you there?"

"I need to go," Amanda said. "I'll call when I have something."

She opened the door of her hotel room and handed the phone to Thomas, who hadn't moved from where she left him. "I'll meet you in the lobby in thirty minutes," she snapped.

She slammed the door, hoping a shower might help.

Rivers of sweat streamed down Matt Steelman's forearms as he hurled blow after blow with his hickory-handled axe, muscles straining with flagellant intent, his tortured mind trying to navigate its latest interval of turbulence. He split nearly a half cord of timber before he decided it was time to go back, finally convincing himself he could endure Amie for at least another hour or so within the small confines of the cabin.

As he walked through the bright morning sun, cradling a dozen thick pieces of fir, the thought of his son suddenly covered him with a dark, dense cloud of guilt and shame. The infant, guiltless and pure, had done absolutely nothing wrong to him. For that matter, his wife was innocent as well.

Matt told himself he would try harder. He needed to do better.

He entered the cabin to find Amie sitting in the living room, casting a hollow glare out of the window, Aaron's head buried beneath a blue handmade baby blanket as he nursed on her breast. She slowly turned her eyes toward Matt, staring at him as though he was an object of curiosity.

"Who is Chloe Morrand?"

Matt walked slowly toward the stove and placed the bundle of wood on the granite slab resting beneath it. "She's an employee of mine," he said as he dropped to one knee and declined to look at her. "Why do you ask?"

Amie reached beneath the blanket and adjusted Aaron's head on her breast. "Was she in some kind of trouble?"

Matt stopped stacking the wood and turned toward her. "What do you mean?"

Amie reached over to a wooden end table next to the couch, retrieving Matt's cell phone. "You're correct—your cell phone reception is rather sketchy."

Matt felt the color leave his face. His chest pounded. He turned away from her, slowly placing the split logs inside the stove. "You answered my cell phone?"

"Yes, I did," Amie said, furrowing her brow as she cocked her head to the side. "Do you have a problem with your *wife* answering your phone?"

Matt stood and placed his hands on his hips. "Let's not play games, Amie. Who called? Was it . . . Chloe?"

"No, it wasn't Chloe," Amie said as she placed the phone back on the end table. She tugged Aaron up from under the blanket and positioned him on her shoulder, lightly tapping the bottom of his diaper. "It was someone named Gwen."

Matt squinted. "Gwen? From the ranger station? What did she want?"

"Well, first of all, she seemed a little upset that I answered your phone." Amie looked away from him in apparent thought, casually running her tongue along her top lip. "She seemed to get more upset when I informed her I was your wife."

Matt never wore a ring at work, nor anywhere else. No one thought he was married, probably because he didn't act like it. "Gwen works for me," he huffed dismissively as he walked to the end table and picked up his phone. "What did she say?"

"She said she needed to talk to you right away—about Chloe Morrand. She said it was urgent." Amie paused for a second. "She started to cry. She was sobbing, actually."

"Sobbing? About what?" Matt glared at her as he felt his jaw muscles tighten. His anger was returning. Amie nonchalantly shrugged her shoulders.

"I think something bad may have happened to Chloe. All that this Gwen lady said was that they *found* her." Amie shook her head as she continued to tap Aaron's bottom. "Do you think she might be dead?"

An ice-cold chill crawled up the back of Matt's neck as he turned back to the stove. He dug into his jeans for a blue-tip match and struck it on the granite, the odor of sulfur filling his nostrils as he reached inside to ignite the fire.

He shifted his body to shield himself from Amie, lest she notice his hand was trembling.

CHAPTER 31

THE LATE-MORNING SUN WAS quickly warming the snow that blanketed the Shadow Lake trail, causing Charlie Duchesne to mumble profanities beneath labored breaths. Whatever footprint traps he hoped to examine and photograph at the Sawtooth were either buried or trampled, likely leaving them indistinguishable on the well-traveled footpath. Caleb Tidwell had butchered this one but good.

"Obstruction of justice," Charlie muttered to himself, still seething after his altercation with the young sheriff.

From a brief conversation he had with Billy Renfro, Charlie gathered that the sheriff's office was assuming Chloe's death was a suicide. It was Charlie's practice never to assume anything, and even though he was familiar with Chloe's past travails, he didn't find the initial conclusion of suicide overly credible. In fact, he wasn't buying it much at all.

Charlie had begun a long, caffeine-addled night with a radiological autopsy. While he discovered two separate fractures on Chloe's skull, she had suffered no other broken bones, which Charlie found odd for a victim who supposedly fell—or was pushed from— one hundred fifty feet from the top of a cliff. In addition to the relative absence of fractures, Chloe seemed to have limited internal injuries, the most notable being some bruising on her lower back. Further, the relative absence of abrasions on her body was not consistent with a fall that would surely have included contact with the serrated layers of rock that lined the face of the Sawtooth.

Charlie stopped on the trail, his heart thumping as he sucked in the cold, thin air. Removing his hat and brushing sweat from his brow, he cursed the arrival of early season snow, which had left a maze of mushy, useless tire tracks in the trailhead parking area. He had found Chloe's SUV shrouded by tree branches at one end of the lot, the door unlocked and the keys lying on the floor. *Had she come up here alone? Did she leave her car there, or was it moved? Did she drop the keys because she was under duress, or did she leave them there because she simply no longer cared? When did she arrive? Where was her cell phone?*

Charlie resumed walking, losing his footing consistently as his weathered brain continued to bombard him with questions to pose when he evaluated the scene. Experience had taught him that his was not so much a business of discovery as it was one of elimination, and the process could often be lengthy and tedious.

He glanced at his watch. He had told Billy Renfro he would meet him in the parking area, but he decided to forge ahead on his own, especially given the events of the previous night. In the days when Big Jim Tidwell was in charge, Charlie had functioned well in conjunction with the sheriff's department, their various parallel crime investigations often reaching the same seamless conclusions. Since Caleb had taken over, though, things had been different. Charlie still got along with Billy well enough, but he also realized the aging deputy had been putting increasing weight on one foot that had already stepped into retirement.

Charlie stopped again, heaving breaths through the right side of his mouth, his hands pressed against his hips. He was physically spent, those endless cups of coffee an insufficient substitute for a night's worth of lost sleep. His thoughts were scrambled and short-circuited, reminding him of the all-night card games when he was convinced his next hand would square him with the house. A cloud of depression crept over him as he recalled the demoralization of his gambling days, and he willed himself to return his focus to Chloe.

He squinted up the trail, blinded by the reflection of sunshine off the snow. The sky was as brilliant as a sapphire, the only blemish being a single dark cloud casually pausing on the distant horizon. The storm had passed, but Charlie had an eerie feeling another was just beginning.

While searching for a pair of socks in his hotel room, Reiff had unearthed a prescription bottle he had secreted away in his luggage. The vial contained an emergency supply of OxyContin and Valium, procured from an unlawful source and intended to be used in the event his legitimately prescribed painkillers ran out, which occurred with considerable frequency. Taken in unison, the two medications provided both pain relief and lucidity. All Reiff needed to do now was stay away from alcohol, which he promised himself he would.

He had spoken to Rick only briefly that morning, their conversation wooden and awkward before Rick provided directions to the home of one Sage Fontenot, presumably a family friend. After learning at the hotel that taxis in Riverton don't run much on Sunday—or any other day, for that matter—he managed to coax a ride in the bellman's 1995 Chevy Luv, rural Montana's closest answer to Uber.

As the truck sputtered onto the gravel road leading to Sage's house, Reiff loathed the task that lay ahead, primarily because he preferred to avoid situations that involved emotion. In his journey to becoming an accomplished personal injury lawyer, abstaining from genuine human feeling had always been the most prudent course to take. Of course, this approach also spilled into his personal life. He had rarely, if ever, told his wife that he loved her, possibly because he wasn't certain whether he did. He simply would appease her, showering her with gifts while resolutely clearing the balance on her Platinum American Express.

He had always wanted his relationship with Rick Morrand to be different. In Rick, he had found a trusted, loyal companion, a red-blooded Montanan who never wavered from the Cowboy Code even when afflicted with alcohol and drugs. Reiff wanted badly to return Rick's friendship—be a true confidant during this time of desperate need—but he felt constitutionally incapable of doing so, especially at this moment.

After all, his entire trip to Montana was a fraud. While he had presented Rick with this odd business about protecting him from disgruntled client Richard Bledsoe, he had no real concerns about Bledsoe at all. He had come to talk to Chloe Morrand—his good friend's daughter and Reiff's ephemeral lover, a millennial version of Lolita. Despite their considerable age difference, and the obvious moral implications of her being Rick's *child*, he had pursued his whimsical fantasy, convinced Chloe was the only person he had ever truly loved. It was a secret Reiff was determined to take to his increasingly imminent grave.

He hesitantly stepped onto the porch at Sage's house, his legs feeling unstable, as Rick emerged from the doorway to greet him. Reiff edged forward to shake his friend's hand before the men exchanged a clumsy embrace.

"I'm ... sorry, Partner," Reiff stuttered into Rick's ear, feeling a sudden thickness in his throat. His stomach churned, his bootleg medications doing little to allay his feelings of penetrating guilt—a Judas Iscariot greeting Jesus in the garden of Gethsemane.

Sage emerged from the house, startling Reiff as their eyes met. A brief, vacuous silence followed.

"Sage, this is Reiff Metcalf, my former law partner," Rick said, turning toward her.

"We've met," Sage said, looking at Reiff skeptically. "At least, I've met *him*."

Reiff hesitated. "That's right!" he said, snapping his fingers and pointing at Sage. "At the saloon. You're the bartender."

"Actually, she's the owner," Rick corrected. Indeed, Sage had acquired The Spur from her third husband—an insurance man by profession. She'd kept the bar; he'd kept his mistress.

They stepped inside. "Can I get you a beer?" Sage asked Reiff, her knowing tone suggesting he could use one. "A Bloody Mary, perhaps?"

"Lord, no, way too early for me," Reiff replied, causing Sage to smirk. "Water would be just fine."

Reiff scanned his surroundings. The home was small yet tidy and inviting. A gentle fire crackled in the fireplace. The black dog lying next to the stone hearth rested his chin on his paws as he trained his eyes on the unfamiliar visitor.

Rick's eyes were desolate, his face tired and drawn. "I was surprised when you called from the hotel," he said. "You should have stayed at the hospital."

"I'm fine," Reiff answered with a wave of his hand. He noticed his fingers tremble slightly when he snatched the glass of water offered by Sage, who shot him a tight smile.

As they moved toward the living room, Reiff heard a door open, and he noticed a young girl peering into the hallway. She was staring intently at him. He felt an eerie sensation shudder through him, astounded by her resemblance to Chloe. Shortly after their eyes met, the child ducked from sight.

"Is that . . . Abby?" Reiff asked, edging forward in his chair as he pointed down the hall.

"My granddaughter," Rick said. He cocked his head. "Have you ever met her?"

"Uh . . . no."

"C'mere, baby," Rick said down the empty hallway. "I want you to introduce you to someone."

The child slowly emerged. She pushed her fine hair behind one of her ears, averting eyes that appeared swollen from crying. Reiff's chest grew thick. He had never bargained much in pity, but this must be what it felt like.

"Abby, this is Mr. Metcalf. He is an old friend of mine."

"Hi," Abby said quietly, raising her hand slightly while her eyes remained fixed on the wood floor.

"Hello, Abby," Reiff said with a measured smile. He started to move forward but stopped. He felt an urge to give her words of comfort, somehow console a child who had lost her mother, but he found himself incapable of doing so. His stomach grew queasy, and his forehead warmed as sweat began to bead.

Abby folded her arms across her stomach, her trembling fingers massaging the splotchy skin on her elbows. Her face was ghostly white. She seemed like she was freezing cold. Her wet, dull eyes remained focused on Reiff, as though there was something she desperately wanted him to explain. His lips quivered. He remained silent.

Abby turned to her grandfather. "May I go back to my room now?" she asked. Rick nodded. Without speaking, she turned, her bare feet pattering on the floor as she ambled down the hall.

Reiff sat on the couch, dabbing his forehead with a handkerchief. He took a deep breath through his nose and sipped his glass of water, knowing it was too soon for his next dose of OxyContin and Valium.

"Is there is anything I can do? Arrangements?"

"No, but thank you," Rick replied somberly. "Sage made some calls this morning. The vigil is Wednesday night, and she'll be . . . buried . . . on Thursday. When are you going back to California?"

"Not right away," Reiff said quickly, shaking his head. "I'm going to stay. I'm *definitely* going to stay."

Rick rubbed his jaw as he studied Reiff's eyes, just long enough to fill Reiff with unease. "What else can you tell me about this ex-client of ours, this guy Bledsoe?"

Reiff exhaled a sigh that felt like relief. He shrugged. "Not much to add beyond what I already told you. He harassed some of the people at our office, and now no one is quite sure where he is."

Rick leaned forward in his chair. "How well do you know his wife? Can you reach out to her, find out if she's heard from him?"

Reiff nodded eagerly, as though the request was simple. "Sure, absolutely, I can do that." He shot a glance a brief toward Sage, who was watching him without expression. "Is there anything else I can do?"

Rick paused in thought. "Actually, there is something you can do—if you feel you're up to it."

"Anything."

Rick sat back his chair. "I have this court appearance coming up. Against my strongest wishes, I represent a guy by the name of Buddy

Rivers. He has a bad habit of killing buffalo that come anywhere remotely near his cattle. That doesn't sit too well with law enforcement."

"Buddy Rivers," Reiff said, rubbing his chin and edging forward on the couch. "I heard about him when I was in the . . . at the hotel. He doesn't seem all that popular with folks in general."

"Most people around here just let him be. As for those protesters—wildlife advocates, I guess you'd call them—they're pretty much outsiders. Our judges are pretty territorial. They don't appreciate people meddling in local affairs. I would expect that if Buddy pleads guilty, he'll eventually get off with a fine."

Reiff considered the request. "I don't have a law license here, Rick. Besides, this sounds like criminal law."

"I just need to you to stand in, get a continuance," Rick said. "The judge likely will grant it—gives him a chance to get these protesters out of town."

Reiff stared at his former partner, his chest thick with remorse. He felt a tinge of pain in his abdomen but managed to ignore it. He wanted to do *something*.

"I'll be there," he said, nodding confidently.

Rick tilted his head. "You sure?"

"I'll be there."

Abby had been set up on Sage's fluffy queen bed in the other room, equipped with a Diet Coke, a Snickers, and a remote. Nipping a small bite from her candy bar, she stared blankly at the TV screen, the laugh track from a show on the Disney Channel doing little to budge her downturned lips.

The grownups were still talking in the living room. Pa-Pa's friend was nice, even if he seemed to sweat a lot. She had never met him before, but she felt like she knew him from somewhere. Maybe Pa-Pa had talked about him, and she'd heard his name.

She blinked her eyelids, gummy and crusted from tears that had seemed to fall like intermittent rain. She shivered, her body cold, her stomach feeling the way it did when she would stay home from school. She tugged the comforter up beneath her chin, the sheets and blankets smelling like Sage. Her eyes grew moist as she remembered what her mom smelled like, the unmistakable blend of shampoo, perfume, and chewing gum shielding the distant yet honest odor of cigarette smoke. She longed for that scent again, to have her mom wrap her tightly in her arms.

Pointing the remote at the TV, Abby lowered the sound, hoping to glean snippets of conversation from the other room, maybe more information about what happened to her mom. All she heard were muffled voices, everyone serious, no laughter.

Weary of the happiness on the Disney Channel, Abby started clicking the remote, no particular destination in mind. She landed on a Bozeman station, which showed a lady with a microphone standing in front of a crowd of people who were yelling and holding signs.

The door to the bedroom was cracked open, so she jumped off the bed to close it. The grown-ups were still talking in the living room but not about her mom. She thought she might have heard the name of Buddy Rivers, the weirdo who was always shooting buffalo.

Abby shut the door and moved back toward the side of the bed. As her eyes returned to the TV, her mouth fell open, the remote dropping with a thud onto the rug-covered floor. The news lady and crowd of people were gone, replaced by a full-screen photo of her mom. She didn't look pretty, or normal. She looked sick, kind of like Grandma did when she had cancer and was going to die. Her hair was messy, her skin white as chalk. She seemed as though she had been in some kind of trouble.

With her eyes glued to the screen, Abby squatted toward the floor, her trembling hands picking up the remote. Glancing at the closed bedroom door, she turned up the volume.

The picture of her mother got smaller, and a lady was talking. She used a word Abby had heard before. She thought she knew what the word meant, but she wasn't sure. She wanted to look it up, but Sage had hidden the computer. Abby hoped the word meant something other than what she thought.

She ran into the living room, the remote still in her hand. The grown-ups were at the front door, where Sage and Pa-Pa were saying good-bye to his friend. When Abby entered the room, all three of them stared at her.

Her hands and shoulders trembled. She felt warm tears stream down her cheeks as she struggled to breathe. Between heaving sobs, she finally spoke, her voice quivering.

"Pa-Pa?" she asked. "What is suicide?"

CHAPTER 32

R ICK STORMED PAST THE DISPATCH desk at the sheriff's office, fists balled and face hot with rage. Before Helen could even lift the phone to alert Caleb he had a visitor, Rick was already past her, leaving her doe-eyed and speechless, the receiver dangling limply in her hand.

Rick barged through Caleb's door to find him leaning back in his oak swivel chair, boots on his desk and a smirk across his face as he chatted lightheartedly on the phone. His voice sounded flirtatious, meant for a woman. Rick slammed the door, nearly shattering the frosted glass with the word "SHERIFF" arched across it. That got Caleb's attention.

Caleb pulled his feet down, his face turning ghostly pale as he muttered, "I'll call ya back," his shaky hand clattering the receiver into its cradle. He rose from his chair, appearing to brace himself for whatever assault Rick was prepared to deliver.

"Suicide?" Rick shouted. "*Suicide?* What in the hell is the matter with you?"

Rick had just spent a heart-wrenching hour consoling Abby, attempting to explain what suicide was and why people did it. He kept telling Abby the news report wasn't true—that her mother hadn't taken her own life—but the shattered child was hardly convinced. Rick had struggled to harness his anger as he spoke to her, finally excusing himself by saying he needed to meet Charlie

Duchesne. Instead, he bolted straight to the sheriff's office, convinced Caleb had leaked erroneous news.

"Mr. Morrand, you're going to need to calm down," Caleb said, a nervous tremor in his voice. He took a step backward as Rick leaned over the desk, an accusatory finger piercing the air in front of him.

"You told the news station that my daughter committed suicide? Before you even conducted an investigation?"

Caleb drew a few short breaths, his arms outstretched and palms opened wide in an attempt to keep Rick at a distance. "I haven't told them anything."

"Bullshit!"

"I haven't told them anything," Caleb repeated, his voice now sturdy and rising. "But maybe there is something you want to tell me."

Rick stood rigid, tilting his head. "What are you talking about?" he asked with narrowed eyes.

Caleb reached forward and picked up a clear plastic bag on his desk. It contained a cell phone.

"We found your daughter's phone on a hitchhiker we picked up in the valley early this morning. There was a text message on it from Friday morning. It was a text message to you. I'd like you to explain—"

Rick blinked rapidly, wagging his head. "Wait a minute. Her phone wasn't with her? You found it on a hitchhiker? How did a hitchhiker get her phone? Who is he?"

Caleb took a deep breath, shifting his eyes toward the phone. "His identification says he's from Arkansas. He was panhandling down at The General Store in Cottonwood, and he became too . . . aggressive. Clint Roswell brought him in. We found the phone in his backpack."

"How did he get it?"

Caleb shrugged. "He says he found it."

"*Found* it? Where?"

"Down near Gardiner."

"Is he a suspect?"

Caleb frowned. "Suspect for what?"

Rick rolled his eyes. His jaw tightened. "A suspect for harming my daughter!"

"He's suspected of marijuana possession, and he's guilty," Caleb said. "Which means we'll probably let him go."

"How do you know he didn't hurt Chloe?"

Caleb put his hands on his hips. "'Cause he was in jail in Jackson all night Friday—I checked out his story. He was just making his way up here to join the other protesters."

They stood in silence. Rick stared at the cell phone, the same one Chloe had in her hand on Thursday night, the same one Abby had used to play video games. A shiver crept up his spine. It was the same phone that Chloe used to call him on Friday morning—the call he didn't pick up.

He nodded his chin toward the plastic bag. "I want to see it."

Caleb shook his head. "No can do. It's evidence."

Rick edged closer to the desk. "Give me the damn phone, Caleb! There could be a text message I recognize."

"Oh, there's a text message you'll recognize."

"What's that supposed to mean?"

Caleb picked up a pad of notebook paper resting beneath the bag. Flipping past the first sheet of paper, he read, "Dad, it seems like no matter how hard I try, I still disappoint you and myself. I feel so hopeless I can barely stand it. I am so sorry . . ."

Rick shook his head. "You're not serious."

Caleb set the pad down and tapped on it. "You would have received this text on Friday morning. I'm sure you saw it. Why didn't tell me about it?"

"It wasn't important."

Caleb raised his eyebrows. "Not important? Some people might interpret that as a note."

"What kind of note?"

"A suicide note."

Rick's nostrils flared. "Are you kidding me?" he said through a clenched teeth, his voice rising. "She was apologizing to me!"

Caleb cocked his head, squinting his eyes with curiosity. "Apologizing for what?"

"For Thursday night," Rick said, his tone now somber. "We had an argument when we left the restaurant Thursday night."

"An argument? What *kind* of argument?"

Rick sent a searing glare toward Caleb. He thrust his forefinger at the sheriff.

"Fuck you, Caleb!" he shouted. "I don't know what kind of shit you're trying to pull—"

Caleb took a step back, far enough to rattle the blinds behind his desk. He rubbed the back of his neck, scratched his chin, and cleared his throat, all within seconds. "There's no call for that kind of language."

"Fuck you, Caleb!"

Caleb's face reddened. He looked away briefly, then back at Rick. "Mr. Morrand, I'm afraid I'm going to have to ask—"

Rick raised his hands and took a deep breath, indicating a promise to calm down. He removed his hat and stared at the crease, smoothing it with his fingers.

"What about the news report?"

"I can't help you with that," Caleb said. "I didn't tell them anything."

Rick returned his hat to his head. He took another deep breath and burned a hardened stare into the eyes of the young sheriff.

"Chloe didn't commit suicide, Caleb," he said, his tone thick and fierce.

Caleb set down his notebook and stared at his desk. He glanced up briefly before averting his eyes once more. "We're conducting an investigation," he muttered. "We haven't reached any *final* conclusions."

Rick walked toward the door. He turned toward the sheriff one last time, teeth bared.

"She. Didn't. Commit. Suicide."

CHAPTER 33

COURTNEY CLAMPED HER EYES SHUT as she gingerly lowered herself onto the couch in Chase Rettick's trailer, her crawling skin wrapped far too tight around her skeletal frame. She bent forward, nostrils begging for fresh air but finding only the acrid odor of methamphetamine and vomit. Her arms cradled her hollow stomach, its final contents having been retched into the kitchen sink.

"Do that in the bathroom next time, will you?" Chase said with irritation from across the room. "Talk about fuckin' *gross.*"

Courtney lifted her eyes to witness Chase inhaling deeply from a filthy resin-coated glass pipe, tossing his lighter on the coffee table as he held his breath for a euphoric four seconds, his bloodshot eyes rolling backward until his pupils vanished into the darkness of his abandoned head. Her hair soaked with sweat, she tried to fight off another oncoming wave of nausea, uncertain whether it was her latest attempt to kick or the sickening sight of Chase Rettick that lay at the root of her discomfort and despair.

As a ghostly white billow exited Chase's mouth and floated toward her face, Courtney turned away, eyes teary and downcast, her besieged brain sentenced to consider how her once-promising future now appeared to have gone up in smoke.

Her parents had never planned it this way—not by a long shot. Her father being a preacher, she had been raised in a household that was strict but loving, built on a deep faith in a powerful God who seemed reluctant to provide yet plenty eager to punish. She feared God almost as much as she feared disappointing her father, and for a good while that kept her in check. She had been an obedient child, or at least so she thought. Her only real rebellion had been her initial resistance to piano lessons, long before she realized the instrument might be her ticket out of Riverton. Her father had made big plans for her, urging her to attend one of the private music schools back East, places she could barely pronounce. He'd kept close tabs on her, having her play hymns each week for three or more Sunday services. TV? No way. IPhone? Uh-uh. Boys? Forget it. Daddy's little girl was going places, headed for big things. She'd watch her father beam with pride in her presence, showering her with so much love and affection that he may as well have buried her face beneath a pillow.

Feeling smothered, it didn't take much for her to drift to the wild side. All exterior pretenses aside, her insides blew hollow. Satan's serpent arrived in the form of a fellow student named Jackie Ewing, a new girl in town who had lost weight using crystal meth. Perpetually concerned with her appearance, Courtney offered only mild resistance before deciding to *experiment* with the drug. She became instantly hooked, which sent her careening down a winding, unpaved road that led to the predatory Grim Reaper named Chase Rettick.

"I should have told him the truth," Courtney said, staring vacantly at Chase. He jabbed the meth pipe toward her, but she shook her head, declining. "I shouldn't have lied."

Chase took another hit and held his breath. "What are you talking about?"

"Mr. Morrand. I told him you were with me Friday night."

"So what?" Chase asked, eyes squinting in disbelief. "What difference does it make?"

"A lot of difference. You weren't with me Friday night. I don't know where you were."

Chase exhaled another cloud of smoke, placing the pipe on the table. He stared at Courtney.

"You did the right thing," he said. "The guy was out of control."

"I shouldn't have lied."

"You didn't lie. Not really."

"Yes, I did."

Chase held the pipe out in front of him. "C'mon, babe, take a hit."

Courtney shook her head again. She didn't like Chase calling her "babe," as though he truly cared for her, the way her father cared for her. She thought of her parents, likely worried sick about her whereabouts. They deserved better.

Another queasy feeling rumbled into her stomach. Her skin felt clammy, and an irritating itch raced throughout her body. She wanted badly to scratch her forearms, her neck, her face, the veins on the back of her hands. She knew that taking a hit of the meth pipe would solve everything, if only for a little while.

She resisted. She felt so alone.

Chase set down the pipe and picked up a small plastic bag, the kind that earrings came in at the swap meet. The bag was empty, its edges flecked with powdery traces of meth, causing Chase to stare at it with annoyance. He stood up unsteadily, walked over to the kitchen table, and plunged his hand into a khaki canvas backpack supposedly used by his grandfather during the Korean War.

He pulled out a fistful of plastic jewelry bags, each filled with tiny white crystals. Courtney stared at him while he examined his plunder, contemplating which package to choose. He shot a wild, menacing glare in her direction. An ice-cold flood of fear ran through her body, causing her to quickly look away.

Chase returned to the couch and picked up the pipe. He filled it and took a hit, which seemed to help his demeanor. Courtney watched him silently before summoning the courage to speak.

"Don't you . . . care?"

"Care about what?"

Courtney sighed. "The mother of your child is dead."

Chase picked up his lighter and prepared to reignite the pipe but stopped. "All I care about is my kid."

"You do?"

Chase delivered the same vicious glare she had seen moments earlier. This time, Courtney stared back at him. "Why did you go to see her? Why did you go to see . . . Chloe?"

Chase sighed, as though tired of the conversation. "Like I said, I wanted to see my kid."

"What did you argue about?" Courtney asked. "Mr. Morrand said you argued."

"She was giving me shit about child support, okay?"

"Do you even pay child support?"

Chase averted his eyes. "I'm working on it."

Courtney shook her head, sighing disgust as she studied her decadent surroundings. She stared at the backpack, the one filled with plastic bags, before looking at the Formica kitchen counter cluttered with dirty dishes. Sunlight shone through the kitchen window, suggesting pleasant autumn weather, but the world outside seemed so far away. She rubbed her forearms vigorously, trying to arrest the sensation of a thousand tiny creatures marching beneath her skin. She suddenly felt cold and wondered whether someone had left open a door or window.

"I didn't kill her, babe, if that's what you're thinking," Chase said calmly. *Babe* again. "Whatever happened to Chloe Morrand, she brought on all by herself."

She wanted to believe him, but Chase and the truth were not well acquainted. He'd lied to her about going to see Chloe, and he probably lied about *why* he went to see her. No matter how jealous Courtney was of Chloe Morrand, the woman hadn't deserved to die. Someone needed to know that Chase wasn't home on Friday night. Her parents had taught her to always tell the truth, regardless of the consequences.

Chase continued to stare at her with his wicked raven eyes, causing her to shudder. The consequences of crossing *him* would not be pleasant—she was certain of it.

Courtney lowered her chin, shoulders slumped. Deep-gray hopelessness rushed over her, delivering the overpowering certainty of impending doom. Of all the feelings when trying to kick, she hated this one the most.

Chase extended the pipe toward her, and she reached for it.

It would solve everything, if only for a little while.

CHAPTER 34

RICK'S TRUCK SKIDDED ON THE gravel as he pulled into the parking lot of Chloe's apartment complex, his grill narrowing missing the sticker-covered rear bumper of an ancient Datsun pickup.

Charlie Duchesne was leaning against his SUV, arms folded across his chest and a cigarette between two of his fingers. He squinted into the sun as Rick approached, giving him a Popeye-like semblance as he funneled smoke through the opening on the side of his mouth.

The men shook hands in silence, Rick's grip firm and abrupt as he continued to boil from his visit to the sheriff's office. As Rick pumped short bursts of air from his nostrils, Charlie studied him quizzically, as though trying to crack a code.

"You know, you're going to have to stand down at bit, or you'll get yourself in trouble," Charlie said, stamping out his cigarette out in the dirt.

"What do you mean?"

Charlie's eyes widened. "What I mean is, I just talked to Helen at the sheriff's office. She said you caused quite a bit of commotion over there."

Rick removed his hat and scratched the back of his head. "I don't much care for Caleb," he said, turning back toward the coroner.

"I don't care for him either, if you haven't guessed."

Charlie wasn't the enemy. Instead, he was a good friend, someone who knew Rick inside and out. Rick wondered whether that was such a good thing. He cast a thumb toward Chloe's apartment and placed his hat back on his head. "You ready to go in?"

"Not so fast," Charlie answered. "I'll be the one going in—*alone.* I invited you here as courtesy. I also have a few questions."

"Such as?"

"Such as, to your knowledge, was Chloe taking her meds?"

Rick froze. He shot a glance toward his truck, where Chloe's untouched prescription was stashed inside the glove box. He fixed his eyes on the ground in front of him before looking up at Charlie.

"Yeah, as far as I know, she was."

"You sure?"

"Positive," Rick said with more conviction.

Charlie nodded slowly, hardly appearing persuaded. He dug behind a pack of cigarettes in his shirt pocket and produced a small spiral notepad. "What medication was she on?" he asked, clicking a pen.

"Seroquel."

Charlie nodded, scribbling the name on the paper.

Rick took a deep swallow. Did you test . . . you know, for illegal drugs?"

"I did," Charlie said, still looking at his notepad. He paused, eyebrows pinched, as though he was trying to remember how to spell Seroquel.

Rick's heart raced, the skin of his forehead suddenly feeling tight. "And?" he asked hesitantly.

"She was clean, Rick. Totally clean."

Rick exhaled, nodding with relief. Charlie pulled the pack of cigarettes from his pocket and tossed one into his mouth. Rick flicked a couple of his fingers, welcoming a smoke. Charlie hesitated at the request, then furrowed his eyebrows as he extended the pack.

"Tell me, Rick," he said, lighting their cigarettes, "did Chloe have a boyfriend?"

Rick took a drag, pausing to consider Charlie's question before he exhaled. "Not anyone I met recently. Why?"

"Well . . ." Charlie said. He stopped.

"Well what?" Rick asked, moving closer. The coroner stared back at him, appearing reluctant to speak. "My autopsy revealed that she'd had sexual intercourse. And it was within twenty-four hours of her death."

"She was raped?" Rick asked, his voice straining. He thought of his daughter suffering. His stomach grew queasy. Pellets of sweat gathered like dew on his forehead.

Charlie shook his head rapidly. "I didn't say that. I said she had sex."

"Is it possible she was assaulted?"

"It's . . . I don't think so. The sex may have been slightly rough, but I don't think it was an assault."

Slightly rough? Rick winced, his eyelids closing tightly as air left his lungs. Charlie may as well have punched him in the gut. "What does slightly . . . never mind."

A dense cloud of shame darkened him. Chloe's hypersexuality was a grim, unpredictable trait of her illness, soaring to frightening levels of intensity during episodes of mania. Her sexual exploits, dating back to high school, were well chronicled in Riverton and throughout the valley, leaving her with a reputation that had only just begun to mend.

Rick took a long, hard pull on his cigarette, causing the tobacco to flame into a bright orange. He brushed his thumbnail across his forehead as he exhaled a stream of smoke.

"There's her boss down at Yellowstone—a guy named Matt Steelman," he said. "Chloe seemed pretty enamored with the guy."

"Have you met him?"

"Not yet," Rick said with firmness as he took another drag. "I haven't met him—*yet.*"

He watched Charlie scribble in his notebook. *Matt Steelman.* Rick's jaw muscles grew taut as he considered the name. He hadn't met many of Chloe's suitors, primarily because the relationships rarely took lasting flight. In many instances, such as the case of Chase Rettick, that was a good thing.

Matt Steelman. When Chloe had mentioned him, she insisted he was the real deal. If he was such a standup guy, why didn't he return Rick's phone calls? Perhaps it was time to pay him a visit.

Charlie's eyes rose abruptly from his notebook, as though Rick's brain was speaking aloud. "Don't start getting any ideas, my friend. You're going to have to let law enforcement handle this."

Rick pushed smoke out his nostrils, his eyes wandering toward the door of Chloe's apartment. "Law enforcement doesn't move very fast around here."

"We do the best we can with what we got. You need to understand that." He placed his notebook back into his pocket, the ash from his cigarette tumbling onto his shirt. He followed Rick's eyes to Chloe's door.

"How was her demeanor? Was there anything in her statements or actions that might lead you to believe that she might harm herself?"

Rick flattened his lips and wagged his head. "Nope."

"I know this is hard, but think a minute, Rick. Nothing at all?"

"Nothing at all," he said, his voice unsteady. Rick looked away, blinking back wetness in his eyes. "Abby's birthday is next weekend, Charlie. Chloe was planning a big party for her."

"I see," Charlie said as he folded his arms across his chest. "Even so, you and I both realize—"

Rick shot an intense glare that stopped Charlie mid-sentence. He edged closer to the coroner. "Chloe didn't *harm* herself, Charlie," he said, his voice laced with bite. "Somebody *did this* to her."

"Easy, Rick. I'm just trying to do my job."

Rick looked toward the Chloe's apartment door, which was covered with an X of crime scene tape. He swallowed hard. Throughout her short life, Chloe had always stood out, marked as different.

"Billy stopped here earlier, and not a moment too soon," Charlie said. "The landlady was about to go in and poke around. Minnie leans a little toward the nosy side." He cast a nod toward the door. "You mind opening it up?" Rick paused a moment before trudging forward. He turned the key, just like he had done the day before.

When Sheriff Tidwell received the call from Maggie Townsend, he assumed that Draper had laid another beating on her, and perhaps this time she would be willing to finally press charges. That would likely be enough to send Draper back up to Deer Lodge for six months or so, temporarily cleansing the valley of an unwanted varmint and thus making Caleb's job a little easier.

Maggie had urgency in her voice when she'd called, insisting that an audience with the sheriff couldn't wait. His heart still pulsing after his fiery confrontation with Rick Morrand, Caleb reluctantly agreed to see her, convincing himself he could probably stand some fresh air.

Caleb would have preferred to bring Billy along with him, or any other deputy not named Clint Roswell. He didn't relish the notion of a direct encounter with Draper Townsend, even though Maggie assured him that the ex-con wouldn't be there. As he exited his vehicle, Caleb put his cell phone in his shirt pocket and brushed his hand across the grip of his holstered oversized gun.

He found Maggie in the precise condition he had anticipated, wearing a nasty bruise high on her cheekbone to go with a swollen, busted lip. She opened the screen door to reveal discoloration extending from her elbows to her wrists, likely caused either by Draper seizing her or perhaps Maggie raising her arms in self-defense. Caleb took a step back, casting his eyes around the corner of the house to confirm there were no parked vehicles in the driveway. He turned to Maggie, shaking his head with dismay as he accepted her invitation to step inside.

Caleb initially waved off a cup of coffee Maggie had prepared but then accepted it out of sympathy after looking into Maggie doleful, lifeless eyes. Glancing around the kitchen, he pulled out a chair and sat down at the table.

"Where's your husband now?" he asked.

Maggie took a sip of coffee, cringing as it passed across the cut on her lip. "My *husband* took off about an hour ago, drunk and headed south," she said in an acrid tone. "I would imagine he's seated at the first open saloon in Gardiner."

Caleb nodded, pleased to learn Draper was far away. "How can I help? Do you want to press charges?"

Maggie lit a cigarette from a pack on the table, sending a stream of smoke in Caleb's direction. "Press charges?" she asked with a frown. "You mean, for this fall I took in the shower? No, Sheriff, I don't want to press no charges."

"Why not?"

"Why not?" She sucked her cigarette as if trying to pull the tobacco right through the filter. "I'll tell you why not. He gets arrested for beating me up, and he'll be right back here in no time to do this to me all over again."

"So, Draper *did* do this to you? It didn't happen in the shower?"

Maggie's eyebrows furrowed in disbelief, indicating Caleb's question did not deserve an answer. She placed her cigarette in a yellow ashtray, placed her elbows on the table, and interlocked her fingers in front of her face.

"Look here, *Sheriff*," she said. "I'm fully aware that I'm the poster child for domestic violence in this valley. I get that. But I sure didn't call you out here to chat about spousal abuse."

Caleb picked up his coffee but quickly put it back down. "What then?"

Maggie leaned forward, twitching her head to chase a wisp of graying hair off her forehead. "I believe that he had something to do with the death of that girl."

"Chloe Morrand?"

Maggie nodded.

Caleb tightened his eyebrows as he lifted his cup and took a sip of coffee. It was hot but woefully stale. He pondered Maggie's assertion. Billy Renfro had mentioned something about Jack Kelly seeing a guy on the trail. The man was said to be gruff and unshaven, hardly a peerless description in rural Montana. *Still, could that have been Draper?*

"What makes you say that your husband was involved in Chloe Morrand's death?"

Maggie took a drag, then flicked cinders into the yellow ashtray. She rested her bruised forearm across her stomach, using her wrist to prop up the hand holding her cigarette.

"Draper was on the trail to Shadow Lake late Friday. He was out there all night. Ain't that when she died?"

Caleb returned his coffee to a stained saucer. "We don't know that for certain. But, yeah, it looks like that's when it happened."

"That's definitely when it happened," Maggie said, exhaling another billow of smoke.

"We don't know—at least, we don't think . . . that she was murdered," Caleb said

"You mean, 'cause she was Chloe Morrand and she was found at the bottom of that cliff?" Maggie asked. "You think that means she killed herself? Trust me, Sheriff—that girl was murdered."

Caleb swallowed, his throat coated with the bitter aftertaste of Maggie's coffee. He tilted his head with curiosity. "What makes you so sure?"

Maggie shrugged. "He told me," she said. "He told me he did it."

Caleb leaned forward, squinting at her. "Draper?"

Maggie rolled her eyes. "No, Teddy Freakin' Roosevelt!" she snapped. "Yes, Sheriff . . . *Draper*."

Caleb head jerked backward, eyelids blinking rapidly, the sudden bite in Maggie's voice giving him a start. "When did Draper tell you this?"

Maggie took out another cigarette and lit it from the one she was about to finish. She pointed the pack toward Caleb, assuming the entire world smoked. He declined.

"I don't know if you noticed, Sheriff, but Draper likes to do his share of drinkin'," Maggie said. "And when he's drunk, and he's not busy beating the crap out of women, he tends to do a lot of talkin'." She sat rigid in her chair, placing her elbows back on the table. "He told me flat-out that he murdered that girl."

"What *exactly* did he say?"

"He said that if I didn't watch out, he'd do me just like he did Chloe Morrand."

Caleb focused on Maggie's eyes, attempting to gauge her credibility. Despite his representations to Rick Morrand, he had proffered the notion that Chloe's death was a suicide. Maggie had certainly complicated things.

"Are you willing to testify?" he asked.

"You arrest Draper Townsend for murder, and I'll be more than willing to testify."

Caleb sipped his coffee, then wished he hadn't. It was no longer hot, but it was still bitter. "You realize," he said, "that we haven't seen any evidence to suggest that she was murdered. Even if you testify, the case still is circumstantial."

Maggie huffed. "You happen to check out Draper Townsend's circumstances these days?" she asked with an uneasy chuckle. "I guarantee you that he committed this murder, and I'll testify to that."

Caleb took another sip of bad coffee. "It's still circumstantial," he repeated.

Maggie took a drag of her cigarette, casually placed it in the ashtray, and rose from her chair. She walked toward a small room off the kitchen, where a tired washing machine could be heard laboring through the spin cycle. She returned with a pair of tan suede work gloves, then dropped them on the table in front of Caleb.

"These are the gloves Draper was wearing that day—last Friday. Who knows? Maybe he might have left one of 'em at the scene?"

Caleb stared at the dirt-stained gloves. He took a deep breath, his nostrils filling with the stale odor of dead fish.

"You're suggesting I plant evidence?"

Maggie's face flushed with emotion, her eyes filling with a fiery mix of anger and frustration. She pounded her fist on the kitchen table, causing Caleb's cup of coffee to dance. Her lips began to tremble.

"I'm suggesting that you plant Draper Townsend's ass in prison, Sheriff!" she shouted, tears gathering in her eyes. "You need to plant his ass in prison once and for all."

Caleb sat stunned. Maggie wasn't finished.

"Can you tell me one good thing Draper Townsend has ever done for this valley?" she asked, jabbing her index finger toward him. She pushed her wounded face closer, near enough for him to feel her hot breath reeking of coffee and cigarettes. "Look at me," she continued, pointing at her face. "Look at me! He's evil, Sheriff. *Eeevil!*"

Caleb was silent, paralyzed as he stared at Maggie's face. His brain replayed his confrontation with his fiancée, Tessie Lou—a pregnant woman, no less—the thought causing him to become sick with guilt. He wondered how much different he was from Draper Townsend.

He watched as Maggie stepped back and collapsed into her chair as if overcome with exhaustion from a lifetime's dose of Draper. She stared at Caleb with plaintive eyes, tears flowing down her weathered, weary cheeks.

"I swear he killed that girl, Sheriff," she said in a firm, subdued tone. "He told me he did, and I'll testify to it. All you need to do is go and arrest him."

CHAPTER 35

RICK HEADED BACK OUT TO the valley, his mind haunted by the cold decisive X of yellow tape across Chloe's apartment door, her turbulent existence now crossed off like bad debt on humankind's harsh and dispassionate balance sheet.

The chill of the morning had given way to warm abundant sunshine, but Rick felt himself surrounded by dense gloom, the finality of his daughter's death continuing to hammer its way into his head and heavy heart. His jaw tight, lips pursed, an anvil on his chest, he fought to harness his emotions as he clenched the steering wheel of his truck, keeping his watery eyes fixed on Highway 89.

The turnoff to Sage's place came and went, Rick incapable of facing his confused and grieving granddaughter. He felt guilty—cowardly—knowing he should comfort her, the child needing someone of the same blood now more than ever. But he just couldn't, not at this moment. Each time he had looked into Abby's eyes, he only saw Chloe.

As he reached for his sunglasses, he noticed a CD on the console. It was a gift from Chloe, a collection of songs she insisted he would like. He had neglected to listen, convinced it would be more songs from Coldplay, which she had given him before.

He loaded the CD into his player, and turned up the volume. The hard opening strains of "Yellow," her favorite song, were too much. His jaw muscles tightened as he choked off a sudden surge of emotion. He searched the CD for a different track, landing on the more gentle "Fix You."

Rick remembered when he first tried to fix Chloe. She'd been fifteen. It was right after a suicide attempt. She was in lockdown, and she insisted she wanted to die.

Reiff Metcalf had recommended a psychiatrist—Dr. Jonas Silverman. "This guy's supposed to be the very best," Reiff explained, handing Rick a business card. "He's a Jew, which is always good." Whatever that meant.

Rick recalled sitting in a waiting room, a sedated Chloe at his side. Her sandy hair was matted, her eyes empty, her face ghostly white and drawn. She wore the same Def Leppard shirt of a week before, and she needed a shower. Real bad.

His daughter was led through a hollow dark-brown door, her head bowed and her thumbs planted in her back pockets. Rick watched her disappear, then cast a dull gaze at his surroundings. In addition to framed certificates reassuring visitors of Dr. Silverman's credentials, the walls were covered with tacky posters of whales and dolphins, cartoonish sketches in cheap gold frames depicting joyful underwater scenes that could never possibly exist.

He remembered Chloe walking back out to the waiting room, bored, plopping into a chair. It was Rick's turn. He was led down a hallway and into an office marked "Private."

A stout bespectacled unmade bed of a man with long wiry gray hair rose to greet him, offering a weak handshake. His palms were soft and sweaty.

"Hello, Mr. Morrand," Silverman said. "Sit down, please."

Rick sat to one side of a three-seat leather sofa, interlocked his hands, and placed his elbow on the armrest. As Silverman returned to a worn burgundy leather chair, he straightened a faded charcoal cardigan sweater that could have been inherited from his father. Maybe even Sigmund Freud.

Rick noticed a rockslide of breadcrumbs that began below Silverman's mouth and cascaded down a disheveled beard onto his sweater, survivors from the lunch that apparently had preceded their one p.m. appointment.

"I was looking at your questionnaire," Silverman said, referring to paperwork Rick had filled out. "We asked if there was any mental illness in the family. You didn't mark yes or no."

Rick hesitated. He felt like he'd been caught cheating on an exam.

"There was my Uncle Phillip, I guess," he said with reluctant irritation. Dr. Breadcrumb tilted his head forward and furrowed his thick silver brow, looking for more.

Uncle Phil, his father's fraternal twin brother, gave Rick his first football. Rick had loved Uncle Phil—for a while, anyway.

"He killed himself," Rick said flatly. "Shot himself in the chest with a .44."

"Do you know why?"

"He was depressed."

"Did you notice signs of depression?"

"Not when he was around me."

A brief silence. Rick took a deep breath. There was something else.

"I remember my folks talking about him in the kitchen, saying how he needed a job," he said. "When he wouldn't come around, they would talk to each other about him going through a season . . . or a valley. Something like that."

"Was it a season or a valley?"

"Does it matter?"

"Not really."

Silverman reached for a prescription pad and began scribbling on it as he braced it in his lap. He tore off three pieces of paper and handed them to Rick.

"The first is an antidepressant, the second an antipsychotic, and the third something that can help her sleep," he said. "I suggest you administer all three for now, especially the third one."

Rick looked at the three pieces of paper, unable to read any of them. He folded them and placed them in his shirt pocket.

"So, what's the plan?" Rick asked, turning his eyes back toward the doctor.

"The plan?" Dr. Silverman asked, seemingly amused by Rick's choice of words. "The plan is to try to keep her *alive*."

The *plan* had failed. Driving through the peaceful valley in his truck, Rick turned up the volume on the CD.

> *When you try your best but you don't succeed.*
> *When you get what you want but not what you need.*
> *When you feel so tired but you can't sleep.*
> *Stuck in Reverse . . .*

He tightened his grip on the steering wheel. He remembered the bright smile Chloe wore when she had given him the CD. He had nodded and accepted the gift, knowing he probably wouldn't listen. He'd play some Tim McGraw instead, figuring Chloe's music could wait. Now, it couldn't wait.

> *Lights will guide you home.*
> *And ignite your bones.*
> *And I will try to fix you.*

His chest tightened. He felt as if he couldn't breathe. He closed his eyes tightly, trying to barricade his tears. He remembered his daughter as a young girl. When she would cry, he could take care of her. He could *protect* her.

"Damn it, Chloe!" he shouted as his truck slid to a stop off the side of the road. "I'm so sorry. Please forgive me!"

Rick pressed his forehead on the top of his steering wheel and sobbed. He repeatedly hit the wheel with his open fist, burying his face in the back of his glove. He should have done more. He should have fixed her.

He turned off the CD, blinking his eyes and dabbing them with the canvas sleeve of his jacket. "Sittin' here cryin' like a damn baby," he told his empty cab.

He sat back in his seat. He breathed.

When he stared over the hood of his truck, he lurched forward, eyes squinting in disbelief. No more than twenty yards in front of him, a buffalo stood broadside, warily watching him with its left eye. This wasn't the same place Chloe had seen the two bison on Friday—

that was at the Double-U, which was a good six or seven miles farther down the valley.

Rick continued to watch the eye, then noticed the buffalo start to flinch. Its right front leg was caught in the lower two wires of the fence. The more the animal struggled, the worse its predicament became.

Rick got out of the truck, tossing his jacket on the front seat. He reached into a toolbox in the bed, emerging with a pair of wire cutters. He walked purposefully at first, slowing as he drew closer to the animal.

"Easy, boy," he said in a gentle voice.

As he stooped to cut a wire, the buffalo waved its snout powerfully, narrowly missing Rick's throat with a horn before it nearly dislocated his shoulder. The wire cutters flew from his hand as he fell to the ground and clutched his wounded clavicle.

"Goddamn it!" he yelled at the leviathan beast. "I'm trying to help you! Can't you see, you dumb shit? I'm trying to help you!"

He lowered his voice, but it remained intense. "I'm trying to *help* you."

After a brief search, Rick retrieved the wire cutters from the tall grass behind him. He approached the buffalo again, this time on his hands and knees, his shoulder pulsing with pain. After two quick cuts, the animal was free.

At least, it was free from the fence. As it kept its eye fixed on Rick, the buffalo looked less than appreciative.

"You're welcome," Rick said dryly. He rose to his feet and dusted off his jeans. The struggle had left him out of breath. "Why are you here?" he asked the animal. The eye remained fixed on him, the proud animal seemingly wondering the same thing.

Suddenly, a gunshot rang out, and the eye descended into a daze, the buffalo wobbling like a punch-drunk prizefighter before collapsing onto its side. Rick froze, staring in shock as blood drenched the fur in front of the animal's shoulder. The buffalo lay still, its long tongue falling limp in its mouth as it begged for air through labored breaths. Rick whirled, trying to trace the source of the gunfire.

Another shot. This one clanged off the inside of the truck bed, leaving a bulge in the metal. Rick eyes opened wide, stunned that the bullet had nearly punctured the steel. A hunting rifle, his mind told him. Air bolted from his lungs. A *powerful* hunting rifle.

He scrambled toward the truck, bracing himself against the front tire. A third shot rang out, this one shattering the passenger's side window. Rick's heart pounded. Whoever it was, they were firing at *him*. The bison was collateral damage.

He edged toward the driver's side door, hoping to reach a weapon, but a fourth shot crashed through the rear window of the cab, chasing him back.

Heaving rapid breaths, he leaned hard on the tire, sandwiched between the fear of death and the surge of adrenaline urging him to fight.

He waited. No more shots. Silence.

He rose with caution, his face sliding past the door handle and peering over the side rail of his truck. Several hundred yards away, across a range sprinkled with cattle, he saw dust rising from a ridge as a truck—a dually, it looked like—disappeared from sight. *Was it black? Dark blue?* He spun back around, his sweat-soaked shoulder blades flush against the cold metal of his truck, the buffalo lying motionless less than twenty feet away.

What was he—or *she*—shooting at? The buffalo? Doubtful. Did this have something to do with Chloe? Were they after him and his family?

A sudden thought jolted him with panic. *Sage! Abby!*

Rick yanked open the door of his truck and lunged for his cell phone. His hands trembling, he pushed Sage's number using speed dial. Bursts of air thrust from his nostrils as he waited through three endless, agonizing rings.

"Hi," Sage said.

"Are you in the house?" Rick panted.

"No, we're outside. We were going to sit by the river and—"

"Get in the house, lock the door, and call the sheriff's office."

"What?" Sage asked, fear creeping into her voice. "Why?"

"I've just been shot at."

"You've been *what*? By who?"

"I don't know. Just grab Abby and get in the house."

"But—"

"You still have your gun?"

"Yes."

"Keep it nearby, just in case. I'll be there as soon as I can."

Chapter 36

Rick's half-ton fishtailed onto Sage's gravel driveway, bounding recklessly through potholes before skidding to a stop in front of the house. He burst from the truck, his jaw tight with fevered intensity, the barrel of a long rifle riding on his remaining healthy collarbone.

Sage's house appeared to be silent and peaceful, the only sound coming from the distressed cackles of two chickens being pursued by a mischievous Blue Heeler. Rick's heart pulsed. The place felt way too quiet. His eyes trailed up the river and scanned the surrounding foothills, manically searching for signs of danger.

Sage and Abby appeared on the front door and stepped onto the redwood porch, Sage cradling a .12 gauge under her bent arm. Rick exhaled. He rushed toward them, dropping one knee as he pulled Abby close, his heart weighted with self-blame for failing to provide Chloe with greater vigilance. He winced as the child's chin fell onto his sore shoulder, but he ignored his pain.

Abby suddenly pulled back.

"Pa-Pa, what happened to your truck?" she asked, pointing at the shards of glass framing the vehicle's shattered windows. Rick didn't respond, rising to his feet and placing his palm on Sage's cheek. "You okay?"

His hand was coarse, more rancher than lawyer, but Sage pushed her skin against his, her deep, abundant eyes blending confusion and fear. "What's going on?" she asked.

Rick placed his rifle against the railing and took the shotgun from Sage. He cracked it open to find the chambers empty. "No shells?"

Sage snatched the shotgun, snapped it shut, and set it down. She wagged her head with exasperation. "Got 'em in my pocket. I usually don't load a .12 gauge until I know what I'm shooting at. Can you *please* tell me what's going on?"

Rick began to answer, but he heard the sound of tires grinding stone behind him. He grabbed his rifle and whirled, eyes keen, frayed nerves having put him on edge. He slowly lowered the barrel when he recognized a black-and-white law enforcement SUV.

Billy Renfro emerged at his own pace, shooting a frown at Rick's rifle. "I was headed back from the Sawtooth and got a dispatch," Billy said, casting a thumb over his shoulder. "Everything okay?"

Rick nodded toward his truck. "Does it *look* like everything's okay?"

Billy followed Rick's eyes toward the wounded vehicle, taking a few steps closer to study the shattered rear window. "No, I don't suppose it does," Billy said. His index finger stroked the bulge on the side panel. "Care to tell me what happened?"

Rick hesitated, turning toward Sage. "What don't you go ahead and take Abby inside?"

Sage shook her head. She opened her mouth to speak but remained silent.

"Please," he repeated. Sage placed her arm around Abby's shoulders and disappeared through the screen door. Rick walked past Billy toward his truck, warily eyeing the foothills as he walked. He opened the door to the cab and placed the rifle inside.

"It's like I told you the other night, Billy—Chloe didn't take her own life," he said. "Someone was after her, and now they're after me." He cast his eyes toward Sage's house. "Or maybe they even might be after my family."

Billy used his thumb and forefinger to smooth his bushy mustache. "You said you had a run-in with Draper Townsend?"

"At the Pines. On Thursday."

Billy nodded. "Sheriff called me a little while ago and said he has reason to believe Draper was out at Shadow Lake on Friday night."

Rick felt a coldness ripple down his spine. "He was?" he said urgently. "So it was Draper?"

"Not so fast—I don't have details," Billy replied. "Caleb and I were cut off, and then I got the radio call to come here. Tell me about the gunshots. Did you see where they were coming from?"

"It was someone tucked among the brush in the foothills," Rick said. "They were a fair distance away."

Billy bent over to take a closer look at the side panel. "A .30-06 maybe?"

"More powerful than that," Rick said. "I'm thinking some kind of seven millimeter. That bullet almost went through two layers of truck."

Billy stood, which seemed to take some effort. He sighed. "We'll probably need to remove the panel to find a shell." He peeked through the driver's side window. "You find anything inside the cab?"

"Haven't looked."

"Did you see a vehicle of any kind?"

"A truck," Rick said. "It was dark-colored. Black, or maybe blue, I think."

Billy nodded again. "I'm not sure what kind of truck Draper is driving these days," he said. "He always picks up a different beater each time he's released from the pen."

"Where is Draper now? Do you plan to bring him in?"

Billy drew a deep breath that leaned more toward exasperation than oxygen. "We're trying to locate him. For the moment, all his is guilty of is going fishing." The deputy pulled a toothpick out of his shirt pocket, where he always seemed to have a limitless supply. He twirled it in his mouth, crinkling his forehead as he appeared to search for inspiration. "Tell me more about this guy from California."

"Bledsoe?"

"That his name?" Billy produced a weathered notebook from his back pocket. He clicked a pen. "He was an ex-client, you said?"

"Yes," Rick said, watching Billy scribble. "B-l-e-d-s-o-e. First name is Richard."

"And you think he might be in Montana?"

"That's what my old law partner says."

"What's the law partner's name?"

"Metcalf," Rick answered. "Reiff Metcalf,"

"How long has he been in town?"

"Couple days, I guess. Why?"

"Hmmm . . ." Billy flipped back to the front of his notebook. "Sheriff and I took a look at Chloe's cell phone. I ordered the CDRs— Call Detail Records?—but I won't have those back for a couple of days. There were a couple of numbers that stood out."

Rick lifted his chin, urging Billy to proceed.

"In addition to Chloe's place of work, there were several calls to the 801 area code, which is Utah. When we tried it, all we got was a voice mail that repeated the number. You happen to know anybody from Utah?"

"Utah," Rick repeated, rubbing his temples as he studied the ground. "Wait!" he said, his eyes snapping back toward Billy. "Her boss. He's been there less than a year. I think Chloe told me he came from Utah. Guy named Matt Steelman?"

"Matt Steelman," Billy muttered.

"You talk to him yet?"

Billy chuckled. "How would I have talked to him? I just heard his name."

"Charlie didn't tell you about him?"

"No."

"You need to talk to him."

Billy pulled the toothpick from his mouth. "Easy, Rick," he said, raising a palm as if he planned to take an oath. "If that's who it is— Steelman, is it?—if that is his number, it wouldn't be all that unusual for Chloe to have called her boss."

Rick exhaled. "I can't be sure, but he may have been something more than her boss."

Billy raised his bushy eyebrows. "Oh?"

"Charlie Duchesne said that Chloe had . . . sex . . . within twenty-four hours of the time she died," Rick said, his voice colored with defeat. "Chloe seemed to like this Steelman guy, and he may have taken advantage of the situation. I tried to contact him, but he didn't return my call. Guy seems pretty shady. You *really* need to talk to him. If you're not going to do it, I'll go talk to him myself."

Billy frowned. "I'll talk to him, but *you* need to have some patience. In case you haven't noticed, we're stretched pretty thin—especially with all these protesters in town."

Rick ground his teeth, his eyes hardening into an angry glare. Billy's pace was far too leisurely for Rick's liking. "I don't care about protesters. I care about my daughter and what happened to her. You should too, Billy, unless you're like everybody else, and—"

Billy flicked his toothpick onto the ground, his version of throwing down a gauntlet. "Now hold on, Rick," he said, his tone rising with ire. "I haven't come to any conclusions about anything."

Rick held his eyes on Billy for several seconds before drawing a slow breath and nodding. The deputy had been a fishing companion of Rick's father and a loyal family friend. Billy deserved his respect, and his trust—especially after what he did for Rick those many years earlier, following the accident. It seemed every time Rick looked at Billy, he remembered that night, a younger version of the deputy glaring at him through the cold, misty rain, the flashing lights of emergency vehicles bouncing off Billy's tightened features as he shook his head with a peculiar mix of disappointment and compassion.

"I apologize, Billy. I'm just a little frustrated, that's all. I just know—I'm *positive*—Chloe didn't . . ."

Billy nodded but didn't speak.

"What was the other number?" Rick asked. "You said there were a couple of numbers that stood out."

Billy pulled a fresh toothpick from his shirt pocket and placed it in his mouth. "Actually, it wasn't a number," he said. "It came up as 'Restricted.' Could be anybody, I guess. We won't know the exact number and source until we get the CDRs."

Rick stared blankly at Billy before a sudden thought jolted him. He fumbled in his pocket for his cell phone, shielding it from the sun as he squinted at his call logs.

"You know anyone with a restricted number?" Billy asked.

"Yes . . . no. Well, maybe."

Billy lifted his eyebrows with expectancy, waiting for a more definitive answer. Rick stared a moment at his phone, nodding as he placed it back into his pocket.

"My ex-partner. When he called the other day, it was a restricted number."

Billy nodded. "This Metcalf fella?"

"Yes."

"Will he be in town for a while?"

"Sure. He supposed to sit in for me on a court case tomorrow. He'll be around. But why—"

"We'll need to talk to him. Maybe even get a DNA sample."

Rick cocked his head. "DNA?"

Billy nodded. "No doubt Charlie found some DNA in Chloe's vehicle, and maybe even on her clothes—though, with the rain and snow, that's probably not as likely."

"You don't think—"

Billy folded his arms across his chest. "You want the truth, don't you, Rick?"

"Well, of course, but Reiff—"

"We find out what's true by eliminating what ain't."

Rick stared at the river, its crystal waters tumbling with pride and purpose over gold-colored stones. He flinched when a falcon flushed from a cottonwood tree, the raptor oblivious to him, wings welcoming the wind, flight effortless and carefree.

He turned toward Billy. "And Matt Steelman? You'll talk to him?"

Billy shook his head with frustration, his eyes signaling impatience. "I'll talk to Steelman myself," he said. "We'll find Draper, and we'll question him. We'll also get our hands on a photo of this Bledsoe character and find out if anyone has seen him around."

The deputy crammed his notebook into the back pocket of his uniform slacks, then nodded at Sage's house. "You go on ahead and take care of your loved ones," he said gently. "Let us do our job."

Rick studied Billy's soft, pleading eyes, measuring sincerity. He nodded, then turned to walk away.

"If you don't mind," Billy called after him, "I'm going to go ahead to take a look inside the truck."

"It's all yours," Rick said without turning back. "As you can see . . . it's open."

Rick plopped onto the edge of Sage's front porch, forearms resting on bent knees. He watched as Billy tugged a pair of nitrile gloves over his pudgy hands—perhaps he was hoping to find a bullet somewhere inside Rick's truck. A bullet might have prints.

The screen door creaked open behind him. It was Abby. She sat down, her head snuggling below his shoulder in a desperate search for affection. His eyes darted in all directions, wondering whether she would be safe. He placed his arm around her and pulled her close.

"Is that Deputy Renfro, Pa-Pa?"

"You know him?"

Abby nodded. "He talked at our school last year. He's really nice."

"Yes," Rick said, eyes considering Billy, "I suppose he is."

"What is he doing?"

"Looking for evidence."

"Evidence?" she asked. "That's what they look for on the crime shows. What kind—"

"You shouldn't be watching crime shows."

"Mommy said it was okay."

The mention of Chloe chased them into a silence that lasted for several endless seconds. Abby peeked up at her grandfather, wetness gathering in her eyes. "What kind of evidence is he looking for, Pa-Pa?"

Rick drew a deep breath and caressed Abby tiny shoulder, her collarbone as wispy as a switch of willow. "What do you say we talk about something else?"

Abby didn't press him. She adjusted her head slightly, her eyes staring straight ahead, seemingly into nothingness.

"Pa-Pa? Do you think my Mommy's in heaven?"

Rick felt a surge of painful emotion inside him. He swallowed hard, moistened eyes blinking rapidly.

"I have absolutely *no doubt* your Mommy's in heaven," he choked through a tight jaw. "Why do you ask?"

Abby hesitated, her gaze still distant.

"I heard a man tell Sage that people who, you know . . . do what Mommy did . . . don't go to heaven."

Rick felt blood rush to his forehead, his sadness burned off by anger. He squared himself toward Abby, placing his hands on her shoulders. "What man?"

Abby seemed startled by the change in Rick's tone. "A man who came to the house," she said cautiously. "I think his name was Clarence."

"Clarence Avery? From the funeral home?"

Abby shrugged. "I guess. All he said was, if Mommy died the way everybody says she did, then she would be going straight to hell. Is that true, Pa-Pa?"

Rick's forehead tightened. "Clarence Avery doesn't know what he's talking about," he snapped. "And we don't know for sure how your Mommy . . . passed on."

Abby released a deep sigh, seemingly approving of the answer. "So, Mommy won't be going to hell?"

Rick tugged Abby closer, squeezing her as he rocked gently, half of her face buried against his ribs. "No, she's not going to hell," he said, barely above a whisper. "She's already been there."

CHAPTER 37

R EIFF FELT RELATIVELY FRESH FOR his Monday morning court appearance, the product of a rare night of sleep. More accurately, perhaps—he had passed out earlier than normal. He did allow himself a brief stop at the hotel bar, where he threw back a pair of cocktails, the liquor fomenting a mischievous hope that the newswoman might appear.

Reiff's nine a.m. request for a taxi was met with a spirited chuckle at the Riverton Grande's front desk, reminding him to track down the bellman with the Chevy Luv. The Oxy-Valium combo still seemed to be performing admirably and likely would continue to do so, provided Reiff kept his alcohol intake at a manageable level.

He exited the truck in front of the Dexter County Courthouse, leaving the bellman staring wide-eyed at a twenty-dollar gratuity. Briefcase in hand, Reiff brushed off the sleeves of his royal-blue Armani and turned to face a small media gathering. To his pleasant surprise, Amanda Westin Cobb stood front and center. He removed his sunglasses just long enough to provide her with a self-assured wink before proceeding into the courthouse without comment.

Once inside, Reiff sat down at the defense table and put on a pair of reading glasses. He reached into his briefcase and removed a thick manila folder that had been delivered to the hotel that morning. As he thumbed through the file, he was distracted by the sound of uneven whistling, a disturbing cacophony of mismatched notes barren of melody.

A man with long gray hair and thick black-rimmed glasses was poring over the pages of a notebook, as if studying highly classified information. He used a scorpion bolo tie and leather vest to formalize his flannel shirt and jeans, and his brown ropers were old but clean. As he continued his unnerving whistle, he tapped the sole of one of his boots on the edge of the counsel table, apparently having determined that his one-man orchestra required percussion.

Reiff squinted over the top of his reading glasses. "Who are you?"

The man stopped whistling momentarily, his expression indicating that Reiff's intrusion was rude. "Who am I? Who are *you?*"

Reiff removed his glasses. "My name is Reiff Metcalf. I'm—"

"Where's Morrand?"

"Mr. Morrand couldn't make it. He had a family emergency."

"Yeah, I know," the man said without much emotion. "His daughter."

Reiff extended his hand. "So, you must be Buddy Rivers?"

The man glanced at Reiff's hand but didn't shake it. He nodded. "You heard about Rick's daughter?"

"Sure—everybody has. It's a shame. She was a really pretty girl."

Reiff tilted his head. *Pretty girl?* "How did you know her?"

"Rick brought her with him up to the house once, and I seen her around town," Buddy said matter-of-factly. "She was a real pretty girl."

Reiff felt an odd chill rattle up his neck, something about the way Buddy uttered the words "pretty girl" making him uneasy—in a protective, if not *possessive*, kind of way. He stared at Buddy, wondering whether the guy was retarded or psycho. Blowing out a lengthy breath, he shook his head and turned his attention back to the file folder.

"So what I'm going to do, Mr. Rivers, is simply ask the judge for a continuance, maybe for a few weeks. That will give Mr. Morrand time to get back and offer proper representation."

Buddy had placed his notepad on the defense desk, yanked his shirttail out of his pants, and started cleaning his glasses. "I don't want no continuance."

Reiff shrugged. "It's our only option, sir. I'm not licensed to practice law in Montana. I'm going to politely ask the judge to issue a continuance."

Buddy put his glasses on the table and tucked in his shirt. "I don't want no continuance," he repeated. "I don't like coming in here, being around all these people."

Reiff glanced at the gallery. The courtroom was full. "I understand your position, sir. But we really need to just ask for a continuance."

"I ain't guilty. I was just protecting my cattle and my land."

Reiff sighed. He tapped his pen on the file, searching for a new strategy. He noticed Buddy lean forward and fold his hands on the table.

"Did you know that 997 American soldiers were killed on their first day in Vietnam?" Buddy asked. "Nine hundred ninety-seven."

Reiff didn't respond. *Vietnam?*

"There were another 1,448 killed on the day they were supposed to come home. Bet you didn't know that, either?"

Rick had mentioned that Buddy had been in Vietnam, but Reiff didn't expect this.

"Out of the 58,267 soldiers killed in Vietnam," Buddy continued, "a total of 33,103 were just eighteen years old."

Reiff stared straight ahead and pursed his lips, his eyes fixed beyond the judge's bench at the Seal of the Great State of Montana. Rick apparently had left out the fact that Buddy Rivers was a certifiable whack job.

"You know, I greatly appreciate your service to our country, Mr. Rivers," he said dismissively as he reopened the file. "According to the allegations here, you shot the bison because you were concerned they would infect your cattle with brucellosis?"

"There's no doubt they would infect 'em. I have to defend my cattle—that's my livelihood."

Reiff nodded. "But you shot them with a .22. That's a small-caliber rifle, so you would have needed several shots. That means those animals probably suffered."

Buddy cocked his head with curiosity. "Where you from, Mr. Met— What was your name again?"

"Metcalf. I'm from California."

"That would've been my guess. I used a .22 'cause it was the only gun I had—I was out lookin' for varmints."

Reiff shook his head as he returned his eyes to the file. "It just doesn't seem fair to the buffalo, that's all."

"You know, Metcalf, a lot of things ain't fair. Guys come back from wars these days, and they throw them a parade or salute 'em at football games. Sure wasn't that way when I came back from Vietnam."

More Vietnam. Reiff felt perspiration gather on his forehead, a throbbing pain evolving in his abdomen. He was losing patience.

"As I mentioned, Mr. Rivers, I appreciate your service. However, I—"

"All rise!" a bailiff bellowed, catching Reiff by surprise. In walked Judge Samuel Wade, all five foot six of him. As he sat behind the behind the bench, he adjusted his round tortoise-shell glasses and glanced around the courtroom, seemingly surprised it was so full. The courtroom lights glistened off of his shiny pate, which was surrounded by a hula skirt of thick graying hair.

"Good morning, everyone," he said as he scanned the docket. "We have a fairly full calendar today, so I ask that we try to move things along as efficiently as possible."

Wade lifted his eyes toward Buddy Rivers, who had returned to thumbing through his notepad. "Mr. Rivers," Wade said, letting out an exasperated sigh. "It was our sincere hope that you wouldn't be returning to my courtroom anytime soon, but here you are."

He glanced at Reiff. "I see you had the decency to bring counsel, although this man doesn't look familiar."

The pain in Reiff's abdomen was increasing. "My name is Reiff Metcalf, Your Honor," he said, suppressing a wince. "I'm here because—"

"Where's Mr. Morrand?"

"He's had a family emergency, Your Honor. His daughter—"

"So I've heard," Wade said, disinterested. He opened a manila folder in front of him.

"Your Honor, if I may, I'd like to ask—"

Wade raised his hand to silence Reiff, then motioned that he should sit down. Reiff plopped into his wooden chair, his hand reaching beneath his suit coat to try to sooth his stomach.

Wade turned his attention to the court file.

"Mr. Metcalf, at the recommendation of the Department of Fish, Wildlife, and Parks, your client has been charged with possession of an illegally killed game animal, waste of a game animal, and unlawful hunting during a closed season. How do you plead?"

Reiff glanced at Buddy, who shook his head. "I don't want no continuance," he said in a loud whisper.

The pain in his side nearly caused Reiff to double over. He'd about had his fill of Buddy Rivers. His painkiller clock was ticking. There wasn't much time.

"Mr. Rivers pleads guilty, Your Honor."

A roar of approval erupted in the courtroom. "Stop the flood of bison blood! Save the buffalo!"

Wade slammed his gavel. "Order!"

Reiff glanced at Buddy. "You shouldn't have shot those buffalo, Mr. Rivers. That was downright mean."

Buddy rose from his chair. "I ain't guilty! This guy ain't even my lawyer."

Wade furrowed his brow as studied Reiff. "Tell me, Mr. Metcalf. Are you with a local firm?"

"No sir. I'm from California," Reiff said as he seated himself and poured a glass of water. "The reason I'm here—"

"You *are* a member of the State Bar of Montana, are you not?"

"That's what I tried to explain, Your Honor. I—"

Wade pressed on. "You're *not* a member of the State Bar of Montana?"

"No, Your Honor." He sipped his water. "If you would give me a moment, I can explain."

Wade's beady eyes peered over the top of his glasses. "So you come into my courtroom, enter a plea on behalf of a defendant, and you are not even licensed to practice law in my state?"

Reiff winced as he rose from his seat, his stomach on fire. "That's what I've been trying to explain, you damned hick!" he said as he slammed his glass on the defense table. "Are you deaf? I'm just here to help a friend."

"Mr. Metcalf, I am holding you in contempt!" Wade said, throwing down his gavel for emphasis and looking at the bailiff. "Travis!"

A behemoth of a man bursting out of his green bailiff uniform was distracted. He was staring at the young court reporter, who was batting her lengthy false eyelashes and chewing her gum as though she was angry at it.

"Travis!" Wade growled, this time louder. "Take this man into custody!" The judge shifted his attention to Buddy Rivers. "Mr. Rivers, how do you plead?"

Buddy quickly rose to his feet. "Not guilty, Your Honor!"

"I am releasing you on your own recognizance," Wade said. "You are due back in this courtroom three weeks from today."

A raucous blend of boos and hisses echoed through the courtroom.

"Order!" Wade shouted, slamming his gavel. Reiff looked out of the corner of his eye to see Travis closing in. It was senseless to resist. "You gotta be shittin' me!" Reiff yelled.

Wade's eyes opened wide. "You dare to use vulgarity in my courtroom? That's a one-thousand-dollar fine, Mr. Metcalf!"

"What kind of backwater, inbred town is this?" Reiff sputtered as he was being cuffed.

Another slam of the gavel. "Two thousand dollars!"

As Travis cuffed him and led him away, Reiff glanced at Buddy Rivers, who wore a wry smile. "I told ya I wasn't guilty," Buddy said.

CHAPTER 38

WELLS FARGO WAS NORMALLY A comfortable place where Rick would visit with everyone, from the sleepy security guard to the loan officers and tellers. But when he entered the bank around midmorning, he was greeted by faces offering only silent, sympathetic nods. He felt toxic, as though the death of his daughter had given him a disease no one wanted to contract.

He searched for a familiar face and found one in Sandra Billingsley, whom he had met about six months after Christine died. Sandra had lost her husband about a year prior, and some well-meaning friends thought the two would hit it off. They had shared dinner, followed by ambitious—and hasty—sex, as they both yearned to shed loneliness, if only for one night. Rick quickly realized that he was not quite ready to let Christine go, and he declined to call Sandra again. There were some hurt feelings, but Sandra soon met James Billingsley, a wealthy rancher whom she married a year later. From then on, she and Rick had been cordial, figuring no one needed to know their full history.

Sandra didn't necessarily have to work, but she wanted to keep busy. As a loan officer for Wells Fargo, she was well liked, or at least as well liked as a loan officer could expect to be.

"Morning, Sandra," Rick said as he quietly sat down in front of her glass-topped oak veneer desk.

Sandra tensed her lips into a tight smile and folded her hands in front of her. "Rick, I'm so sorry for your loss," she said, the suntanned skin surrounding her eyes tightening into genuine sorrow.

"Thank you, Sandra."

Awkward silence followed. Rick considered asking how Sandra's husband James was doing but decided he wasn't all that interested.

"Can I get you some coffee?"

"No, I'm good," Rick said, flashing the palm of his hand. He found himself looking awkwardly around the bank, as if checking to see if someone was watching. He eased forward in his chair.

"Chloe had a checking account here," he said, just above a whisper. "I'd put money in it every week or so."

Sandra turned toward her computer, her fingers rattling across the keyboard. "Computer's slow," she said, taking a sip from a coffee mug emblazoned with the image of an Irish setter. "Ah, here it is. Do you want the balance?"

"Sure."

"Twenty-three dollars and seventy-four cents."

Rick sat back and propped his elbows on the arms of his chair. Tilting his head, he reached into his shirt pocket and withdrew the deposit slip he had removed from Chloe's dresser two days earlier. "That doesn't make sense," he said as he handed the piece of paper to Sandra.

Sandra glanced at the deposit slip. "This is a different account," she said. "This is a savings account."

Rick leaned forward and studied the slip. He hadn't bothered to look at the account number, assuming that Chloe had made the deposit into her checking account. He looked at Sandra, who had returned to her keyboard to access the other account.

"Whoa!" she said.

"Whoa what?"

"That's quite a number," Sandra said, pulling a pen from a lacquered wooden cup next to her computer screen. She turned over the deposit slip and wrote on the back. "This is the current balance, including that last deposit."

When Sandra pushed the paper toward Rick, he squinted at it as though his eyes were failing him. He felt the color quickly drain from his face.

The total amount, written in black ink, was $163,947.

Rick felt his eyes widen as he looked at Sandra. "Do you . . . How often were there deposits?" he muttered.

Sandra turned toward her screen and scrolled her mouse. "Looks like about once a month. Most of them are for the same amount, fifteen-hundred dollars. But there were a couple of bigger ones in recent months. Ten thousand each."

"Cash or check?"

"I can't be sure."

"Is it possible to find out where the money came from?"

"That will take some time."

Rick left the bank in a trance, nearly broadsiding a truck as he left the parking lot. As he drove through town, he kept reaching into his pocket and pulling out the deposit slip, staring at the number written in Sandra's tidy feminine handwriting.

$163,947.

"That's ninety-nine cents, sir," a voice said, interrupting Rick's thoughts. He found himself inside the Exxon station, buying a Coke while his truck filled with gas. His brain had briefly danced with the idea of buying something stronger, but he managed to dismiss it. A husky twenty-something man with a thick reddish beard too long for his age was waiting for Rick to pay for the drink.

"What?" Rick said in a daze.

"Ninety-nine cents," the young man replied. "Unless there's something else?"

"Uh, no, sorry," Rick said, returning the deposit slip back to his shirt pocket and pulling out a five-dollar bill. He picked up the Coke and turned to walk away.

"Sir?" the red beard said a little louder.

"Yes?"

"Your change," he said, extending a burly auburn-haired hand that held four crinkled bills.

Rick nodded, stuffed the money in his jacket, and left the store. As he stepped into his truck, his mind suggested explanations for the large sum of money, and none were encouraging. The most prominent source he considered—and the most plausible, he feared—was drugs. That might explain her continued willingness to interact with Chase Rettick, who had proven far more talented at dealing dope than at being a father.

Rick felt both angry and betrayed. Perhaps sadness would come later.

His phone rang. A local number he didn't recognize. He answered. It was Reiff.

"You're where?"

"In jail, Partner," Reiff grunted. "The judge of yours is a real piece of work."

"How did you end up in jail?"

"Things got complicated."

"How? All you needed to do was ask for a continuance."

"I tried. But Judge Wade didn't like the fact I don't have a Montana law license."

"You had Wade? That's not good."

"No it wasn't."

"Didn't you explain?"

"I tried, but he wouldn't let me speak," Reiff said. "So I just entered the guilty plea."

"Guilty plea?"

"Buddy Rivers is an asshole. Not to mention a nut."

"I get that," Rick said. "But . . . never mind. Did they say when you'll be released?"

"Not anytime soon."

"Why not?"

"As I mentioned, things got more complicated."

"What do you mean?"

"I was carrying a couple of prescriptions—one for Oxycontin, another for Valium," Reiff said.

"What's wrong with that? You have cancer, for God's sake."

"The prescription didn't have my name on it."

Rick pinched the bridge of his nose, his forehead starting to throb.

"Since the prescription was from a pharmacist in California," Reiff said with a sigh, "they're claiming I transported illegal drugs across state lines."

The line was quiet except for the sound of Reiff's labored breathing. "I'm not doing too good, Partner," he said. "I managed to dry-mouth a couple of pills before they took my stash, but I don't think they're going to last too long. You need to get me out of here."

Rick didn't answer. He stared at his face in his rearview mirror. Dark circles hung beneath glazed eyes. He bowed his head and gathered himself. "Let me see what I can do."

CHAPTER 39

WHEN BILLY RENFRO PULLED UP to Jack Kelly's barn, the former detective had just lowered the iron blade of his splitting maul through an eight-inch section of fir, sending two healthy chunks of timber catapulting in opposite directions through the crisp autumn air. After placing the firewood on a nearby stack, Jack tugged off his gloves, removed his weathered Rutgers hat, and dragged a plaid flannel sleeve across his sweat-covered brow.

"You seem to be convalescing quite well, Mr. Kelly," Billy said as he used the side of his door to haul himself out of his SUV. "Good to see you are doing better."

Jack's place was tidy in appearance, the parcel consisting of about ten acres nestled against the velvety foothills. A custom cedar-framed house matched the sizeable barn, both structures surrounded by a wire-covered split rail fence designed to prevent deer and rabbits from munching on flowers and other carefully manicured vegetation. The exterior of the fence was lined by dense groves of aspen trees, their branches tickled by toasted golden leaves clinging to the final vestiges of fall.

"Morning, Deputy," Jack heaved between short, deep breaths as he extending a large, sturdy hand. "How's the investigation coming along?"

Billy leaned against his vehicle and reached into his pocket for a toothpick, but after fumbling around with his index finger, he concluded he was out. He folded his arms across his chest. "That's what I wanted to talk to you about. You and I managed to discuss a few things in the ambulance the other night, but neither of us quite had our wits about us. Now that we've both had a couple of days to recuperate, I was hoping to get some additional details."

Jack took a seat on a thick stump and plopped his hat back onto his freshly shaved head. "I'm all yours, Deputy," he said, resting his forearms on the front of his muscular thighs. "Let me know how I can help."

Billy's lips curled into a smile. He'd only met Jack once, but he liked the man. Having been a detective in Jersey, Jack likely had seen his share of scrapes, and his impressive physique told Billy that Newark probably wasn't been the best place to be one of the bad guys. With Caleb less than passionate about the case, Billy had been leaning on assistance from Charlie Duchesne, and the coroner was always eager to assist. But perhaps Jack Kelly could be of help as well.

Billy reached through the driver's side window of his SUV, grabbing a manila folder off the dash. He took a few steps closer to Jack, showing him a photo printed on computer paper. "Ever seen this man before?" he asked, handing him a mug shot of Draper Townsend.

Jack tightened his brow, tilting his head as he examined the photo. "Is he someone I should know?" he asked, turning his deep-brown eyes toward Billy. "Are you thinking this is the guy I saw coming from Shadow Lake?"

"For now, I'm just asking if you've ever seen him."

Jack calmly took the photo from Billy and pulled it closer to his face. He squinted as he studied the ex-con's soulless glare, Draper wearing the mystified expression of the lost man that he was. After several seconds, Jack blew out a long breath and shook his head. "Can't be sure. The guy I saw had a hoodie, and he was wearing aviators—the cheap ones, like they sell at the Exxon station? I wasn't able to see his face all that well."

"How tall would you say the guy was?"

"Maybe five nine."

"How old?"

"Late forties. Maybe fifty."

"White?"

Jack smiled. "Ya think?" he said with a chuckle. "I don't think I've seen a black or Mexican since I moved here."

Billy shrugged. "I suppose he could've been an Indi— Native American."

"Nope. He was white."

Billy tapped the notebook with his pen. "Do you happen to recall if he was wearing gloves?"

Jack glanced away in thought. "I don't recall. He was carrying a stringer of fish—more than the limit, it looked like. I didn't really notice his hands." He handed the photo back to Billy. "Is this the guy you're looking at?"

"He's the *only* guy the sheriff seems to be looking at," Billy said. "Draper Townsend is his name. Caleb seems to think he's responsible for Chloe Morrand's death. He claims Draper more or less confessed to the crime."

"Not sure what you mean by more or less. Did he confess?"

Billy stroked his moustache. "He *supposedly* confessed to his wife. And his gloves were *supposedly* discovered at the scene."

"You don't sound convinced."

"I didn't see any gloves up there. Did you?"

Jack flattened his lips and shook his head.

"A couple of days ago, the sheriff was saying Chloe took her own life," Billy said. He jabbed a forefinger at the photo. "Now, he says it's this guy. If you haven't noticed, Caleb is still a little wet behind the ears. I like to be a little more thorough about things. And so does Charlie."

"Charlie?"

"Duchesne. The coroner."

Jack nodded. "Right." He looked toward the house, where a woman was staring out the window. Must be Tamara Kelly, the woman who had called in a panic, Billy presumed. Jack waved at her, as though signaling he would be in soon. She nodded and closed the curtain.

Billy rubbed the gray stubble on his chin. "You said you arrived at the trailhead on Saturday morning?"

"First light."

"Where there any vehicles parked there?"

"There was one I saw—an old Chevy, or maybe a GMC."

"Color?'

"Light brown, maybe even tan, as I recall," Jack said. "Had the crest of the Aryan Brotherhood on the rear window. Lot of people don't recognize that symbol, but I sure as hell do."

"Sounds like Draper," Billy mumbled. "Except the truck's the wrong color."

Jack's eyebrows tightened. "How so?"

Billy pulled out his notebook and thumbed through the crinkled pages. "Seems that somebody took a shot at Rick Morrand yesterday," he said. "Rick spotted a truck driving away, but it was dark blue or black."

"You're thinking whoever shot at Rick would be the same person who might have harmed his daughter?"

"Makes sense, doesn't it?"

Jack nodded. "Is there anyone else you're looking at?"

"There a guy from California, an ex-client of Rick Morrand's," Billy said. "Seems they had some sort of falling out. We have reason to believe the guy is up here."

Jack adjusted his ball cap. "Tell me—have you reviewed any surveillance of the area? I mean, she worked in Yellowstone, and she was found halfway up the valley. Maybe she stopped somewhere."

Billy looked away, heaving an exhausted sigh. Things were getting more complicated by the minute. Maybe he should have called it quits after Big Jim died, before Caleb took the reins. His mind wandered to his late brother-in-law, Leon, who once went down to Mexico, to a place called Puerto Vallarta. Leon caught a 175-pound swordfish and mounted it on the wall, right next to the head of a five-by-six elk. Billy suddenly wished he was retired, fishing down in Puerto Vallarta.

"Surveillance?" he asked with a false chuckle. "No, we haven't reviewed any surveillance. This ain't New Jersey, Detective. We're not that well-staffed to begin with, and right now we're a little stretched."

"Maybe I can help."

Billy didn't answer. Instead, he cast his eyes toward the window where he had seen Tamara Kelly. She didn't seem thrilled Jack was chatting it up with a deputy. Billy'd heard that a lot of city cop's wives were like that—once you'd quit, they wanted you to forget your career ever happened. "I thought you were retired, Jack."

"Well, I am retired, but—"

Billy had more questions. "It's my understanding you also went up top on the Sawtooth?"

"Correct."

"What boots were you wearing?"

"Wolverine, size thirteen," Jack said. "Same ones I have on now."

Billy glanced down at Jack's boots. They appeared fairly new, except for a few scratches on the toes and mud caked on the sides.

"Did you observe anything that might help—you know, when you went up top?"

"I took some pictures," Jack said with a shrug. "I called the sheriff and offered to email him what I found, but he didn't seem all that interested. He said he took his own."

"Pictures of what?"

"The hiking boots—women's boots—for one thing," Jack said. "I didn't want to move them, so I took a picture with my phone. Then, of course, there was the ankle bracelet."

"The what?"

"The ankle bracelet."

Billy tilted his head and raised his eyebrows. He felt a shudder, as though someone had just thrown a bucket of ice water in his face. "*What* ankle bracelet?"

Jack fished into the pocket of his jeans and pulled out his cell phone. After thumbing the keys for a few moments, he brushed his thumb and forefinger on the screen to make an image larger.

Billy squinted at the picture. "Desiree," he said barely above a whisper. "Can you email that to me?"

"Of course. I'm sure the sheriff has it—maybe even the coroner. It was sitting right out there in the open. It could have been dropped by a hiker or anybody, of course, but you never know."

Billy shook his head. "It's not rusted or weathered. It must not have been out there long."

He reached into the back pocket of his snug uniform pants and wrestled out his wallet. He produced a business card, which he handed to Jack. "Email that to me—please," he repeated. "And maybe any other photos you might have?"

Jack nodded. "Sure."

The two men stood in silence. Billy noticed Jack look at the window of the house, where Tamara was again staring out the window. "You need anything else, Deputy?"

They exchanged a firm handshake. Billy turned to enter his SUV, his mind skimming through a mental phone book of the female residents of Riverton, the town in which he'd spent his entire life.

He'd never met anyone named "Desiree."

CHAPTER 40

WHEN HE WAS LED TO one of two jail cells at the sheriff's office, Rick found his one-time law partner casting a despondent stare at the cracked concrete floor beneath him, his elbows planted on his knees as he sat on a two-inch vinyl pad that served as the lower bunk. After running his fingers through his washed-out hair, Reiff raised his yellowed doleful eyes, manufacturing a tight smile as he stared at Rick through ancient iron bars caked with decades of gunboat-colored paint.

"How you holding up?" Rick asked.

"Been better."

Rick sat on a wooden bench across from the cell. "I'm trying to get you in front of the judge as soon as possible. As of right now, you're being held without bail."

Reiff stared straight ahead, rubbing his cupped hands across his silver-stubbled jaw. "I need to get out of here, Partner. I need to get out of this jail, and I need to get out of Montana."

"Looks like the earliest we'll get into court is Friday."

"Friday!" Reiff shouted, whipping his eyes toward Rick. "That's four days from now."

"It's elk season."

"Great."

The men sat in silence. They once had been inseparable partners and friends, engaging in countless court battles as they built a legal juggernaut that brought both wealth and notoriety. Those days seemed so far away.

"I need to ask you something," Rick said.

"Shoot."

"When we met last Saturday, you said you'd just got in. When did you actually arrive in Montana?"

Reiff hesitated, averting his eyes. A solitary light on the ceiling cast a gleaming reflection off beads of perspiration gathering on his forehead. "I guess it was Friday, late morning."

Rick leaned forward. "Did you call Chloe on Friday?"

Reiff glanced briefly at Rick, then darted his eyes away. "What makes you say that?"

"Chloe got a call Friday morning—a restricted number. Don't you have a restricted number?"

"A lot of people do." Reiff shrugged. "No, I didn't call Chloe."

Rick nodded. More silence, save for the dripping sink next to Reiff's bunk. "What's going on with the investigation?" Reiff asked as he rubbed his side. "Do they have any idea what happened?"

"Nothing yet. They say they're preoccupied with the wildlife advocates in town. You know, the buffalo protesters?"

Reiff seemed grateful for the change of subject. "There was a ton of them in court. What's up with that, anyway?"

Rick sat back on the bench, interlocking his hands on his lap. "The cattlemen are convinced that the infected bison destroy their herds. If brucellosis spreads, it can have big ramifications on the entire industry. They want the population managed so the bison don't spill out of Yellowstone Park, which means the buffalo go to slaughter."

"I assume the protesters have a problem with that?"

Rick nodded. "Big issue around here. The wildlife advocates argue that brucellosis is all a hoax, that it's just an excuse to slaughter the bison. Chloe was on the side of the protesters, of course. She really loved those bison. She even had a website and wrote a regular blog. She was known as the Buffalo Gal."

Reiff massaged his chin. "There was a guy in here yesterday, busted for possession. Looked kind of pissed. He said he came all the way up here from Arkansas to join the demonstrators, but now he wouldn't get paid."

"Paid for what?"

"To protest."

Rick's eyebrows furrowed. "Who was paying him?"

"Not sure. I've heard of unions paying people, but not wildlife activists."

Rick edged forward. "Where is the guy now?"

"They let him go this morning. Told him to leave town." Reiff drew a short gasp, grimacing as his hand again touched his side.

"You okay?"

"Not really."

"You should have stayed in the hospital."

"I don't like hospitals."

Reiff pursed his lips and exhaled. He removed his trembling hand from his abdomen. "How well do you know this Buddy Rivers?"

"Since I was a kid. He had a rough upbringing—drunk mother, abusive stepfather, the whole package. He actually *enlisted* to go to Vietnam. Really messed him up."

"The guy made my skin crawl."

"How so?"

"When we were in court, he mentioned Chloe a couple of times. He kept talking about how pretty she was."

Rick considered Reiff's comment, then shook his head. "Buddy's pretty harmless."

"You sure?"

"Pretty sure."

Reiff forced a chuckle. "Bet the buffalo don't think he's harmless."

Rick offered a faint smile, then rose to his feet. "I'm going to do everything I can to get you out. In the meantime, you need some medical help. I want them to get a doctor to—"

Rick stopped abruptly, interrupted by a loud banging sound on the metal door leading to the cell area. Through the foot-wide wired-glass window, he could see uniformed officers struggling with an unruly prisoner. After a few more slams against the gray door, the man appeared to be subdued. Rick assumed it was one of the protesters.

The door flew open, making Reiff jump from his seat on the lower bunk. Caleb Tidwell and Billy Renfro burst into the cell area, each gripping a shackled arm of Draper Townsend. Rick watched in stunned silence as Draper passed within inches of him, his snarling, unshaven face reeking of alcohol, cigarettes, and sweat.

"Rick, you need to get out of here," Billy shouted breathlessly. "Now!"

Rick moved toward the door, fixing his eyes on Draper. The parolee offered one final thrust of energy, attempting to break free of the sheriff and the deputy before they stuffed him into the cell and slammed the heavy iron door behind him. Reiff watched uneasily from the adjoining cell, pressing his back against the bunks.

Draper flailed around the cage like a crazed captured beast, finally pressing his face between two bars of the cell. He heaved the deep, pained bellows of a wounded animal, his black, satanic eyes glaring at Rick. He let out a long guttural sound as he gathered mucus from his sinus tract, then launched a gruel-colored stream of spit in Rick's direction. Rick sidestepped the disgusting scud, then lunged toward the cell before being intercepted by Caleb and Billy.

"Out you go," Billy said as they quickly wrestled Rick from the cell area. He took one last glance at Reiff, who had taken a seat on the lower bunk, now watching Draper in dumbstruck wonder, apparently confident the thick bars of his cell would hold.

Caleb tightened his grip on Rick's bicep. "Calm down, Mr. Morrand."

Billy leaned against the wall, sucking air and shaking his head as he slid toward the concrete floor. "I'm way too old for this shit." Under his breath, he wheezed, "Sorry, Melba."

Rick fixed his eyes on the wired glass window that led to Draper. "How did he violate parole this time? Domestic violence? Drugs? Drunk in public?"

"It's a little more serious than that," Billy mumbled from the floor.

Rick looked at Caleb, eyes narrowed. "How so?"

Caleb drew a deep breath, glanced at Billy, then fixed his eyes on Rick. "Draper Townsend is under arrest for suspicion of murder, Mr. Morrand."

"Murder? Murder of whom?"

"Your daughter."

Caleb's words seemed to echo endlessly off the yellow cinder-block walls of the claustrophobic room, like dull sounds of a cast-iron bell tolling midnight. Rick's mouth hung open, his synapses unable to fire. His chest ached as his mind volleyed between the relief that his daughter might not have taken her own life and the sickening concept that Draper Townsend had brutally stolen it from her. *You failed to protect her.* He felt Chloe dying again and again and again.

The searing pain of her loss was suddenly swept away, replaced by a surge of irrepressible rage. Blood flooded into Rick's head, his heart racing as he dove toward the metal door. He tugged the handle repeatedly, the door clanging as the lock held firm.

"You lowlife bastard!" he screamed through the glass. "I'll kill you!"

Billy had struggled to his feet, assisting Caleb as they battled to bring Rick under control. "Easy now," Billy whispered. "Easy."

"How do you know?" Rick grunted frantically through gritted teeth. "Did he confess?"

"Not yet," Caleb said. "But we have some pretty convincing evidence that places him at the scene. Even Maggie says it was him."

"You're sure?"

"Yep."

With a final burst of adrenaline, Rick pounded his fist twice against the metal door. His pained eyes took one final look through the window, Draper Townsend branding him with a venomous smirk destined to forever persecute his mind.

CHAPTER 41

A MANDA WESTIN COBB SWEPT HER tongue beneath her upper lip to ensure no lipstick would smear her teeth, a longtime ritual she had performed since she first broke into broadcasting. When Thomas gave her the signal, she instinctively pushed her customary avalanche of personal issues into the recesses of her brain, offering viewers the bright, carefree smile they had trusted for decades.

"This is Amanda Westin Cobb reporting from Central Montana, where wildlife advocates and cattlemen are squaring off in a heated debate over the revered Yellowstone buffalo," she said with seasoned intonation. "Eyewitness News Denver has exclusively learned from an unidentified source that several head of cattle north of the park have tested positive for brucellosis, a virus that is transmitted by bison and causes cows to abort their fetuses. The crisis threatens to place the entire state on quarantine status, meaning none of Montana's two million cattle will be allowed to ship across state lines without costly vaccinations and testing.

"The disruption couldn't have come at a worse time for the state's beef producers, who are preparing their herds for auction. And, for consumers nationwide, it appears that beef prices may soon be on the rise."

As Amanda spoke, protesters gathered behind her, carrying signs and chanting their familiar anthem. *"Stop the flood of bison blood! Save the buffalo!"*

Amanda glanced over her shoulder, brushed a wisp of wind-blown hair from her forehead, and elevated her voice. "The discovery of infected bison has done little to dampen the fervor of these demonstrators, who have been in Montana for several days to protest the slaughter of buffalo that wander out of Yellowstone Park and onto private land."

"Stop the flood of bison blood! Save the buffalo!"

Amanda now had to shout. "This crippling blow to the state beef industry likely will only intensify the war of words between cattlemen and bison advocates. Eyewitness News will continue to bring you developments as they occur."

As Thomas lowered his camera, Amanda dropped her microphone to her side and began walking toward their news van. "That ought to keep Harvey happy for a while," she grumbled, alluding to her station manager. "He wanted a national story, and he's got one."

"Right," Thomas muttered flatly.

Amanda furrowed her brow. "Now what's your problem? We're about to send him an exclusive."

"Terrific. An *exclusive*."

Amanda stopped and glared at Thomas. "That's right."

Thomas drew a deep sigh. "It's an exclusive, but is it true?"

"Of course it's true!"

"Really? So who is your *unidentified* source?"

"You don't need to worry about that."

"Right," Thomas grumbled. "I just need to hold the camera."

"And drive the van," Amanda snapped as she jumped into the passenger side and slammed the door.

"Jack, where are you?" Tamara Kelly shouted from the kitchen.

"I'll be there in a minute," came a muffled response. Tamara followed the voice into the garage, where she found Jack wearing a faded New York Giants sweatshirt to go with paisley pajama bottoms—his traditional outfit for Monday Night Football.

"What have you been doing?" she asked as she watched him angrily rummage through a stack of cardboard boxes. "You're not even dressed yet?"

"Do you know where the VCR is?"

"VCR? I didn't even know we still had a VCR. Who the hell still uses a VCR?"

"The General Store down in Cottonwood, that's who. I called and asked to check out their surveillance tape from last Friday, and they told me no problem—except it's a VHS."

Tamara raised her eyebrows. "At least they let you have the tape. I mean, it's not like you're *official* law enforcement."

Jack threw a penetrating glare at Tamara, her comment making a direct hit. She would throw that zinger at him from time to time, reminding him that he had voluntarily surrendered his badge—albeit far earlier than he'd wanted to. She saw it as a brand of tough love, done for his well-being, although he knew deep down that she was terrified of him ever returning to any form of police work.

Jack dragged his eyes away from her, biting hard on his bottom lip as he opened a new cardboard box.

"Why are you doing this?" Tamara asked. "You're retired, remember?"

"I've doing this for Rick."

"You sure about that?"

"Yeah, I'm sure."

"What do you expect to find?"

Jack tossed aside the box he was holding, placed his hands on his hips, and perused an array of containers around him. "I solved a lot of cases by reviewing surveillance tape," he said. "Just about anyone who comes through the valley stops at that general store, whether it's for gas or whatever. There's a chance Chloe might have been there. Or, maybe someone else."

"Did anyone actually see Chloe there?"

"No one remembered seeing her. But maybe she pumped gas and didn't come inside."

Jack reached into an open box and began yanking on an electrical cord. A dust-covered VCR emerged from a jumble of videotapes, some of them clattering onto the garage floor. "Here we are!" he said, staring at it as though he were admiring a trophy trout. "I hope it works."

CHAPTER 42

R ICK STARED THROUGH LIFELESS EYES across the steering wheel of his truck, scanning the confused clutter of advertisements littering the front window of Horseshoe Liquor and Lounge. Whether it was the Montana State Lottery, Skoal chewing tobacco, Budweiser, or Black Velvet, the small establishment boasted a limitless array of products to satiate any urge, indulge any pleasure, or bandage any pain.

At one point, Rick's drink of choice had been a simple ice-cold beer, perhaps even a Heineken or Becks once his pockets had grown deep. Toward the end, when he no longer had a choice, he would drink straight vodka, the brand being of little consequence.

Eager patrons filed in and out of the store, many appearing to be on their way home from work. He tugged the front of his Stetson lower on his head, tears of gloom beginning to blur his vision as he considered his initial encounter with Draper Townsend, the standoff that happened down at The Pines. Rick should have immediately contacted the sheriff's office, reported the threat, and protected his daughter. Instead, pride had told him that his barroom bravado would have bulled Draper into standing down.

The fact that Caleb Tidwell had delivered a murder suspect—a remarkable reversal for a sheriff who'd suspected Chloe took her own life—did little to soothe matters. Rick's final verdict was that his daughter was dead, forever gone, and his chest would be eternally crushed beneath a weighty burden of blame. *You failed to protect her.*

Rick glanced at his truck's console, where his one-ton Blackberry rested next to his wallet. He had been taught in his recovery that a man in crisis should pick up that phone, no matter how heavy it was, and seek a lifeline from another alcoholic who might listen and help. The Big Book echoed in his mind: *"The alcoholic at certain times has no effective mental defense against the first drink."* An icy chill rippled down the center of his spine. It had always been some other guy on the phone who was in trouble—never him.

Rick reached toward the phone, then pulled back, returning his eyes to the storefront window. An ad for Tanqueray gin drew his attention. He drank gin and tonics once, before the paralyzing hangovers got to him. Maybe now, these many years later, things would be different.

He closed his eyes, clenching his teeth as he felt warm tears tumble onto his cheeks. From the depths of his despair, he thought of Chloe and how she would loathe seeing him like this. There also was Abby. He needed to take care of Abby. He clutched these thoughts as though gripping a rope leading from a dark, viper-infested pit.

Reaching for his phone, he scrolled through his contacts and punched Charlie Duchesne's number. Three rings took forever.

"Rick?" Charlie answered, slightly out of breath. "How you doing?"

"Not good."

"What's going on?"

"I'm coming up with some bad ideas. Real bad ideas."

Charlie seemed to understand the code. "Where are you?"

"Sitting in front of Horseshoe Liquor."

"Stay where you are. I'll be right over, okay?"

No answer.

Rick's shoulders curled forward as he slumped in a booth at the Forty-Niner, the nearby diner where Charlie insisted they go to talk. Though Charlie was a longtime trusted friend, Rick found himself flushed with embarrassment, the ability to ask others for help not among his more salient skills.

"I probably shouldn't have bothered you, Charlie. I overreacted."

"That right?" Charlie said, lifting his eyebrows.

Rick forced a faint smile. Whether you were an alcoholic or compulsive gambler, the lies you told yourself were all the same. He stared at the grounds floating on the surface of his coffee, as though the ceramic cup held some deep, penetrating truth. "I should have done more," he finally mumbled, the sound of his own words blowing a gale of emptiness through his chest.

"What exactly do you think you could have done?"

"I should have protected her."

Charlie furrowed his brow. "Protected Chloe? How?"

Rick didn't answer.

"You ever hear of the difference between guilt and regret?" Charlie asked. Rick looked away from the table with disinterest, but Charlie proceeded anyway. "You feel guilt when you intentionally— that's *intentionally*—do something to cause another person harm or pain. Regret is when you wish you somehow acted differently, that you could have done something to change an outcome. You may have *regrets*, Rick, but you shouldn't feel any guilt."

"I should have done more."

"You're not responsible for your daughter's death."

Rick lifted his coffee, but put it back down. "The guy threatened me, and he threatened my family."

Charlie leaned forward, his face tightening into a frown. "What guy? You mean, Draper?"

Rick nodded.

Charlie shook his head. "Is that what this is about?"

"Draper Townsend hated my guts," Rick said, staring at his coffee. "He didn't like me before his sister died in the accident, and he sure didn't like me after. I should have seen this coming."

"Seen what coming?"

Rick raised his eyes and squinted with disbelief. "The guy *killed* my daughter."

Charlie scanned the restaurant and blew out a breath. "Yeah . . . Right."

Rick cocked his head as he felt warmth rush to his face. "I just came from the jail, Charlie," he said, his voice growing intense. "They arrested the bastard this morning. His wife is willing to testify, and Jack Kelly may have spotted him near the scene. They said they have other evidence."

"Yeah, I've seen their *evidence*."

Rick's eyes widened. "Well, what is it?"

"A glove," Charlie said with a long sigh. "They gave me a work glove. Caleb said it belonged to Draper and was found beneath the Sawtooth, near the spot where Jack saw Chloe."

Rick frowned. "You don't believe him?"

Charlie took a sip of coffee. "The problem I have is that Jack Kelly didn't see a glove, Billy Renfro didn't see a glove, I didn't see a glove, then all of a sudden there's a glove."

Rick felt his heart begin to race, as though he was the foil in a cruel scheme of deception. "You don't think Draper did it?"

"I removed fingerprints from Chloe's SUV and sent them to the crime lab," Charlie said. "No matches for Draper." He took another sip of coffee, brushing away dribble with the back of his sleeve. "Billy managed to pry a bullet out of the dashboard of your truck. We found prints on it. I don't know whose prints they are, but they ain't Draper's."

"How about DNA?"

"I'm working on it."

"There has to be his DNA," Rick said, his voice quickening into a panic. "You said there was sex. He probably . . . *assaulted* her."

"The folks in Missoula promised me they'd fast-track the DNA," Charlie said firmly, "but my gut tells me there won't be a match for Draper. And, as I told you before, I'm fairly sure Chloe hadn't been raped."

"What makes you so sure?"

"There weren't any bruises on her wrists, her arms . . . her neck," he said. "I just didn't see what I normally see when there's a violent sexual assault."

Rick's fist slammed onto the table, causing cups and saucers to clatter. He lurched forward, tightening his jaw. "Then, what the hell happened, Charlie?" he hissed through clenched teeth. "You're basing this all on your *gut*?"

Charlie drew a breath and looked at the lunch counter, where a man in a ball cap and overgrown moustache had stopped eating and turned toward them. Charlie's glare sent him back to his own business.

"Easy," the coroner said as he turned back toward his friend. "I haven't finished my investigation. It's just that I've been doing this a long, long time, and I have my doubts that Draper Townsend was involved."

Rick placed his elbows on the table, rubbing his temples. "The guy hated me, Charlie."

"I get that," Charlie said. He took a long drink of coffee and pushed the cup toward the edge of the table. "I just don't like the narrative."

"What narrative?"

"The story. I mean, Draper Townsend is going to kill Chloe—why would go all the way up to the Sawtooth?"

"Maybe he followed her there."

"Let's say he did," Charlie said with shrug. "Then what? He just so happens to bring along his camping gear? He commits a murder, then he pitches a tent a few miles from the scene? Even Draper ain't that stupid."

A waitress appeared at the table with a full pot of coffee. Charlie nodded at her as she filled his cup, then he pulled his saucer closer. Rick shook his head to decline.

"Draper Townsend is an ugly, angry, vicious man," Charlie continued as he stirred sugar into his coffee. "He surely would have—forgive me for being indelicate—he would have raped Chloe, shot her numerous times, perhaps bludgeoned her. If he wanted to somehow stage a suicide, he would have just . . . thrown her off the cliff." Charlie sipped his coffee, scowled at it with disappointment, then added more sugar. "Besides . . . Draper Townsend has been out of prison plenty of times over the past thirty years. If he wanted revenge, wouldn't he have already gotten it by now?"

Rick shut his eyes tightly, his heart suddenly thick with grief. He balled his fists, praying to awaken from his nightmare. His eyelids opened to find Charlie still there.

"What do you think happened?"

"Well, I don't think she jumped. And I don't think she slipped. Fact is, I don't think she went off that cliff at all."

Rick swallowed hard. "What then?"

Charlie interlocked his fingers, stared out the window, and pushed a deep breath into the side of his mouth. "I believe she died at the top of the Sawtooth. Her boots were up there, and I found several drops of blood."

The word *blood* jolted Rick. Emotion rose from his chest, trying to claw its way into his eyes. "How *did* she die?" he forced from his mouth.

"She either fell onto the ground, or someone struck her. She was hit once, probably twice. But it all happened up on top."

"How do you know?"

"Her injuries," Charlie said with a shrug. "Her internal and external injuries just weren't consistent with a fall from that height."

Rick stared at the table in front of them, a sudden coldness scaling his neck. The arrest of Draper Townsend as a murder suspect, as horrid as it was to accept, had at least opened a small window to closure. The window was rapidly slamming shut.

"So how did she get down below?"

"That's the thing," Charlie said. "When I examined Chloe, I found that not only was the occipital bone at the back of her skull fractured but also the temporal bone above the ear. I expected it to be one or the other."

Rick shook his head, confused.

"If it was a suicide," Charlie explained, "you would assume that the deceased died from blunt-force trauma when her head struck an object on the forest floor below the Sawtooth. If that were the case, then either the occipital bone or temporal bone would be fractured, having struck the object—let's say a rock. But it is unlikely that it would be both—unless, of course, the skull was crushed, which it wasn't."

Rick's felt nauseated. Cold sweat gathered on his forehead. "So, both bones being broken means what?"

"If two bones were broken, that means the skull suffered blunt-force trauma two different times. But that couldn't happen if the deceased only hit the ground once. There also was no indication from her injuries that she hit the side of the cliff."

Rick studied his empty cup. He leaned forward and focused his eyes intently at Charlie.

"So, what you're saying is, Chloe was *struck*—at the top of the Sawtooth, then someone *carried* her down below to make it look like a suicide?"

Charlie nodded. "That's what the evidence tells me."

Rick glanced away for a beat. "And you're convinced it wasn't Draper Townsend?"

"We both know I wasn't a very successful gambler," Charlie shrugged. "But Draper? I wouldn't bet on it."

In the wake of Rick's dance with his demons at Horseshoe Liquor, Charlie had suggested they go to an AA meeting. Rick politely declined, opting to get in his truck and drive the streets of Riverton, his mind hurled into chaos by the theory the coroner had presented.

As he turned onto Highway 89 and headed into the valley, he hit a sudden slowdown, the bison advocates out in force once again. He glared at them as he crept by, reading their placards while their loud chants streamed through the bullet-shattered windows of his truck.

"Stop the flood of bison blood. Save the buffalo!"

He hit his horn repeatedly, flashing his brights and pumping his brakes as his truck lurched forward. He glanced at the Winchester lying among broken glass behind his seat, wondering whether he might need to use it again.

"Stop the flood of bison blood. Save the buffalo!"

Rick's thoughts turned to Chloe, which brought a plaintive smile to appear on his face. If she were alive, she would have been right there with the protesters. Being the Buffalo Gal—the most outspoken voice in the valley when it came to the bison controversy—she perhaps would have even been *leading* them.

Rick slammed on his brakes, staring blankly at the dash of his truck. A chilling thought rewound and played again. *She would have been leading them.*

He inched forward impatiently, willing his way past the final few protesters. With an open Highway 89 in front of him, he punched his accelerator, speeding toward Sage's house.

"Do you have your laptop handy?" Rick asked Sage as he burst through her front door.

She was standing at the stove, stirring a pot of what smelled like chili. "Hi Pa-Pa," Abby said from the living room sofa, where she was reading a book. She didn't look up.

"I need to use your laptop," Rick repeated.

Sage's eyebrows furrowed briefly. She nodded calmly. "Okay. I put it away, but I'll go grab it."

Abby turned from her book toward her grandfather. "Can I use the computer when you're done, Pa-Pa?" she asked. Rick recalled his earlier decree to Sage that Abby be kept off the Internet.

"We'll see."

Sage emerged from the hallway, booting up the laptop as she walked. "What's going on?"

Rick took the computer from her and sat down at the kitchen table. He waved his hand in a circular motion, urging the MSN home screen to appear. He typed rapidly, feeling a comforting warmth as Sage positioned herself over his shoulder and rested her arm on the back of his chair. The home page of a website appeared, Chloe's face prominently displayed in a banner across the top. A rush of penetrating sadness stampeded through his chest, but he managed to fight it off.

"The Buffalo Gal," Sage said quietly, her voice thick with lament.

Rick scrolled down the page, then back up again. He nodded, his theory proven correct. "Look at her web page. There's not one thing on here about protests in the valley. She posted last Thursday, but she's spewing some statistics about bison in Colorado. Absolutely *nothing* about anything going on here."

Rick turned toward Sage. "If there were protesters coming to Montana, wouldn't Chloe have at least *known* about them?"

Sage moved closer to the screen, her hair falling onto Rick's shoulder, the scent of her skin filling his senses. "You're right," she said, looking into his eyes. "But what do you think it means?"

Rick shook his head. "I don't know what it means. It just doesn't make sense, that's all. She knew everything—I mean, *everything*—that was going on with those animals."

Abby appeared at the kitchen table, leaning on Sage's hip as she stared at her mother's face on the computer screen. "If Mommy's not here, who is going to take care of the buffalo?"

Rick glanced at Sage, who tugged Abby closer to her. "Your mommy sure did take good care of those buffalo, didn't she?"

Abby nodded. There was a long silence.

"Pa-Pa? Where am I going to live?"

Rick drew air into his lungs. He closed the laptop, stealing a moment to gather himself, his chest aching with sorrow for his granddaughter. He reached for Abby's hand and pulled her toward him. She slid off Sage's hip and tucked herself beneath his arm. "You're going to live with me. You know, out at the ranch."

Abby pushed her head against his ribs. "Am I going to go to the same school?"

Rick nodded and smiled. "Sure, you can go to the same school."

"Can we stay here with Sage?"

Rick shot a quick glance toward Sage, feeling a flush flow into his face. "This is Sage's house," he said awkwardly. "We have our own house."

Sage stroked the back of Abby's hair, her other hand gently touching Rick's shoulder. "You both can stay as long as you like."

Rick looked at her, his face finding a smile. Sage looked back at him, the intimate, soothing solace of her eyes making the long journey into his heart.

CHAPTER 43

COURTNEY WILLIAMS SNAPPED AWAKE TO the latest chapter of her living nightmare, the putrid meth-and-Marlboro breath of comatose Chase Rettick assaulting her nostrils. Something told her it was Tuesday, but she couldn't be sure.

As she stared at the hopeless addict through the predawn darkness, his colorless, unshaven face flecked with pinprick sores, she was overcome with an unforeseen interlude of lucidity, her brain instructing her in unambiguous terms that she had finally and firmly arrived at rock bottom—and it was time to stop digging.

She rose quietly from the sweat-soaked sheets, her eyes fixed on Chase as she felt her way along the hollow bedroom wall of the double-wide. Her hand swept onto the floor, where she snagged her blouse and jeans. She slipped into the bathroom. A sudden rush of nausea sent her crumbling to her knees, small slices of shattered mirror grinding into her tightened skin. Leaning over the toilet bowl, she could only force a couple of hollow wretches, her stomach as empty as her soul. She rolled over and leaned against the wall, waiting for chilled sweats to pass as she prayed—*begged*—that her dizziness might be caused by drug use rather than pregnancy.

Her mind turned to her father, the heart-shattered reverend, forced to preach to his flock each Sunday while his most precious lamb had been lost. She wondered how she could ever return to him and her mother, how she could ever heal wounds seemingly beyond suture and running so unfathomably deep.

Chase's thick breathing continued from the bedroom. Courtney clutched the bathroom sink and rose to her feet, turning on the faucet so he wouldn't hear her getting dressed. She pulled her unwashed blouse over her head and slipped into her jeans, jamming her hand into her right pocket to feel for her car keys.

She turned off the water and listened. *A sound?* Her heart thumped. Movement in the bedroom. She froze, breathless, and waited. Finally, a deathly cough rattled from Chase's charred throat, succeeded by an extended groan. He mumbled something unintelligible and peacefully returned to oblivion.

Courtney exhaled. She slid through the bathroom door, using the carpet to brush fragments of glass off her feet. Guided by a lonely beam of moonlight filtering through the kitchen window, she felt her way down the hallway.

Chase's backpack rested on the kitchen table. She snared it and threw it over her shoulder. The front door creaked as she pushed it open, straining on its rusted spring. She pressed her eyes closed, stood quietly, and listened. Releasing a deep breath, she passed through the screen door, holding it tightly so it wouldn't slam shut.

Frost covered the metal porch steps, stinging her bleeding feet, but she edged forward across the frozen dirt, her keys now balled in her hand. "Please, God, please," she whispered aloud as she slid into her Toyota and tossed Chase's backpack on the passenger seat. Her words brought shame, her neglect of God slapping her as coldly as the morning air. "Please, God," she persisted.

Her teeth chattered as her trembling hand struggled to put the key in the ignition. She stared through the frosted cracked windshield of her once beautiful car. "Please, God, please."

She turned the key. *Nothing.* She slapped the steering wheel. "No!" she muttered. Another try. The ignition clicked, then tried to find life. Courtney pumped the accelerator furiously, but the car wouldn't turn over. She squinted at the dash—the gas gauge was on empty. Short bursts of frozen air streamed from her mouth as she tried the key again.

She stopped. A light went on in the bedroom of the trailer. She saw the torn curtain move, followed by the thud of Chase's fist pounding the wall.

"Oh God!" she shouted inside the car, tears of terror forming in her widened eyes. She turned the key again. After a brief grinding sound, the engine gasped, then whirred alive. Her hand trembling mercilessly, Courtney managed to shift into Reverse. Chase burst from the front door, clutching a lead pipe, a weapon he had kept handy since Rick Morrand's unscheduled visit.

"You bitch! Get your ass back here!"

Dogs started barking. Courtney pushed down on the lock of her door and put the car in Drive. The engine hesitated briefly, threatening to stall. *"God, please!"* The car lurched forward.

Chase drew closer, his dark satanic eyes shooting tremors of terror through her body. As Courtney's tires spun on the frozen ground, he reared back, preparing to deliver a blow to her window. She closed her eyes, preparing for impact. Miraculously, the car thrust forward, causing Chase to miss the mark, the pipe shattering the rear passenger window. "You bitch!" Chase shouted again as Courtney sped away.

She took one final look in the rearview mirror, her vision clouded by tears of joy and sadness as she watched Chase kneeling in defeat, lead pipe at his side. She turned in the direction of her parents' house, which was only fifteen minutes and a world and eternity away.

She would beg for forgiveness—from her parents, from God, from anyone who would listen. No one wanted to end up like Chloe Morrand.

Rick stoked a morning fire, sipping coffee as he watched the dancing flames. His back felt stiff after another night on Sage's couch, reminding him that it would soon be time to head back to the ranch, where he and Abby would commence their uncharted life beyond Chloe. The thought carried grief, fear, and a sudden lonely gloom as he wondered how he was going to raise a second child when he'd hardly done an admirable job with the first.

"You ready for some breakfast?" Sage called from the kitchen.

"In a bit," Rick muttered over his shoulder. "I'm good with coffee for now."

Sage held a mug of coffee as she walked into the living room, her eyes fixed on a copy of the *Riverton Herald*. "I see that they arrested Draper Townsend. You didn't say a word about it last night."

Rick shrugged. "Nothing much to say."

"This article claims they have some pretty convincing evidence."

"Not according to Charlie Duchesne."

Sage raised her eyebrows and creased her lips, but she didn't speak. Rick winced as he rose from his crouch and rested the iron poker against the stone fireplace. He sat down in a rocker, Sage's dog, Bear, sidling up next to him, welcoming some morning affection.

"Charlie's still waiting for some forensics, but he has his doubts," Rick said with a heavy sigh. "Myself, I thought Draper was a pretty good candidate."

Sage sat on the couch, laying the morning paper on the coffee table. She took a sip of coffee, then leaned forward as she cradled the mug in her hand. "What is it with you and Draper Townsend? Why does he hate you so much?"

"The accident."

"But the accident was just that—an *accident*," she said, shaking her head. "I remember when it happened. The homecoming dance, wasn't it? There was freezing rain. The roads were icy. It wasn't your fault."

Rick swallowed hard. "That's not necessarily true."

"What do you mean?"

Rick looked into Sage's eyes, then turned away. His chest grew tight as he considered just how complete of a confession he was prepared to make. He stopped rocking in the chair, leaning forward as he rested his elbows on his denim-covered knees.

"I was drinking that night. I don't know if I was necessarily drunk, but I probably shouldn't have been driving."

Sage frowned. "There was never any mention of drinking at the time."

"There were empties in the backseat, but Billy Renfro chose to ignore them," Rick said, lifting his eyebrows. "Billy knew my dad, and he also knew I had a scholarship. I guess he made a judgment call, figuring alcohol wasn't the cause. It was the eighties—nobody made a big deal about drunk driving back then."

Sage fell silent, staring into her coffee. Rick took a deep breath and bit the inside of his lip. "I shouldn't have even been with Julianne Thompson that night. I asked her to the dance at the last minute."

"Who were you supposed to go with?"

"Mandy Westerfield," Rick murmured, turning his eyes toward the fire. "We broke up out of nowhere. I'm not even sure why." He shook his head. "That was the week after I missed the field goal against Bozeman High—would have been a huge upset. Maybe that was it."

"She dumped you over a missed field goal?"

Rick shrugged. "Who knows? Right after that, she disappeared. Left the school and everything."

"Right," Sage huffed with a roll of her eyes. "Now I remember. Good old Mandy. You took that pretty hard."

"Yeah, I did," Rick said haltingly. He drew a breath. "But then Julianne came along. I guess she had a thing for me."

"A lot of girls had a thing for you," Sage said, her eyes filling with an odd mischief as her smile welcomed him in. Rick felt a rush of warmth flow into his face. They held an uncertain gaze before he turned back toward the fire.

"I should have just left Julianne alone. I was selfish."

Sage sipped her coffee. "How did you ever get over it—you know, the accident?"

"I drank a lot."

"Does anybody else know about this besides Billy?"

Rick forced a smile. "You do. And, of course, Charlie."

"How does Charlie know?"

"I told him during my Fifth Step."

Sage's eyes furrowed. "Fifth Step—that an AA thing?"

Rick chuckled. "Yeah, it's an AA thing."

Sage brushed hair off the side of her face, more out of habit than function. "So, why does Charlie have his doubts about Draper?"

"He said it was pretty much a gut feeling. He just doesn't think Draper did it."

Sage put her coffee mug on the table and interlocked her fingers. "I guess you must really trust Charlie."

Rick nodded slowly. He stared wistfully into Sage's tranquil loyal eyes, his damaged heart an unstable listing vessel in desperate search of safe harbor. "Yeah, I trust Charlie—just like I trust *you*."

Sage tried to hide her blush. She fumbled with the diamond-studded wedding band she often wore on her right hand, a remembrance from one of her marriages. The ring not only had understated elegance but also utility, since Sage would shift it to her left hand when she believed a customer at The Spur was hitting on her. She had a habit of tugging the ring when she was nervous, seemingly unsure whether it belonged on her finger or not.

Her face broke into a shy smile that had spent a lifetime begging for honesty, faithfulness, and hope. As she placed her soft hand into his, Rick stared into her eyes, his heart telling him to pull her closer. Perhaps her warmth could somehow assuage the penetrating ache he felt over the loss of his daughter, if even just for a moment. He gently caressed her fingers, her soothing gaze enveloping him with temptation. Suddenly, strangely, he resisted.

Abby's feet pattered down the hall. Rick gently released Sage's hand.

"I'm *so* hungry!" Abby said.

When Tamara Kelly had arranged for the purchase of a Sony sixty-five-inch plasma flat-screen TV, her stated intent was for her husband to enjoy endless hours of football. Considering Jack had pointed himself toward a restful retirement, she likely never bargained that he would use the gift to watch surveillance tapes playing on an ancient rickety VCR.

"Did you ever come to bed?" his wife asked. He glanced away from the grainy screen in front of him, watching his wife's eyebrows tighten as she forcefully tied the bow of her white silk robe. He normally liked seeing her in the morning, before makeup, when he could drink in her natural features. Ten years his junior, she had maintained her youthful, shapely figure, and her allure was only enhanced by her robe. She did have a point—he *should* have come to bed. Without speaking, he looked back at the screen.

"Jack!" she repeated, her voice loud and sharp. "Did you even watch the game last night? Have you had any sleep?"

"Give me a second, honey," he replied, disregarding her tone. He had the VCR remote suspended in the air, his forefinger volleying between Forward and Reverse. "I think I'm getting close to something here."

Jack rose from the couch and moved closer, his eyes glued to the TV. He brushed aside a few magazines on the coffee table, providing him with a front-row seat. Tamara eased closer to him, placing her hands on her hips as she watched over his shoulder.

"Check this out. I've gone through a full day of tapes from The General Store, all kinds of different angles. Most of the cars stopping for gas have license plates from Montana, Wyoming, or Idaho, maybe one or two from Utah. Tourist season is pretty much over. These people are locals, or maybe just passing through."

Jack rewound the tape and hit Play. "Look at this guy from California. Watch the way he's looking around. Kind of seems on edge, doesn't he?"

Tamara drew a deep sigh. "O-kay," she said, her voice lacking commitment.

Jack stared at the tape. After inserting the nozzle into his gas tank, the man began rummaging through the bed of his truck, as though he was searching for something in a duffel bag. He emerged with two boxes of ammunition, which he placed on top of a backpack resting on the passenger seat—next to what appeared to be a hunting rifle.

Tamara shifted impatiently, folding her arms across her chest. "So he's a hunter—what a coincidence. It just so happens it's hunting season."

Jack glanced over his shoulder, hit Pause, then clicked the tape forward a couple of frames. "He's loading the rifle," he said, pointing at the screen. "Any experienced hunter knows you don't load your rifle until you're in the field. This guy doesn't look like he's going hunting—he's acting more like he's going to war." Jack shook his head and pressed his lips. "There's just something about him I don't like."

"Well, there's something about your retirement that I don't like," Tamara said brusquely. "You're not acting very *retired*."

Jack ignored her, reaching for a pencil and pad of paper on the coffee table. Dropping to one knee, he leaned forward so his face was inches from the screen. He began jotting down the license number. "I can't tell if that's a five or an eight," he mumbled. He looked toward Tamara for assistance. She didn't budge. He sighed with exasperation.

"Honey, I'm trying to help Rick. The deputy told me there's was a guy in California—an ex-client of Rick's—who might have had it in for him. I still have some contacts—I'll have someone run the plate and see what turns up."

"Seems like a reach to me."

"Maybe," Jack replied. "That's why it's called an investigation."

"But it's not *your* investigation."

Tamara sat down on the front edge of a chair next to the coffee table, calmly straightened her robe, and placed her folded hands in her lap. "Let's say you do find something," she said in a measured tone. "What happens if people around here start making some calls, looking into *your* background? You know . . . back in Jersey?"

Jack's jaw tightened, a stern expression spreading across his face. "So what if they do? I have nothing to hide."

Tamara took a deep breath. "You didn't exactly go out on your own terms."

"Are we going to go through this again?" Jack snapped, tossing the paper and pencil onto the coffee table.

Tamara remained calm. Despite Jack's immense size, he knew she didn't fear him. She considered him a kind and gentle man, regardless of how Newark's Internal Affairs may have characterized him. She placed a hand on his large, solid bicep.

"Baby, I'm not the enemy," she said, her warm hazel eyes pleading with him. "Trust me—I'm on your side. It's that, well, I thought we left all of this behind us. That was the whole idea of moving out here, wasn't it?"

Jack bowed his head, exhaling as he pulled Tamara toward him. "Like it or not, I'm the guy who found Chloe. Rick Morrand is my friend. Tomorrow night, he'll be having a vigil for his daughter, and on Thursday morning he will bury her. Don't you think he deserves to know what happened?"

Jack hesitated, swallowing hard as moisture gathered in his eyes. "If anyone can understand that," he said, his voice filling with emotion, "it would be us."

"I'd like to speak to Matt Steelman."

Billy Renfro was driving south on Highway 89, bound for Yellowstone Park and thinking about sex. Not sex in his own regard, of course, because, despite the image he sought to project, he hadn't been with a woman in the biblical sense since Melba passed those many years ago. There had been a little necking here and there, even once with Helen, but not much else.

No, Billy was more interested in the person who had sex with Chloe Morrand. Before Sheriff Tidwell asked his deputy to assist in the unexpected arrest of Draper Townsend, Billy had Matt Steelman squarely on his radar. There were indications, primarily from Rick Morrand, that Chloe and her boss may have had more than a simple workplace relationship. In light of there being no conclusive forensics, and Draper currently doing more spitting than talking, Billy saw fit to continue his due diligence.

"I'm sorry, he's not in today," said a woman who had identified herself as Gwen. "Can someone else help you?"

"This is Deputy Billy Renfro from the Dexter County Sheriff's Office. Is it Mr. Steelman's day off?"

"No sir."

"Did he work yesterday?"

"No sir."

"Is he sick?"

"No sir."

"Well, what then?"

"He's taking a couple of personal days."

Billy looked into his rearview mirror so he could watch himself roll his eyes. "*Personal* days," he repeated with thinly veiled contempt. "Do you have a home address?"

Gwen hesitated. "Actually, I . . ." she said nervously. "I'm not sure I can—"

"Of course you can," Billy said. He looked at his watch. "I can come down there, show you my badge, if you prefer."

"Just . . . just a moment please, sir," Gwen said as she put Billy on hold. A full minute later, she got back on the line.

"Is this your cell phone, Deputy Renfro?" Gwen asked.

"It is."

"I'll text it to you."

"Much appreciated."

Billy stuffed his phone into his shirt pocket, curious who Gwen was and why she seemed on edge. The thought drifted from his mind as he felt a vibration in his chest pocket. He glanced at the text. Matt lived on the north side of Gardiner, meaning Billy was just minutes away.

His radio crackled. "Two, Seven-Four-Zero," Helen's voice said. "Billy, are you there?"

"Seven-Four-Zero, Two. Go ahead, Helen."

"Has Caleb been in touch with you yet? He said he wants a deputy here at the office while he keeps those protesters in check, and he wanted me to track you down."

"I'm down near Gardiner, following up on a lead in the Chloe Morrand investigation—just as I said I was going to do."

"That's what I told him, but he didn't seem to like that answer. In fact, he got pretty angry. He's convinced that Draper Townsend committed that crime."

Billy bit the side of his lip and shook his head. "We don't know that for sure just yet. We're still waiting on forensics. Until that happens, we need to—"

Billy slammed on his brakes as he skidded past Rams Horn Drive, the road that led toward Matt Steelman's cabin. He threw his SUV into Reverse, then fishtailed onto loose gravel. "I'm trying to complete my investigation."

"Sheriff's acting like it's a done deal," Helen persisted. "He said we need to focus on these protesters. He figures the whole Chloe Morrand case is a distraction—it's only going to bring the valley unneeded attention."

Blood rushed to Billy's temples. He closed his eyes with agitation as he considered Caleb's latest demonstration of incompetence. "Distraction or not, we need to complete the investigation. I won't be gone long."

Billy accelerated, leaving a trail of dust behind him. There were only two cabins he knew of off Rams Horn Drive, and one of them belonged to Drake Billings. The other was several miles farther. It was a summer rental, Billy recalled, so Matt Steelman must have leased it long-term.

As he rambled down the gravel road, Billy's thoughts drifted to Caleb—more specifically the sheriff's peculiar eagerness to pin a murder rap on Draper Townsend. Even though Billy fully endorsed the notion of sending Draper away for good, he was suspicious of Caleb's haste in rushing through what was becoming an untidy investigation.

After navigating a few miles of dense forest, Billy pulled to a stop in front of a modest cedar-sided cabin. As he approached the covered porch, he double-checked the house number on his phone. He spotted two vehicles, one of them with plates from Utah. The curtains on the windows were drawn, but a light was on inside. Resting his right hand gently on the grip of his firearm, Billy rapped his knuckles on the wooden door.

He was surprised to see a woman open it.

He glanced again at the number beside the front door. "Good afternoon, ma'am," he said, removing his hat and stroking his hair. "I'm Deputy Billy Renfro from the Dexter County Sheriff's Office. Perhaps I have the wrong place—I was looking for a Matthew Steelman?"

The woman wore a long flowered dress buttoned up to her neckline. She offered a polite, innocent smile. "Oh no, Deputy, you have the right place. Matthew was taking a shower. Let me—"

A man appeared behind her, his hair dripping wet. After zipping his jeans, he nervously began buttoning a shirt as rivulets of water streamed down from the base of his neck. Billy noticed a tattoo on the upper right side of his chest, a blurry lightning bolt signifying the crest of the Army Rangers. Below the tattoo, along his rib cage, there appeared to be a pair of pink-colored abrasions. The man swallowed, then manufactured a cough as he eased onto the front porch. "Can I help you, Deputy?" he asked tentatively.

Billy looked at the woman and then at Matt. "You're Matthew Steelman?"

"Yes, sir, I am."

"I'd like to ask you a few questions."

Matt turned toward the woman. "Why don't you go back inside, honey. I'll talk to the deputy out here—so we don't wake the baby."

Billy lifted his eyebrows. *Baby?*

"The baby's fine, Matthew. I think I'll stay out here."

Matt glanced at Billy, then heaved a sigh as he turned back toward the woman. "Honey, I really think you should—"

"I said no, Matt!" she snapped, her voice rising. "I think I'll stay right here."

Color crept across Matt's face. "This is my wife, Deputy. Amie Steelman."

Billy nodded. He stroked his thumb and forefinger along his lower lip, studying the couple. "I didn't realize you were married."

The woman huffed. "Neither do most of the people around here," she said, her tone as sharp as a rapier.

Billy blinked his eyes as he reached for his notepad. "Mr. Steelman, can you please tell me your whereabouts on Friday night?"

Matt began scratching the back of his neck, averting his eyes as though looking at Billy was like staring into the sun. "Is . . . this about Chloe?" he stuttered. "Did something happen to her?"

Billy measured Matt for several seconds, then cleared his throat. "I'm sorry to say that Chloe Morrand was found dead."

Matt rubbed his forehead, his hand shaking. "Dead?"

Billy cocked his head. Matt seemed surprised, but not quite surprised enough. "You hadn't heard?" Billy asked. "It's all over the news."

Matt stared at the porch floor. "I . . . *we* . . . don't have TV—or Internet," he mumbled. "W. . . What do you think happened?"

Billy stayed the course. "Can you tell me where you were Friday night?"

Matt's lips quivered as he stared into the distance. "I was here."

The deputy turned toward Amie. "Do you live here with your husband, ma'am?" he asked. He nodded toward the side of the cabin. "What I mean to say is, I noticed one of the vehicles over there has Utah plates."

Amie stared at him with cold, hard eyes. "The baby and I are visiting—for now."

Billy scribbled on his notepad. "And you arrived when?"

"Friday night."

Matt whipped his head toward her, somehow unsettled by her answer.

"I arrived Friday night," Amie repeated. "About an hour after supper time."

Billy tightened his brow as he studied her face, drawing a deep sigh. "You drove all the way up from Salt Lake?" She nodded.

"Did you stop for gas?"

"Yes."

"Use a credit card?"

"Cash."

"Do you remember the station? Or maybe what town it was in?"

Amie pursed her lips and gazed at the porch ceiling, as though in contemplation. "Somewhere in Idaho. Small town. It was an Exxon, I think. Or maybe a Phillips 66? The baby was crying. I just don't recall."

Billy nodded slowly. He looked at Matt. "Can you tell me the last time you saw Chloe Morrand, Mr. Steelman?"

Matt drew a deep breath and placed his hands on his hips. "On Friday, late afternoon," he said. "Down in Yellowstone."

"At the end of her shift?"

"More or less."

Billy tilted his head. "Can you be more specific?"

Matt flicked an uneasy glance at his wife. "We . . . *talked* . . . for a while after her shift."

Billy squared his stance and folded his arms across his chest, waiting patiently for Matt to look directly at him. As Matt slowly raised his eyes, Billy nodded toward the ranger's abdomen.

"Were those scratches I saw on the side of your body, Mr. Steelman?"

Matt's chin dipped as he swallowed slowly. "It's possible." He shrugged. "I was fishing the river. There's a lot of brush down there. It could have happened then."

"May I take a look at the scratches?"

Matt hesitated, then began slowly unbuttoning his shirt. Amie stepped in front of him, clutching his forearm. "Is my husband in some kind of trouble, Deputy?"

Billy eyed her with curiosity. He tabled her question, instead casting a nod toward Matt's torso. "I'd just like to take a look at those scratches is all."

Matt brushed her hand aside. "It's okay, Amie," he said with resignation. "I have nothing to hide."

Billy took a step closer and examined the deep abrasions, following them with his eyes as they trailed around Matt's rib cage. "Those don't look like they came from a bush, Mr. Steelman."

Amie stepped forward again. "Deputy, does Matthew need a lawyer?"

Billy sighed with exasperation, burying his thumbs in his pockets. "That's totally up to you and your husband, ma'am. I'm just asking some simple questions."

Matt lifted his chin and glared at his wife. "I don't need a damn lawyer, Amie!" He sneered. "Please go inside and let me talk to Deputy Renfro. I can clear this up right now."

Billy pressed forward, undeterred. "Those scratches look like they came more from a grizzly than a bush, Mr. Steelman. But they didn't come from a grizzly *or* a bush, now, did they?"

Matt stood silent, eyes downcast. "Did you and Miss Morrand have some kind of quarrel?"

"No. Not really."

"Not really?"

Matt bit the inside of his mouth. "We had an argument, but that's not what caused the marks."

Billy stared at his notebook, where he had underlined the word "scratches" several times. He rubbed his forehead, considering Matt's answer. "Is it fair to say you and Miss Morrand had a . . . relationship—you know, outside of work?"

Matt turned toward his wife. "Amie, please go inside," he said sternly. Amie's mouth tightened, her face growing flush.

"Answer the question, Matthew," she said through clamped teeth. "I believe I know more about Chloe Morrand than you might think."

Matt shoulders slumped. He heaved a deep breath, as if searching for the right words. "Yes," he said with an exhale, "we had a relationship."

"Was it sexual?"

Matt glanced at Amie. Her eyes desperately clawed for hope but portended heartbreak. He turned toward Billy and nodded.

"Did you have sex the time you saw Miss Morrand? Last Friday?"

Another nod, followed by silence. Amie glared at Matt. Her lips quivered as she blinked back tears, her face wavering between humiliation and fury. Life seemed to drain from her face. She drew a series of shallow breaths, as though she had confirmed something she already knew but was woefully unprepared for the words that had tumbled from her husband's mouth. Slowly turning the knob of the cabin door, she stepped inside without a sound.

Billy grimaced, his sympathies lying far more with Amie than Matt. Hard to feel sorry for a man courting another woman while his wife was with child. "I'm sorry that had to happen, Mr. Steelman," he said flatly. "I reckon you'll probably be needin' Doctor Phil."

Matt's eyes narrowed as he glared at Billy. "Do you have any other *questions*, Deputy?"

Billy glanced at his notebook. "Did you stop anywhere on the way home? You know, for groceries or anything?"

Matt paused a beat, then nodded. "I bought a fishing license at the fly shop. Then I got something to eat."

"Can you tell me the name of the fly shop?"

"Rescue Creek Outfitters," Matt said. "Only one in town."

"And you said you stopped somewhere for supper?"

"The Skillet."

"I assume you own a cell phone?" Billy asked. Matt nodded, digging into his jeans and handing his phone to Billy. The deputy scrolled to the call logs and squinted at the screen. "This 801 phone number I see—is that your wife's phone?" He turned the screen toward Matt, who shook his head.

"That's her mother's house in Salt Lake. That's where's she's been staying."

Billy scribbled on his notepad. He pointed to another entry on the screen. "This other 801 number—is that your wife's cell?" Matt nodded. Billy jotted the number down, then handed the phone back to Matt. Tilting his head to the side, Billy curled the edge of his moustache and tried to read Matt once more. "When you last saw her, what was Miss Morrand's general demeanor?"

Matt shrugged, looking at everything except the deputy. He started to fold his arms, then returned them to his side. "She seemed ... fine," he said, shaking his head rapidly. "I mean ... she was Chloe. She had her different ... *moods*."

Billy fished a toothpick out of his breast pocket, tucked away his notepad, and straightened the flap of his uniform shirt. "That's all I have—at least, for now," he said as he turned to leave the porch.

"Deputy?" Matt said, his voice unsteady. "What do you *think* happened to her?"

Billy focused his eyes intently on Matt. "We're not sure," he said, holding the toothpick an inch from his lips. "She may have harmed herself, or maybe she . . . let's just say we're not sure."

Matt stood in silence as Billy's SUV pulled away from the cabin. When he walked inside, he found Amie sitting at the kitchen table, hands folded as she stared straight ahead in catatonic stillness. Matt pulled out the chair across from her and sat down.

"I was trying to break it off," he mumbled. "That's what caused the argument."

Amie glanced at Matt and rose from the table, appearing as though the sight of her husband made her nauseated. She gazed out the wooden multipaned window, the sun casting striped shadows across her face and chest.

"Why did you *lie* to him?" Matt said in a loud whisper. "You and Aaron arrived on Saturday. Why did you lie?"

Amie glowered at her husband, her eyes wondering what made him an authority on truth-telling. She blew out a breath and folded her arms. "I told him what he needed to hear at the time."

Matt's jaw tightened. "I didn't do anything wrong," he said. Amie fired another icy glare, causing him to reconsider his words. "I mean, I didn't *harm* her."

Amie walked slowly toward him, making him uneasy as she stood behind his chair. She placed her hand on his shoulder, touching him lightly, perhaps concerned he might confuse the gesture with affection. "I know you didn't harm her, Matthew," she said in a cryptic tone. "I know."

CHAPTER 44

RICK WAS FURIOUS AT CHLOE.

His anger burst forth like a mighty untamed river surging through a fissure in a weakened, decaying dam. As he knelt before her tranquil, motionless body, staring at the rosary placed inside her milky childlike hands, he despised himself for feeling that way, and he was unnerved by how quickly his seemingly bygone emotions had returned.

It was Wednesday evening, less than a week since the last time he had seen—and argued—with his daughter. His intent was to spend a few moments in solemn prayer in front of her casket, but instead of finding peace, his mind danced with fury. The fuse of his anger ignited when his thoughts had drifted to Christine, whose vigil a few years earlier was the last one he had attended. Christine had been everything to him, and in many ways he blamed Chloe for taking her away.

It was Christine who could be unsparingly honest with Chloe, but also loving and gentle. Christine had nurtured her, clashed with her, and worried about her. She'd paced the floors at night and stared out the window for hours, wondering where Chloe might be, who she was with, whether she was safe. Rick was convinced that it was this constant mental anguish that eventually caused his wife to fall ill.

Chloe had maddened him so—the way she humiliated him, strained his marriage, and filled his life with incessant uninvited drama and pain. There were times, and plenty of them, when he'd wished she simply wasn't there. And now, she no longer was there. Chloe lay in front of him, surrounded by white billowy silk in a lavender casket, no longer a torment to anyone, least of all herself.

He begged himself to remember that this wasn't her fault. She had done no harm to herself—someone had done this *to her*. But then, if you asked Chloe, *nothing* was *ever* her fault. He felt another gush of bitterness course like poisonous venom though his veins. What made her go to the Sawtooth? Why did she go alone? How could she put herself in danger like this?

He didn't want to be here. Not in this place, not in this moment. Chloe had left him behind—not to mention Abby—and he was struggling mightily to forgive her.

As he stared at her through watery eyes, he was struck by how young she looked. Even though Clarence Avery—third-generation owner of Avery Funeral Home—was now in his seventies, he still knew how to properly present a loved one to family and friends. Clarence was an artist of sorts, possessing a unique talent of bringing out true beauty—even personality, perhaps—of the deceased. It appeared that Clarence knew Chloe well.

Rick had requested a wake—or a vigil, as everyone preferred to call it—in keeping with his Irish roots. The Morrands were Catholics, or at least Rick's mother had described them as such, even though they only attended church on Christmas and Easter. Rick's mother, the former Maureen O'Shea, would have preferred to attend Mass more often, but his father was a reluctant participant even on holidays, claiming *his* church was found at ten thousand feet while seated on the back of an Appaloosa.

To the Irish that Rick had known, the vigil was not intended to be a solemn occasion but rather a joyous one. With plenty of food and alcohol on hand, the purpose was to celebrate the life of the individual, virtually ignoring the corpse that was present and the circumstances that delivered it there.

Such a celebration had been challenging at the wake for Rick's uncle, Philip Morrand, who terminated his life with a Ruger .44 following years of sporadic depression. That gathering at the

Morrand home was one in which the pouring of alcohol far outdistanced the serving of food, and the consumption of spirits was done with great purpose. The end of the evening was abrupt, when Rick's Uncle James—younger brother of his father and Uncle Phil— was defeated by knockout in a fistfight with beloved Aunt Claire.

Rick held Chloe's wake at a funeral home, just like the one he'd arranged for Christine, and he certainly had no plans to serve alcohol. He simply wanted friends to have an opportunity to come together and remember his daughter. Any "celebration" of her life would be more daunting. After all, it was difficult to celebrate a life when no one was completely certain just how that life had ended. At this moment, sadly and painfully, Chloe Morrand's life was an unfinished song.

"You okay, hon?" a gentle voice behind him asked.

It was Sage. Before turning his head, Rick thought he recognized her perfume. He wasn't positive it was her, since the "hon" thing was new.

"I'm fine," he said, wiping the edges of his eyes with his forefinger and thumb.

"There're a lot of people coming in. You probably want to start saying hello."

Rick nodded and moved away from the casket, turning to steal one final glance at his child.

The parlor was filling up quickly. Rick felt hot, his chest suddenly heavy, and he found it difficult to breathe. He wanted to go outside, draw in some fresh evening air, but he knew that wasn't possible. He wedged two fingers beneath his buttoned collar, trying to loosen his multicolored Jerry Garcia necktie—a fashion accessory he wouldn't be caught dead wearing were it not a birthday gift from Chloe.

In front of him appeared the tanned, leathery face of Bull Redmond, the man who had lost his son, Ryder, in the not-too-distant past. Their eyes connected with a compassionate sorrow that only parents of a deceased child could understand. "I'm sorry for your loss," Bull croaked, his deep voice reflecting his own residual pain. "I am sure this can't be easy."

"No, I guess it's not, Bull," Rick answered as he felt his hand get swallowed up in Bull's massive grip. "Sorry I wasn't available to talk to you about your horse. Did you ever get anything worked out?"

"Not yet," Bull said quietly, his sad brown eyes peering out from beneath his wide-brimmed Stetson. "There was a time when I didn't want to let that horse go. Now, I can't seem to get rid of him."

Rick forced a smile. "I may still be interested. Give me a day or so."

Bull nodded, Rick patting him warmly on the shoulder. As the large man stepped away, Rick felt a rush of blood flooding into his head. His eyes sharpened as he found himself standing directly in front of Caleb Tidwell. When he noticed Caleb's fiancée, Tessie Lou Hunter, standing next to the sheriff, well on her way to motherhood, he reminded himself of the need for civility.

"Hello, Sheriff," Rick said without emotion, extending his hand. "Thank you for coming."

Rick was surprised to see Tessie Lou in public, since Caleb had kept her more or less sequestered once it had been determined she was with child. When she did venture out, she'd had her share of embarrassing incidents. The latest word around Riverton was that she was a bit of a shoplifter, hardly an impressive attribute for the fiancée of the local sheriff. Rick nodded at her and said her name, but she only offered a shy half-smile.

"Good evening, Mr. Morrand," Caleb answered routinely, following their abrupt handshake. "I'm sorry for your loss." Awkward silence followed. Caleb looked around the funeral parlor as though he wanted to be somewhere else.

"What's the latest with those demonstrators?" Rick asked, filling the empty air. "They still keeping you busy?"

"Oh, they're still around," Caleb said wearily, continuing to survey the room.

Rick nodded. He felt his jaw tighten. Caleb's preoccupation with the protesters—ones Chloe didn't even know about—contributed to the young sheriff's failure to properly investigate her death. Rick drew a deep breath. "How are you feeling, Tessie?" he managed to say.

"Fine." Her face was ashen, her eyes stuporous as she cast them toward the floor. Her hands rested over her bulging stomach, her fingers tense as thought she was trying to protect her unborn child from being suddenly snatched away.

Rick met eyes with Sandra Billingsley, his friend from the bank. He gave her a hug, then shook hands with her husband, James, a large, serious-looking man with a thick head of silver hair. The Billingsleys made a tidy couple, although their marriage seemed almost contractual—James wearing a younger, attractive wife on his arm, and Sandra displaying a huge rock on her finger, an accessory to her enormous ranch house and two Arabian show horses in the barn. Both parties appeared satisfied with the arrangement, so perhaps James was a skilled businessman after all.

"I didn't know your daughter, Rick, but my wife here says she saw her quite a bit," James said politely. "I know she went through some hard times, but Sandy said she had turned her life around."

Rick flashed a tight smile and nodded his head. He hung on the words "quite a bit." It appeared that Chloe was a regular visitor to the bank, Rick unaware she had *two* accounts there.

Sandra touched Rick's forearm. "When you have a chance, I have some more information for you. Now is probably not the time."

"No, please," Rick said quickly. "It's okay."

Sandra leaned forward slightly and lowered her voice. "That money—those checks—came from a Zions Bank account in Salt Lake City. Do you know anyone there?"

Rick cocked his head backward. "Utah? Whose account is it?"

"I don't know just yet. I'm still working on that part."

"Utah," Rick repeated pensively. "When you find out more, can you let me know?"

Sandra nodded, and Rick offered a grateful smile. He scanned the parlor, now full. It looked like the whole town was there, and likely it was. He spotted Jack Kelly and his wife, Tamara, coming through the front entrance. Rick moved toward them before someone else caught his eye. Standing in the corner of the room was a man in a uniform. Not a law enforcement uniform but one worn by employees of the National Park Service, the same attire of which Chloe had been so proud.

Rick eased his way through the crowd. The man was listening with little interest to Burl Simpson, owner of the only hardware store in Riverton. Rick all but turned his back to Burl as he extended his hand toward the ranger. "My name is Rick Morrand."

"Uh, yes, hello, Mr. Morrand," the man said uneasily. He had thick blond hair and blue eyes, his cleft chin covered in a thick shadow of beard. He curled a burly arm around his barrel chest to shake Rick's hand, his grip dry and firm. "I'm Matt Steelman. I'm . . . I was Chloe's boss down in—"

"I know who you are," Rick said. He nodded toward the funeral home's chapel. "You mind if we talk?"

Matt seemed unnerved by the request. He hesitated to answer, his eyes racing around the room as if he were in search of someone. "Sure."

He slowly made his way toward the stained-glass chapel door, glancing warily as Rick followed behind him. A converted storage room, the chapel was cramped, featuring a modest altar and a few wooden pews. It likely was designed as a secluded setting to say a few private prayers, but Rick wasn't in there to pray. Once inside, he drew close to Matt's chest, his furrowed eyebrows inches from the young man's face. "You're not very good at returning phone calls," he said with a snarl. "The first time I called you was on Saturday. For all I know, my daughter was still alive."

"I'm sorry about that, Mr. Morrand," Matt mumbled cautiously. "I've been busy."

Matt edged backward as Rick continued to move toward him. Soft organ music crackled over the chapel's tiny wood-encased speakers, with little effect. "I'm surprised you even showed up."

"What would you have thought if I didn't?" Matt answered firmly. "I have nothing to hide."

Rick's eyes narrowed. "You sure about that?"

"I already talked to the deputy this afternoon. A Deputy Renfro? I told him everything."

"What kind of *everything* did you tell him?"

"About the sex."

"What sex?"

"Chloe and I liked to have sex, okay? That's *all* it was. We liked to . . . hook up."

Rick's nostrils flared as blood pulsed into his forehead. He thrust his forearm across Matt's neck, pinning him tightly against the walnut-covered chapel wall.

"Hook up?" he said through grinding teeth. "Is that what you call it? Like a couple of animals? That's my daughter you're talking about. My daughter! The woman lying in the next room!"

Rick's chest ached, his heart crushed beneath an anvil of shame. Matt had presented yet another stark reminder that Chloe measured her worth by her ability to remove her clothes. *Hook up?* The words echoed in his head, which felt like it was about to explode.

"You need to take your hands off me," Matt warned, placing a firm grip on each of Rick's forearms. Rick pressed harder, causing Matt's face to redden.

"You were the last one to see her alive. What did you do to her?"

"I said, get off me!" Matt shouted, thrusting his weight forward. Rick lost leverage, desperately clutching the ranger's collar as they crashed over the first two rows of chapel pews. Wood shattered around them. Matt steadied himself on top of Rick and held his fist in the air, prepared to deliver a blow.

"Get off him! Now!"

Rick followed Matt's eyes toward the chapel door, where Billy Renfro had his gun drawn. A blond-haired woman, holding an infant, stood wide-eyed beside the deputy. Matt unclenched his fist and extended his right arm, his open palm urging Billy to remain calm. He slowly rose to his feet. Rick followed him, heaving for air as he dusted debris off his shirt and dress pants.

"Rick, this is Amie Steelman," Billy said, nodding toward the stunned woman at his side. "She's Matt's wife." Amie looked warily at Billy as her infant began to whimper. "And this is their son, Aaron."

Rick stared at the woman and her baby before delivering a scumbag glare at Matt. Placing his hands on his hips, he tilted his head as he looked at Billy. "So what are you trying to tell me?" he growled. "Are you saying this man spent a quiet evening with his wife after having sex with my daughter?"

Billy rubbed his chin, as though the pause might somehow calm Rick down. He shook his head. "Not quite."

"Well, what then?"

"I don't believe Mr. Steelman harmed your daughter," Billy said flatly. "He claimed he bought a fishing license in Gardiner on Friday night and then had a meal there. His story checks out. I believe he spent the whole evening near Gardiner—a good forty miles or so from where Chloe was found."

Matt brushed off the front of his uniform. Having secured vindication, he shook his head with disgust. He glowered at Rick, raising his eyebrows as though expecting an apology, but none would be forthcoming. "C'mon Amie," Matt murmured as he stepped over rubble on the floor of the chapel. "We need to go home."

"Not just yet, Mr. Steelman," Billy said, lowering his eyes while raising an index finger. "I need to ask your wife a few questions."

"Questions? About what?"

"Mrs. Steelman said she arrived at your cabin on Friday night, but that's not exactly true, now, is it?" Billy tilted his head expectantly, but Matt returned only a stupefied gape. "Fact is, your wife was in Gardiner on Friday night, but she *wasn't with you.*"

Matt glared at Amie, seeking an explanation. His wife averted her eyes, turning her focus to their child.

Billy pulled his notebook from his pocket. "Using that number you gave me yesterday, I went ahead and placed a call to Mrs. Steelman's mother in Salt Lake City. According to her—Barbara Olsen is the woman's name—Mrs. Steelman left Utah on Friday morning and checked into the Riverside Motel late Friday afternoon. In fact, Mrs. Olsen made the reservation herself—even used her own credit card."

All eyes focused on Amie, who rolled her bottom lip as she bobbed her baby in her arms. After several seconds, she lifted her eyes, glancing briefly at Rick before brushing a cautious stare past her husband.

"I wasn't sure whether I could get here by nightfall," Amie said to Billy, a slight tremor in her voice. "I didn't want to try to find his cabin in the dark—not with the baby and all."

Billy scratched his forehead with the corner of his notebook. "Your husband could have met you in town, Mrs. Steelman. Fact is, it's pretty obvious your husband didn't even know you were coming."

Amie released a long sigh and nervously adjusted Aaron in her arms, the infant having fallen asleep. "You're right, Deputy," she said, her voice acquiring an edge. "My husband didn't know I was in town, and I planned it that way. In case you haven't figured it out by now, I don't trust him all that much. For that matter, my mother doesn't either."

Matt's shoulders slumped as he stared at the ground. He opened and closed his fists for several seconds before lifting his gaze, his forehead flushed. "Deputy, I think we've answered enough questions," he stammered. "Amie, let's go!"

Rick took a couple of steps forward, blocking Matt's path. The ranger shot a biting glare at him, indicating he was more than ready to go another round. Billy glanced at both of them, his frown demanding decorum in front of the woman and her child.

As he edged closer to Amie, Billy's protruding stomach pressed against the arm that cradled Aaron. Gentleness drifted across his face as he studied the infant. "Looks like he's completely out," he said in hushed voice. "You know, I read somewhere that newborn babies can sleep up to eighteen hours a day. Is that what you've found?"

"He does sleep quite a bit," Amie said with the hint of a grin, Billy's gentle tone seeming to disarm her. "He sleeps, eats, and, of course . . ."

"Poops," Billy blurted out with a chuckle. He glanced over his shoulder at the small altar behind him. "Not sure if that's okay to say in a chapel." He smiled and shook his head slowly as he watched Aaron in apparent wonder. "I remember when my kids were young. My son, Evan, was a little colicky. It was tough for him—and us—to get any sleep. What Mabel and I would do was take him for a ride around town, right during the middle of the night." His eyes twinkled as he savored the memory. "Worked every time when she did that. He went right out."

Amie glanced at Aaron. "I've heard that works," she murmured.

Billy's smile vanished, his face turning serious. "Is that the reason you left your motel last Friday night, Mrs. Steelman? You know, maybe you were trying to get your baby to fall asleep?"

Amie's eyes grew wide. She looked toward her husband, his jaw muscles pulsing. "What are you implying, Deputy?" Matt asked.

"Settle down, Steelman," Billy shot back. "The desk clerk at the motel said your wife left her room about an hour after checking in. By the time she got back, it was after dark, and the weather had turned." He looked at Amie. "Ma'am, you mind telling me where you went?"

Amie shifted Aaron in her arms, innocence fading from her face. "It was like you said, Deputy—I went for a drive," she said defiantly. "When it started raining, I came back."

Billy raised his chin. "And I'll bet the baby was asleep the whole time?"

Before she could answer, Matt shoved his way past Rick. He put his arm around his wife, and ushered her toward the door of the chapel. Billy put his hands on his hips. "I would appreciate it if you didn't head back to Salt Lake City just yet, Mrs. Steelman," he said. "At least, not for a few days." The couple left the chapel without a response.

Rick looked at Billy. "Good luck with that." As Billy shook his head and rubbed his temples, Rick noticed Sage standing at the door, a solemn expression on her face. He wondered how long she had been there, what she might have seen. "Will you be coming back out here soon?" she asked. "There are a lot of people asking for you."

Rick nodded. He scanned the splintered wood on the floor. "Looks like I'll be writing Clarence an extra check." He followed Billy out of the chapel.

The parlor was filled beyond capacity with the mourners of Chloe Morrand—almost all of them not knowing how she had perished. Rick was certain at least one of them knew.

CHAPTER 45

WHEN RICK INFORMED ABBY THEY would be spending Wednesday night back at the ranch—"home" is what he called it—the child staged a mild protest. She immediately demanded that Sage pack a bag and follow them, a plan that made perfect sense since the burial service would be held the next morning farther south in the valley.

Rick welcomed Sage's presence, knowing she would provide a buffer of sorts between him and his granddaughter. His limited moments with Abby had featured lengthy silent spells cluttered with agonizing internal thoughts. Between his failure to choose the right words and his fear of betraying his own decimated emotions, he'd been of little help to her. Abby needed a mother, and she no longer had one.

They didn't arrive home until almost midnight. A light rain that began earlier in the evening had turned to snow, leaving a feathery dusting that glittered beneath the star-flooded Montana sky. The ranch was hushed in a peaceful stillness.

As he watched a translucent cloud brush the moon, Rick remembered that it was almost Halloween, which arrived each year on the day after Abby's birthday. He and Chloe would laugh when Abby insisted on a distinct separation between those two occasions, never wanting to dilute the spoils of either one.

"I would love a cup of hot tea," Sage said as they came through the front entry and walked into the kitchen. "Do you keep tea in the house?"

Rick pointed to a weathered hickory cupboard. "I got tea with your name on it."

Sage reached into the cabinet and pulled out a small lime-green can. When she showed the label to Abby, they rolled their eyes and giggled. "Sage Tea," Abby said, reading the front of the can. "Real funny, Pa-Pa!" Rick winked at his granddaughter and they smiled. Smiles were good.

"You need to get ready for bed, young lady," Rick said. "You must be pretty tired."

Abby looked at Sage, seeking a second opinion, but received only a wag of the head. "You listen to your grandpa. I'll be in after a while to say good night."

Abby opened her arms as she trudged toward Rick, who leaned down so she could hug his neck. She held him longer than normal, perhaps sensing that he needed the hug as much as she did. "I'll be out in the living room," he said. "I'm going to start a fire."

He lingered a moment, watching Sage put the tea kettle on the stove. She had discarded her customary boots and denim, having donned heels and a black silk dress for the vigil. Her curled hair looked rich and full, and her eyeliner illuminated her emerald eyes.

Abby poked her head back into the doorway after dawdling her way out of the room. "Do I have to brush my teeth?"

Sage put a hand on her hip. "Yes, you have to brush your teeth. The last thing you want is to have someone in your dreams saying you have bad breath."

Abby giggled again. "Oo-kay," she said, trudging down the hall. Rick chuckled at Sage's comment as he left the kitchen. It sounded like something Chloe might say. His smile faded quickly, drowned beneath rolling waves of sadness.

"Are you going to sing to me?" Abby shouted from down the hall, her speech slurred by the toothbrush in her mouth.

"Of course I am, darlin'. Right after you say your prayers."

Sage was without her guitar, but her voice was a rare and delicate instrument in itself. For Abby, she chose "My Heart Will Go On," somehow making it sound country. Sage had rented a DVD of the movie *Titanic* when Abby stayed over once, and Abby insisted Sage learn the song, even though they'd both been left in tears when Jack Dawson disappeared into the icy depths of the North Atlantic. When Chloe had been with them, she would join Sage in harmony, Chloe having a pretty fair voice of her own.

Every night in my dreams I see you, I feel you.
That is how I know you go on.
Far across the distance
And spaces between us
You have come to show you go on.

Near, far, wherever you are,
I believe that the heart does go on.
Once more you open the door
And you're here in my heart
And my heart will go on and on.

She sang only two verses before Abby was out, and Rick was sad she stopped. Sage was a tough girl—*a real Montana girl*—but her timbre was always as sweet and gentle as the warm summer wind. Rick blinked his moistened eyes, keeping them trained on the fire when Sage entered the room. Once the kindling in the fireplace had begun to crackle, he took a seat on the couch as she placed a pair of cups on the coffee table.

Rick never figured Sage to be much of a tea drinker—at least not tea that was all by itself. When he decided to get sober, Sage's enthusiastic support carried a disclaimer that she had no plans to give up drinking herself. After all, she considered alcohol use, severe hangovers, and ill-conceived spontaneous decisions simple hazards of her profession.

"Sorry I don't have something for you to put in that," Rick said, trying to be hospitable.

Sage frowned. "I don't *need* anything to put in it."

Sage hadn't had any alcohol since Chloe's death. Some people could cut it off like that. Not Rick. For him, it was all or nothing. He felt a shudder as his brain wandered to the day before, when he was sitting in front of the liquor store in Riverton. He had dodged a bullet, that was for sure. He prayed it would stay that way. Abby needed him. He was no good to her drunk.

He and Sage sat in silence, staring at a painting above the fireplace—a cowboy on horseback crossing a creek on a gilded autumn morning. The piece was done by a local artist, James Ressler, and it was said to be inspired by Fire Creek, which was lined with radiant aspens as it ventured down a narrow canyon from the snow-covered peaks guarding Shadow Lake. There was the hint of a rock outcrop seeping through the trees at one side of the painting. It could have been the Sawtooth, but no one was quite certain.

Sage turned toward him. "Is it true Chloe could paint?"

"She told you that? I thought that was a big secret."

"She told me plenty of secrets," Sage said, her face turning impish as she drew a sip of tea.

"Oh yeah? Like what?"

"If I told you, they really wouldn't be secrets, now, would they?"

Sage put down her cup and pondered Rick's question. "I'll tell you one secret," she said, pointing her finger toward him. "She absolutely adored her daddy—she told me so."

"Really," he answered, unconvinced.

"It's true. She loved you because despite all the crap she put you through, you always stuck by her. You never gave up."

Rick choked back emotion as he looked back up at the painting. "So," Sage asked, "was she any good?"

"Who?"

"Chloe. Was she any good at painting? Was she a good artist?"

Rick took a sip of tea, which he didn't drink often. It seemed to calm him. "You never saw any of her paintings?" Sage shook her head.

Rick put down his mug and pointed with his thumb outside the house, in the general direction of the detached structure where his office was located. "Well, I guess I haven't either—at least, not lately. Let's go have a look."

Sage followed Rick out a side door off the kitchen. The stone walkway was icy, so he extended his hand to her. She interlocked her fingers with his, then wrapped her other hand around his upper arm, pulling herself close to him. "Your hand is cold," she complained lightheartedly. They proceeded forward with caution, Sage tightening her grip on Rick's bicep whenever the sole of her boot would slip.

Chloe had shown promise when she took painting lessons in California during early adolescence, but she abandoned her art— along with everything else—when she descended into the darkness of her illness and drugs. She started painting again after she got clean, and Rick eventually offered to let her set up shop in the shed, once used to store feed. She readily accepted, with one pointed request—no one, not even Rick, was allowed to view her work until it was *finished*.

By her own measure, Chloe had come close to completing one painting—a portrait of Abby at three years old. Rick loved it and wanted to hang it in the house, but Chloe had adamantly refused. She was self-conscious about it, not wanting others to see it until she had touched it up. Several months had passed, and it remained in the shed.

"Look at beautiful little Abby," Sage gasped as Rick turned on the light in the studio. "Why didn't you hang it?"

"She said she wasn't done."

In addition to a palette and various art supplies, there remained two easels, each covered with a powder-blue bedsheet. He lifted the cloth covering the first easel, revealing a portrait of a tan horse leaning its head over the top rail of a wooden fence. "Lady," Rick and Sage said in unison.

Lady had died a couple of years earlier. She was a gentle, attentive Bay who was especially trustworthy with children. Her long cream-colored mane tumbled over the top of her head and around her ears, almost covering her eyes. Chloe would always comb Lady's hair forward, as if she was giving the mare a hairdo. The ritual never failed to get a laugh out of Abby.

"She was . . . she's *really* good," said Sage. Rick folded his arms proudly, soaking in all aspects of the painting. "Look at the detail of the markings, the hair, the eyes," he said. "She totally captured that horse's personality."

Sage frowned. "Chloe considered this unfinished? It sure looks finished to me."

Rick looked at the lower right-hand corner of the painting, where "CHLOE" was written in small letters. "Well, she signed it," he said with a shrug. "She should have given herself more credit."

He proceeded to the next painting, which was a bit larger than the first. He lifted the sheet to reveal a rodeo clown standing in a wooden barrel in the middle of an arena. Two cowboys were chasing a bull that appeared to be headed straight at the clown. "Good ol' Cleo," Rick said with a smile.

"Cleo?"

"The clown in the barrel. His name was Cleo."

Sage leaned forward for a closer look. "How can you tell?"

"The face—it's definitely Cleo. He had a sad face. All of the other clowns had a happy face, but Cleo was always sad."

Rick's lips quivered as he clung to the word *sad*. He found himself pulling Sage closer to him. She leaned against his ribs, lightly brushing her fingernails back and forth across his back.

He released a long exhale. "She always felt bad for Cleo, even when she was a little kid," he said, a tremor in his voice. "She couldn't figure out why everybody there was having so much fun—it being Independence Day and all—while Cleo had to be sad. It only made things worse when everyone laughed at him."

Rick replaced the cloth over the painting. Sage curled in front of him, wrapping her arms around his waist and putting the side of her head against his chest. He returned her embrace, pulling her closer. She was warm and soft, and he grew aroused as her breasts pushed against him. She looked up at him through watery eyes, and he found himself close to her lips, so close that it only seemed natural that they should kiss.

Her mouth stirred his senses even more, and he pressed himself against her. Sage took a half step back, propped herself on a worktable and squeezed her legs around him. He kissed her harder, every fiber of his being begging for more of her touch.

Then, suddenly, he stopped. His mind raced. Was this wrong? Did they want this? How would this *change* things?

"Don't!" Sage said emphatically, as if she could read his thoughts.

Rick obeyed. He shut off his mind. With everything that had gone wrong, this somehow felt right. No more guilt.

He pawed for the light switch. In the darkness, he unbuttoned his shirt as Sage did the same. He reached around to the back of her bra, but she removed his hands and unsnapped it herself.

"Easy, Cowboy," she said in a tempting whisper. "Let's take it nice and slow."

The full moon cast its light across Sage's breasts, still pure and well-proportioned in spite of her age. Rick had sometimes wondered, depending on what she was wearing, what love-making with her might be like. He would attempt to dismiss the thought, reminding himself that she was *Sage*. But there she was, and here they were— together in a beautiful moment that seemed both true and secure.

They giggled mischievously as she reached below her dress and slid off her panties. Their foreheads touched, and their lips played at a tempting distance, close enough for them to steal each other's breath. He drew his chest against hers, the touch of her skin unchaining his desire. He swallowed her into his arms, never wanting to let her go.

He moved closer, and they were one.

CHAPTER 46

CHLOE LIKELY WOULD HAVE PREFERRED her ashes sprinkled over the falls of the Grand Canyon of Yellowstone, or perhaps scattered to the wind from the summit of Electric Peak. But in death, as in life, Chloe never seemed to get what she wanted.

They had never fully discussed it, but Rick was uncomfortable with the notion of cremation, the thought of incinerating a body conjuring up images of burning in hell. Instead, he decided to bury Chloe in one of the family's two remaining plots at Cottonwood Cemetery, right between her mother and troubled Uncle Phil.

Thursday morning was cold, damp, and gray, useful for nothing other than a funeral. As Rick watched Chloe's casket being lowered into the ground, his weighted heart descended with it, the grim, cruel thought of no longer seeing his daughter still impossible to comprehend.

"A parent should never outlive a child," Father Andrew Dolan said, his words making Rick feel as though he had gained membership in some dreadful exclusive club. Rick's jaw tightened as he bit down hard on the stark reality that he had lost both parents, a child, and a devoted wife—not to mention his favorite uncle—and he wondered just exactly how God and Father Dolan might go about explaining all of that.

Rick and Father Dolan had never met—the priest was fairly new to the valley—and it had been ages since Rick had darkened the doors of a church. Rick half-expected a service filled with meaningless canned clichés, but to his surprise, Father Dolan not only knew Chloe but also Abby, whom he greeted warmly by name. It turned out that Chloe had been volunteering at the church's food bank for more than a year, her daughter by her side.

"Chloe *did* matter," Father Dolan instructed the small gathering who'd braved the wind and rain. "Her life was not wasted. She made a difference, and she will be remembered."

She would be remembered. But how?

The crowd gradually dispersed, friends offering final good-byes. Rick stood motionless in front of Chloe's grave, staring in a stupor at the muddy ditch. He suddenly flinched, a loud gunshot echoing in the distance. Fear rumbled through him as his brain snapped back to a few days before, when a sniper dropped a buffalo and shot Rick's truck to bits. *Somebody is still out there.*

His eyes darted around him, searching for Abby and Sage. They stood only a few steps away. They stared at him quizzically, likely seeing panic on his face.

A second shot was heard, this one farther away. He drew a deep breath, remembering hunting season was in full swing. Deer and elk hunting was part of life in the valley, and life was marching on.

Sage and Abby watched him silently, their mournful eyes fixed on him in allegiance, wind and rain be damned. Behind them, an attractive woman clutched the top of her black raincoat, her eyes shielded by large dark sunglasses.

"Hello, Rick," she said in a quiet, soothing voice. He hesitated, squinting through the mist, almost in disbelief. "Mandy?"

She moved forward and boldly embraced him. "I'm so sorry for your loss."

He hugged her gingerly, offering a nod of thanks. She extended a gloved hand toward Sage, who wore a wary, protective frown. "Amanda Westin Cobb," Mandy said.

"Right," Sage replied, nodding skeptically. Awkward silence hung in the misty air. Sage turned toward Rick. "We'll be in my truck."

Rick hadn't spoken to Mandy in more than three decades. He only recognized her from seeing her on TV a few years before, when the network had her covering the theater shootings in Aurora, Colorado. She still boasted a nice figure, albeit one sustained with manmade assistance. Her lips were fuller than Rick remembered, and her blond hair was now brunette, a color perhaps more easy to maintain.

"I really appreciate you coming," Rick muttered, his voice betraying his sudden uneasiness. "Are you still in Denver?"

"Yes, Denver. After Ricky and I split up, I took a job in Albany, but it wasn't right for me. So I moved west."

Rick wasn't aware Mandy had married "Ricky," let alone divorced him. Perhaps that's where the Cobb came from, he reasoned. He looked out toward Sage's truck, which they chose to drive that morning since it still had windows. Sage stared at him without expression, which spoke volumes. She turned her head away and gazed out the front windshield.

"What brings you to the valley? It's been a long time, hasn't it?"

"Yes, it has," Mandy said, drawing a deep sigh. "I came here to cover the bison controversy."

"Right. The bison."

He had plenty of things he wanted to ask Mandy, but his questions were thirty-five years old. They were concerns of an immature eighteen-year-old spurned by his first true love, and they seemed to matter little now. She removed her glasses, revealing the deep and dangerous blue eyes he had been powerless to resist as a teenager. His muscles tensed, his body becoming rigid. He buried his balled fists in the pockets of his overcoat, suddenly feeling the first trickles from a distant, swollen river of anger and hurt.

"Look," Mandy began, shifting her weight and glancing at the ground, "I was hoping that maybe we could get together. You know, to talk."

Rick flicked his eyes toward Sage's truck. "Talk?"

"It's important," Mandy said, moving closer. Her eyes were reaching inside him now, as if placing him under an odd spell. The smell of her perfume reminded him that their one-time love affair had been constructed principally on lust, and traces of that desire strangely lingered. Rick stood silent, staring dumbfounded as she reached into her purse and produced a business card.

"My cell phone is on the back. There is something I *really* need to tell you."

Rick accepted the card. He felt uneasy and didn't like it. He hiked his chin. "If it's so important, why not tell me now?"

"This isn't the time and place," she said as she walked away.

He flipped over the business card. The back not only included a cell number but the words "Riverton Grande, Room 201." His eyes followed her before he turned back toward Chloe's grave one final time. He made the sign of the cross, even though he wasn't quite sure why.

He exhaled a sigh and walked back toward Sage's truck. As he approached the passenger side, he saw Rev. Richard Williams standing there. The pastor's daughter, Courtney, was next to him, her eyes fixed on the ground. Seeing her made Rick want to cross himself again.

When he last encountered Courtney, she was brandishing a butcher knife inside Chase Rettick's trailer. As she shivered beside her father at the cemetery, she looked better, albeit not much. Her face remained deathly pale, and she had her hands wedged into the front pockets of her jeans, likely to keep them from shaking.

"Hello, Rick," Rev. Williams said. "I was hoping to see you here. We've just come from the sheriff's office. Courtney has something she would like to say to you."

The teen stood motionless for several seconds, like an actress who had missed her cue. Or, worse—forgotten her lines. Rev. Williams nudged her elbow. "Go ahead, honey—tell him." Tears flooded her frightened eyes as she prepared to speak.

"I . . . I'm sorry, Mr. Morrand," she said through whimpers. "I'm sorry about the way I acted."

Her father patiently stared at her, indicating her confession was far from complete. Courtney wiped her eyes on the sleeve of her wool coat. "I . . . lied to you, Mr. Morrand," she said between short breaths. "Chase Rettick wasn't with me on Friday night."

She seemed relieved she got the sentence out, though Rick wasn't particularly stunned by her news. "Do you know where he was?"

She shook her head, causing her father to clear his throat. He glared at Courtney. "I'm sorry, did you say something? Mr. Morrand asked you a question."

Courtney looked at her father, then at Rick. "He doesn't just use drugs—he's a dealer. He may have been making a delivery. I don't know."

Rick's forearms tightened as he opened and closed his fists. "Do you know where he is *now*?" Courtney shook her head and began to sob, so Rev. Williams intervened. "The sheriff said he was going to take a ride out to his trailer, but I don't know when."

Rick bit down hard, warm blood surging into his temples. Chase Rettick had been in contact with Chloe a lot more than he'd let on. But why? Something told Rick there was more that involved her than child support. He needed answers. He wondered whether he could locate Chase first, before the sheriff got to him.

He studied Courtney. Her hands were now trembling as she continued to shiver. Rick had seen this before. He waved Rev. Williams over. "She needs some medical help," Rick told the pastor, barely above a whisper.

"What kind of medical help?"

"She's having withdrawals. Trust me—she needs help."

Rev. Williams seemed bewildered. "Withdrawals? From marijuana?"

The man's heart already broken, Rick saw no need to shatter it further. The pastor would find out soon enough. "Promise me you'll take Courtney to the hospital. They'll know what to do. Will you promise, Reverend? *Please*?"

Rev. Williams looked curiously at Rick, then nodded. Taking his daughter by the hand, he trudged away.

As Rick's eyes followed them, he caught sight of a distant solitary figure dressed in black. The man was leaning against a gray World War I cannon stationed among a group of gravesites designated for veterans. Once discovered, he quickly turned to leave.

"Buddy?" Rick said as he squinted through the mist. "Buddy! Wait!"

Buddy Rivers moved away briskly, like an animal startled by a predator. Within moments, he had disappeared among the tombstones. Rick cocked his head. He was sure the man had heard him. Sure, Buddy wasn't what you'd call social, but everyone was gone. Why did he run away?

Rick turned and headed toward Sage's truck, his thoughts returning to Chloe and her relationship with Chase Rettick. The skin on the back of his neck tightened. His mind sprinted to the hidden bank account at Wells Fargo. He tried to remember the exact figure—something around $160,000. Where was Chloe getting that kind of money? Courtney said Chase was dealing drugs. Had Chloe been involved?

Sage started the engine. "You okay?"

Rick glanced over his shoulder at Abby sitting in back on the bench seat. "I'm fine."

Sage put the truck into gear.

He wasn't fine at all.

Charlie assumed that the doorbell on Maggie Townsend's house hadn't worked since the Reagan administration, so he rapped his knuckles on the peeling lime-colored paint of the wooden front door. He had received forensics from Missoula that morning, confirming his suspicion that there was no trace of Draper Townsend's DNA anywhere near the crime scene, aside from the mysterious glove that Caleb had produced—a glove that contained no DNA from Chloe Morrand.

That meant a case against Draper would balance heavily—if not, solely—on Maggie's testimony, and Charlie wanted to hear for himself the intricacies of Draper's alleged "confession." Though he was fairly certain he had a homicide on his hands, Charlie remained unclear just exactly who had done the killing and how.

His delay in determining a cause of death did not sit well with Sheriff Tidwell, of course, but Charlie found that of little concern. Having just left the funeral for the daughter of his long-time friend, he was determined to get this case right, regardless of how long it took.

Charlie knocked on the door again, sending snowy paint shavings floating onto the sleeve of his black suit. He brushed off his forearm and knocked again, his efforts more robust. "Maggie! Maggie? You in there?"

Charlie drew a deep breath, unbuttoned his collar, and loosened his tie. He had phoned ahead and spoken to her, so Maggie should have been expecting him. He leaned off the porch, shielding his eyes as he peered into the living room window. Placing his hands in his pockets, he creaked across the unstable wooden steps and squinted at the house.

A rustling sound beneath the porch startled him. He jumped backward, only to see a barn cat emerge in pursuit of a field mouse. He flicked his black boot toward the cat as it ran by, missing the mark as he muttered expletives beneath his breath. Charlie preferred dogs to cats.

He walked around the side of the house to look for Maggie's car, which he didn't recall seeing when he drove up. It wasn't there. His eyes followed the driveway toward the detached garage. The wooden door was old and weathered, much like the entire property. A hole had been kicked in the lower corner, no doubt compliments of Draper Townsend. Small wisps of smoke seemed to be drifting from the opening.

Charlie froze momentarily, an icy shudder racing through him. He shook his head, mouthing the words, "No, no, no," his purposeful stride breaking into a run. As he drew closer, he heard the sound of a running engine. He reached the side door of the garage, where he rattled the locked metal knob. Peering through the dirt-covered glass-paned window, he was barely able to see the front of Maggie's faded green Taurus through the murky darkness. "Damn it, Maggie! No!"

Bending his elbow, he shattered one of the window panes, then reached through the remains of a spiderweb to open the door. He tugged a white handkerchief from his back pocket, covering his nose and mouth. With exhaust stinging his eyes, he spotted Maggie sitting motionless behind the steering wheel. He slapped his open palms against the roof of the truck. "No, Maggie! Why?" he heard himself wail.

Charlie's trembling hands fumbled to open the lock of the passenger door. Gagging on fumes, he threw open the door and lunged toward the ignition, shutting off the engine. The garage fell eerily quiet. He placed his fingers on Maggie's neck, begging for a pulse.

Raindrops began to tap the tin roof above him, slowly at first, then rhythmic and steady. Charlie's chin fell onto his chest, a damp, dark gloom descending over him.

Lifting his eyes toward Maggie's ashen face, he pulled his hand away.

CHAPTER 47

RICK GLARED OUT THE FRONT windshield of Sage's truck, hypnotized by the cadenced *thwack* of wipers pushing a sudden downpour off the glass, his besieged brain rolling an imaginary unedited video of a meth-dealing daughter.

As they entered the ranch house, Sage took a call on her cell phone, mindlessly clanking her keys on the kitchen counter. Rick sought brief refuge in the bedroom, where he threw on a Pendleton shirt and pair of jeans. After emerging to exchange a few volleys of monosyllabic dialogue, he announced he would be taking a ride into town, suddenly concerned about the physical well-being of Reiff Metcalf.

What he really needed to do was breathe.

Sage eyed him curiously, folding her arms across her chest. She nodded toward Abby's room. "You mind taking her with you?"

Rick hesitated. "Yeah, sure. I just thought, since the truck windows were broken—"

"She needs to be with you—I'm not sure if you get that or not," Sage said flatly. "Besides, I need to go to The Spur. I just got a call— it got trashed last night."

"Trashed? How?"

"They had the news on, and some talking head said the buffalo had contaminated all the beef in the valley. That didn't sit too well with the cowboys sittin' at the bar. A few of those bison activists started clapping, and the rest is history."

"Brucellosis doesn't harm beef."

Sage threw him an impatient look. "I understand that. The news reporter obviously didn't do her research. All I know is that the felt on my pool table is shredded, and the mirror behind the bar is shattered. Worse yet, someone tried to bounce a longneck off my flat screen, and I need to get it replaced. We *are* in the middle of football season, you know."

Rick stared at Sage for several seconds, a peculiar awkwardness suddenly enveloping them. Her defeated eyes told him that she considered the previous night to be a mistake, their lifelong bond of friendship forever scarred, but his heart insisted that just wasn't so. He promised himself he would talk to her, reassure her that her affections were warranted, her trust and devotion not squandered.

She raised her eyebrows, her taut smile inviting him to speak. He paused, then let the opportunity pass, his frayed emotions somehow still not equipped for a return to prime time. For now, he would keep his secrets and she would have hers. "Let me know if I can help," he said clumsily, the comment doing little to fill the vacant air.

Abby initially resisted the idea of going into town with her grandfather, but at Sage's urging, she complied. The promise of a stop at the ice cream parlor seemed to help, if only a little. Rick felt a dull ache in his chest, knowing full well that it would take a lot more than a scoop of Moose Tracks to mend his grandchild's wounded heart.

He duct-taped pieces of cardboard across the rear of his cab, his truck a metaphor for his life in disarray. They drove down Highway 89 in silence, the only sound coming from wind whistling through cracks in his makeshift windows.

Abby stared with hollow eyes as she traced her finger along the metal Dodge emblem on the glove box. The cold, definitive permanence of Chloe's departure seemed to overpower the joyless cab, Rick and Abby journeying together into their new, uncharted void. It was one thing for Pa-Pa to spoil his granddaughter all weekend and then return her to Mom. But what now, with Chloe no longer there?

"Want to listen to the Disney Channel?" Rick finally asked, grappling for enthusiasm.

"You hate the Disney Channel."

"I don't mind."

Abby shook her head.

"Have you thought about what you want for your birthday? We're only a couple days away."

Abby's lips quivered. "I just want my mom," she said, her voice shaking.

Rick's eyes blinked at the road in front of him. He extended an open palm toward Abby. She resisted at first, appearing confused. He grabbed her hand and enveloped it in his.

"I miss her, too, Abby—trust me," he said, forcing words barely above a whisper. "But things are going to be okay. I promise." She looked up at him, her innocent face painfully unconvinced, her eyelids pinching tiny teardrops onto her cheeks. "I promise," he repeated, unsure whether to believe himself.

They rode a few more miles in deafening silence. Rick tried again. "What kind of ice cream are you going to have?"

Abby hesitated. "Moose Tracks," she muttered.

"You always have Moose Tracks."

"It's my favorite."

"Forever and always?"

"Forever and always."

Rick leaned toward Abby, trying to make eye contact. "Do you know what my favorite ice cream of all time was?"

Abby shook her head as she stared out the passenger window.

"Vanilla."

Abby glanced at him, crinkling her nose. *Bor-ing*.

"I was in the hospital having my tonsils out. When I got back to my room after the operation, they gave me this tiny carton of vanilla ice cream. It was *magical*. I can still remember the taste of it, sliding off that little wooden spoon. Pure heaven."

Abby pursed her lips in thought. "I want to get my tonsils out."

"No, you don't. Trust me."

"I do!" Abby insisted. "I want to get some of your magic ice cream!"

Rick forced a light chuckle. He lightly squeezed Abby's tender hand. "Getting your tonsils out hurts," he said, releasing a deep breath. "Life will deal you enough pain without you going looking for it."

The truck grew quiet again.

Billy Renfro was waiting in the lobby of the sheriff's office, boots spread wide, thumbs buried beneath his belt. He winked at Abby— "Hey, darlin'," he said in an efficient tone—then turned his eyes toward Rick. "We need to talk."

Rick gave him a skeptical nod. "Abby, can you sit out here a minute? I need to speak with Deputy Renfro." Abby trudged across the tile floor with slumped shoulders, then plopped onto a wooden bench.

Rick trailed Billy into his office, closing the door behind him. Billy motioned toward a seat in front of the desk, clearing his throat as he sat down in his squeaky metal chair. "Why didn't you tell me?"

"Tell you what?"

"About the money."

"What money?"

Billy stroked his moustache and looked toward the window, his stomach swelling as he leaned back and drew a massive breath. "Seriously?" he asked, whipping his head back toward Rick. "Are we really going to do this?"

Rick interlocked his fingers and leaned forward in his chair. "Do what?"

Billy reached into his top pocket for a toothpick. "I went to Wells Fargo," he said with exasperation. "I wanted to see whether Chloe had made any ATM withdrawals. Maybe she was followed, got robbed––"

"Robbed?" Rick huffed. "In the valley?"

Billy's eyes narrowed. "I was trying to be *thorough*," he said, irritation in his voice. "Sandra Billingsley told me that there were no withdrawals from Chloe's checking account. But then she mentioned a savings account—a fairly *large* savings account. She told me you knew about it."

"Sandra said that?"

"After some prodding," he said. Billy leaned forward, twirling the toothpick beneath his burly moustache. "I was hoping the money was from you—a college account for Abby, maybe. But Sandra said that's not the case."

Rick exhaled. "I apologize, Billy—I should have mentioned it. I guess I didn't want you to jump to any conclusions."

"I'm *paid* to jump to conclusions!" Billy snapped. He leaned forward, resting his elbows on his desk. "Sandra says regular deposits were sent from Utah, an LLC named Yellowstone Investments. Ever heard that name before?"

Rick shook his head.

"Any idea *why* Chloe would have that kind of money?" Billy pressed. "Do you know if she was involved in drugs?"

Rick rubbed his jaw, stealing time. He had the same suspicion, but denial made him unwilling to embrace it. He decided to hold his cards. "I find that hard to believe."

"You know Chase Rettick is dealing drugs, don't you?"

"Why haven't you arrested him?"

"We've had him on our radar for a while," Billy said. He removed his toothpick, examined it, then returned it to his mouth. "We're actually working with other agencies, trying to nail his supplier."

"I thought he made the stuff himself."

Billy shook his head. "Chase ain't much of a cook, at least as far as I know. If he was, that rat hole trailer he lives in probably would have blown sky-high by now. No, the stuff he moves likely comes from across the border."

"Mexico?"

"Yep. Drug cartel. Into Arizona, up to Utah, then here. That's why an LLC in Utah is intriguing. Ogden is somewhat of a popular way station, if you will."

"I thought all these guys deal in cash," Rick said softly.

"Not if they want to spend it, they don't. They run it through lawyers, real estate agents, even Indian poker machines. If they want to be sophisticated, they may even form an LLC."

"An LLC called Yellowstone Investments? That's a *drug cartel?*"

"What would you expect—Drugs-R-Us? These guys are trying to blend in. A gringo name like Yellowstone Investments would be perfect."

Rick's heart raced, his brain in sudden disarray as he tried to process Billy's words. "You think Chloe was involved?"

Billy rolled his bottom lip beneath his moustache and raised his eyebrows. "As you may have noticed, Chase Rettick isn't exactly the sharpest tool in the shed. Figuring out how to launder cash might not necessarily be his forte. Your daughter, on the other hand, was a smart young woman—college material, I would say."

Rick's heart sank as he thought of Chloe's chaotic life, retracing for the one-thousandth time what might have been. He cocked his head. "So, what? You think he was dealing, and she was somehow handling the books?"

Billy pointed at him affirmatively. "It might be worse than that. Up until a couple of years ago, Chloe's savings account had plenty of withdrawals. But in the past couple of years, no money has been taken out—just put in. We're thinking that maybe she was holding out on him."

Rick's eyes tapered into a cold glare. "You're saying Chase may have harmed her?"

"It's possible. We're trying to track him down. No luck so far."

Rick lowered his head and pressed his eyes shut, white knuckles gripping the arms of his wooden chair. His brain replayed the last time he had peered into the dark, depraved soul of Chase Rettick— he should have taken care of that tweaker then and there.

He raised his eyes toward Billy. "Are you still holding Draper Townsend?"

"Oh yeah," Billy replied with an uneasy half-chuckle. "Sheriff thinks Draper is his prime suspect, but Charlie and I disagree—the forensics just aren't there." Billy pulled his shredded toothpick from his mouth and tossed it into the wastebasket. "We do still have Maggie's claim that Draper said he did it, but that's about all we have."

Draper's unholy visage drifted hauntingly into Rick's mind as he considered the threat the felon might pose to Abby and Sage. "So you still plan to hold him?"

"No doubt," the deputy answered. "Fact is, I'm worried what he might do to Maggie if we cut him loose, especially if he realizes she had something to do with his arrest in the first place."

Billy rummaged through some papers on his desk, producing a large mug shot printed on copy paper. "There's also this guy. You happen to recognize him?"

Rick felt blood leave his face as he stared at the printout. "Richard Bledsoe," he muttered. "He's the guy I told you about at Sage's place—right after I got shot at."

Billy nodded. "Your friend, Jack Kelly, was kind enough to review surveillance tapes from The General Store in Cottonwood. He spotted this guy getting gas, and we tracked his plate. This mug shot is from his California driver's license."

"Is he a suspect?"

"For now, we're referring to him as a 'Person of Interest.'"

"What kind of car was he driving?"

"Not a car—a truck," Billy answered. "A black Ford F250." The deputy rifled through the jumbled stack on his desk, shoving another piece of paper in Rick's direction. "Here's a photo Jack took of a frame on his big screen. Kind of grainy, but that's the truck."

Rick squinted at the photo. "Is that a dually?"

Billy reached for a pair of cheaters. He leaned forward and nodded. "I believe so."

Rick shook his head slowly. "That might be who shot at me," he said, barely above a whisper.

Billy furrowed his brow. "You saw a truck? Was it a Ford?"

"Not positive. But I'm pretty sure it was a dually. The back wheel wells were wide."

"Was it black?"

"Maybe. It's hard to notice details when you're being shot at."

Billy's moustache twitched back and forth as he considered Rick's testimony. He rose from his chair, strolled toward the window, and stared pensively into the parking lot, as if he hoped Bledsoe might suddenly drive right in and clear things up. "Well, we're trying to locate him, I can assure you that."

Wedging his pudgy fingers deep into his shirt pocket, Billy emerged with a fresh toothpick, perhaps the last of his current supply. "How long have we known each other, Rick?"

"A long time."

"If there is *anyone* you should be able to trust, it's me. Don't you think you *owe* that to me?"

Rick stiffened, his jaw muscles growing tight. He didn't want to owe anything to anybody. Sure, Billy had made the accident with Julianne Townsend go away, but it never really did—the deputy had a habit of making sure of that. Rick sometimes wished he'd been arrested back then, forced to take his medicine. Maybe he could have balanced the books, made amends, dropped the rock. Instead, he continued to haul around his weighty guilt-riddled burden, and karma remained a bitch.

"Is there anything else you haven't told me?"

Rick bit his bottom lip, scratching his wrist while he scanned the barren room. Billy had only one file cabinet, likely used to warehouse toothpicks. A brown trout was mounted on the wall, compliments of Big Jim. "She was off her meds," Rick said flatly as he returned his eyes to the deputy.

Billy squinted in disbelief from beneath his overgrown eyebrows. His face reddened. "How do you know?"

"I found her meds in the drawer at her apartment. They're in my truck."

"And you withheld this information because . . . ?" Billy said as he cocked his head. He glared at Rick, then raised an open palm like a crossing guard. "Wait. Don't tell me: you didn't want us jumping to any *conclusions*."

Rick's face turned to stone, his eyes igniting as he focused them on Billy. "She didn't take her own life," he growled through gritted teeth.

Billy nodded. "I know—you've made that thought abundantly clear." He ran his fingers through his disheveled hair. "And I have to say that I agree with you."

Billy placed his beefy forearms on his desk. He picked up a pen with both hands and stared at it, rotating it in his fingers. "Tell me. Any idea why your friend back there in the jail cell would call Chloe on the day she went missing?"

Rick's forehead tightened. "Reiff called Chloe? He said he didn't. I don't even know why he'd have her number."

"He erased it from his call log, but we verified it on phone records."

Rick pursed his lips as he considered Reiff's deception. "Did you ask him about it?"

"He said he called her trying to find you—to let you know he was in town," Billy said with a shrug. "He got pretty huffy over the whole thing. He volunteered a DNA sample, and we took him up on it."

"Son of a bitch," Rick spit out as he shook his head. "He's the reason I'm here—I was hoping to get him before the judge tomorrow, have him released on bail."

Billy tossed his pen on his desk. "He isn't going anywhere, I assure you. Seems as though Judge Wade's hunting trip got complicated—he fell down a ravine and fractured his arm in two places. He'll be delayed a day or two."

"But another judge—"

Billy shook his head vigorously. "Nobody releases Judge Wade's prisoners except Judge Wade."

Rick released a deep sigh. "Reiff looked pretty sick when you locked him up."

"Looks fine to me, now that he ain't drinking."

"But he has cancer."

"You sure about that?"

"You have doubts?"

"I'm a deputy, not a doctor. But—"

The phone jangled. "Excuse me," Billy said, raising a finger and picking up the receiver. "Renfro here."

As Billy listened, his face grew ghostly pale. He wrapped a thick hand around his forehead, his fingers massaging his temples. "I'll be right there," he mumbled, then hung up.

Billy sat in numbed silence for several seconds before rising from his chair. "I need to go."

"What's up?"

Billy drew a deep breath, resting his hands on his hips. "Let's just say that the case against Draper Townsend—if there ever was one—just got weaker."

Rick frowned. "What do you mean?"

"Maggie Townsend won't be testifying."

"Why not?"

"She's dead."

CHAPTER 48

"**A**RE YOU OKAY, PA-PA?"

Rick stared out of the front windshield of his parked pickup, his weathered face lost in a dazed stupor. Sweat gathered on his forehead as his bloodless knuckles massaged the steering wheel, his mind under siege from a ceaseless assault of rapid-fire emotions.

Maggie. Draper. Reiff. Bledsoe. Chloe. Chase. Their faces exploded like laser-guided bullets through his brain. Maggie was gone, an *apparent* suicide. But why? Would Draper go free? Was Reiff telling the truth about Bledsoe? Why did Reiff call Chloe? Was Chloe dealing drugs? Where was Chase Rettick *now*?

His swirling thoughts came to rest on Chase with all the surety of an ivory roulette ball landing on a winning number. His eyes flamed with wrath as he considered the meth dealer, a loathsome creature who had decimated the lives of so many innocent victims. People like Courtney Williams. People like Chloe Morrand.

No, in answer to Abby's innocent question, Rick was not okay. His search for answers would begin—and hopefully end—when he found Chase Rettick. Billy said the cops were looking for him? *Yeah, right.* Rick was going to look a little harder, hopefully find him first.

"Pa-Pa?"

Rick whipped his head toward his granddaughter, jolted from his trance. "I need to take you to The Spur, so you can be with Auntie Sage. There is something I have to do."

Abby's face crinkled into a confused frown. "What do you have to do?"

Rick turned the key to his ignition and threw the truck into Reverse. "There's just something I have to do."

Abby slapped her hands on the front of her thighs, drawing a deep sigh as she stared straight ahead. After a moment, she turned toward Rick, tears pooling in her dispirited eyes. "Why are you always trying to get rid of me?"

Rick glanced at her as he pulled from the parking lot. "I'm not trying to get rid of you. I love you, baby. You know that."

"No you don't! You keep leaving me with Sage." Her lips trembled. "Who is going to take care of me?"

Rick swallowed, his heart sinking like a stone. As he stopped at a traffic light, he turned toward Abby. "I told you," he said barely above a whisper. "*I'm* going to take care of you."

"How about my dad? I do have a dad, don't I?"

Rick felt his jaw tighten. "Yes, you do have a dad."

"Can I go live with him?"

"No, you can't."

"Why not?"

"Abby, please."

Abby held her fire for a moment, just long enough to reload. "So, where are you going?"

"I can't say."

"Why can't I come with you?"

"You . . . just can't."

They rode in silence. Rick turned the corner onto Main Street, thankful to find a parking spot directly across the street from The Spur. The inside was lit, in spite of the window sign claiming "Closed."

"You need to stop treating me like a little baby, Pa-Pa," Abby protested. "I'm almost nine, you know!"

Rick turned off the ignition and drew a deep breath. He turned to his granddaughter and cupped her tiny hands in his. "Look, Abby, you just have to trust me. People are saying bad things about your mommy. I'm trying to help her. *Please.*"

Abby cast her eyes downward, moistening her lips as she considered his words. Finally, she nodded. Rick gently squeezed her hands. "Let's go."

Sage was standing behind the bar, holding a remote as she stared at the blank cracked screen of her wounded plasma.

"How's it look?" Rick asked as he and Abby walked in.

"Not good," Sage answered, setting down the remote. "I probably need to go to the Walmart in Bozeman, pick up something on sale."

"Can Abby ride along with you? Maybe spend the night at your place?"

Sage glanced at Rick as she wiped the bar, shaking her head as her lips tightened with disappointment. "Sure," she said curtly, her shrug saying the request didn't completely surprise her. He started to speak, wanting desperately to reassure her, tell her that he was going to see Chase Rettick. But he couldn't, not in front of Abby.

Rick watched Sage wring murky water from the bar rag, the room becoming drenched in an awkward silence. The mirror behind her was cracked in several places, and shattered bottles of liquor were strewn beneath broken shelves. Rick's nostrils filled with the thick aroma of alcohol, a sensation that both teased and tormented him.

"How bad is it?" he asked, puncturing the quiet with a foolish question.

Sage glanced around at the obvious. "Pretty bad. In addition to everything out here, the bathroom doors were ripped off their hinges."

Rick put his hands on his hips and cocked his head. "This all happened because of an argument over *bison*?"

Sage dropped her rag into the sink. "And it probably is going to get worse around here." She tossed a copy of the *Bozeman Chronicle* onto the bar. "Check this out."

Rick stared at the headline, written in block letters across the top of the front page: "CATTLEMEN SAY LOCAL BEEF NOW WORTHLESS."

As he began to read the article, Sage offered a verbal recap. "That's how my plasma got broke. All that story does is repeat the news report on TV—a report done by none other than Mandy Westerfield."

The news story did indeed reference the TV report and named the reporter: Amanda Westin Cobb. Rick looked up from the paper. "Does anyone know for sure that cattle have been infected?"

"I don't know that the cattle have even been *tested*," Sage said, shaking her head as she leaned on the edge of the bar. "From my understanding, it was assumed because of the bison that have been popping up in the valley that the cattle are infected. Looks like your friend Mandy didn't quite do her homework."

"She's not my friend."

Sage raised her eyebrows. "Oh?"

Rick had wondered whether seeing Mandy at the cemetery had sparked jealousy in Sage, and apparently it had. He brushed aside her remark, staring at the newspaper. Mandy had butchered the story, no question about it. She should have known better, being a local girl. Due to her carelessness, ranchers were going to suffer. Their cattle likely would be quarantined, taken off the market. The whole state could be affected. He felt his jaw muscles tighten as he pushed bursts of air out of his nostrils. Tucking the paper under his arm, he glanced at Sage. "I won't be gone long."

He strode purposefully toward the door, suddenly feeling as though the dark low-ceilinged bar was suffocating him. He burst onto the sidewalk, drawing a deep breath of brisk autumn air, eyes squinting into the late afternoon sun. Across the street, just beyond his truck, was the Riverton Grande. Rick fished into his front pocket for the business card belonging to Mandy Westerfield. *Room 201.* He snared the newspaper from underneath his arm and rolled it into his fist. Chase Rettick would have to wait—at least for now.

When he entered the hotel, Phyllis Danielson stood behind the registration desk. "Phyllis, I'm looking for one of your guests. Have you seen, uh, Amanda Westin Cobb around?"

Phyllis rolled her eyes. "You mean Mandy? Yeah, Rick, she's around. Let me ring her room." As Phyllis turned to use the phone behind her, Rick darted for an elegant staircase next to the elevator.

"The line's busy," he heard Phyllis call behind him. "If you give me a minute—"

Rick stormed across the second-floor balcony that ringed the lobby, then headed down the hallway. As he arrived at Mandy's door, he raised his arm, hesitating a moment as his wiser instincts told him to retreat. He knocked firmly, and the door opened almost instantly.

Mandy stood before him, wearing only a white terrycloth robe that had been hastily secured. She wore no makeup. Her eyes opened wide as she froze before him, her hand clutching a towel she was using to dab her hair. "Oh!" she gasped. "I thought you were room service."

Rick stared a moment, stunned by her appearance. Her once-alluring eyes were barren, weighted down by dark circles normally guarded from public. Her cheekbones seemed large and unnatural. Botox was her close yet unreliable friend.

Rick's eyes chased a droplet of water as it trickled down her neck and onto her chest, her robe revealing more than he would have preferred. He raised the newspaper gripped in his fist, reminding himself the purpose of his visit.

"The beef is not contaminated," he stammered through clenched teeth.

"Excuse me?"

"The beef—the cows—they're not contaminated just because they come in contact with a buffalo."

Mandy squinted at him, shaking her head rapidly. "What are you talking about?"

Rick took a deep exasperated breath. "Your story! Your goddamned news story! You said the buffalo had contaminated all the beef in the valley. That's not accurate. Now, all the newspapers have picked it up! Don't you even *care*?"

"Of course I care!" Mandy said, folding her arms across her chest. "I think you might be overreacting a little bit."

She moved out into the hallway. Rick took a step back, staring at her as he recalled all that lay beneath that robe. He remembered the sex—that unbelievable, passionate sex—especially when they'd argued, and they'd argued plenty. It had been a long time, but he remembered.

"Overreacting?" he snapped, trying to remain focused. "No, Mandy, I'm not overreacting. These are real people around here. Of course, what would you know about real people?"

"What's that supposed to mean?" she asked, narrowing her eyes.

"Remember high school, Mandy? You were as shallow as a September crick."

"September *crick*? How . . . *rural*."

Rick began walking away. Despite her attire, Mandy stormed after him. "High school? You're talking about *high school*?"

He stopped and turned toward her. They had squared off in the balcony above the lobby. Two elderly hotel guests seated below interrupted their reading to gaze at the commotion overhead.

"I missed a field goal, Mandy. A freakin' *field goal*. It cost us a football game. So what? I was just a kid. I really needed someone to stand by me, and you disappeared."

She went quiet, her face suddenly shrouded in sadness. She was hurt for some reason, and he felt a strange desire to comfort her. He resisted, keeping a safe distance.

Mandy started to cry, beginning slowly at first, then progressing to deep sobbing. Rick tilted his head to the side, his forehead tightening in confusion.

"It wasn't my fault! I had to leave!" she shouted loudly, slamming her hand on the dark-stained wooden railing. "I was pregnant!"

Rick felt the color run from his face. *Pregnant?* He stood paralyzed, his brain firing a cartridge full of thoughts. Did she have the child? Was it his? Did he have another daughter? Or a *son*?

He felt his heart thump as he tried to speak. "Who . . . I mean, how—"

Mandy stopped sobbing, her expression becoming sober and resolute. She shook her head, waving her hands in front of her. "I can't do this right now." His mind flashed back to their teenage years. This was straight out of Mandy's high school playbook. When things got difficult, she would run.

Rick's eyes opened wide. "What do you mean you can't do this right now?" he shouted. "Don't play that game with me, Mandy! You *need* to do this right now!"

Sage had just started her engine when Abby spotted Rick's truck. "My backpack! I don't have my backpack, Auntie Sage. Do you think Pa-Pa has it?"

Sage nodded. "I'll be back," she said, sliding off of her seat. She crossed the street and peered through the front window of Rick's cab. Nothing. She looked into the backseat, but all it contained were bluish smithereens of window glass. After glancing up and down the street, she entered the Riverton Grande.

Sage met eyes with Phyllis and started to ask her if she had seen Rick. Their eyes shot in tandem toward the balcony, where an altercation appeared to be growing more intense. Rick was speaking loudly with a woman clad only in a robe—a woman who looked like Mandy Westerfield. She was shouting something at him as she walked away. He stormed after her.

Sage felt nauseated. She looked at Phyllis. "Is that Mandy?" she asked. Phyllis nodded grimly.

Rick glanced into the lobby and met eyes with Sage, a stunned look sweeping across his face. He stopped for a beat, eyes darting about as though he'd somehow lost his bearings. He continued down the hall.

Sage scrambled for the door. She wanted badly to be angry, but warm tears on her cheeks told her something else.

After Mandy had slammed her hotel door in his face, Rick scrambled down the stairs and out the front door. He was too late.

He stood breathless on the sidewalk as Sage sped away, his hands seizing his hips as his shoulders melted into dispiritedness. He wondered what she'd heard—and what she thought. He'd find out soon enough.

He looked over his shoulder at the second floor of the Riverton Grande, trying to process the news he'd just received from Mandy. He took a half-step toward the front door of the hotel, then stopped and whirled toward his truck, his focus returning to the whereabouts of Chase Rettick.

The addict's trailer would be a good place to start.

Rick's chest heaved short breaths as threw his truck into gear, his forehead about to detonate from the onslaught of emotions cascading through his mind. The streets seemed eerily empty, the invading bison activists apparently deciding to give the small town a brief reprieve. As he watched the final lonesome leaves of autumn dance past the high beams of his truck, he felt as though he were the only man left in Riverton, the valley, maybe even all of God's universe.

His senses snapped awake to the wail of sirens. From a half mile away, he saw dense smoke. A cold shudder of shock ran through his veins. As he drew closer, he saw tongues of fire prancing from the windows of Chase Rettick's mobile home. Rick's eyes widened as a sudden explosion sent a ball of orange spewing from the roof of the structure, throwing him back in his seat. He skidded to a halt, watching as a pair of volunteer firefighters retreated briefly before aiming their overmatched hoses back toward the powerful inferno.

Rick jumped out of his truck, shielding his eyes as he felt the intense heat of the blaze. He edged toward the firefighters, instinctively searching for some way to help.

"I'm going to need you to stay back, Mr. Morrand," a voice behind him shouted. Rick turned to see Caleb Tidwell slamming the door of his SUV and walking toward him.

"This *is* Chase Rettick's trailer?" Rick asked, futilely hoping he's made a wrong turn.

"It is," Caleb answered. "There's been a series of explosions. It appears that Mr. Rettick decided to take his meth operation in-house."

"Was he in there?"

"Not sure. We probably won't know until the fire burns out."

"Could he survive?"

"Doubtful."

Rick's eyes blinked with disbelief. Chase Rettick dead? *No, damn it! Not now!* He buried his hands in the back pockets of his jeans and turned toward the fire, the gushing arcs of water helpless against the blaze's dogged destruction. He exhaled in defeat, glancing one last time at Caleb, who stared stone-faced at him, the reflection of flames flickering in the young sheriff's cavernous eyes.

CHAPTER 49

A S HE SQUINTED AT THE DNA markers beneath the lens of his microscope, Charlie Duchesne scratched his balding head in confusion. He drew a mouthful of sturdy black coffee from his stained yellow mug, his third refill of the morning.

Fridays were usually light, but this one wouldn't be. He'd spent a good part of the previous night out at the Townsend place, evaluating the circumstances surrounding Maggie's death. Even though he was the one who'd discovered the body, he hardly considered the case a slam dunk. Despite Draper being locked up, something told Charlie that the felon's treacherous tentacles were somehow wrapped around this one. *Did Maggie feel guilty for turning Draper in? Did she fear him? Did she decide she still loved him?* As a physician, Charlie had encountered enough battered women to know how difficult it was to uncover the secrets held captive within their souls.

Charlie drew a deep breath and peered back into his microscope. For the moment, he would have to focus on the Morrand case—more specifically, the DNA belonging to Reiff Metcalf, the lawyer from California. Charlie had been reviewing the markers for the better part of an hour, and something didn't seem to add up. He rubbed his weary eyes, his fatigued body begging for sleep. Heaving a lengthy sigh out of the side of his mouth, he wondered whether he could have made a mistake.

As he examined the DNA that he had found inside Chloe Morrand's vehicle, he had found a match for Chloe's markers, as well as those for her daughter Abby, all of which made perfect sense. That's when things got complicated. Charlie was fairly certain that Reiff had not been inside Chloe's vehicle, but he was struck by how similar Reiff's DNA was to that of Chloe's daughter. It was so similar, in fact, that Charlie felt compelled to check his science numerous times. He almost wished he hadn't.

Charlie removed his readers from the top of his forehead and began chewing one of the tips. He impulsively reached for his cell phone and dialed Rick's number. Voice mail. Probably for the best. He had no idea how he was going to break the news that Rick's former law partner and one-time best friend had fathered the child of Chloe Morrand.

Rick propped his shoulder against the top rail of Bull Redmond's paddock, his hand stroking the soft chestnut face of Big Sky, the docile animal transmitting a peaceful tranquility only a horse could provide.

"He sure is a gentle giant, isn't he?" Bull said in his thick rolling voice. "I suppose I'll probably miss him."

Sadness washed over the deep lines of Bull's grizzled face, his moist, dull eyes betraying the shattered spirit he had inherited following the death of his son. Rick wondered whether the grief that comes from the loss of a child ever faded, or if it was a permanent fissure in the heart that would never fully close. He and Bull were innocent men, convicted of crimes they didn't commit, each handed an unjust, lifetime sentence they probably didn't deserve.

"You sure you want to do this?" he asked Bull.

The large man nodded, his cracked lips downturned. "It's time."

They stood in silence, Rick continuing to stroke the side of Big Sky's face. "Abby is sure going to love him. This will be a nice surprise."

Bull stared at the horse, stuck in an odd trance. After several seconds, he suddenly snapped awake, tapping his ring on the metal rail of the paddock as if tolling a final bell. "You remember Reno, don't you Rick?" he asked, nodding to a ranch hand standing a dozen feet away. Reno spewed a lengthy stream of tobacco, his smile exposing a jumbled row of yellow teeth that seemed at home beneath his untamed handlebar moustache. "Reno and one of the boys can bring him out to your place this afternoon. They can walk him around a bit, let him get used to his new surroundings, prepare his stall. I would suggest you don't try to ride him for about a week or so."

Rick rubbed the stubble on his jaw. "I pick up Abby from school between three thirty and four. I probably won't be back until close to five, if that will give them enough time."

Bull nodded as Rick handed him a check. He folded it in half and stuffed it in his shirt pocket without looking at it. His attempt to trudge forward in life without Ryder had nothing to do with money.

The men shook hands firmly, sharing a common bond they would forever loathe.

Amanda Westin Cobb leaned against the red-brick corner of the Riverton Grande, sucking on a Virginia Slim as though it were her last. Her room was non-smoking, as fate would have it, and rather than face the wrath of the front-desk Medusa named Phyllis Danielson, she reasoned it was prudent to step outside.

Her cell phone rang. Harvey, her boss. Third time that day. She hit "Ignore" and stuffed the phone back into her coat pocket.

She stared across the street at an old train station, which now served as a Greyhound bus stop. The vehicle that caught her eye was not a Greyhound bus but a luxury coach suited for touring retirees, or perhaps even a country music band. This vehicle carried neither—instead, it poured out modestly dressed passengers onto the street, many of them carrying backpacks.

The first group was replaced on the bus by similar travelers, albeit ones who appeared fatigued. Some of them carried picket signs, which they tossed into a careless pile on the sidewalk as they stepped on board.

Amanda drew another deep drag on her cigarette, contemplating the browbeating administered by Rick Morrand. He was likely correct—she had no definitive evidence that any cattle in Montana were tainted. Her amateurish report had touched off a beef scare that likely would have a ripple effect across the nation. Her desire to pacify her boss had made her reckless. *Journalist?* Not quite. She deserved to be out of a job.

She watched as two of the new arrivals began to cautiously cross the street, looking around in wonder as though they had just cleared customs in a strange land. One of the men glanced toward Amanda, who seized the opportunity to shift to a more alluring pose. Tossing her cigarette onto the sidewalk, she walked directly toward the newly arrived pilgrims.

"You guys visiting?" They nodded simultaneously, eyes scanning her goods. She sensed an opportunity. "You must be tired. How about I buy you a drink?"

They looked at each other, then back at Amanda. "You a hooker?" one of them asked in a deep Southern accent.

Amanda cocked her head and sighed. "No, I'm not a hooker," she said, remaining focused. "I'm a reporter. A television reporter."

Heckle and Jeckle looked at each other again. "I don't think we're supposed to talk to any reporters," the second one said. He also had an accent. Boston, maybe?

"I'm not on duty," Amanda lied. "Consider it a social call." She nodded toward the hotel's bar entrance. The men shrugged and followed her inside the Riverton Grande lounge, where she hoped alcohol might loosen their lips. Within fifteen minutes, Amanda managed to ply the men with four shots of Jose Cuervo while she nursed a margarita.

"Coming all the way out here, this buffalo issue must mean a lot to you," she said as she stirred her drink. Her comment brought roars of laughter from both men.

"Buffalo?" said the guy with the Southern accent, the tequila offering newfound bravado. "I'm from Columbus, Georgia! I've never even *seen* a freakin' buffalo!"

"I don't give a damn about buffalo nee-tha," said Mr. Boston. "I don't even like the *city* of Buffalo!"

The men rumbled into another spate of obnoxious laughter. Amanda stared at them blankly, then turned toward the bartender, nodding at him to fill another round of shots. They slammed their glasses on the bar, wincing as the tequila went down. "Ahh, smooth," said the Southern guy, who appeared ready to throw up.

Amanda interlocked her fingers, turning toward them. "So, let me get this straight, gentlemen. You came all the way out here from the East Coast. You're replacing people who have been here almost two weeks, staging protests to save the buffalo. But you don't *care* about buffalo?"

"Nope," the Boston guy said, shaking his head as he sucked on a lime. "We just go where they tell us to go. It's usually the unions who call us up—that way, their guys can keep getting paid. This one is a little different."

"You guys are hired feet?"

"Hired feet?"

"Yeah," Amanda said, leaning closer to them. "You know, astroturfers. You don't care about the cause—you're just here to bring attention to it." She took a sip of her drink. "But why?"

The Southerner began to answer, but the Boston guy nudged him in the ribs. He looked at Amanda and turned more serious.

"Look, lady, we don't know all that much, except that we need this job. I had a decent career driving a truck until the recession. I lost my house, my wife, everything." The bartender approached with the bottle of tequila, but the man waved him off, turning toward Amanda, his doleful eyes pleading with her. "We're just trying to pay our bills."

Amanda nodded with feigned sympathy, distracted by the thoughts and emotions barreling down the carpool lane of her brain. Her cell phone went off, its vibration causing it to rattle on the bar. It was Harvey. She had ignored him earlier, but no more. "Excuse me," she said as she casually slid from her stool, tossing a twenty on the bar. She took a deep slug from her margarita, figuring the fortification might come in handy.

"You set me up," she said into the phone as walked out to the hotel lobby.

The line remained quiet for a beat. "Set you up? How?"

"You told me you had a source that said the cattle were infected!" she snapped, her rising voice flush with rancor. She turned a few heads in the lobby, causing Phyllis to stare at her from the front desk. Amanda fearlessly returned her glare, then went back to her phone. "Thanks to you, Harvey, I've caused a complete shit storm!"

"I . . . I did have a source," Harvey said, attempting to steady his voice.

"Yeah? Who, Harvey? Who is your source?"

"Someone in New York."

"Who, damn it! Tell me who."

The line was quiet. "Look," Harvey finally said. "You're going to need to calm down. You did a nice job—the network picked it up. *It's working*. Now, you need to do a follow-up."

"What's working?"

Silence.

"Harvey! *What* is working?"

More silence.

She tapped her phone's speaker button and held the phone in front of her. "Harvey, what have you done?"

"Amanda, you're going to need to calm down," Harvey's voice crackled.

"Calm down? Tell you what, Harvey. You want a follow-up? You can bet your ass I'm going to do a follow-up!" Her voice echoed through the lobby. Phyllis narrowed her eyes from the front desk. Amanda defiantly flipped her the bird, causing Phyllis's eyes to widen.

"Amanda, I'm going to tell you again—you need to calm down," Harvey pleaded. "You need to calm down or else."

"Or else what?"

She heard Harvey draw a deep sigh. "Or else you'll be fired."

Amanda shifted her weight, as though Harvey was standing right in front of her. "Oh yeah, Harvey?" she screamed. "You know that little fling we had? It's called sexual harassment! You'll be hearing from my lawyer!"

She stood panting, as if the conversation had exhausted her. An elderly couple who had been reading on the sofa nodded approvingly in unison. Amanda was on a roll.

"And, Harvey?" she said with a smile. "You don't have to fire me—I quit!"

A gaggle of gleeful children poured from the front door of Abby's school late Friday afternoon, their spirits buoyed by the promise of a carefree weekend ahead. Abby waved weakly at a couple of her friends, then bowed her head as she walked joylessly toward Rick's truck.

She said nothing as she climbed into the passenger seat, other than when she looked over her shoulder and asked whether he ever planned to get his windows fixed.

"Soon enough," Rick mumbled. "I just haven't had a chance."

"It's kind of cold in here."

"Sorry," he said, turning up the heat.

It would only get colder when the late-autumn sun settled behind the Gallatin foothills. Still, Rick bided his time, stopping first for gas, and then at Town & Country, hoping to give Bull Redmond's men ample time to get Big Sky settled in the barn.

Though she tried to disguise it, Abby seemed to be favoring her right hand, opening and closing it as if she were squeezing an imaginary tennis ball. As they headed down 89, Rick noticed her wince as she tried to make a fist.

"Let me see that," he said, extending an open palm. Abby briefly resisted before blowing out a breath and lifting her arm toward him. She had two cuts across her knuckles, which had turned purple and begun to swell.

"What happened?"

"I fell."

"What *happened?*" Rick repeated, his voice carrying an edge.

"I punched Ronald Cassidy. A couple of times."

"You punched a guy?"

"You've always said no one should punch a girl."

Rick drew a deep sigh, shaking his head as he looked out the driver's side window. He snapped his head back toward Abby. "Why did you punch Ronald Cassidy?"

"He made fun of my mom," Abby said with a shrug. "He said she was crazy."

Rick felt blood rush to his face. "He said that?"

"Yep."

He tightened his grasp on the steering wheel. "Ronald was wrong to do that. But Abby, you can't go around hitting people—not girls, and not even boys."

"Maybe boys need to watch what they say."

Rick allowed himself a taut smile. "Did Auntie Sage say she'd be coming tomorrow?" he asked hesitantly, wading into dangerous waters.

"Yep. She said to tell you she would bring a cake."

Rick nodded with relief. Perhaps he and Sage could talk. He reached toward Abby. "Let me see those knuckles again."

"Ow!" Abby squealed as he tapped his thumb on her bruised hand.

"Doesn't seem to be broken, but I can't be sure," he said with a frown. "We'll put some ice on it when we get home—that should reduce the swelling." He released her hand, smiling as her nose wrinkled with scorn.

"Do me a favor, will you, Abby?"

"What?" she said, staring at her hand.

"Remind me to teach you how to throw a proper punch."

Abby flashed a sly grin at her grandfather. He smiled back, studying her innocence. His heart ached to assure her that she forever would be safe and protected, that she would suffer no more pain, that everything for the rest of her life would be okay. That same broken heart reminded him that life offered no such guarantees.

They rode in silence down the road winding toward the ranch house, the cedar roof a mere silhouette in the day's final light. As Rick's truck climbed a small hill past the faded gray barn, Abby turned toward him, a curious look on her face.

"What was that sound? Was that a horse?"

Rick stared straight ahead. "I didn't hear anything."

Abby lowered her window. A loud neigh could be heard, followed by an agitated snort. "I heard a horse."

Rick glanced over his shoulder, trying to maintain his innocence. Beyond the barn, he noticed the front grill of a truck, one he didn't recognize. Was it Bull Redmond's man Reno? Was there a trailer?

"Abby, you go ahead and go inside," Rick said, putting his truck into Park. He stared at the barn. The horse continued to snort, clearly disturbed. Rick heard the crack of splitting wood, a signal the animal was kicking in its stall.

"Why can't I go with you?" Abby asked, slamming the door of the truck and slinging her backpack over her shoulder.

"Abby, please."

Abby trudged toward the house, shaking her head as Rick watched her go inside. After reaching into the back of the truck for his rifle, he walked toward the barn. He placed his hand on the cold metal latch, the door already slightly ajar. He glanced back toward the house, spotting the outline of Abby's body as she watched him from her bedroom window.

Rick tugged the latch, the barn door groaning as it edged along its rusty rails. "Reno? Bull? Anybody in here?" He stepped into the blackness, wishing he'd brought a flashlight, perhaps a lantern. Big Sky was in his new stall, his head dancing wildly as his front legs stabbed at the wooden gate in front of him. "Easy, boy," Rick said as he edged forward.

Rick heard movement behind him. Before he could turn around, an object thudded against the back of his head. He staggered, his ears flooded with a dull ringing sound. His rifle soared from his grasp as he collapsed forward, his cheekbone bouncing off the thin layer of hay covering the concrete barn floor. He lay on the ground, unable to open his eyes, let alone move.

"Dumb bastard!" said a voice hissing with venom. The tone was raspy, almost hoarse.

Rick struggled to place his arms on the ground, wanting urgently to rise. He lifted his throbbing head slightly, only to collapse again, his bleeding skull caught in a ceaseless, nauseating spin. His eyes blinked as he recognized a familiar scent, one that stung his nostrils. *Gasoline.* He heard the heaving sound of a metal gas can splashing fuel onto the barn floor. Big Sky kicked relentlessly, trapped between fear and fury, desperately trying to break free. The barn had a yellow glow that was rapidly growing brighter, the hay having been ignited.

"Pa-Pa!"

Rick's eyes opened wide in shock as he heard Abby's voice. His heart raced, his instincts urging him to act. He tried to push himself up, only to have the steel toe of a work boot kick one of his arms out from under him, sending him crashing back down onto the unforgiving concrete slab. His assailant delivered a potent blow to his Rick's ribs, an excruciating exclamation point.

"Abby!" he groaned as loud as he could. "Abby! Run!"

The child responded only with a deafening scream. Rick's woozy head swayed when he raised it, his eyes squinting through the dense smoke as he feverishly tried to shake his double vision. He watched helplessly as the man dragged Abby by her collar.

When he pulled back the barn's rear door, the man loosened his grip on Abby. She seized the opportunity, grabbing his hand and biting down hard on his finger. "Ahhh!" the man yelled. "You little—"

Abby broke free, the intruder gagging as he fled the blaze. She choked for air as she raced toward her grandfather, tugging at the top of his jacket as the flames dared them to find an escape. "C'mon, Pa-Pa! You have to get up!"

Rick shook his head, gasping for oxygen but inhaling only smoke. He rose to his feet and staggered through the haze. He stopped.

"Wait!" he shouted. "The horse!" He shoved Abby out of the barn, so forcefully she tumbled to the ground. Covering his face with his sleeve, he stumbled toward Big Sky's stall. When he unlatched the gate, the horse knocked him backward with a desperate burst for freedom. The massive animal headed straight for Abby, who curled into a fetal position as she braced for impact. Rick froze, smoke searing his eyes as stared in horror at the twelve hundred pounds of horseflesh thundering toward his granddaughter.

In perfect stride, Big Sky gracefully sailed over Abby, galloping harmlessly into the darkness. Rick's knees buckled as he nearly collapsed with relief. He lurched ahead, his lungs searching desperately for air as he fled the advancing flames. Pulsing with adrenaline, he picked up Abby in a single motion and carried her out of harm's way. They fell onto the freezing ground, Rick's arms wrapping tightly around Abby's shivering body as a brilliant inferno swallowed the barn.

Rick heard the rumble of tires spitting gravel. He jumped to his feet and began running toward the sound. "Pa-Pa, don't leave!" Abby screamed in panic. "I'm scared, Pa-Pa! Please!"

Rick stopped, glancing toward his trembling grandchild. He couldn't leave her. He *wouldn't* leave her. He watched helplessly as the dark-colored truck started to speed away. The fire from the barn ignited the darkness, enabling him to see the vehicle more clearly. He swallowed hard, his heart pounding.

It was a Ford truck. A dually.

Rick dug his cell phone from the pocket of his jeans and searched for a number. Abby rose to her feet and ran toward him, throwing her arms around his waist and burying her face into his side. He tugged her close to him.

"Helen? It's Rick Morrand," he said between short breaths. "I need to talk to Billy. Or the sheriff. Whoever is there."

"I'm sorry, Rick," she answered. "Neither of them is here."

"Where are they?"

"Billy's tending to a bad wreck on Highway 540," she said. "And Caleb trying to get a handle on those protesters—looks like they've started up all over again."

Rick started to ask for Clint Roswell, but decided that would be useless. He blew out a sigh. "Ask Billy to give me a call, will you, Helen?"

"Any message?"

Rick paused. He considered the truck he saw, and the voice he had heard. "Yeah, I have a message," he said. "Tell Billy I just had a close encounter with Richard Bledsoe."

Rick slipped his phone back into his pocket. He could feel Abby shivering, likely from fear more than cold. He held her tighter, his hand gently stroking the side of her face, his fingers feeling the wetness of her tears. An ear-splitting crack startled them from the direction of the barn. They whirled to see the ridge beam fall to the ground in a glowing shaft of flames. He released a defeated sigh. The fire wouldn't spread, but the barn was lost.

Abby's eyes blinked through moist eyes as she looked up at her grandfather. "Who did you say that man was, Pa-Pa?"

Rick stroked the back of her head. "It's not important," he said. "Let's just say he wasn't a nice man."

"Was it Buddy Rivers?"

Rick furrowed his brow and tilted his head to the side. "Buddy Rivers? What makes you say that? Have you ever even *met* Buddy Rivers?"

Abby tightened her grip on Rick's waist. "Well, no. But I heard he hates animals, and that man was going to hurt that horse. Besides, everybody says Buddy Rivers is crazy."

"I thought we agreed it wasn't good to call people crazy." He shook his head, placing an arm around Abby's shoulder as they began walking toward the house.

"Pa-Pa?" Abby asked, wiping her tears. "Was that horse for me?"

Rick nodded. "Yes, baby, that horse is for you. His name is Big Sky."

Abby hugged him with all her might, plunging her face into his jacket. "Will he come back?"

Billy Renfro finally called around midnight.

"So you figure it was the same truck that was on the videotape from The General Store?" the deputy asked.

Rick stared out his window at the smoldering embers of what used to be his barn. "It was dark, but I'm fairly certain it was the same one," he said, adding with bite, "I would imagine he's in Idaho by now."

Billy sighed. "I got back to you as quick as I could, Rick. We're pretty strapped, as you know."

"Right—the protesters."

Rick paced the dark fir-covered floors of his ranch house. His phone connection was silent for several seconds, save for the sound of Billy's labored breathing. "I'll get this description out to area law enforcement," Billy finally said, "and also alert the media."

"The media," Rick repeated flatly, thinking of Amanda Westin Cobb.

"They can be helpful in these situations."

"I see."

More silence. "I'll keep you posted," Billy said.

Rick dropped his phone into his pocket and walked down the hall toward Abby's room. Cracking the door slightly, he squinted inside. She was sleeping.

He returned to the kitchen and reached into a cabinet above the refrigerator. He produced a .45 Taurus Judge, his self-defense revolver. He flipped open the cylinder, confirming that it was loaded with .410 shotgun shells. It was a ritual he had performed twice already that night.

He peered out the kitchen window once more, wondering if Richard Bledsoe really was in Idaho.

CHAPTER 50

DARRELL GREER WAS FEEDING HIS chickens Saturday morning when he noticed a horse munching on grass just beyond his tool shed. A few phone calls later, Big Sky was returned to its latest owner, just in time for Abby's ninth birthday party.

The fire had claimed the Morrand's century-old barn, but it spared the metal corral, enabling Rick to provide a temporary home for the prized chestnut. Rick adjusted his Stetson as he stared at the darkened rubble, the smell of charred wood filling his nostrils. He scanned the surrounding mountains, their snow-covered peaks foretelling an ambitious winter. A new structure would need to go up quickly.

Abby rested her chin on the second rail as she peered wide-eyed at Big Sky prancing confidently around his new surroundings. The horse played to his audience of one, raising his head boastfully as the late-morning sun glistened off his shiny bronze coat.

Rick's cell phone rang. He answered without looking at the number.

"It's me," Mandy Westerfield said. "We need to talk."

"Not a good time, Mandy."

"It's important," she persisted. "Didn't you get my voice mail?"

"Not now," he said, ending the call and putting the phone in his pocket. He fixed his eyes on Abby, clutching the rare sliver of joy delivered by the child's glimmering smile. This was *her* day. "You're

gonna catch cold," Rick said to Abby. "I'm going to get you a jacket."
She didn't respond, mesmerized by the splendor of Big Sky.

Sage was in the kitchen unpacking groceries, having brought the
cake as promised. She didn't look at Rick when he entered the house.

"The girl's so excited she forgot her jacket," he said uneasily,
lifting a lavender parka off a hook next to the door. Sage had been at
the house for more than an hour and hadn't uttered a word.

"That's way too much horse for that girl," she said without
looking at him.

"She won't be riding him right away."

"Too much horse," Sage repeated. "A nine-year-old doesn't need
a horse like that—unless you're trying to *spoil* her."

"So, what if I am? Maybe I should spoil her a little."

Not a good start. Sage shook her head. After unpacking the
groceries, she reached into a drawer and pulled out a large carving
knife. She placed a melon on the cutting board and began
aggressively slicing it as if it had wronged her somehow. "I don't
really care," she said flatly. "It's none of my business."

Rick sensed hurt in her voice, most assuredly caused by the
episode with Mandy Westerfield the previous afternoon. He walked
toward her, as if approaching an animal wounded in the wild, its
defenses up in the interest of self-preservation.

"Can we talk?"

Sage shrugged. "What is there to talk about?" she replied,
forcefully halving the melon.

"It's not what you think."

Sage looked away from the melon, staring down at the floor. As
she turned back toward him, her eyes signaled anger. "How do *you*
know what I think?" she asked, pointing the knife for emphasis.
"Maybe that's your problem. You know what everyone thinks, and
how they *feel*."

She hammered the knife twice more through the melon. The
blade made a loud, banging sound as it hit the cutting board. Sage
reached into the refrigerator and emerged with a head of lettuce, two
tomatoes, a cucumber, and an onion. She suddenly seemed eager to
sever anything in sight.

Rick swallowed, rubbed his temples, and tried again. "Don't shut down, Sage—please," he said. "The other night, you and me, it wasn't a mistake. It *meant* something."

Sage stopped cutting and glared at him. "Oh?" she asked, cocking her head. "And what does it mean now?"

Rick drew a deep breath. "If you're referring to Mandy—"

"Like I said, that's none of my business," she said while assaulting another innocent vegetable.

"Sure it's your business. I *want* it to be your business." Rick moved forward, placing Abby's coat on a chair. "I went to talk to her about the bogus report she made about the bison. The next thing I know, she tells me she got pregnant when we were younger."

"Great," Sage said flatly. She lifted her eyebrows and tilted her head, her eyes blinking as if holding back emotion.

Rick sighed. "I don't even know if she had the baby."

Sage jerked her head back. "Don't you *want* to know?"

"I guess—I mean, of course I do," he said softly. "Thing is, I just lost a child."

Sage lips trembled, her eyes beginning to moisten. "Do you think you're the only one who's hurting right now?"

She put down her knife, resting both of her hands on her hips. She seemed to soften—at least, that was his hope. He studied her features, realizing just how attracted he was to her. When he'd lost Christine, the likelihood of ever replacing her was so dim he never made an effort. He considered himself a luckless prospector, destined to stake claims that would never again yield the mother lode. All the while, the brightest of gems was right in front of him. His selfishness and self-pity hadn't allowed him to see her. Rick started toward her, wanting to hold her, comfort her. Sage stiffened slightly. He stopped. *Not yet.*

"Mandy has called me twice already today, saying she wants to meet. I'm sure I'll find out what's going on soon enough."

Sage turned her eyes from Rick toward the tall front windows of the ranch house. He followed her gaze, his stomach sinking as he saw Mandy Westerfield coming up the walkway.

"I'll be outside," Sage said as she snared Abby's coat off the chair and slung it over her arm. "Guess you're going to find out sooner than you think."

Sitting in the cafe in Gardiner, Bledsoe peeled back the bloody bandage covering his finger, studying a wound that wouldn't seem to close. The little girl had sunk her teeth into him like a rabid pit bull, her bite slicing through skin and tendons nearly all the way to the bone.

"You care for more coffee, sir?" Fawn said as she approached his table. She frowned as she noticed his finger. "Oooo, that's a nasty cut. How'd that happen?"

Bledsoe quickly replaced the bandage over the wound, fearful that Fawn might notice human teeth marks. "I dropped a glass in my motel room. I got careless when I picked up the pieces."

"Well, there's an Urgent Care—"

"I'm fine," Bledsoe answered, cutting her off. "I think I'm ready for my check." Fawn nodded, glancing once more at his finger before walking away.

Bledsoe tugged several napkins from the dispenser and stuffed them into his coat pocket. He took a long sip of coffee, heaving a sigh as he sat back in his booth and turned his eyes toward a soundless black-and-white television being ignored in the corner. Steve McQueen and James Garner were in a Nazi concentration camp, brainstorming in *The Great Escape*.

The bells on the front door jingled. It was Herrera, the priest. He still had that stupid carefree grin pasted on his face. He plopped onto a stool at the lunch counter, Fawn looking all atwitter as she poured him a cup of coffee. When he saw Bledsoe, he nodded enthusiastically and began to rise from his seat. Bledsoe shot him a glare that made him stay put.

"You staying away from the bears, Padre?" Fawn asked him with a smile. "From what the paper says, they've been walking all over town, picking through dumpsters and whatnot."

"Ah, los osos," Herrera said quietly, staring into his coffee. The subject seemed to unnerve him. "Los osos son peligrosos."

"Peligrosos?" Fawn asked, furrowing her brow.

"Dangerous."

"You're damn—darn—right they're peligrosos, Padre! I hear there's not only black bears out there but also grizzlies."

Bledsoe's jaw tightened as he stared at them, the use of Spanish igniting anger—especially him being from Southern California. *Don't they know this is an English-speaking nation?* Herrera was far too self-assured for Bledsoe's liking, reveling in the worship he received from the likes of Fawn, acting like some beacon of virtue against which the rest of humanity should be measured. He projected an unattainable purity to which all could aspire, a holiness you just wanted to touch. It was the same innocence that had been portrayed by Father Tim, though, in Bledsoe's mind, Father Tim wasn't innocent at all. More than likely, neither was Herrera.

Bledsoe cast his eyes back toward the television. Steve McQueen and James Garner were gone, replaced by a blond newswoman. Next to a logo of a Bozeman station, the words "BULLETIN: Police Search for Murder Suspect" stretched across the screen. The picture cut away to a driver's license photo of Bledsoe pasted next to a mug shot of Chloe Morrand.

Bledsoe dropped his eyes toward the table, his heart racing with panic as he lowered the bill of his baseball cap. Morrand must have made it out of the barn and somehow identified him. He scanned the diner. Fawn and Herrera were still talking about bears, ignoring the TV. A man in the corner, absorbed in his newspaper, seemed unaware of everything—including the ketchup dribbling down his bearded chin. Bledsoe's eyes darted back to the TV. He breathed a sigh of relief when Charles Bronson appeared on screen.

He lowered his head again as Fawn approached. "Here you go, sir," she said as she laid his check on the table. "Are you sure I can't get you anything else?"

Bledsoe's eyes remained focused on the table. He wagged his head briskly, relieved as he watched her apron move away. His cell phone vibrated in his top pocket. He glanced at the number. *Susan.*

He sent it to voice mail, just as he'd done all week. At first, he had felt guilty about ignoring his wife, but no more. He had ventured to a grim, distant place from which no one—not even Susan—could possibly bring him back. He was alone in the darkness, and he had become comfortable, as though he belonged there. Satan felt nearer than God.

Bledsoe slid from his booth and began walking toward the door. As he passed the lunch counter, Father Herrera turned toward him. "Hello again, my friend. Will you be joining us for services tomorrow?"

Herrera's voice unnerved him, a stiffness roping its way up Bledsoe's spine. He considered continuing on his way, but a sudden thought halted him. "We'll see, Father," he answered politely, eyes averted. "Tell me: Didn't you say you offered confession on Saturdays?"

"Five o'clock, today and every Saturday," Herrera declared. The priest's answer made Bledsoe bristle. Herrera sounded as though he received some voyeuristic pleasure listening in on the transgressions of others.

"Five o'clock," Bledsoe repeated. He turned up the collar on his jacket and walked out the door.

Mandy and Rick stared at each other as though they had never met. She stood outside the front door for several seconds, Rick's brain filled with a litany of questions he didn't necessarily want answered. "May I come in?" Mandy finally asked, her hand shielding her face from a sudden blast of wind.

Rick took a step back. "I'm sorry. Please." He gestured her inside and offered her a seat at the kitchen table. "Can I take your coat? Would you like something to drink?"

Mandy pushed strands of hair away from tired eyes colored with exhaustion and defeat. She shook her head and sighed. "I won't be here long." Rick swallowed and studied her face, a strange emptiness filling the depths of his stomach.

"You were right about the story I reported," Mandy began, drawing a deep breath. "I was totally inaccurate—there is nothing wrong with the cattle in the valley or anywhere else in Montana."

Rick nodded politely. He'd all but forgotten his original purpose for storming into the Riverton Grande.

"My story was picked up by other news organizations, as well on the Internet, and nobody checks their facts. The result was a beef scare that has affected prices across the country. I—"

Rick found himself growing impatient. He held out an open palm, shaking his head in disbelief. "Wait a minute. Why are you telling me this? You came all the way out here to talk about *cattle*? I thought—"

"I was used, Rick. The story about brucellosis, the protesters in the valley—it was all a hoax. The activists were sent here to draw media attention. The buffalo popping up all over the place were actually *planted*. Once the news organizations were here to cover the protesters, all they needed was someone to report that the cattle were contaminated. Unfortunately, that someone was me."

Rick furrowed his brow. "Who exactly is *they*?"

"A group of brokers on Wall Street set all this up," Mandy said. "The details are a little complicated, but it appears that they buy up stocks tied to futures contracts for beef. After they pull the trigger on a 'scare,' those contracts skyrocket in value. Remember the salmonella outbreak in the Midwest a couple of years ago, when they said the source was pork? The supply tightened, and prices went up. That was these same guys."

Rick pulled his chair forward and rested his elbows on the table. "How do you know all this?"

"I used to be married to Ricky Cobb, the baseball player for the Yankees. I'm sure you've heard of him?" Rick hated baseball. Still, he nodded his head. "When Ricky retired, he got into trading stocks. His celebrity status opened a lot of doors."

"Is he involved?"

"Thankfully, no," Mandy insisted, "but I consider him a reliable source. I got suspicious when I saw a new group of protesters coming into town yesterday. After I talked to a couple of them, I started making some phone calls."

Rick shook his head. "Wouldn't government regulators be on top of this?"

Mandy pursed her lips. "For all I know, they're in on it," she said with a nervous laugh. "This whole idea started with Occupy Wall Street. Some brokers got together with the leaders of the Occupy movement and devised a way that they both could benefit. Money always talks, doesn't it?"

"Let me get this straight—you're telling me that you started this beef scare?" Rick said, his eyes squinting. "Why did you make that report?"

"I was . . . *sloppy*, to say the least. I based my story on a source provided by my former boss. For all I know, he's in on it too."

"Your *former* boss? Were you fired?"

"I quit. I'm not sure exactly how I'm going to get the word out, but I fully intend to make this right."

Rick rose from his chair and walked over to a pot of coffee that had been made that morning. It looked like mud, but he didn't care. He filled two cups and brought them back to the table, setting one in front of Mandy. He released a breath as he stared at the yellow mug, stroking the side of it with his thumb. His eyes rose toward Mandy.

"So, that's the reason you came all the way out here? To tell me about a beef scare?"

Mandy looked away from him, her eyes reaching out to the surrounding foothills. "No," she said as she shook her head. "I needed to talk you to you about . . . us."

Rick raised his eyebrows. "You mean, you being pregnant, back when we were kids?"

Mandy turned toward him and nodded. "Yes, I was pregnant."

Rick sipped his coffee. It tasted like burnt firewood. "Did you have the child?"

"I did," Mandy said, her eyes filled with surrender.

Rick clutched his forehead, his thumb and forefinger pressing on his temples as though he feared his blood vessels might burst. *Do I have . . . another child?* In an odd, aberrant way, the thought seemed to soothe him, as though granting him a temporary reprieve from the viselike stranglehold of grief. His brain flashed with visions of Chloe, her face glaring at him, washed in disappointment and sorrow, as though he was betraying her. He slowly lifted his eyes toward Amanda, trying to move his lips but producing no words.

"When my parents found out I was pregnant," she continued, "they sent me to live with my aunt in Seattle. Once the baby was born, I gave her up for adoption."

"Her?" Rick heard himself say.

"Yes. Her name is Victoria. She lives in Chicago. She's a lawyer."

Rick eyes widened slightly. "A lawyer?"

"A very successful lawyer. She received both her undergrad and law degrees from Northwestern. That's how she ended up in Chicago."

Rick rubbed his grizzled chin. "If she was adopted, how do you know all this?"

"She contacted me. She's fairly *aggressive*, I guess you'd say. Her investigator tracked down the adoption agency in Seattle and found out I was her birth mother. You're on the paperwork as the father."

He leaned forward, placing his forearms on the table. "She must be in her mid-thirties."

"Thirty-six."

"So why did she contact you now?" he asked. "If she's a successful lawyer, it sounds like her adoptive parents did a good job."

"Like I said—she's aggressive. She seems like someone who gets what she wants."

Rick shook his head. "Well, what does she *want*?"

"A kidney."

"A what?"

Mandy drew a deep breath. "She has some kind of rare kidney disorder. It's worsened over the years, and now she needs a kidney transplant. If you have a relative as a donor, the organ tends to last longer." Mandy forced a laugh. "Here I thought she wanted to have some warm and fuzzy relationship with her birth mother, but that apparently wasn't the case. What she wanted was my kidney."

"And?"

"She has Type O blood," Mandy said. "I have Type A. I wasn't a match. When she found that out, Victoria wanted to contact you—or better yet, your daughter. The younger the kidney, the better, I guess."

Rick's head began to spin. *She wanted to contact Chloe?* "No one named Victoria has contacted me," he muttered. "Besides, I'm Type B."

"How about your daughter? Chloe? What blood type is she?"

Rick felt the skin tighten on the back of his neck. He hesitated to answer, his throat suddenly as dry as dust. "Type O," he managed to say.

Mandy lifted her thick eyebrows. "Do you know if Victoria called your daughter?"

Rick wagged his head slowly, his eyes staring into nothingness. "Not that I know of."

Not that I know of? Rick realized he knew everything about Chloe, yet he knew nothing. His brain scurried through a maze of scrambled thoughts. *Did Victoria contact her? Did she ask Chloe to donate a kidney? What if Chloe refused?* He veins ran cold as he remembered Sandra Billingsley telling him about recent deposits in Chloe bank account. Large deposits. Fifteen thousand dollars each. *Did Victoria offer money? What if they had an agreement and Chloe changed her mind? Who is this "investigator" Victoria has?*

"I asked her not to contact you—either of you," Mandy said, her voice snapping him from his daze. "I told her I wanted to talk to you first." She paused, clasping her hands beneath her chin as though she were about to pray. "Rick, I never planned to ever come back to Riverton, or Montana, for that matter. I only took the bison story so I could meet with you, talk to you face-to-face."

Rick shook his head. "Talk to me? Why? If this Victoria is my daughter, why not just let her call me?"

"That's just it." Mandy's lips quivered as she lowered her eyes. "I . . . I'm not sure that she's yours."

Air abandoned Rick's lungs, color running from his face. Mandy Westerfield—*Amanda Westin Cobb or whatever her damn name was*—had done it again. His stomach filled with the queasy, doomsday sensation of a teenager who just learned his girlfriend was cheating on him—in this case, decades after the fact. His brain raced through a yearbook's worth of male classmates, his shock melting into a mix of anger and odd humiliation. He hated liars, and he despised drama, but Mandy had come to town with a suitcase filled with both.

"You're telling me that you don't know if I have a daughter or not?" he asked. His own words jolted him, a cloud of guilt moving in like a mountain storm. He had just lost Chloe, his dear Chloe, and he had been all too ready to replace her like some spare part. He scolded himself for his selfishness, his desperate desire to run from his grief.

"I'm sorry, Rick," Mandy said, her voice unsteady as she started to weep. "Victoria is convinced you are her father, but I had to tell you the truth." She pulled a tissue from her purse and swabbed it across her cheekbones, doing her best to wipe away the mask of Amanda Westin Cobb, her despairing eyes seeming to reach for vulnerability. "I can't lie anymore, Rick. My whole life has been a lie. I have to make things *right.*"

Make things right? He looked out the window toward the corral. Sage was greeting children as they arrived for Abby's birthday party. How would she feel when she found out he might have a daughter—with Mandy Westerfield of all people? He desired to be with Sage more than ever, if she would still have him. He drew rapid breaths, suffocating beneath the crushing fear of losing her.

Mandy rose from her chair. "I should go," she said, casting a melancholy gaze out the window toward the carefree children. She turned her eyes toward Rick. "I haven't heard from Victoria in several days, and I may never hear from her again. It's my suspicion that there was only one thing she was after. Like I said, she's very aggressive. Very *driven.*"

Rick stared out the window again, this time spotting Abby. Grief received him once more, his heart weighted as his mind found its way back to Chloe. "I suppose you can't begrudge someone for wanting to stay alive," he said flatly.

Amanda opened the door, the room filling with a chill wind. "Good-bye, Rick," she said.

Rick stood in solitude on the front porch, a penetrating burst of frigid wind placing a chilling exclamation point on his sudden isolation. He drew a deep breath and looked toward the corral, where Abby was showing off Big Sky to her arriving playmates. Sage glanced briefly at him, her eyes distant, her smile nonexistent. She looked away.

"Hey, stranger," a female voice said. He turned to see the smiling face of Sandra Billingsley, red-haired boy in tow. "Rick, this is my grandson, Ely," she said as she looked at the child. "Ely, this is Abby's grandpa, Mr. Morrand." Ely seemed unimpressed, offering a weak wave before scurrying off to join the other children.

"So, what's up with the barn? That just happen?" Sandra asked.

"Last night. Guess it was time for a new one."

He looked at Sandra's profile, her long auburn hair tied in a ponytail that trailed from a brown felt hat, her skin still smooth and fresh despite her age. Just about every time he saw her, she wore a beaming smile, as though she didn't have a care in the world. He wondered whether she was really that happy, of if anyone could ever be that happy.

Sandra turned toward him, her hands plunged inside the pockets of her suede jacket. "I found out a little more about that LLC."

"Which LLC?" Rick asked, head in a daze.

"Yellowstone Investments."

"Right-right-right."

"I left Billy a voice mail late yesterday, but I guess he's preoccupied with the situation involving Maggie Townsend. Poor, troubled soul—may she rest in peace." Sandra paused, as if to offer Maggie a moment of silence. "Anyway, we managed to find the owner of that LLC. It's a law firm."

Rick's forehead tightened. "A law firm? Are they out of Chicago?"

Sandra squinted in confusion. "Chicago? No, not Chicago. This law firm is in Southern California. The name of the firm is Metcalf and Associates. Ever heard of them?"

Rick turned toward Sandra, eyes narrowed. "Who?"

"Metcalf and Associates."

Blood pulsed into Rick's forehead, his face flushing with anger. *One hundred sixty thousand dollars? From Reiff Metcalf? Why?*

"Have you heard of them?" Sandra repeated, her ever-present smile replaced by a concerned frown. "Rick, are you okay?"

Rick averted his eyes and clenched his fists, his fingernails digging deep into his palms. His jaw clamped shut as he grasped for composure. Staring at the toes of his boots, he slowly shook his head.

"No, Sandra. I haven't heard of them."

CHAPTER 51

FATHER HERRERA HAD BEEN AT his new parish in Montana for more than a year, but he remained ill at ease when it came to bears.

There certainly were no bears around where he grew up—in a one-room shanty in a dusty settlement outside Laredo, Texas. Plenty of rattlesnakes, yes, but no bears. His two-bedroom cedar cabin on the outskirts of Gardiner—luxurious by Laredo standards—was located about 350 yards from the back entrance of St. Thomas Aquinas Catholic Church. The two structures were connected by a narrow footpath that took several blind turns as it wound through a stand of tall, dense spruce trees, eerie braids of moss dripping from their branches. The route received limited sunlight during the day and quickly grew darker when the late-afternoon sun would fall.

"Father Ernie" walked briskly, not only because it was a few minutes before five o'clock—the start of Saturday confession—but also because he had to make the foreboding trek through the shadowy forest. Recent reports of bear activity in the area elevated his anxiety.

During his brief tenure, he had deduced that his parishioners in Gardiner either were equipped with stainless souls or they no longer believed in the age-old Catholic ritual of confession. A few of Herrera's flock—mostly women—would occasionally offer up their wrongdoings to him in private, where his warm and gentle countenance would make them feel at ease. Attendance at Saturday confession, however, was typically light.

When he entered the church, he noticed only one person waiting for confession to begin—the man from the diner. He was sitting far enough away that any audible greeting would have been improper, so Herrera offered a simple, comforting smile. The man declined to acknowledge the priest, instead turning his eyes toward the altar.

Herrera slipped behind the sculpted wooden door of his confessional and waited patiently. He heard the stranger approach then turn the brass knob and step inside the adjacent compartment. Once the man knelt down, Herrera opened the sliding wooden door that separated them, casting gentle light through the wicker screen. The priest closed his eyes and rested his folded hands on his lap, the silence inviting the man to speak.

"Bless me, Father, for I have sinned," the man began, his voice uncertain. "My last confession was—"

He stopped, the confessional awkwardly quiet before the priest put him as ease. "It is all right," Herrera said in his soothing Hispanic accent. "Please proceed." He waited, but there was no sound. "It is all right," he repeated. "You can *proceed*." More silence. The priest thought he heard soft sobbing, sounds of anguish, perhaps even a touch of anger?

After a half minute, Herrera heard a rustle on the opposite side of the screen, as if the visitor were preparing to leave. When he heard the door open, he began to rise himself, hoping he could perhaps persuade the despondent man to stay. But before the priest reached his feet, the door to his compartment flew open. A large body was upon him, pushing him against the back wall and pressing a long Bowie knife firmly against his Adam's apple.

Herrera felt air leave his lungs, fear rumbling through his limbs. He twisted his shoulders, attempted to break free, but the man had his forearm pinned against the priest's chest, crazed eyes lasering from six inches away.

"Please be calm, Brother," the priest pleaded, attempting to mask his terror as he squeezed words from his throat. "Please tell me what troubles you."

"What troubles me? You want to know what *troubles* me?"

"Yes . . . please," Herrera stammered through short breaths.

The attacker pushed the knife harder onto the priest's skin. "Let me tell you what *troubles* me, *Padre*," he spewed with derision. "What troubles me is that my son was molested by a priest, a man who was supposed to be a friend. The priest denied it, but I don't believe him. Because of this *priest*, this person we *trusted*, my son ended up getting into drugs, and now he's *dead*."

Herrera's eyes opened wide, his pounding heart about to detonate. He desperately tried to speak, hoping to offer words of comfort. The man wouldn't allow it, pushing his forearm higher on Herrera's chest, just below the knife.

"I wanted to blame the lawyers who represented my son. I figured I should go after the daughter of the man who let the priest walk—kind of an eye-for-an-eye thing, you know?" The man released a huff of air, his breath carrying the stale odor of alcohol. "I wanted to kill her, but someone beat me to it."

Herrera looked away from the assailant's vacant eyes. Quaking with fear, he stole a glimpse at words of hate spewing through gritted teeth from a mouth surrounded by a weathered, unshaven face. "It was all for the best," the man growled. "When I got here to your town—when I saw you in the diner—it occurred to me that the lawyers weren't the problem." He paused for emphasis, focusing his eyes on Herrera. "It. Was. The . . . *priest!*" he shouted, his voice rising with each word.

"Wait!" Herrera pleaded. "Please! Maybe I can help you!"

"Help me? Yes, I think you can help me. I figured that since my innocent son was harmed by a priest, perhaps I can make things right by finding an innocent priest to harm. What do you think? Are you innocent, Padre?"

"Please," Herrera muttered through his hoarse throat. "You do not want to do this. Please! It is not too late." He knew better. It *was* too late. He needed to act.

Although he had limited knowledge of bears, Herrera had learned plenty about firearms growing up in South Texas. In order to ease his anxiety while walking to the church from his cabin, he had acquired a Smith & Wesson .44 Magnum. Herrera knew the diocese would frown on such a weapon, especially considering he was Franciscan. But in light of the current bear threat, he was rarely without it, easily concealing the pistol beneath his bulky wool vestments. Should danger lurk, he reasoned, God and the .44 would make a formidable tandem.

Herrera hesitated. The revolver was meant for beast, not man. Discharging his firearm would be justifiable in the eyes of the law, but what about the eyes of God? He felt the blade start to break the skin of his throat, a trickle of warm blood beginning to wander down his neck. He raised the barrel of the gun beneath his vestments, innate instincts blurring doctrine.

The priest lightly tugged the trigger. The gun exploded with rage.

The man's eyes filled with a peculiar dismay. He seemed startled not only by the gun's deafening sound but the feeling of being propelled backward. Herrera quickly fired again—as he had once been taught—then watched as the man catapulted away as if falling uncontrollably into an abyss.

With a thundering crash, the man hurtled out the confessional door, nearly knocking it off of its hinges. He ended up sprawled across a pew, still wearing the perplexed expression he had when the first shot rang out. He had been struck square in the stomach, where a snarling, crimson hole was gurgling blood. The second round had struck his chest, just below the right shoulder, its hollow point most assuredly claiming tendons and flesh as it rocketed through his body.

Herrera rose to his feet, gasping for breath as he edged his way out the doorway of the confessional, the relief of having secured his own survival quickly supplanted by the horror of taking another man's life. The weapon dropped from his trembling hand, echoing through the church as it landed on the stone floor.

His lips quivered as he stared into the man's eyes, so angry a short time before but now seeming to plead to him. The man was alive, but barely. He moved his lips weakly, lacking the oxygen to produce any sound.

Herrera had welcomed the security of his firearm but never dreamed of ever having to use it on any creature, least of all a human being. His throat grew thick, tears filling his eyes.

Taking the man's hand in his, Herrera began to administer the Sacrament of Anointing of the Sick, once known simply as last rites. "Oh Lord, Jesus Christ, Most Merciful, Lord of Earth, I ask that you receive this child into your arms," the priest whispered urgently, quoting the Gospel of John. "As Thou hast told us with infinite compassion: Let not your heart be troubled. Ye believe in God, believe also in Me."

The dying man squeezed the priest's hand, drawing it closer to his chest, signaling his surrender and approval. As Herrera felt the warm flow of the dying man's blood, he tearfully struggled to continue. "My Father's house has many rooms," he uttered. "If that were not so, would I have prepared a place for you?" The man gripped his hand tighter, much like an eager child raptured by a bedtime story. "And if I go and prepare a place for you, I will come back and take you to be with me that you also may be where I am."

The man lifted his head slightly, once again trying to speak. His eyes were fixed on Herrera as the life drifted away from him. His face fell motionless. The priest rested his hand on the troubled man's forehead, then gently closed the eyelids.

CHAPTER 52

A S MUCH AS SHE ENDORSED her husband's decision to steer clear of racetracks, cards, and casinos, Dora Duchesne wondered whether Charlie's job had become his new vice. When one considered the number of hours he put in—especially in a town where homicides were few and very far between—she sometimes feared she had swapped a compulsive gambler for a workaholic.

To keep herself busy, Dora spent twenty hours each week at the office of Dr. Thomas Brunson, a seventy-eight-year-old third-generation family physician who had welcomed more than half of Riverton's residents into the world. When not working for Dr. Brunson, or toiling with her latest quilt, she focused her laser-like attention on her beloved Charlie.

"I brought a club sandwich—your favorite," Dora said as she whisked through the door of Charlie's office late Sunday morning. "I fried up the bacon fresh—less than an hour ago."

Dora still had the fast-paced stride from her days as an ER nurse in Upstate New York, when she became smitten with the dashing young intern named Charles Augustus Duchesne. Now approaching sixty, she had maintained her perky well-toned figure, a fact not overlooked by her husband. Charlie had no idea what Pilates was—nor did he care to find out—but he always insisted Dora keep doing what she was doing.

Her lips curled downward when Charlie barely acknowledged her, taking a swallow of coffee from his discolored mug while he stared at a photo printout he clutched in his hand. "Charlie, did you hear me?"

"I'm sorry," Charlie said, shaking his head as if she'd splashed icy water on his face. He glanced at the sandwich. "Thank you. That was very thoughtful of you."

Dora took a seat in front of his desk. "That was so sad, what happened to Maggie Townsend. Were you able to reach her family?"

"Yes and no," Charlie mumbled, his eyes still studying the photo. "She has a cousin, down at The General Store in Cottonwood. Apparently, this woman was the only member of the family still talking to Maggie. There are other relatives, but they seemed to have pretty much disowned her."

"Well, I suppose she had her share of complexities, getting mixed up with Draper Townsend."

Charlie laid down the photo and sat back in his chair. "Maybe, maybe not."

"What do you mean?"

"Not important."

Dora leaned forward. "Please, Charlie. Tell me."

He released a deep breath, folding his arms across his chest. Dark circles surrounded eyes racked with fatigue. "I called Helen at the sheriff's office, asking whether Maggie had come in to visit Draper. I figured maybe she'd had a change of heart or somehow felt guilty—it wouldn't have been the first time. But Helen tells me that Maggie hadn't been in."

Dora tilted her head with curiosity. "And?"

"Helen said that the only visitor Draper had in the last week was Darrell Pittman, an old cell mate."

Dora nodded. "O-kay. His friend came to visit. What's so unusual about that?"

"Pittman may have paid Maggie Townsend a visit as well," Charlie said. He adjusted himself in his chair, appeasing his perennially sore spine. "The sheriff's whole case against Draper was based on Maggie's testimony. When Draper found out about his glove being found at the Sawtooth, he had to know that Maggie was involved. It's possible the cell mate may have—"

Dora thrust up her empty hands. "Okay, Charlie, stop. That's enough. You can't be serious."

"It's just a theory, but—"

Dora rolled her eyes, her pleasantness abandoning her as she glared at her husband. He could get like this. No sleep, not much to eat—next thing she knew, he'd pack his bags and drive right off the reservation.

Dora took a breath. "You said yourself that Draper wasn't involved in Chloe Morrand's death," she said in a soothing tone. "I mean, Maggie was a troubled soul, Charlie. She must have had her reasons for doing what she did. Was there a note?"

"No note."

"But you were *there*, Charlie! You were the one who—"

"Found her?" he snapped, his eyes piercing her. "Yes, Dora, I was the one who *found* Maggie. Thanks for reminding me."

"I'm not the enemy."

"I hate when you say that."

Charlie dropped his chin as he slumped back into his chair. They sat in silence for several seconds before he lifted his bloodshot eyes. Dora returned a sympathetic gaze. They had built a nice life together, conquering untold trials along the way, and there was no certainty just how many years might be left. No sense wasting time being at odds.

"Charlie, honey, do you think maybe you're making things a little *complicated*? I mean, are you even sure Chloe Morrand was murdered? Are you absolutely certain that she didn't—"

"Take her own life? Yes, Dora, I'm certain."

Dora rose from her chair and walked around Charlie's desk. She stood behind him, gently rubbing his shoulders. His neck muscles were twisted in knots, shoulders as hard as stone. "Maybe you need to just get some rest."

"I need to do my job—that's what I need to do," he grumbled. "I'm no closer to solving this Morrand case than when—"

"Wait!" Dora said. She leaned over Charlie's shoulder, her eyes focused on his desk. She reached for the photo. "May I?"

Charlie shrugged. "Go right ahead. I've been staring at that photo for the last three hours. Billy Renfro passed it along to me. It was taken at the top of the Sawtooth, not long after they found Chloe."

The photo showed a tiny anklet lying in gravel, the shiny metal scripting the word "Desiree." Dora continued to stare at the photo.

"Most of the hikers who go to the top of the Sawtooth are locals," Charlie said. "For the life of me, I can't think of anyone in town named Desiree."

Dora threw a glance at him. "Maybe it's someone from out of town?"

"Maybe."

Charlie began opening the wax paper wrapped around his club sandwich. The paper wasn't always easy to come by, but Charlie preferred it over Ziplocs. He was peculiar that way.

"Yes!" Dora said. She dropped the photo onto the desk, pointing her finger at it. "I think I've seen this before."

Charlie shoved his sandwich aside and stared at her, his thick silver eyebrows colliding in confusion. Dora pursed her lips as she studied the printout once more.

"I know," she said, snapping her fingers. "I saw this—I'm not saying it's the same one—but I think I saw this being worn by Tessie Lou Hunter."

Charlie cocked his head to the side. "Tessie Lou? You mean Caleb's Tessie Lou?"

"Yes. She came into Dr. Brunson's office about a month ago— she said she had been experiencing some discomfort with her pregnancy." Dora bit the side of her lip, eyes focused as she recalled details of the scene. "When Dr. Brunson was examining her, I noticed a piece of jewelry—I believe it was this one—on her ankle. When I asked her about it, she said that was the name she had chosen for her baby."

Charlie leaned forward, staring intently at Dora. "Are you absolutely sure this was the anklet?"

Dora winced. "*Pretty* sure. I was standing right there, and her ankle was in a stirrup. It was kind of hard to miss."

Billy Renfro emerged from his office, thumbs plunged under his belt as though they'd been severed. The news Helen had delivered to Rick Morrand had been ill received, so she'd buzzed the deputy's intercom, seeking reinforcement. "What seems to be the problem, Rick?"

Rick glared at him, squaring his stance. He removed his Stetson and held it with both hands, his finger stroking the crease. "Reiff Metcalf has been released? How could that happen? Where's Judge Wade?"

"Judge Wade is out of the picture. This one came straight from the governor's office. Apparently, your friend is fairly well connected."

Rick's forehead tightened. "What happened to the drug charges?"

Billy sighed. "Given Mr. Metcalf's overall physical health, the district attorney was, shall we say, *ambivalent* about moving forward."

"But isn't Reiff a suspect?"

"Suspect of what?"

"Murder, damn it! What about the money he was sending to Chloe? Something must have happened. There must have been a disagreement—"

Billy's face reddened, his jowls appearing to inflate with air, his patience losing tread. "There is absolutely no evidence that Mr. Metcalf had any physical contact with Chloe—at least not during this trip to town."

"What is that supposed to mean?"

Billy rolled his eyes. "It means that there was no physical contact. As far as the money goes, you need to take that up with Charlie."

"Take it up with Charlie? What do you mean, Billy? I'm taking it up with you!"

Billy's face hardened. "Rick, I *said* you need to take it up with Charlie."

"Where's Caleb?"

"Caleb's not here."

"Where the hell is he?"

Billy folded his arms across his chest. "He had to go down to Gardiner—there was a shooting there last night. He should be on his way back up this afternoon."

Rick placed his hat firmly on his head and pulled out his Blackberry. He scrolled in his call log for the restricted number Reiff had used to contact him a week earlier. He pressed the Send button and listened. "The subscriber you are trying to reach . . ." He shoved the phone back into the front pocket of his Wranglers. "And where's Reiff Metcalf now?" he said to Billy through gritted teeth. "The hotel—or the airport?"

"None of my concern—and none of yours, either. Don't be getting any ideas."

They glared at each other for several seconds, the opening of the front door ending their standoff. Clint Roswell entered the sheriff's office, one hand gripping the bicep of a handcuffed prisoner. The man's head hung from his shoulders, his eyes cast toward the floor as his long, dark hair shielded his face. It wasn't until he glowered menacingly at Rick and Billy—flicking his hair to the side—that Rick recognized him.

Chase Rettick?

Rick jerked his head back as he turned toward Billy, his skin crawling after spotting a ghost. "I thought he was dead."

"Sorry to disappoint you. If he's dead, he died and went to Billings. That's where they picked him up."

Rick wagged his head. "He wasn't in the fire at the trailer park?"

"That's what he hoped we would think, but it didn't work out. He might have gotten away with it if he hadn't been busted for possession."

Billy watched in disgust as Chase was led through the metal door leading to the cell area. "You wouldn't believe what this guy told the cops in Billings." He huffed a breath. "He claimed that he could give them some valuable information if they would just let him go."

"What kind of information?"

"According to Mr. Rettick, he'd been working for Sheriff Tidwell. He claims that Caleb had him dropping off bison in various places up and down the valley."

"Dropping off bison," Rick repeated. He stared at the floor, rubbing the grizzle on his chin. His mind flashed to his conversation with Mandy. He lifted his eyes toward Billy. "Did Rettick give you a reason he was doing this?" he asked. "And why would he be doing it for Tidwell?"

"He said he wasn't sure," the deputy said. "All he knew was that he was supposed to mix them in with the cattle." Billy pulled a toothpick from his top pocket and placed it in his mouth. He slowly shook his head. "I'll tell you—these tweakers will say anything to save their own ass."

Charlie had barely sunk his dentures into the first bite of his club sandwich when Rick barged into his office. Dora was gone, which was probably good.

"I need you to tell me about the money."

"Hello, Rick," Charlie said through a mouthful of food. "What money would that be?"

Rick burned steel eyes into Charlie. "Why was Reiff Metcalf sending money to my daughter?"

Silence. Charlie wrapped up his sandwich and placed it to the side of his desk. He chewed his food slowly, his eyes focused on Rick. He swallowed. "How much money?"

"What difference does it make?"

"How much?"

"A hundred and sixty grand."

"One hundred sixty thousand dollars?"

"That's what I said."

More silence—only the sound of Charlie drawing short breaths from the side of his mouth. Finally, he heaved a long sigh. "I should have told you sooner. I *wanted* to tell you sooner."

"Tell me what?"

"There was . . . an arrangement between Metcalf and your daughter."

Rick's stomach churned, his heart beginning to pound. "What kind of arrangement?"

Another sigh. "You might say that money was child support."

Rick leaned forward, placing his knuckles on Charlie's desk. "Child support? For what?"

"Chloe and Metcalf had a child together."

Rick shook his head with confusion, trying to awaken from a bad dream. "What are you talking about, Charlie?" his voice rising as he stood. "Chloe had only one child."

"That's correct."

Rick's face grew flush, his mouth agape as though he'd been punched in the throat. He edged closer again, the coroner easing backward in fright. Rick's lips quivered as he tried to speak. "You mean to tell me," he said haltingly, "that Reiff Metcalf is Abby's father?"

By the time Charlie mustered the courage to answer, Rick was already gone.

As Rick's truck skidded to a stop in front of the Riverton Grande, bellman Tommy Bryant was loading a piece of designer luggage into the back of a Chevy Luv.

Rick reached under his seat, grabbing the Ruger he kept to put down injured deer struck on the highway. He stuffed the pistol into the left side of his jeans, covering it with his jacket. "Tommy, is that Reiff Metcalf's bag?" Rick asked as he slammed the door of his truck.

"Hi, Mr. Morrand," Tommy said politely. "Yes, it is."

"I got it," Rick said as he snared the luggage from the pickup. "Mr. Metcalf is a good friend of mine. I have some time, so I'll take him."

Tommy's face sank into disappointment. "I'd really like to drive him, Mr. Morrand. He's a pretty good tipper, and I could use the money."

Rick fished into his pocket and peeled off a couple of twenties. He opened one side of Tommy's coat and stuffed the bills into the bellman's shirt. "Mr. Morrand, I really can't—"

"Sure, you can," Rick said with a smile, gripping Tommy's shoulder blade. "Now why don't you go ahead back inside?"

The bellman shrugged briefly before trudging toward the entrance of the hotel. He passed Reiff, whose smile was replaced by a look of puzzlement. "I got you covered, Partner," Rick said as he slung Reiff's bag into the back of his truck.

Reiff shook his head as he walked toward Rick. "Oh no, I can't let you do that. Let the kid take me. You probably have other things to do."

Rick pursed his lips and pulled open the side of his jacket, enabling Reiff to see the Ruger. "Get in the truck, Reiff."

Reiff swallowed hard, his face growing pale. "What—?"

"Get in the truck, Reiff," Rick repeated, more firmly. He opened the passenger door and watched as his former partner reluctantly climbed inside. Rick held his glare, studying Reiff's profile. He observed the bone structure around Reiff's eyes, the curvature of his nose. In his mind's eye, he could see similar features in Abby, right down to a tiny, subtle bump at the base of Reiff's ear. A shudder ran down the back of Rick's neck.

Abby didn't much resemble Chase Rettick, but she did look a whole lot like Reiff Metcalf. *How did I miss this?*

Reiff's eyes pleaded with him. "Partner, what's this about? What's going on?"

Rick didn't answer. The passenger door slammed shut.

CHAPTER 53

CHARLIE CALLED THE SHERIFF'S OFFICE and was informed that Caleb was in Gardiner. That suited the coroner just fine.

The anklet photo had come from Jack Kelly, by way of Billy Renfro. When Charlie had questioned Caleb about the piece of jewelry, the sheriff claimed he'd never seen it.

Charlie concluded it was best that he speak to Tessie Lou Hunter alone.

As he drove into the valley, he kept glancing at the picture he held in his hand. For some reason, the anklet looked oddly familiar. Playing a hunch, Charlie called Melody's Cards and Gifts, where he'd often dropped in to purchase a gift for Dora, whether it be to celebrate a special occasion or mend a minor misdeed.

"Melody, it's Charlie Duchesne," he told the singsong voice that answered the phone. He deduced that Melody was having a pleasant day.

"Charlie, is it your anniversary again already?" she chirped. "We just received some wonderful—"

"Actually, Melody," he interrupted, "I need to ask you about something." He paused, tapping his brakes as his eyes gauged the movements of two skittish deer a hundred yards up the highway. "Is it your place where I saw these little gold . . . anklets, I guess you'd call 'em? They have the person's name—"

"Sure, I have a whole rack of them, in alphabetical order," Melody said. "Let me see if there's a Dora."

Charlie chuckled. "No, not for Dora—I'm not sure those are her style. What I was looking for was one that said, 'Desiree.' That's D-E-S-I-R-E-E."

Melody paused. "Desiree? Now Charlie, you're a little old to have a girl on the side, aren't you?" They both burst into laughter. After a beat, Charlie's voice turned serious. "I'm wondering whether you may have sold an anklet with the name Desiree."

"Hmmm . . . don't see one on the rack," Melody answered. "Let me check the computer." She started humming "Amazing Grace," apparently confident enough in her musical skills that she saw fit to share them with Charlie. He rolled his eyes and checked his watch before returning his focus to the road in front of him.

"That's weird," Melody said. Charlie saw himself raise his eyebrows as he looked in his rearview mirror. He slowed his SUV and took a right onto Deep Creek Drive, less than a quarter-mile from the Tidwell place.

Melody stopped humming. "Damn it!" she said, her carefree day seeming to take a turn.

"Something wrong, Melody?"

"Damn it!" she repeated. "We did have an anklet that said Desiree. My sister brought it in on a special order. Problem is, it ain't here and we never sold it."

Charlie felt his eyebrows tighten. "Does it show who ordered it?"

"Sure as hell does!" Melody shouted, her tone no longer full of grace. "It was that Tessie Lou Hunter. I keep telling Billy Renfro that woman is a damned thief! If the sheriff doesn't—"

"Thanks, Melody," Charlie said quickly, ending the call. He tossed the phone on the dash, as though it were on fire. He felt his heart thump in his chest, hair rising on the back of his neck. His brain blurred with confusion. *If Tessie Lou Hunter was indeed a thief, and if the anklet was the same one Dora had spotted at the doctor's office, how did it end up on the top of the Sawtooth?*

He felt as though he was traveling in slow motion as he approached the entrance to the Tidwell property, reluctant to turn in, hardly relishing the task at hand. He swallowed, his chest growing heavy as his mind trailed to his ill-fated visit to Maggie Townsend a few days before. Rolling slowly up the gravel driveway, he spotted Tessie Lou's truck parked off to the side. Charlie licked his dry lips and nodded his head. *Showtime.*

The small house was freshly painted, the front yard ringed by an optimistic white picket fence. Charlie eased his way through the gate, gently closing it behind him. The flower beds within the yard lay barren, the hopeful blossoms of summer now a distant memory.

He stepped onto the porch, clutching the manila envelope in which he had placed the printout. He heard the opening of a dead bolt but couldn't detect a face, the glare of bright sunshine reflecting off the aluminum storm door. "Caleb's not here, Charlie," Tessie Lou's muffled voice said through the glass. "Would you like me to have him call you?"

Charlie paused a moment, biting the inside of his lip as he squinted at the distant mountains. "Actually, I'm not here to see Caleb," he said, turning his eyes back toward the face he couldn't see. "Is it okay if I come in?" He waited in silence for several seconds before the storm door opened.

"Sure."

Tessie Lou watched Charlie over her shoulder as she led him into the kitchen of the rented home. He had known her since she was a small child. She'd been a bright and happy girl, coming from good stock—church-going folks, those Hunters were. To Charlie's knowledge, both her parents were still alive. He wondered whether Tessie Lou was still in touch with them, given her parturient condition and its surrounding circumstances.

The small home was immaculate, as though it was cleaned several times a day. *Nesting, isn't that what they call it?* A pleasant aroma wafted from the stove, where a large silver pot released wisps of steam as it simmered above a blue-yellow flame. An iron skillet rested on the back burner, a half-dozen strips of bacon immersed in a slow contented sizzle. As she walked, Tessie Lou pressed her hand firmly on the small of her back, the burdensome tug of her unborn child apparently taking its toll. Charlie's eyes trailed past the hem of her dress, down her bare calves, stopping above feet covered by red canvas flats. No sign of an anklet.

"Can I get you some coffee?"

"No, Tessie. No coffee."

She picked up a wooden spoon and stirred the pot on the stove. "I'm making elk chili—it's Caleb's favorite," she said with the glint of a smile. "Are you sure you don't want me to call him? He really should be home at any time."

"That won't be necessary." Charlie rubbed the back of his neck and glanced toward the door, wondering how long "any time" might be. He took a seat at the kitchen table, setting the envelope in front of him. "Tell me, Tessie—how have you been feeling? Are you taking good care of that baby?"

"Oh, yes," she said, shooting a quick glance at Charlie as she continued to stir. "I had a part-time job at the feed store, but Caleb insisted I give it up—you know, so I can get my proper rest and all? He's so excited about having a daughter."

Charlie raised his eyebrows. "So it's a girl? Congratulations."

"Yep, it's a girl," Tessie said as she lifted the spoon to her lips to sample the chili. "I wanted the gender to be a surprise, but Caleb wouldn't have it. He insisted we do one of those . . . what is it called?"

"Ultrasound?"

"That's it—ultrasound," Tessie said with a nod. "I always forget that word for some reason."

Charlie cocked his head to the side and tightened his brow. "Any names yet?"

"Oh, yes," Tessie said, her face aglow. "I was thinking—"

She suddenly froze. Her jaw muscles tensed, her eyes fixed on the pot of chili. She reached for a paper towel, folded it neatly, and placed the wooden spoon on top of it. "Actually, we haven't decided on any names just yet," she said hesitantly, her voice uncertain.

Charlie nodded. "I see." The room fell silent, aside from the murmur of bacon cooking. He drew a deep breath as he picked up the envelope and removed the printout. "Tessie Lou, I'd like you to take a look at something."

She watched him curiously as she wiped her hands on the front of her apron. He pushed the photo across the table. "Have you ever seen this anklet before?"

Her face grew pale. She shook her head. Charlie paused, studying her. "You don't own an anklet that looks like this?" he asked. "Are you sure?"

She averted her eyes, wagging her head more decidedly. "I wonder where Caleb is," she said, looking at the front door. "He should have been home by now."

Charlie reached out and gently touched her wrist. "Tessie, please sit down." She resisted, pulling her arm away. "Tessie, please," he repeated, pulling out a chair for her and gently guiding her into it. Tessie avoided looking at the photo, staring straight ahead, her body numb.

"Tessie, can you tell me about the last time you saw Chloe Morrand?"

She turned toward Charlie, drawing short breaths as her eyes glazed over with a blend of spite and mistrust, her inner being seemingly overtaken by aliens. "Chloe Morrand was not a good person," she said in a deep voice.

Charlie swallowed, spooked by her cryptic tone and the demonic look on her face. "Can you tell me the last time you saw Chloe?"

"She was *not* a good person," Tessie repeated sharply. "She was trying to take Caleb from me—my future husband, the father of my child! We're a family, don't you see? We're a *family*! She wanted to take that away!" Her lips quivered as she shot a glance toward the door. "I know Caleb is coming home soon. I just know he is."

Charlie gripped her wrist. "Tessie, you're not in any trouble. I'm just trying to find out what happened."

"It wasn't my fault," Tessie murmured, calmer now. "It was *her* fault. She should have left Caleb alone."

Charlie's forehead tightened. *What wasn't her fault?* He nodded toward her, trying to remain calm. "Okay, I know it wasn't your fault, Tessie," he said in a soothing tone. "Please tell me what happened."

Her anger seemed to dissipate, replaced by a sudden gush of remorse. She blinked back tears as she pressed her fingers to her lips, burying her face in her hands. "Caleb had nothing to do with this," she sobbed. "He tried to stop me."

Charlie felt a shudder ripple through him. *Stop her? From what? Did she kill Chloe? But how?* Chloe was killed at the top of the Sawtooth, Charlie was sure of it. How could Tessie have killed Chloe and then—

"She should have left Caleb alone," Tessie said again.

Charlie stared in the direction of her womb, his gaze slowly rising toward her tormented eyes. He gently stroked her forearm, her skin cold. "Nobody's accusing anybody of anything, Tessie. I just want to help you if I can." He tapped an index finger on the photo printout. "This anklet belongs to you, doesn't it?" She nodded. "You were up on top of the Sawtooth?" She nodded again.

Charlie drew air through his nostrils. He leaned forward, trying to make eye contact. "Why were you and Chloe there?"

Tessie took short gasps, trying to catch her breath. "She left a voice mail for Caleb, saying she wanted to meet with him. I waited at the trailhead, and when Caleb showed up, I . . . I hit him with a shovel handle."

Charlie's eyes opened wide as he instinctively slid backward in his chair. He snuck a furtive glimpse at the door. "Then what happened?"

Tessie brushed tears from her eyes and calmed herself, folding her hands on the table. "We went up to the top of the Sawtooth, and I told her to jump."

"You told Chloe to *jump*?"

"I told her that if she didn't do as I said, I would harm her daughter. She wanted to harm my daughter, so I was going to go after hers."

"Your daughter. You mean Desiree? How was Chloe going to harm Desiree?"

"My daughter needs a daddy. I told you—Chloe Morrand wanted to break up my family."

Charlie eased forward again, cupping his hands over hers. "What happened next, Tessie?"

"I told her to jump, but she wouldn't do it."

"And Caleb was there?"

"He tried to stop me. He wanted to let her go."

Caleb had been there. Charlie swallowed hard, his heart thumping in his chest. *What if Caleb showed up now?* Charlie resisted the urge to spring from his chair and look out the kitchen window.

"Caleb tried to stop you from doing what, Tessie? Making Chloe jump?"

Tessie Lou didn't answer. She glared at Charlie, her eyes flooding with fury. "I think you need to leave," she said through grinding teeth. Charlie pulled his hands away, as though he'd touched a burning stove. His eyes widened as the innocent Tessie he had once known seemed to take leave of her soul, her vessel inhabited by another hostile visitor he did not recognize.

Charlie raised his palms, trying to calm her. "Tessie, I want to help you." Her jaw muscles tensed, her body growing rigid. "I said you need to leave!" she shouted, slamming her fists on the table. "You need to get out—now!"

Charlie jumped up from his chair, an eerie chill rattling through him. "Okay, okay," he said, his hands in front of him. "I am going to leave, but before I go, I want to get you some help."

"I don't need any help, damn you!" She buried her face in her hands and began crying again, as if her strange, sudden interloper had granted her a reprieve. "Can't you see?" she blubbered. "She was trying to take my family from me!"

"I know, Tessie Lou, I know," Charlie said, gingerly touching her shoulder. He reached into his breast pocket for his flip phone, then speed-dialed the sheriff's office. He edged away from the table toward the front door, glancing over his shoulder as Caleb's fractured fiancée continued to sob, chin resting on her chest, her hands now caressing her expanded stomach.

"Helen, it's Charlie Duchesne," he whispered into his phone, turning his back to Tessie Lou. "Is Caleb still in Gardiner?"

"I'm not sure. Why?"

"I need an ambulance to come out to the Tisdale place. It's seems Tessie Lou has had some sort of . . . breakdown."

"What kind of breakdown?"

"She needs medical help. I want to get her to the hospital—I don't want her to harm herself or her baby."

"What happened?"

"It's some kind of psychosis. Perhaps it's related to the pregnancy, I don't know. For now, please just send an ambulance. I'll stay here with her."

"Should I call Caleb?"

Charlie wagged his head rapidly. "No, no. I'll call him. You call the ambulance."

"I really think I should call Caleb."

"Helen, *please*. I promise I'll call him. Just get the EMTs out here. Now!"

Charlie closed his phone. As he lifted it toward his pocket, a nauseating thwack shattered the air, a crushing blow connecting with the back of his head. The phone flew from his hand, bouncing across the tile floor. His vision blurred, a loud ringing filling his ears. He watched helplessly as streaks of bacon grease streamed down the yellow enamel wall. Dropping to his knees, he tried in vain to regain his balance before collapsing in a heap. He lay motionless, a stream of warm blood flowing across his forehead and forming a dark crimson pool in front of his face.

"I'm sorry, Charlie," his swimming head heard Tessie Lou say. "I just can't let you harm our family."

CHAPTER 54

REIFF STARED WARILY AT HIS one-time law partner, Rick's crazed eyes igniting the pavement as they sped southbound on Highway 89.

"Where are we going?" Reiff asked nervously. "I have a plane to catch."

"I think you're going to miss your flight."

Reiff shook his head in disbelief. "Can you at least tell me what this is about?"

"We need to go have a little talk—in *private*."

"What kind of talk? About what?"

Rick didn't answer, his face a boiling cauldron of rage. Reiff's muscles stiffened, his stomach churning. In all the years he had known Rick Morrand, he had never seen him so full of venom.

"You always thought you could solve problems with money," Rick said through clenched teeth. "If you just threw enough money at something, eventually it would go away, right?"

"What are you talking about?"

Rick lifted his Ruger off his lap and positioned it inches from Reiff's face. "I'm talking about the one hundred and sixty grand you sent my daughter."

He knows. Reiff's eyes widened as he stared down the dark gun barrel. He pressed his shoulder against the passenger window, his heart pounding as he tried in vain to squirm out of range. For nearly a decade, Reiff had been able to keep this dark secret hidden from his best friend, cloistered deep within his soul. He had convinced himself he could take care of Abby, and of course Chloe, and Rick would never have to know. Chloe's death changed all that. The moment Reiff feared more than death had finally arrived. *Rick knows.*

"Partner, wait a minute," Reiff sputtered. "I wanted to tell you, I really did."

"You sure took your sweet time about it, didn't you? Ten years is a long stretch."

"Can't we talk about this?"

"Trust me—we're going to talk about this," Rick said, returning the Glock to his lap. "For now, you just need to shut up."

"But—"

Rick shoved his weapon back in Reiff's face. "I said, 'Shut up!'"

Reiff stared out the window, gasping for air in short breaths as his chest tightened. Dizziness enveloped him, his abdomen reminding him he was a dying man. He watched from the corner of his eye as Rick lowered his gun once again. He exhaled, welcoming the stay of execution, convinced this would not end well.

Charlie opened his eyes to see a tiny spider emerging from a crack in the baseboard of Tessie Lou's kitchen, the creature somehow having persevered in the spotless home. As the insect inched toward the puddle of blood that continued to spill from his throbbing, wounded skull, Charlie wondered which of them stood a best chance of survival.

"He's lying on the floor right now—I think he's unconscious," he heard Tessie Lou say. He turned his head cautiously to see her talking on her cell phone and examining the contents of the refrigerator, as though whacking Charlie with an iron skillet merited some kind of snack. "Do you still keep that gun in your nightstand? Is it loaded? Good. I'll keep it on him until you get here."

Caleb. The bastard.

Charlie's cheekbone remained pressed against the cold floor, his forehead covered with cold sweat. He reached for the top of his neck, his stomach roiling as he felt his hair drenched in blood. His mind drifted to Dora and his need to get back to her. His spirits darkened. If the ambulance had been called, it was at least a half-hour away. Caleb likely was closer.

As Tessie left the kitchen, Charlie spotted his flip phone just beyond arm's reach. Eyes pressed closed in agony, he inched along the floor and clutched it. His trembling hand speed-dialed Rick Morrand's number, heart pounding as he waited for a ring. Charlie winced. *Voice mail.* He heard Tessie coming back down the hall, gun in hand, no doubt, as he waited for Rick's message to finish. "Rick, it was Caleb and Tessie," he whispered desperately into the mouthpiece. "Tessie Lou killed Chloe . . . and Caleb was in on it."

"Damn you!"

Charlie howled in agony, his cell shattering into bits. The skillet had returned, Tessie fracturing bones in Charlie's hand as she destroyed the phone. He pressed his watering eyes shut and whimpered through gritted teeth. His knuckles trembled uncontrollably, pulsing in pain. The deranged woman he once knew as Tessie Lou towered over him, cookware in one hand and a silver .44 in the other. "I'd prefer not to kill you, but if you're going to act this way, you might not leave me any choice."

She laid the skillet back on the stove and picked up her cell phone, punching a few keys and pressing it to her ear. "Damn!" she said in a loud whisper. "Caleb, why can't you pick up when I'm calling you? Call me back—and hurry. Something's come up."

"Tessie, you don't have to do this," Charlie muttered. "You need help. It's not your fault."

"Oh, I think it's too late for that."

She took a seat at the kitchen table. "Caleb said for me to keep a gun on you and he would get here when he can. I'm sure he's already called dispatch and cancelled that ambulance of yours."

Charlie's temples pulsed, his head on fire. He wondered whether Helen had called for an ambulance at all. Given that Tessie Lou had a habit of getting into scrapes around town, Helen likely had strict orders to call Caleb first.

"No one will believe you," he said with a groan.

"Don't be so sure. Y'all think Caleb's not all that smart, that he's not like his daddy. Take it from me—he can be pretty crafty when he wants to be."

"You killed Chloe Morrand, and now you're going to kill me? What makes you think you can pull that off?"

Tessie laid the .44 on the table. "Now, Charlie, you know as well as anyone that Montana law favors folks who defend themselves. I mean, especially women who are being assaulted."

"What are you talking about?"

"You did try to assault me, Charlie," she said, her voice possessed. "I'm a young, pregnant woman with no criminal record. Not even a parking ticket. And here you come to my house and try to sexually assault me."

Charlie closed his eyes in hopelessness. "You're sick."

"Now, let's not have any talk like that. Like I told you before— me, Caleb, and little Desiree—we're a family."

Her cell phone rang. "What took you so long?" Tessie said, her voice carrying bite. "Who were you talking to?"

Caleb said something that made her take a deep swallow, her face whitewashed with fear. "Now don't be getting mad at me, Caleb, but we may have a little problem," she said, more subdued. "When I went to the bedroom to get the gun, our prisoner here made a call on his phone."

She winced as she listened, fawning now, tears welling in her eyes. "Caleb, please don't yell at me!" She burst into sobs, nodding her head as she tried to catch her breath. "I think I might have heard him say 'Rick.' Do you think maybe he was calling Rick Morrand?"

With one eye on his hostage and the Glock resting on his thigh, Rick picked up his cell phone to check on a call that had gone to voice mail. As he listened, he felt his forehead tighten into a perplexed frown.

"What are you talking about, Charlie?" he murmured while staring at the phone. The coroner had left a confusing message, his voice muffled and strained. Rick listened again, then shook his head. He cast another glance toward Reiff, who was sucking oxygen through widened nostrils, perspiration pouring down his face.

Rick pressed Charlie Duchesne's number. As he placed the phone to his ear, he spotted Reiff lunging for the pistol while yanking the truck's steering wheel hard to the right. Rick dropped the phone in a panic and tightly gripped the wheel. "What the hell are you doing?" he shouted before delivering a desperate backhanded blow to the bridge of Reiff's nose.

The sidearm tumbled to the floorboard. Reiff growled loudly, flecks of red spewing forth from the stream of blood gushing over his mouth and chin. He tugged the steering wheel in his direction once more. This time, the truck swerved out of control, snaking across the center line of the highway.

Rick's eyes widened in terror as a large truck barreled toward them, blaring its deafening horn. He swerved back into his own lane as his truck continued to fishtail. Bloodless knuckles gripping the wheel, his heart pounded as he tried in vain to regain control. He heard a loud thud, followed by a thick grunt as Reiff's head cracked against the passenger side window. The truck soared off the side of the road, bounding through a ditch and into a barrel roll, the valley turning upside down through the fracturing front windshield.

Rick felt weightless, suspended in time, the inside of the cab seemingly without sound. As though awakening from a dream, he heard the violent crash of crushing steel, shattered glass spraying the inside of the truck. Everything went dark.

Rick awoke to find himself pressed against the roof of the cab. He blinked his eyes, astonished he was alive. Placing his hand on his stinging forehead, he felt warm blood stream from an angry gash. He looked toward the passenger seat. Reiff wasn't there.

Rick tried to steady himself, grunting in agony as excruciating pain rumbled up the left side of his rib cage. With gritted teeth, he inched his way toward the passenger window, shards of glass piercing his forearms. He crawled out the window and across the matted pasture, the ground soaked and muddied by melting snow. Slowly, steadily, he rose to his feet.

Shielding his face from the sun, he spotted Reiff staggering toward a dozen cattle, his sights apparently set on a distant barn and ranch house.

Rick balled his fists, taking a few rapid steps before breaking into a run. He buried his head with malice into the base of Reiff's spine, a hunter plunging a spear into his prey. Reiff howled, his arms flailing as his neck whiplashed. In an instant, Rick straddled the chest of his one-time best friend, connecting with a powerful fist to the jaw.

"She was a child, you bastard! A vulnerable child!"

Reiff shielded his face to protect himself from another blow. Fueled by the adrenaline of survival, he pulled Rick toward him, sending them rolling into the frigid waters of an irrigation ditch. They released each other, shaking off the water like drying dogs as they both struggled to find their footing.

"I loved her!" Reiff yelled. "I truly loved her!"

Rick squinted in disbelief. "What did you say?"

Reiff gasped for air. "I said, I loved her!"

The words had hardly left Reiff's mouth when Rick hammered another fist against Reiff's cheekbone. "That's what I thought you said."

Reiff plunged backward into the irrigation waters, Rick's hands placing an iron grip around his neck. He clawed helplessly at Rick's wrists, his eyes opening wide as tiny air bubbles rose to the surface, precious oxygen leaving his lungs.

Suddenly, Rick released his grasp. He wasn't a killer. He'd lost Chloe, but he still had Sage and Abby. Seemingly astonished by his reprieve, Reiff planted his elbows beneath himself, pushing his head and chest to the surface. As he wheezed for air, Reiff's eyes blinked rapidly, as though he was startled by something. Rick followed his gaze, slowly twisting his neck to look over his left shoulder.

Squinting into the blinding yellow sunlight, he saw the barrel of a shotgun pointed at both of them, the weapon firmly in the grasp of Sheriff Caleb Tidwell's hands.

CHAPTER 55

T HE TWO FORMER LAW PARTNERS sat handcuffed in the back of Caleb's SUV, unlikely comrades united once again, this time in the custody of a rogue sheriff.

Rick twisted his hands vigorously, veins pulsing from his bloodied forehead as he attempted to break free of his metal shackles and go about the business of wringing Caleb Tidwell's neck. He winced as a sharp pain stabbed his side of his chest. His mind wandered back to a blind-side tackle during a kickoff in college, one that cracked two of his ribs. This felt a lot like that.

Rick glared at Caleb, the voice mail from Charlie playing in his head. *Caleb was in on it.* Rick watched as the young sheriff's hands fidgeted on the steering wheel, eyes darting nervously as he headed southbound on Highway 89. Caleb was a man without a plan, or so it appeared, once again in far over his head, just as he'd been throughout much of his earthly existence.

Rick needed a plan of his own, and he needed it quick.

"Are we under arrest, Sheriff?" Reiff asked as Rick shook his head in disgust. "If so, what would be the charges?" Caleb didn't answer, instead turning off the highway onto a gravel road. He was headed for the Sawtooth.

"Why did you do it, Caleb?" Rick growled through a clamped jaw. "Why did you kill my daughter? You've left a nine-year-old girl without a mother."

Reiff whipped his head toward Rick, eyes opened wide in disbelief. Rick threw a quick glance at him before returning his glare toward Caleb. The sheriff swallowed, his jaw muscles tightening. "You don't know what you're talking about."

"Why can't you be a man for once in your life? Why can't you stand up and take responsibility for what you've done? Charlie told me everything." Charlie hadn't told him much of anything, leaving only a brief, cryptic voice mail. Rick felt it was enough.

"So, Charlie did call you?" Caleb said as he glanced into the rearview mirror. "That is really unfortunate. It changes things."

Reiff's shook his head rapidly and cleared his throat, his face awash in panic. "What does he mean, it changes things? What has he done? Where's he taking us?"

Rick huffed dismissively at Reiff's cowardice. He fixed his eyes on Caleb, his mind flaming with rage. He said nothing, assuring himself he would find an opening to avenge Chloe's death.

"Really unfortunate," Caleb repeated, shaking his head. Suddenly, he seemed to have a plan.

Billy decided to pull over a good two hundred yards away from the Tidwell house, lest he risk announcing his arrival. He found it odd that Charlie Duchesne, a physician, would call dispatch in search of an ambulance for Tessie Lou Hunter, only to have Caleb Tidwell veto the decision.

Billy figured he best have a look.

He squinted curiously when he spotted Charlie's SUV and Tessie Lou's truck parked outside, Caleb's vehicle nowhere to be found. He pulled his gun and sidled along the detached clapboard garage. Drawing a deep breath, he edged past the two vehicles and closer to the house. He pressed his back against the siding, twisting his neck to peer through a side door that led through a laundry room and into the kitchen.

Tessie Lou was sitting at the kitchen table, a pistol in her hand, her ashen face drained, eyes downcast. Billy followed her gaze toward the floor, where Charlie Duchesne laid prone, a halo of blood surrounding his head. Charlie's eyes were half open. Billy couldn't be certain whether he was alive or dead.

Billy's heart raced, his forehead beading with ice-cold sweat. He lifted his eyes to see Tessie glaring at him. As she gripped her weapon with two hands, Billy ducked from the window. A deafening gunshot rang out, obliterating the glass in the side door. He slammed his shoulder blades against the house, eyes opened wide.

"Tessie! Wait! It's Billy Renfro!" He heaved for air, waiting a beat before peering into the house a second time. Tessie hadn't moved, her gun aiming directly at Billy. He jerked away again, an instant before a second bullet splintered the wood frame on one side of the door. Billy shook his head, wishing he could have somehow made it into retirement without engaging in a shootout with a pregnant woman.

He heard a scream. Looking through the door, he saw Tessie on the ground, wrestling with Charlie Duchesne for control of the weapon. Charlie managed to pull the gun free, sending it tumbling across the linoleum in Billy's direction. The deputy reached through a glassless pane and opened the door, his gun trained on Tessie Lou.

She was on her knees, her chin sinking onto her chest as she caressed the unborn child within her womb. Caleb Tidwell's child. Her head bobbed as she began to weep.

"You don't understand," she said, her lips quivering. "We're a family."

Rick looked over his shoulder at Caleb as he felt the poke of a shotgun barrel in the small of his back. His neck snapped backward when Caleb jabbed him again, this time more forcefully, the sheriff apparently growing impatient with the pace of their trek to the Sawtooth.

Reiff stumbled along the trail in front of them, his dress shoes causing him to lose his footing in the mud and snow. As he gasped for oxygen, he shivered uncontrollably, his clothes still soaked from his plunge into the irrigation ditch.

"This man isn't doing well," Rick said. "He needs medical help."

"He won't be needing any medical help—not after we're done here."

They walked in silence, the canyon growing dim as haunting clouds rolled in, shielding the afternoon's fading sunlight. Despite his wet clothes, Rick's rampant adrenaline conquered the cold, his mind ablaze with hatred and bent on revenge. As they made the final push to the top of the Sawtooth, both Chloe and Abby seemed to be near. He fought back waves of grief fighting to pound their way into his brain, aware that such thoughts were of no use if he was to survive. He *had* to survive. Somehow. Some way.

"You know, your daughter had a knack for sticking her nose where she shouldn't," Caleb said.

Rick stopped walking a few feet from the edge of the cliff. He turned and faced his captor. "How so?"

"Let's just say she saw some things she wasn't supposed to see."

Rick replayed his last communication from Chloe. She left a message about the buffalo. Chase Rettick said Caleb was involved in putting the animals among cattle in the valley. *What if, for once in his life, the tweaker was telling the truth?* Mandy said the beef scare was a scam. So—

"Does this have to do with the buffalo? Someone was paying you off, weren't they?"

Caleb huffed, a smile of resignation creeping onto his face. "I was never going to get rich on my sheriff's salary. And I have a baby on the way."

Rick's eyes narrowed. "You sold out the ranchers in our valley—and killed my daughter—for money?"

"I didn't kill your daughter, Mr. Morrand. I liked Chloe. I really did."

The talk of Chloe's death seemed to awaken Reiff. "If you didn't kill her, then who did?"

Caleb rubbed his chin with the back of his gloved hand. "Tessie Lou."

Rick cocked his head. "Tessie Lou? She's pregnant."

"Six months, to be exact. And she sure has a temper, that one. Chloe followed me that morning, and she saw me talking to some . . . *associates*, shall we say. I asked her to meet me later on, to see what she *thought* she knew. I had no intention of her getting hurt."

Caleb drew a deep breath and shook his head slowly. "Seems Tessie Lou had access to my voice mail, and she knew I was going to see Chloe. She whacked me in the head with a shovel handle—knocked me out cold. She took your daughter up here at gunpoint."

Rick tugged violently at his cuffed wrists, his shoulders writhing as he tried to break loose. His eyes burned at Caleb, his brain flashing images of Chloe held captive, alone and innocent, her father unable to help.

"When I came to and got up here, Tessie was trying to get Chloe to go off the cliff," Caleb said. "Chloe was barefoot—I guess so she couldn't run away. I told Chloe to grab her shoes and go." Caleb heaved a sigh as he scanned the ground, a hint of remorse wandering across his face. "That's when Tessie hit her."

Rick swallowed hard. "Hit her? How?"

"Hit her with a rock—twice. Cracked her skull. She died instantly, as far as I could tell."

Rick's stomach churned, as though he were about to throw up. He shook his head in disbelief. "You are a law enforcement officer, Caleb. Why didn't you arrest her?"

Caleb wagged his head. "Oh, I couldn't do that, Mr. Morrand. I just couldn't have my baby born in prison."

Rick's head slumped forward, air leaving his chest. "So, you staged a suicide."

"Tessie just wanted to throw her off the edge, but I couldn't do that. I carried her down, laid her in the grass. Like I said, Mr. Morrand, I really liked Chloe."

"Do you think your father—"

"Let's leave my father out of this," Caleb snapped, his eyes stewing with anger. "Everyone in this valley always said I wasn't like my father. I get it."

"Wait!" Reiff said eagerly, moving a step forward. Caleb flashed the shotgun toward him, causing him to stop. Reiff swallowed, took a breath, and calmed his voice. "You didn't kill anyone. You covered up a crime, but you had a reason. *You* didn't kill anyone."

Rick shot a bitter glare at Reiff, sickened that his ex-partner would appoint himself defense counsel for a craven sheriff. Reiff returned a knowing look, causing Rick to pause. *Was it a ruse? Was Reiff buying time?* Rick wrestled with the handcuffs behind his back once again, his right hand throbbing as he managed to wedge it halfway free.

Caleb tossed the shotgun off to the side. He reached behind his back, under his jacket, pulling out a Glock that Rick recognized to be his own. Rick swallowed, eyes opening wide. The weapon must have fallen out when the truck rolled. "I'm afraid there's no conventional way to handle this," Caleb said.

Rick watched intently as the sheriff studied the sidearm, briefly popping open the magazine to check the number of bullets. "It's my understanding from my deputy that Mr. Metcalf here is the father of your granddaughter," Caleb said, his numb eyes growing ominous as he stared at Rick. "I would imagine that you didn't take that too well. In fact, I'll bet that's what you two were discussing when I found you in the irrigation ditch."

"What are you getting at, Caleb?"

Caleb inspected the Glock once more, sliding his thumb along the barrel. "What I'm getting at is that you kept a pretty close eye on your daughter—trying to control her every move. Hell, she once told me that herself." He shrugged. "It would seem that when you came to find out that your former partner—your best friend—had slept with Chloe, I would say that you were pretty upset." He raised his eyebrows. "After all, Mr. Morrand, you are known around the valley to have a fairly strong temper—especially in matters involving your daughter."

Rick glowered at the sheriff, but Caleb seemed to ignore him. "So, what I'm thinking is, in a fit of rage, you killed your Mr. Metcalf, using the gun you kept in your truck."

"That would never hold up in court."

"Who said anything about going to court?" Caleb said with a frown. "You were so distraught—having lost your daughter, and having shot your best friend—that you turned the gun on yourself."

"You'll never get away with it," Rick hissed through his teeth as he edged forward. Reiff took the cue, making a bull rush toward the sheriff. Caleb stepped back, firing a bullet into Reiff's chest, causing him to stagger helplessly before falling forward like rotting deadwood. Rick froze, staring in wide-eyed shock as Reiff lay motionless on the gravel, hands cuffed behind him.

Caleb turned the Glock toward Rick. "I'm sorry it has to be this way, Mr. Morrand," he said, moving toward him and burying the gun beneath Rick's jawbone. Rick fixed his eyes on Caleb, nostrils pulsing, anger trumping fear. He yanked the right handcuff once more. *Almost there.* If he could just . . .

Suddenly, Caleb's eyes bulged. Blood gurgled from his mouth as his head quivered. The point of an arrow protruded through the sheriff's Adam's apple. Caleb took two abbreviated steps backward, then fell to the ground, the handgun falling harmlessly at Rick's feet. His body tremored briefly before he lay still.

Rick stared in stunned silence. After a few moments, he heard footsteps on the gravel. Buddy Rivers approached, a crossbow in his hand.

"You okay, Counselor?"

Rick's mouth hung open in disbelief. He nodded, taking another look at Caleb. "Buddy," he mumbled breathlessly. "What did . . . How did you get here?"

"I was tracking a deer, and I thought I saw him come up this way. Once that shot rang out, he scattered." Buddy cast a glance toward Caleb. "When I got to the top, it was looking like this man was fixing to harm you."

Rick looked into Buddy's soft blinking eyes. "Buddy, you saved my life."

Buddy looked at him sheepishly. "Please don't get on me about it not being bow season."

"You saved my life," Rick repeated.

Buddy looked at Reiff's body, lying facedown nearby. "Hey, ain't he that lawyer?"

Rick nodded. "Reiff Metcalf—my former partner," he said with a hint of sadness. He shook his head, lips curled downward. An hour earlier, he'd wanted to kill Reiff himself. "He tried to save us both."

"Well," Buddy said, eyebrows raised hopefully, "you're still my lawyer, ain't ya?"

"Of course, Buddy."

"I figure I'm gonna be needin' a lawyer." He shook his head as he stared at Caleb's corpse. "Looks like I shot the sheriff."

CHAPTER 56

"**O**UCH!"
Rick flinched when Sage tapped his rib cage—the side with the two fractured ribs. She was trying to direct his attention toward Abby, who was standing near the paddock playfully teasing Big Sky with a green apple.

"Ooh, I'm sorry!" She wrapped her hand beneath his bicep and rubbed her cheekbone on his shoulder. "Those ribs still bothering you?"

He cast a tender glance toward her. "Just a bit."

"I thought you were a big tough football player."

"I was a kicker."

Sage shrugged. "Well, even kickers do a little tackling once in a while, don't they?"

"Only when someone else doesn't do their job."

Winter was descending on the valley, having dropped four inches of fresh snow as the calendar closed in on Thanksgiving. The sun had poked through at midmorning, giving way to a clear day that was windless and mild. A sky now drenched in cobalt blue promised that all storms had passed.

Abby continued to feed Big Sky, reaching into a canvas bag as fragments of apple littered the ground beneath them. The horse nodded with satisfaction, bubbles of white foam dripping from the sides of his mouth.

"How many is that?" Sage shouted. "I said only two, remember? He'll end up with a bellyache."

Abby didn't speak. Instead, she raised her index finger in front of her pleading eyes. *One more?*

"He *is* a pretty big horse," Rick offered.

"Okay, but that's it," Sage called to Abby. "Then, you need to put the rest of those apples inside."

Abby whirled back toward her horse with delight. She teased him with the last apple as though she wanted to savor the moment. Big Sky bared his teeth and nipped at her fingers, which she kept a safe distance away.

"She's going to get bit. Abb—"

Rick touched Sage's forearm. "Let her be," he said quietly. "How 'bout we loosen the reins a little?" She shot him a confused look but said no more. They stood in silence before Rick put his arm around her.

"Sure your ribs are going to be okay?" she asked as she gazed into his eyes. His lips rose into a wry smile. "I think I'll be fine."

"Mind if I ask you something?"

"Fire away."

Sage nodded toward Abby. "Do you ever wonder about her?" She paused. "I mean, do you ever wonder whether she'll—"

"Whether she'll have mental illness? Or become an addict?"

Sage shook her head. "I'm sorry. I shouldn't have said that."

"No, it's fine." He sighed with resignation. "Let's see—did I wonder about Abby when she wouldn't sleep as a baby? Yep. Or when she would wet her bed? Oh yeah. Or when the first-grade teacher told Chloe that Abby was always daydreaming? You bet. Truth is, I think about it all the time. We really can't do anything about it right now, can we?"

"We?" Sage asked, raising her eyebrows. "So, there is a we?"

"I sure hope there is."

Sage nestled beneath his arm. She brushed her thick hair away from her face, exposing her inviting eyes. "There is," she said with a smile. "There definitely is."

Abby had spent her last apple. She reached into the canvas bag, casting a wily glance toward Sage. Their eyes met. Sage wagged her head, and the apple dropped harmlessly back into the sack.

"You're going to tell her about her father, aren't you?" Sage asked. "She probably should know that Chase Rettick isn't her dad."

"When she asks about him, I will tell her," Rick said. "I won't ever lie to her, I can promise you that." He drew a deep breath. "I imagine she'll ask soon enough. In the meantime, maybe she can spend a few days being a little girl."

Sage nodded. She pressed her palms together, fingers touching her lips.

"What is it?" Rick asked.

"Nothing."

"C'mon," he said, turning toward her. "What is it?"

"Okay," Sage shrugged. "You heard anything from Mandy? Or her daughter?"

Rick frowned. "Sage Fontenot, are you *jealous*?"

"Damn right I am. Yes or no?"

Rick looked at the corral. "No, I haven't," he said, "and I don't expect I will."

"Not even the daughter?"

Rick shook his head. "No."

"Do you plan to contact her?"

"No, I don't," he answered. "First of all, I don't even know if she's my daughter. Second, even if she is, she was given up for adoption, and she deserves her privacy."

"But surely you have to wonder?"

He paused. "Right now, all I know is that I have . . . had . . . one daughter, and I'll miss her every day for the rest of my life." He blinked rapidly, pushing back emotion. He flicked a nod toward the paddock. "This little girl is going to need all the attention we can give her. She has a lot of healing to do."

He pulled Sage close to him, ribs be damned. "I love you, Sage," he said, diving into her eyes. "You don't ever have to be jealous. *Trust me.*"

Their lips drew close and they began to kiss, the pain and worries of the world around them floating away. Abby interrupted them.

"When can I feed him again?" she shouted as she sprinted full speed, her voice bursting with excitement.

"We'll see," Sage said. "Probably tomorrow."

"Tomorrow," Abby repeated, breathless. "*Tomorrow*."

She wore a hopeful smile.

ACKNOWLEDGMENTS

M Y SINCERE APPRECIATION TO THE dedicated law enforcement officers of Park and Sweet Grass counties, Montana, who have modest resources to protect citizens spread over thousands of square miles of land. Special thanks to Alan Ronneberg, Undersheriff and Search and Rescue Coordinator for Sweet Grass County, for his limitless gift of time and knowledge.

I also want to thank my editor, teacher and friend, Susanne Lakin, for her patience and kindness.

If you have enjoyed this novel, please consider writing a review. That is the best way to thank an author.

Printed in the USA
CPSIA information can be obtained
at www.ICGtesting.com
LVHW091409280224
773024LV00059B/1607